# WELCOME TO
# CARVERNET

## J. J. FRENCH

If you do not know who you want to be, now is an excellent time to begin.

# PROLOGUE

Madison was sore. It had been one of the big days.

She reached up to her record player, and settled the needle into place. As the pressed plate spun, tracking the tiny pinhead through its grooves, warm strains from a long-gone guitar began to play.

She closed her eyes.

*Da-dum, dee dee,*

*Da dada, da-da.*

The record player was one of the few pieces of the old world she kept for herself. The records were fragile, and the sound was hopelessly poor, but she had fallen in love with the tactility of the thing. It was as close as she had ever gotten to touching her own emotions.

As the song's well-worn intro cascaded into a melodious chorus, she picked up her book, a battered, yellowed novel about a spy leading a desperate crusade against powerful businessmen.

She thumbed through the pages until she reached the bookmark, a simple little metallic clip with an etched logo. The inked letters on the paper seemed to fade from view as the story bloomed into her mind's eye.

"I think we might have a problem."

Madison put down the book, annoyed. The fantasy had been shattered before it could even begin.

She swivelled to face the intruder. The movement sent her chair rolling away from her workbench, clattering gently over ridges in the flooring.

"What kind of problem?"

His face was a few years younger than hers. He hooked his fob into its place on the wall, next to several others of its kind. When he looked back at her, she watched his eyes. They looked panicked, she thought. Maybe just nervous.

"Um. Sorry. It's probably nothing."

His voice was unnaturally steady.

Definitely nervous.

Madison shook her head. "Say it, Ricardo."

His fingers were grasping a half-eaten protein bar, flexing as if they didn't quite know how to settle. "It's the new batch in block twelve. The integration isn't…"

"Isn't what?"

He took a half-hearted bite of the ration. "When we had them all ready, I could have sworn I saw a jump in activity on the traces. That shouldn't be happening."

Madison went back to her book. "You imagined it, Ricky."

Her visitor didn't leave, so she looked up again, glancing at a display in the corner for a few moments. "Integration always takes a few days. Acclimation, right? Neural traces can be a little twitchy during that process. Here, take a look."

She turned the display towards him. "See? It's all quiet up there. Block twelve is doing fine. You imagined it."

His troubled look lingered. She smiled kindly.

"Get some sleep, okay? It's been a long day. It's always smooth sailing from here on out."

Ricky slowly nodded. He wanted to believe it. And she *was* right. He had worked hard, getting all the little things sorted out for the coming haul. His bunk was more inviting than it had been in weeks, and if he was quick he might make it back without running into the captain. The captain was, at all costs, to be avoided after long days like this one. Tomorrow would be better.

He nodded one more time, accepting the reassurance. "Block twelve. Normal. Right. Okay."

Madison waved as he disappeared out of her doorway, the sounds of his shoes echoing with his retreat. She glanced at the monitor again, comfortable in her assessment, and rolled her chair back until she could raise her feet. She settled them atop the workbench, crossed her legs at the ankles, picked up the book, and leaned back.

A little while later, she reached a really good bit.

# ONE

I flickered towards consciousness, the world's dimensions colliding at unwanted angles. Dazzling light flooded my eyes, followed by a wave of hot nausea that threatened to overwhelm my senses. A few long moments later it faded, flushed away, replaced by the shock of awareness.

*Bright. Bad.*

I sat up, blinking into the obscene glare.

I was on a bed. Soft-topped mattress, no frame to elevate it. Foam underneath. Soft coverings on the floor. A closet in a corner, a dresser for clothes. Simple chairs, angled towards drawn curtains. A refresher waiting through a door to one side. Off-white composite plating on the walls.

It was *definitely* a hotel room. Simple, minimal, durable, with an emphasis on comfort. Modern standard, they called this look. I'd stayed somewhere very much like it at some point. Visiting…a friend? Family? Couldn't remember. Didn't matter.

Wobbly on feet that weren't quite agreeing with the rest of me, I tested the flooring, sinking down into its coarse weave. It had the texture of something stiff, but yielding. Like straw. My vision smeared, my sense of balance was off. Whatever the hell this was, it wasn't fun.

I looked down, blearily wondering why the bed cloth was sticking to me.

*Oh.*

I was naked. And a little clammy.

I made the mistake of looking up at one of the glow panels, and immediately regretted it. The brightness encouraged a warbling, throbbing pain behind my eyes, and I squeezed them shut.

*What did I drink last night?*

My eyes might not have wanted to focus, but my legs eventually seemed to work. I put one in front of the next, and made it a few steps. The refresher would be an escape. Just had to get there.

I reached the wall, leaning against it for its precious support. It was a nice wall. It didn't mind holding me up.

A muffled chime sounded, somewhere in the distance.

Left foot, right foot. Left foot again. Right foot for balance.

*Happy wall, good wall. Wall friend.*

I reached out, shoving the door open, and stumbled into the mercifully dim nook. Free of the overwhelming glare, I fumbled for the controls, and smeared my finger against the panel, bringing up the brightness bit by bit until there was just enough of it to see clearly. A slim countertop before me was speckled with shiny bits, mocking me, daring me to feel good about myself. They glimmered cheerfully as my gaze tracked up to the mirror.

I stared at the reflection, alarm stirring.

Time slowed, blood rushed, and a surge of adrenaline tingled through the back of my mind.

I recognized my hands. My arms and legs too. Definitely my body. But I didn't recognize the face that looked back at me. Pasty skin. Short reddish-blond hair, brushed back, slightly too lengthy for comfort. Blue eyes. Hint of stubble. A narrow, triangular jawline. Too gaunt. Too *young*. I locked eyes with the man in the mirror, searching for reassurance. He seemed to look right through me.

The face wasn't mine. It wasn't right. It didn't belong to me.

Panic swelled. The walls seemed impossibly close, and fresh sweat started to gather. Heartbeats pounded through my ears, drowning out anything and everything.

I didn't know my name.

The face in the mirror had to have one. It had to exist.

I just couldn't remember it.

*Nothing.*

The thought wormed through my brain with unstoppable persistence. My breathing started gathering speed as the nausea returned, coursing through my limbs and culminating in a dizzy twist as it reached my chest and wrapped it in a knotty grasp. I pitched forward, and let it overtake me.

I held there for a minute, propped against the counter, sweat oozing down my skin, clamminess definitively turning into something stronger. Acid burned in my throat.

*Water.*

The sink responded to touch, releasing a cool stream of liquid goodness without complaint. Gulping down a few mouthfuls, I latched onto the soothing sensations. Water was real. Water was normal. Water was exactly as I needed it to be.

I used that as a place to start.

The shower was simple. A push of a button, a turn of a knob. The middle of the ceiling opened up, spraying down fine droplets to blissfully dance against my skin. I just stood there for endless moments, luxuriating in the dense mist. Another muffled chime came, filtering in from somewhere far away.

The panic receded. Pulsing veins steadied. The water soothed and reassured. And then I stared at the mirror again.

*Freck.*

The spell faded like an enticing dream, and suddenly the refresher was just a claustrophobic closet.

I closed my eyes and looked up, taking in a mouthful of the spray, then shut it off. A soft cloth to one side made for a decent towel, but it was barely needed.

When I stepped out, the lights didn't seem quite as overwhelming. It was progress, if only a little.

A vast picture window hid behind the curtains. From the warm glow in the sky and omnipresent gloom below, it looked to be on the bright side of dawn. Too dark to reveal much detail, but enough to make out trees and bushes. A dewy fog shielded any horizon from view. The word *ghostly* came to mind.

The hotel, only three levels high, was shaped into vast curve, and the long, lazy line of windows came around into view towards the far edge of the clearing. Most of the ones I could see, both above and below my own, were dark and still.

A gust of wind shuddered against the building as a lone leaf swirled outside. Peaceful. A little melancholy.

"Ugh," I muttered, addressing no-one in particular.

I stood there, drying in the open air, and tried to work through the disorientation.

No name to put to my face.

The *wrong* face, for that matter.

No memory of this hotel.

No memories of *anywhere else*.

"Okay," I announced to nobody in particular. "What the *hell* is all this?"

There was no clock or calendar. Or any devices at all, which seemed more than a little odd. There had to be *something* of mine here.

I yanked the sheets off the bed, strewing them across the floor in the hope that something might fall out. Nothing did.

The chairs didn't leave any room for concealing a forgotten gadget. The flooring was even, with no telltale bumps or lumps.

I tried a drawer at random, but found it empty, and dismissed the rest of the dresser. Somehow, I was absolutely certain that there was no way I would have actually *used* it.

I sighed, returned to the window, forced myself to relax, to breathe more easily, and stopped trying to focus on anything. The headache was already more than bad enough. The sight of rustling flora helped, I found. It didn't help a *lot*, but at least it was soothing. I just wished that I could put any kind of label to the landscape beyond that window.

*Okay. I'm alive, and I'm okay, and I'm here. That's enough, right?*

An alarmingly loud noise sliced through my consciousness, reverberating through the room as though it had come from every direction.

*Door chime.*

I blinked, comprehending, and went to go meet it. Hospitality. In a hotel.

*This makes sense,* I thought.

I froze with the door half-open as my state of undress suddenly registered, and managed to get as far as whispering the beginnings of an apology before a fidgety hand flung into view, grasping at the frame. I panicked and reached out, trying to get the hand to go back where it belonged, but it was rapidly followed by a head of loose black hair, dark blue eyes and lips that were starting to ask an evidently important question. The eyes abruptly widened as they found me, and pulled back with impressive speed.

"Oh, shit. I'm *so* sorry."

The woman's words sounded odd, a little low and husky, strangled somewhere in the back of her throat.

I croaked out a noise that I hoped sounded dignified, and forced together the words for a reply.

"My fault, I forgot I was dressed. Naked. I forgot I was naked. Not…Um."

I paused, looking around wildly for a bag or any hint of what I must have worn the previous day. Seeing nothing obvious, I settled on the closet a few feet away, and started towards it. I felt a terrible need to say something to the mystery woman. At least she didn't seem to be fleeing the scene.

"I'm just going to, uh, put something on. If I can."

With the closet open, my next move was to stare at it dumbly. The small space was divided into cubby holes, each containing neatly pressed and folded pieces of fabric. Closer inspection revealed them to be simple hip-length tunics paired with loose trousers. Several color combinations to choose from. A soft pair of slippers rested on the bottom shelf.

At random, I pulled out a white-and-blue set. As the top unfurled, a small metal clip flashed from the neck button. Eyes narrowed, I gingerly pulled it out, peering at tiny letters gleaming in the light:

*CN*

As I inspected it, questions marching through my head, the woman's reply finally came. She sounded more confident now, though it might have been forced. "Maybe, er, try the closet. They have clothes. You know, normally."

Then she added, almost as if forgetting she was still speaking,

"But good luck with *that*."

I stopped halfway into putting on the trousers. "What?"

She was silent for a beat, seemingly at a loss. "I'm sorry. This is weird."

I glanced back at the closet. "Do you work here?"

"Not as far as I know."

"Then can you, er, hold on a minute?"

The woman said nothing, but that was probably a good sign. I finished dressing haphazardly, shivering at the rough fabric tickling against my skin. The cut was strange but fit obediently.

Returning to the door, I straightened, tried my best to feel awake and alert, failed, and opened it. My mystery intruder stood out in the hall, waiting with a look in her eyes that was equal parts suspicious and disoriented. She was tall and lanky, dressed in golden yellows, with hands that seemed perpetually restless.

I tried a question. "Have we met before? Do we know each other?"

She shook her head. "No. That was stupid. I should know better than to barge in on someone. You could be anyone! It's just, today's been really *odd* so far, and that was the first time that anyone's actually *answered...*"

She trailed off, blushing faintly.

I shrugged, still doing my best to stay upright as the throbbing behind my eyes slowly faded.

We stood there awkwardly for a few seconds, and in the silence I took in the hall. A soft, easy, dark green carpet. Crinkly textured walls were interrupted only by identikit doors and number plates spaced beside them. I turned, and spotted the plate for my own door.

"Two-sixteen," I said, quietly.

I hoped it might mean something. It didn't.

I made myself turn back, offering the woman what I hoped was a conspiratorial half-smile to say, *this is weird, but it's okay, right?*

After a beat she started to match the look, and seemed to make a decision. She stuck out her hand. "Can we do this over again? I'm Jennifer. Jen, maybe, if I like you. From room three-thirty, if it helps."

I shook it, awkwardly. "Sure. No idea at all."

"Eh?"

"I don't know who I am. No idea."

"You seem pretty relaxed about that."

"I'm not."

Jennifer shrugged. "Okay, two-sixteen, you're not relaxed, and you have no idea who you are. A reassuring person to be talking to." She paused, bemused, and sounded it out in an odd voice. "*No-ah-dee-ah.* How about Noah?"

"Who's Noah?"

"You. A nickname."

I shook my head, smiling politely. "I don't think our relationship is quite *that* far along yet."

"It could be, until the world says differently. And what else are you going to call yourself?"

She had a point. I pushed past it. "Listen, I'm not feeling great. I'm sure you wanted something, but…do you know where we are?"

Jennifer focused on me, at my expression, a peculiar look sliding across her eyes. "Did I wake you up? And were you a little clammy and a lot sick?"

I eyed her curiously. "Uh huh."

"Yep. Okay."

My thoughts stuttered, then sharpened all at once. "Same for you? With the feeling sick part. Maybe this is a little personal, but did you have any stuff? Any luggage? Anything at all?"

She shook her head, and her posture shifted until she was angled away, inviting me to step out and join her. "Were you in the middle of anything?"

"Uh. No."

"Then would you mind coming with me? I need help with something."

"What? Right now?"

"Yes."

"Why? What's going on?"

"The room next to mine has a dead woman."

I turned around and strode back into my room, shutting the door with a firm *clack*. My feet carried me as far as possible until I was back at the window with its lovely, reassuring scenery.

*Not* my problem. *Definitely* not my problem.

The trees looked nice outside. Calming. Soothing. A model of implacability.

A gentle knocking echoed from the door.

*Nope.*

I said nothing. The knocking continued, persistent.

"Two-sixteen? Please?"

"No!" I said loudly, hoping it would penetrate the layers of wood and metal.

"Noah?" came the muffled reply.

"Nope," I said again. "Definitely not. Find someone who works here for that."

"Nobody works here!"

She kept knocking maddeningly patiently.

Ten seconds later I had opened the door again. This time she didn't try to put her head through it. I appreciated that.

"Look, uh, Jennifer, I don't think I'm the person you need."

"You're the only person I *have*." She held up her hands in that universal gesture of *I-don't-know.* "Please?"

"Can't you ask the staff?"

"You're not listening. There aren't any staff."

I started to shake my head, then caught myself. "What?"

"We're *alone* here."

I studied her as she said the words. She seemed earnest, anxious. But not deceptive. Which meant she was being totally honest. And asking me for help.

"What do you mean?"

Her eyes were wild, and her tone had shifted, becoming slightly unhinged. "I mean I've been walking around this place for hours and I haven't seen a single soul. Except you."

I went to close the door again. "There's probably *somebody* that can help. Somebody better than me."

Jennifer was taking deep breaths, forcing herself to be calm. I relented, just a little. If she hadn't found anyone, or even managed to call for help…

I sighed.

Hell of a way to start the day.

I cleared my throat. "So you think you have a dead neighbor. What do you want me to do?"

"I'm *not* making it up, and I don't know."

"So…?"

"I think I just need someone to tell me I'm not crazy."

"Right. Well, like I said, I don't think I'm the person you need."

"Oh, for god's sake—" she reached out and punched my shoulder. "Be interesting, would you? Can you *please* be interesting and just, you know, *help* with this?"

We stood there in silence for a very long moment, staring at each other.

The walk to her room took us down the long, curving hallway, up a set of stairs, and around a few corners. Our feet padded softly through increasingly fancy decor, with traces of glossy accents starting to appear around the edges of things.

And as far as I could tell, she was right. It certainly looked like we *were* alone.

When we had neared what I guessed was the middle of the building, we passed by a particularly polished section of wall. I made the mistake of glancing at it, and immediately turned away. Whatever I was seeing about myself, it made something in the back of my mind want to curl up and go back to sleep.

*Not an option, Noah.*

I did a mental double-take at my adoption of the name. True or false, it was *a* name, and that seemed to be good enough after all.

I looked back at the distorted, blurred reflection, this time more intently. It wasn't especially *wrong* at all. When I moved, it moved. When I raised a hand, it waved back at me. When I stared at it, it stared back. Alien and unknown, but it was me.

Blood started to thud in my ears again.

I spoke into the looming emptiness, searching for a distraction. I wasn't sure I wanted to deal with a body. At all, in any capacity.

"So," I tried, "where are you from?"

Her reply was tightly clipped, but distinctly sardonic. "I would love to know that."

"You don't know?"

"No. Do you?"

"I do not."

"Then that's…" she drifted away for a moment. "That's okay."

When we reached the door for room three-thirty, Jennifer pushed it open with barely any ceremony. She had left it unlocked.

Her room was bigger than mine, with warm red accents that carved through a sea of beige. Where my window had just included a look at some trees, hers offered views across a sweeping valley.

Higher class. Without a doubt.

Being in someone else's personal space evoked a strange feeling in the back of my mind. The invitation displayed a level of trust, of course. But then, what was she really trusting me *with*?

Another look around, past the obvious luxuries of the design, and I realized that she was really no better equipped than I had been. In fact, despite the lack of *stuff*, it actually looked like she had thrown a *tantrum* at some point.

Her bedsheets were haphazardly untucked, kicked and wrapped around each other, twisted up with a small pile of clothes. A shirt lay crumpled in the corner, presumably a onetime projectile. A pair of slippers rested against the base of the window, one of them upside down.

But there was *not*, I happily noted, a dead body anywhere to be seen.

Then she pointed out the party door beside the dresser. With a tidy little plaque beside it.

Three-thirty-one.

I shivered despite myself, suddenly understanding.

"She's in there," Jennifer said.

"You've been inside?"

"It was unlocked. I was curious."

"That sounds right," I muttered. Then with a trickle of dread, muttered, "Okay. Oh-kay."

Neither of us moved at first. Then she went for it.

Jennifer stepped up against the spot in the wall where the plating was sunken in, and pressed firmly.

It gently swung inwards with all the daintiness of a feather. I half expected a disgruntled shout at the intrusion, but no objections came.

I edged past my host, peering into the room.

It was a mirror image of Jennifer's, with two key differences.

First, it was immaculate. Entirely untouched. That by itself stood out as unlikely. Counter-intuitive somehow, as if phantom stagehands had sorted and posed it, then retreated into the walls.

As I carefully stepped further in, the second difference caught my eye.

A woman lay face-up in the bed, twenty feet away.

She was slender, with dark, straight hair around closed eyes. Older than the two of us by several years, possibly a couple of decades. The soft linen covered her up to the shoulders, where a pillow gently pitched her forward. And she wasn't moving. She lay perfectly still, a lifesize puppet beneath tidy sheets.

Somehow, the sheets made it worse.

The air was still, even borderline stale. A glimpse of warming sunlight dappled through the tops of the curtains.

"Is she breathing?" I whispered.

Jennifer remained in her own room, staring at the older woman's figure. "I think we're related."

"She's *not* breathing. How would being related make this better?"

She looked at me. "It would be nice to know I didn't get here all by myself."

"I don't like this."

Jennifer said nothing.

We approached, tiptoeing forward.

The sensation of approaching her was distinctly uncomfortable, like inspecting a giant doll. In the back of the mind, where the world was unconsciously filtered and categorized, there was no identification of the figure as a *person*.

I backed away.

"We should call someone. Emergency services."

"With what?" Jennifer objected. "I have nothing. If you did, you'd be holding it right now."

"There has to be *something* we can use here."

She shook her head. "Buddy, you are not comprehending what kind of place this is."

I contemplated that, not taking my eyes off the horizontal form. Didn't like what it implied at all. "So, okay, you're not crazy. At least not about her. I think we should leave."

We backed out, and closed the door. Firmly.

It didn't make me feel better.

"I think I need to go," I said.

"Please don't."

"I don't even know you. You don't even know *me*."

Jennifer sighed. "I don't know if you've realized this yet, but there's something extremely creepy about this place, and it's better to…" she searched for the words. "…to have company."

Her tone was placating. And earnest. I surprised myself with a flash of dismissive annoyance. "I don't think I'm good at being that."

"You will be."

I stared at her, suddenly grasping what she had actually said. She looked back, picking up on the unasked question. "Yeah. Look, I am *not* okay here, but you're the first real, *living* person I've seen and talked to. I don't really want to load you down with it."

For the first time in a few minutes, I didn't have anything to say. Then, quite suddenly and easily, I did.

I walked over and tried to give her a hug. It was short, and awkward, and never quite settled. It only lasted a couple of seconds before I stepped back.

"Okay," she said. "Um."

"Sorry," I said. "I thought—"

"Yeah. Look, this isn't—" she broke off, rattled. "Thank you. I think."

"Do you mind if we take this all outside?"

She looked pointedly at the wall concealing the adjoining room. "You mean, go somewhere very far away from here?"

"Yes."

"Then, yes. I know a place. You actually might want to see it."

"Okay," I said.

"It's also weird." she said.

"Okay." I said again.

I gave room three-thirty-one a wide berth as we left, and wondered how many of the countless locked doors in this place contained scenes just like that one.

* * *

The lobby was sterile. Raised ceilings, polished floors. A few bright colors, some softer furnishings. Metallic glimmers from every direction. A narrow reception desk lay empty. Every corner of the entrance was completely still. No distant chimes, no background rumbles, no unseen voices. Nobody to offer a reassuring explanation or give cheerful fake smiles. Any of them would have been welcome.

*Unnerving* would have been too gentle a word.

My guide set her course for the open air, showing no signs of the wobbliness I'd been fending off.

We kept an odd distance away from each other as we walked, somewhere between the polite separation of strangers and the close huddle of scared children. Hard to tell which one of us was dictating it.

With each step towards the exit the cavernous space seemed less and less oppressive. I tried to lighten things up.

"Do you know what CN stands for?"

"Beats me."

"They like the look of their own name, though, don't they?"

This time she nodded, suddenly engaging with the topic. "Even the *laundry* has branding. I had to pull their stupid tags off of everything. Even the socks."

"You had socks?"

Jennifer gave me a troubled look. "The socks were in a drawer. Next to the closet."

"Oh." A moment of silence. "Did you just upgrade or downgrade your opinion of me?"

"Both."

The lobby ended in an opening so wide that it resembled a missing wall. The cool wind invited us outside, carrying vague scents of rain and and pollen. It was soothing. For reasons I didn't quite understand, the open air let me breathe more easily. I craved it. Needed to be out in it, going somewhere other than *here*.

She gestured out at the thinning fog, where a path carved through a meadowy expanse.

"Out there. It's not far."

"Good." Then:

"How many doors did you try before you got to mine?"

I hadn't meant to ask the question. She seemed surprised, but considered the topic with admirable thoughtfulness. "I don't know. A lot. After twenty I stopped counting."

The wind swirled around us, up at the sky, out across the open spaces. The path wound downwards, past a substantial boulder. It seemed reasonable to voice the question that had been nagging me from the start.

"Where *are* we?"

My companion snorted, but her eyes were appreciative. "I don't have an answer, but I think you asked that one a little too soon."

"Too *soon?*"

"Yeah." She said, dryly, and left it at that.

The undergrowth was at least a month or two beyond its last manicure. A smell carried across from the colliding grasses, triggering a memory. I latched onto it, lapsing into an introspective silence as I recalled the imagery.

It was a brightly colored room with a large picture on the wall, of a man in a striped jumpsuit, reaching up with something wrapped around his hand that made it bigger, clumsier. I felt an enticing thrill and lingering bitterness at the sight, a ghost of something warm, yet sad.

I snapped out of the reverie as Jennifer nudged my arm.

At the side of the path sat a trio of metallic cylinders, each squat, perhaps a meter tall, and set into the ground in a paved block. All shared the same dull, unremarkable grey color, with flat tops, no markings, and no obvious hints as to their purpose.

My headache threatened to come back as we paused in front of them.

I looked at Jennifer. "Let's make an agreement to come back to these later?"

She shook her head at that. "I don't think they do anything."

"Maybe they don't. Maybe they do. I'll poke it with a stick when you've shown me this place I should see."

"You *should* see it. It's really damned weird. Like you said, everything is…new." She lingered over the last word.

I opened my mouth to return some kind of snark, but stopped mid-breath.

In the last twenty minutes, she hadn't stopped fidgeting once.

She had to be fighting off anxiety. Or she had already given in to it, and was now trying to put herself right again.

The idea of being awake, alone, amnesiac, and confronted with…*what,* exactly? What was it that we were dealing with? It seemed reasonable to be anxious.

I decided that it would be better to let her voice that topic first. If she wanted reassurance, she would ask for it.

She ushered me forward, and we rounded a gentle bend as the fog started to clear. A grand arch suddenly loomed overhead out of the mist, bold letters curving across it:

*Green Valley*

I lost interest immediately. Beyond it lay something entirely more intriguing.

We were standing at the edge of a vast, man-made square, filled with dormant market stalls and symmetrically bordered by looming buildings, each as tidy, and as unlikely, as the next. I ventured in towards the middle of it all, equally enthralled and spooked.

To our left, a substantial restaurant, its few signs promising an unreasonable range of delicacies. Facing it, an archaic twentieth-century-style cinema. Next to the cinema, an ancient-looking tavern, and opposite the tavern a modern lounge, or maybe a library. The kind of place that might be visited by overconfident students and relaxed business types. Centered across the square from us and halfway distant to everything, sat another trio of anonymous pillars. I pointed them out to Jennifer, who was watching me with guarded eyes.

Beyond the paving and buildings lay more grasses, until the eye reached a wall of trees.

Many, many trees.

Atop silver, grey, and brown bark, their leafy green crowns rose into the distance, indistinctly raising the horizon at every opportunity. Distant cliffs loomed far above, drawing the eye ever upwards.

And it was all deathly silent. Not a bird in the sky or a rustle in the brush.

I mulled it over. No roads. No vehicles. No obvious way in or out, except the footpath we'd used. No people, except us.

It felt surreal, even baffling. I just couldn't get my head around what it implied. I tried different explanations, different ideas, different rationales. *Something* to make sense of it. Nothing did.

Unsettled, my gaze eventually settled back down to Jennifer, her nodding face seemingly minuscule against the unlikely diorama surrounding us.

"Okay," she said, her tone a little softer than it had been. "*Now* you can ask the big question."

"Grand," added a deep voice from behind us. "Where can I get a cup of coffee around here?"

# TWO

The Main Street Diner, as its sign proclaimed, ought to have inspired visions of enticing bites for a vast range of discerning palates.

I doubted it immediately.

On the inside, it was exactly as dark, still, and untouched as everything else. The mystery man had vanished into the back, exploring the kitchen with furious energy. Jennifer and I had claimed a booth along the front windows. Dark green cushions, simple grey table.

I spoke first. "Did you know he was there?"

"No."

"I jumped a little bit."

"Me too."

"What do you make of him?" I jerked my head one side, emphasizing the direction.

"He's loud."

"He snuck up on us pretty easily."

She squinted towards the kitchen, suspicion and indecision swirling behind her eyes. "I think that says more about us than him."

"Hmm."

"What are you thinking?"

"Don't scare him off."

"What?"

I coughed. "Either he's like us or he knows something. Either way it'd be nice to have the company."

"He *did* appear from nowhere. Scared the shit out of me."

A loud metallic clang reverberated across the restaurant, and I was suddenly reliving a half-formed memory. The decor was entirely different, the booths had been a dull, dirty brown, and there had been half as many of them, but I knew with certainty I had been somewhere just like it before. Unnervingly familiar, but the picture's details were maddeningly out of reach.

The earlier flood of adrenaline was working its way out of my system and leaving behind a bitter fatigue.

I sighed, forming a nest with my arms to rest my head. "Is this really happening?"

"I think it really might be happening, yes."

Jennifer was starting to stare off at something only her mind's eye could see when our new addition stumbled over to us. He was pudgy, with a mess of brown hair and wrinkled eyes, dressed in black. He wore a sour expression, but pulled up a chair, and sat himself squarely on it to face us.

"Well," he said, "they don't have coffee."

I raised an eyebrow. "Do they have anything else?"

He shook his head, speaking quickly, as if the topic wasn't worth his time. "Totally, one-hundred-percent empty. Like a movie set. Like nobody's ever cooked *anything* in there."

"A movie set," I repeated blankly, and lost my line of thought just as it was getting started.

Jennifer leaned forward. "So which room were *you* in?"

He stared at her, sourness evolving into uncertainty.

Jennifer settled deeper into the booth. "Let me help. You're lost, kind of dazed, right? Every time you try to focus on something specific, you can't. It's just out of reach, like waking from a dream and trying to tell someone about it. It's scary. So where do you start? Coffee. It's comforting. We get it. What was your room number?"

The newcomer eventually remembered how to put words together. And when he'd decided what to do with them, he reluctantly nodded.

"You're completely right. I can't remember a damn thing." He swallowed. "I was in room two-oh-four."

I nodded in turn. "Same here for us. Nothing but closets full of clothes and a headache for the ages."

He shrugged. "I heard you two talking when you went by my door. I decided to see where you were off to so quickly."

"Do you make a habit of sneaking up on people?" I asked.

He narrowed his eyes at that. Seemed to think about it. "No. How about the two of you?"

I considered him over a long pause, keeping my expression neutral, taking in his fidgeting hands.

*I have to trust people at some point. I just* have *to.*

"I'm Noah, from two-sixteen." I offered, gesturing across the booth. "We think this is Jennifer, three-thirty."

"We think?"

"She thinks."

"Seems that she spends a lot of time thinking. What do *you* think?"

I shrugged. "We invented my name."

Across the table Jennifer gave me a small smile, then looked back at him. "I'm just going to call you Two-oh-four, if you're fine with that."

A long beat later, it was Two-oh-four's turn to shrug as he processed that. "If we're making up names…" He paused. "call me Zed. I'm charmed and a little unsettled." He gave us each a tip of an imaginary hat.

"Zed?"

"You don't like it?"

I shrugged. "I'd have stuck with the number."

"Feel free to do just that, Two-sixteen."

Despite myself, my lips twitched. Banter was more comfortable territory. "So. I'll hear your best guesses about where we are or what all this is, if you've got any."

Zed peered out through the window, scanning the outdoors, perhaps a little bit resentful. Or defensive. Hard to tell.

"We've all been kidnapped and are being held at a resort that ran out of money before it was finished."

"Unfinished resort. Not a *bad* theory. But the hotel is immaculate and it does have power," I pointed out. "Jennifer?"

She slid me a sideways look, then shook her head. "If it was a resort there would be construction stuff, and we'd be able to just walk out. I didn't see any roads. Maybe some walking paths, though. My bet is on cult compound. We're all cultists."

"Cultists. Right."

Zed seemed thoughtful. "Cultists. Out in the middle of nowhere to live a life of seclusion." He looked bemused.

"Maybe that could connect a few dots," I said slowly, working the idea. "You should be called Beans."

He titled his head. "Beans. Coffee? Right on. To the part about waking up with no memory, well, maybe we were drugged." He looked at Jennifer absently. "Oooh. Maybe we did it to *ourselves*."

The gathering warmth disappeared from her eyes. That idea was not safe ground, I noted.

"So," I said, trying to move the conversation along. "We all showed up here, and with no stuff, and wiped out our own memories to…what, force ourselves to start new lives?"

Beans shrugged. "If so, it's working."

I was staring out the window at the brightening day, troubled.

I raised an eyebrow. "Maybe. Doesn't feel right, though."

Jennifer looked at me. "Eh?"

I raised an eyebrow. "It's just a feeling."

Beans shook his head. "On the topic of feelings, I rather feel like a nice bite to eat."

"You're hungry?"

"No. I just like food. It comforts me."

"Maybe you were a chef in that past life of yours," I suggested.

"Let's have it be a *celebrity* chef. We've gone to great expense on these facilities for our private resort, remember."

"Ah, yes, a celebrity chef in an empty diner with no food. You've got yourself the makings of quite a drama."

"Maybe the food gets delivered later? But I was thinking more of a survival competition show."

Jennifer deftly inserted herself into the conversation. "Do either of you have anything *useful* to say?"

Beans looked at her. "My backstory is very important to me."

She shook her head. "No. There's no coffee. There's no food. Aren't you guys getting it? We are *going to have to figure this out*."

Beans' tone was thoughtful. "Of course. First thing I'm sure that we're going to need, is to talk to the outside world. We won't need to go looking for food if we can get it brought to us."

Jennifer was unimpressed. "I was thinking more about *leaving*, not *relaxing*. Find some food. Go foraging. It's important."

She was taut, contained, almost closed. Intense. Beans, for his part, was much more open, but confusing. He kept patting his legs, working too hard at a maddeningly steady rhythm. Either he wasn't used to talking to people normally, or he had something to hide. I decided he was trying to be brave.

I grunted and pushed back from the table. "Talk amongst yourselves. I need a minute."

"Where are you going?" Jennifer asked.

"Not far. I just need a minute."

My feet carried me on a wandering route across the restaurant, ending at the big corner booth. The upholstery shone a vibrant red where the sunlight reached it. An empty napkin holder glinted, its metallic form smoothly molded out of the chromed tabletop.

Jennifer was talking, her voice echoing off the ceiling.

"…fine. So in *your* head, what do we do if more people show up?"

Beans said something snarky back, but I couldn't make it out. I was finding it increasingly hard to listen.

I leaned forward, palms flat, staring down at my distorted self. The hair. The face. The arms. The blue sleeves draped down them.

The eyes, that no matter how hard I tried to ignore them, stared back at me with tired, defiant rejection.

My eyes.

My face.

The longer I looked, the more I knew it. And the less it seemed to belong to me, in the way that saying a word too often would detach it from any meaning.

Something in the back of my mind gave out, and I quietly chuckled to myself. I was going mad. *This* is *what madness feels like.*

Beans was talking again. "We should check out the other buildings. Maybe claim one."

"You want to...*claim* one?" She sounded surprised.

His answer came easily. "If we're starting a new society today, I want to own the movie theater."

"Wow. Well, good luck. I've been in there already."

"When?"

"Earlier."

A pause. "What's it like?"

Jennifer coughed. "It's nice. Very empty."

"Excellent. Then you could own it with me. A business partner."

Whatever her reply was, I missed it. But the tone was a little dismissive.

I deflated, sulking into the squishy, velvety seat. Stared out the window in a stupor, where my mirrored self faintly looked back, contorted and trapped. Far beyond my reflection, sloping valley walls beckoned, even as they framed my face mockingly. I couldn't take my eyes off of a thin line of red hair right at the peak of my forehead, that arched up and away, abandoning the rest of me.

If the sunlight kept coming, and I didn't move, the spot would eventually be cosy.

And for a long time, I didn't move. Just sat there, lost, mind swirling in circles.

I spoke to the table, voice twitching in an unstable whisper.

"If anybody has a smoke, I'll take it."

I didn't know why I said it, or what it really meant.

*Just something mom used to say.*

I blinked at that thought, rapidly trying to trace it back to where it came from. It was like zig-zagging through water, sloshing through an unfriendly current.

And then, abruptly, I was upon the memory in all its wonderful depth.

* * *

A flash, bright and loud. A room, somewhere, dull paneling on three walls. Colors in different shapes, looking down on my bed as a woman sat, holding my gaze. A streak of bright purple wrapped around her.

I reached up to her, my arm impossibly tiny. No matter how tall the room, she could fill it. She may as well have been a god.

She patted the bed, her hand thundering against the mattress. Somewhere in the distance I could sense a wave of cloth rippling towards me.

Then she smiled, and strode away at a pace I could never match. She owned the world, and as she passed out of it, the light vanished.

Whatever she wanted, the world obeyed. And though she was gone, I *knew* it was safe.

Time burst forward, rushing up to surround me, one layer after another. The room became smaller and smaller, the colors resolved into shapes and pictures. Other people flickered by, coming and going. One face, full of freckles and impish grins, lingered a little while longer than the rest. Swirls of decor and perspective as my vantage point moved, different angles on the same setting as things were rearranged.

The once impossibly grand woman became a little less impossible, and a little less grand. The bedroom shrank, and the light started to stay on when she wasn't there. I saw less of her.

The world aged with me. But for a time, I still felt *safe*.

The memory fizzled out.

I picked my head up off the table, realizing that I couldn't hear my companions anymore.

They were gone, leaving behind an empty booth. No hint they'd ever been there, no depressions in the seats.

Odd.

The pads of my slippers clapped against the floor. Stepping outside, the world was darker. Clouds in the sky, gathering in force.

I called out for them, but my shouts went unanswered.

I felt alone. Ignored and forgotten, on some very primal level.

And I felt the inklings of something new.

Anger.

The wind gusted, swirling a cool breeze that carved through me as if my clothes weren't even there. Leaves drifted across the paving stones in search of rest.

But then there was a noise. A simple, beautiful noise.

Birds, somewhere, were singing. And in that dim, stormy isolation, it was the sweetest music.

My veins swelled, pulsing as I lost balance, the world tossing me to one side and the other until a brutal, unseen weight slammed me against the ground.

Then, abruptly, it lifted. Gone.

Befuddled, I stumbled to my feet, wrists and forearms stinging. Scratches covered my skin where it had scraped into the stonework.

The birdsong continued to fill my ears. And suddenly, impossibly, I found I could float, drifting upwards, lighter than the air, until I could see above the treetops.

A melodic voice whispered into my mind, softly enough that it might have been forgotten in the wind.

"Hey, Two-sixteen?"

I snapped awake, startled, and bleary.

I was back in the corner booth. Staring at my reflection in an empty napkin holder.

"Noah?"

Jennifer was standing over me, with Beans nowhere to be seen.

She was leaning against the table, hand lightly resting on my shoulder. She removed it as I straightened. A little cautious, but reassuring, and just within reach.

An image of the dead woman in the untouched hotel room flashed through my mind.

"Hey," I replied. "Hey."

"Are you all right?"

Outside, the sun was right where it should have been. The morning remained calm and still.

I shrugged stiffly, slowly recentering myself. "I've been better."

"You were kind of having a moment there. You were all twitchy."

"Yeah." I wiped at my face, a little surprised at how dry it was. "I think I just remembered my mother."

"That's…that's good? Right?"

My arms still stung. But the scratches were gone. "Um."

She snorted. "Maybe I shouldn't have asked."

"No, not that. It was a good thing."

I looked up, over at the other booth.

"Where's the's other guy?"

"He's outside. You've been out for a little while, and we thought it best to let you sleep. A few more people showed up, though."

I twisted around, looking out through the windows, to where a small crowd was starting to gather out in the sun. "I'll join in a minute."

"If you want to, but they don't know anything we don't know."

"He was right. You were right. We need to explore more."

"Are you feeling better?"

I nodded towards the door, surprised at how resolute my words sounded. "There has to be *something* out there. Maybe some hint about where *here* is. Maybe there's a way out that we just haven't been able to see yet."

I stood up, aware of the dramatic emphasis the movement added. "I'm going to try to reach the edge of the valley. You see out there, towards the south, where the cliffs mellow out and it's just trees at the top? In the middle, that bare patch? I think we could reach that."

Jennifer looked up at me, something unfamiliar in her eyes. "That walk could take *hours*. Plural."

"Maybe, but maybe not. Might not be that far. What could happen? You said it, there's no food for us here anyway so we need to start mapping this place out. Best case, might actually learn something. Worst case, we find out that Beans McChef out there is actually a killer."

Jennifer said nothing for several beats. She just looked out at the gathering group, where Beans McChef was trying his apparent best to stay patient and friendly. She looked back at me.

"Okay," she said. "If you're gonna go, I'll stick with you. Let's go."

# THREE

Jennifer humored my curiosity that morning. At my insistence, we explored (for her, re-visited) the rest of what I was beginning to think of as *the village*. I needed to know what it was that we actually had before leaving it behind. The tavern ended up being a smaller, more rustic version of the restaurant. Something out of an earlier century, with bare shelves stacked behind an empty bar.

The library was a different kind of weird. Sound worked strangely there, refusing to linger or echo back to our ears. Even regular conversation was challenging if one of us drifted too far from the other. As we explored it, bookshelves gave way to a lounge, where high ceilings, smooth woodwork, and armchairs awaited.

It wasn't, in my opinion, all that bad of place to be. I might have happily stayed if it didn't insist on confining us to bubble of whispers.

As we walked out, I noted a sign meant for departing patrons. Its message was simple, and quite clear, and some of the only writing we had seen.

*Thank you for being kind.*

I looked at Jennifer, bemused.

She had nothing but a shrug to offer on the topic.

A small crowd was beginning to gather near the front of the square as more compatriots emerged and found their way down the hill. Beans was at the heart of it, putting on some gregarious voice. We made some introductions, but nobody had much to contribute, and some didn't even speak our language. But the atmosphere was positive, if confused and nervous. A handful of newcomers left to see the place for themselves. One man just sat down against a wall, and didn't talk to anyone. He didn't seem to know what else to do.

I thought about staying, helping the group to establish some kind of order, but Beans was getting on with that happily enough. We lingered by the open edge of the square, watching quietly.

"What are you looking for out there?" Jennifer asked.

I shifted uncomfortably. "We've got water here. Food, who knows. We're not hungry yet. We *have* to see this place. The whole thing. There's got to be more here but we'll never find it if we don't get up high."

"You could just climb the hotel."

"Those cliffs are a lot higher."

"Hmm."

As we spoke, a pair of adventurers peeled off from the gathering crowd and ventured over to us, looking for all the world like twins, with light, disastrous hair and boxy faces. Dressed in easy tunics like mine. He was a little taller. She was a little shorter.

"Hello there!" The taller one called out. He smirked as they reached polite company range.

"Hello yourself." Jennifer replied easily.

The younger one took the lead. "You guys heading out somewhere?"

"Yep," I answered.

"Great." She nodded to the other one. "Told you."

"Yeah, yeah," he chuckled agreeably. "I'm Jazz, this is Tera. We're from two-twenty-six and two-twenty-seven. If you don't mind we'd like to go wherever you're going."

"Why?" I asked, genuinely puzzled.

"It beats this."

"I don't know," Jennifer mused, guarded. "We don't know you."

"It'll be grand, my guys." He insisted. "Nothing to worry about. That obviously means there *is* something to worry about, which is, you know, *death*, but it's not something we're likely to cause."

I sighed. *Fine.* "All right. This is Jennifer, I'm Noah. Two-sixteen, me. If you want to come, that's fine. We're making for the edge of the valley. It'll go faster without anyone else." Beside me, Jennifer relaxed a little at that last part.

"Fantastic. Lead us onward, mister Two-sixteen." Jazz agreed. Tera just gave him a side-on look, but nodded at us with a small smile.

*Harmless,* I decided. Now we were four hopefully decent people with no supplies to speak of.

The crowd was growing, and Beans sounded dangerously close to deciding he actually was in charge of things. Best to get moving sooner rather than later, then.

With a shared mutter of agreement we turned, picked a spot in the forest wall, and covered ground at a rapid pace. The initial burst of energy didn't last forever, and the further out we roamed, the more the terrain seemed disinclined to make life easy. Spots of muck and bits of bramble were unavoidable.

The ground did slope up and away from the village, as I'd guessed. What hadn't been obvious was the sheer scale of the valley. It was proving to be immense. And disconcertingly unfamiliar.

Each step on the forest floor was met with the gentle squish of moss and the crinkle of old, collapsed undergrowth. The trees, monolithic from a distance, were all different up close, varied in color and shape, and I had no names to give to any of them. As if I'd never known anything like them before.

That was, I decided, a surprising thing to learn in its own right. And quietly exhilarating.

The reverie dissolved as Tera struck up a conversation. Her tone, somewhere between petulant and dismissive, was excruciatingly irritating.

"I am going to die in this heat. Does anyone know why the freck we have to wear this cult shit?"

Jennifer looked back at her, evaluating the tunic. "That's…kinda what we said."

The younger woman looked at her, almost accusingly. "I can't help but notice that *you're* not wearing one of these sweat-bags."

"That's because *I* have style and sense."

The brother, Jazz, spoke up then, snorting his way through clipped vowels.

"Shut it, Tera. Like that guy said, it's obviously a cult. And this woman is obviously *running* it. Why don't you try to stay on her good side?"

I resolved to stay out of it. Finding a good path was starting to get harder.

Jennifer shook her head. "Beans, or Zed, or whatever we're calling him, gave you the idea, right? Guys like him are universally full of shit at some level. Do us a favor and forget about it."

Tera wasn't discouraged in the slightest. "That's *exactly* what a cult leader would say. You get us in here, with your nice clothes and your friendly talk, get us to take all the drugs and dress up in bedsheets. And now you just want us to trust you in case it all goes to tits!"

"Okay. Fine. You're right. It's a cult. You're *definitely* not going to be in the inner circle now."

Jazz interrupted his sister's reply with a sweeping curtsey. "Oh, my liege, that seems extremely fair. You are a kind and just ruler."

I couldn't help but snort from my spot up front. Jennifer said nothing.

We trudged onwards.

Around what I guessed to be an hour into the trek, the trees started getting denser, the roots more gnarled. Ferns thinned out, and rocks started to take their place. The walk in the woods was starting to definitively become a hike.

My companions were handling it pretty well, I thought. Tera was moving a little oddly; she didn't pass through nature so much as keep it at a sociable distance. As if she didn't really want to be touching it. Her eyes would drift up towards the thinning canopy at every opportunity.

Discomfort? Or desire? Maybe both. I made a mental note to get to know them all better.

Not that it was the most enticing idea in the world at that moment. The farther out we got, the more little annoyances would start to creep in. An annoyed twitch, a rhythmic cough, or someone getting a little too close for comfort.

Naturally, Tera started talking again.

"This is, like, seriously weird."

Jazz responded, maybe a little dismissive. "Yes. The woods. It's very weird."

"No. Me. Like, I am fine, but not normal."

"I agree. You're not normal."

Tera shifted her target to me, her manner a little more stiff. "Noah, right? Noah, don't you feel...not normal?"

"All the time," I said.

"No, seriously."

"Seriously. So you feel fine, but weird. Seems like that's just how most people are."

She squinted. "You don't feel *exceptionally* weird?"

Jazz again. "I don't think he feels like bitching about it."

Tera shrugged. "I like bitching. Here's a bit of bitching for you: Like, why aren't we walking on a road?'

I coughed. "There aren't any roads."

"Why not?"

Jennifer closed her eyes, sighing. "We don't know that."

A little bit of petulance. "But seriously. Why?"

"A fine question."

"Really seems like there should be some."

Jazz was starting to get short of breath. "Oh, would you buzz off. It's not important."

"You want me to *what*? Let me give *your face* something that's not import—"

I turned. "Enough. See that rock?" I pointed at a boulder, perhaps thirty feet away. It was nestled into a tight clearing. "Go to that rock. Take a minute. Rest. And stop talking. Please."

When they didn't obey, I took my own advice, and picked a clear spot to sit down. Overworked leg muscles ached.

Jennifer remained standing, squinting at my pained expression.

"I guess you're not big on exercise?"

"I guess not," I said.

"How much further do you think we've got?"

I considered it, mentally mapping the route against what I'd seen from the diner. "We're really starting to climb now, and I think that happens around the two-thirds mark. We're probably close."

One of the others tossed a few pebbles, causing a small, furry creature to dart through the brush at unfathomable speed, racing for shelter.

Jazz ignored it and crouched down, studying a plant.

"This plant," he declared, "is spiked, and has berries. Kind of a dark purple. Like lots of little round balls. Looks ripe. Anyone want one? Could be poisonous. Could be nice."

We all declined.

He tugged at one, but it clung to its branch, then squished under his grip, sending some juice flying out to splatter on the ground.

Not to be dissuaded, he squatted down in front of the plant, and aimed the next berry at his mouth before squeezing.

"Sweet," he said. "And little sour."

Jennifer didn't have to voice her thoughts for the rest of us to hear what she was thinking. Her expression said it all: *idiot*.

Tera glared, punching him in the arm. "What's wrong with you? That could kill you!"

He shrugged, unrepentant, and did it twice more.

A few minutes later we left the rock behind, pushing onwards. I lingered at the rear of the group, trying to massage my leg out of a cramp. Jazz and I swapped, and he took up the position in front.

The berries, for whatever it was worth, didn't seem to be poisonous.

Before too much longer, we reached our first real obstacle. The shallow slope abruptly terminated in a wall of stone, mottled grey and green. A solid ledge, perhaps ten feet tall, that ran off into the distance in both directions.

Jazz paused before it, momentarily stumped, and started pacing back and forth, looking around for a way up. Then, just as the rest of us caught up, he found it.

A twisted collection of roots snaked out along the stone where a tree was making an endearing effort at life. Between them, they made a haphazard ladder that reached a little less than halfway up the climb. Not enough to make it easy, but enough to bring the top within reach.

Jazz made quick work of the challenge, only grunting twice as he scrabbled against the rock, slowly grasping for purchase with his fingertips. But then he found a handhold, dug in his fingertips, and hauled himself up over the edge. Flakey brown debris clung to his tunic as he turned around to offer a hand.

Jennifer looked less than enthused by the prospect, but she accepted the offered hand, and clambered upwards without much complaint.

Tera was next, scrambling up the stonework as if she'd done it all her life.

I went last, the party disappearing from view as I looked for how to slot into the shallow handholds. Just as I had finished testing my grip, and started to heft my weight away from the ground, Jazz spoke up from somewhere overhead.

"Huh."

I ascended the distance quickly, though, perhaps less than gracefully. Nobody offered me a hand. That irked, but I soon understood why.

A river, perhaps twenty feed wide and half as deep, carved straight across the hillside at a furious pace, matching the curve of the steepening valley wall in a way that just looked *wrong* to my eyes.

On the far bank, between the water and the base of the cliff, a long strip of lazy grassland beckoned. Luxuriously spaced trees and bushes were joined by fluttery stems from wild grasses. Much further upriver, perhaps a hundred meters, I could just glimpse the crest in the hill where it peeked over the edge.

We were close.

The rippling, sparkling sunlight made the water look wonderfully inviting, but a small thought in the back of my mind was warning me against trying to get in it.

"Uh," I said. "I don't feel confident crossing *that*."

"Me either," said Tera.

Jazz was looking upstream, to where a series of boulders rose from the surface. He pointed. "What about down there?"

Up close, the rocks were a collection of different sizes. All hard angles and washed curves.

Tera slowly nodded. "I could climb those."

"Are you sure?" Jennifer asked.

For once, Tera's tone was plainly serious. "I'm the smallest one here. If *I* can make it…"

"Right." I nodded, a little reluctantly.

The current was stronger than it looked at first glance, crashing on and through obstacles as it rushed past. Bits of white spray licked up at us the closer we got.

Tera searched for a path, then, apparently finding one, placed her right foot gingerly onto the first stone.

Stable. No wobbling.

She brought herself up, and with a cautious twist, balanced on top, then squatted, tilting forward dangerously far, until the next boulder was in reach.

*Careful*, I thought.

Forming an arch with her body, she pulled a leg forward, then lunged, rebalancing herself on the second boulder. Just two more to go. There was an enviable smoothness and confidence to the motion.

Tera scooted across her rock to the far side, then tentatively crab-walked forward, reaching out with a lone leg. The next stone was more flat-topped, but low against the waterline, and its reddish hue shone in the sunlight where splashes had made landfall.

She extended towards it, and her slipper promptly abandoned its foot to plop into the current below.

If it gave her pause, that didn't show.

"Be careful!" Jazz shouted.

Tera leaned across to the next boulder.

And nearly toppled in as her support shifted beneath her. I involuntarily leaned out with one arm, aware of the uselessness of the gesture.

But the stone didn't go far, and she pitched forward, then back, wobbling, and then slowly lowered her torso to match her arms, fighting the change in angle by using more of her body for grip.

Jazz called out to her, trying to be reassuring. "Hey, hey! Steady! Be steady. You're all right."

And she was.

Tera looked back at us, and smiled, somewhere between cocky and bashful.

Only one more step to go.

She hauled around to the other side, cast a leg forward, and lunged, easily landing on the far bank.

Tera wiped her hands on her tunic and looked back at us, grinning. It wasn't an entirely innocent look.

"See? Easy as a one night stand with a bottle of calana."

And then, in the space of a blink, she disappeared.

For a beat, nobody moved.

"What?" Jennifer asked, disbelieving. "Where did she…?"

"Tera?" Jazz called out. He was already halfway across the river, mimicking his sister's route with impressive speed.

Jennifer and I replicated the effort with varying degrees of care. We got considerably more wet, but it couldn't have mattered less.

My feet hit the far bank with an unsettling *squish*, the damp soil sucking at the slippers. We spread out, moving forward, unsure of where to step or what to look for.

"Hey. Hey!"

Behind us, perhaps thirty feet away beneath a lonely tree, Tera was suddenly *there*, standing and shouting, eyes wide, shaking.

Jazz closed the gap rapidly, arms outstretched to hold her steady. But he wasn't fast enough. Half a second before he was close enough, Tera was gone again. Vanished from the world. And Jazz was left reaching for empty air.

He didn't seem to know what to do. None of us did. So he just lingered there. No matter what direction we looked, no matter where we searched, there was no trace of her.

I hated that I didn't have a clue what to do or say. I was useless. Worse, *helpless*.

Jennifer stayed close, whether for comfort or security I couldn't say. The temperature dropped by half a degree every few steps. The wind too seemed to fade, dropping away as we left the water.

"What," she quietly demanded of no one in particular, "in the *most absolute of unexplained nonsense* is this?"

I glanced at her. "Good words."

And then Tera was *back* again, right where she had been, sagging into Jazz's reach, babbling indistinctly through a mess of tears.

I counted to five. Then to ten. She remained with us, shattered, no matter how much her brother comforted her. But at least she was here.

"How…?" I whispered. "What just happened?"

Nobody had an answer. No sane reason for why they might.

As we gathered around Tera, my ears were suddenly alive with the song of a dozen birds, all perched in faraway trees, as if they had all filtered into existence alongside our companion. The four of us lingered there, together in the warming sun, calmed by the gentlest patch of nature.

"Tera," I said, "what happened? Where did you go?"

She looked up at me, confused, and suddenly very young. "Where did *you* all go? I was just…here. But it was dark. And it was cold, and wet. And I was alone. And there was a voice."

Jennifer's turn to ask a question. "A voice? Like one of us talking?"

Tera nodded, a little more sure of herself. "There was a voice. I don't know what it was saying, but it was…in my *head*, and outside it. Uhm."

Jennifer started tuning out before Tera had finished. The withdrawal was clear as the daylight across her face.

Surprised, I leaned back, waving a hand in what I hoped came across as *hey, buddy, are you still here?*

The other two couldn't be abandoned right now. The clarity behind Tera's eyes had collapsed, her mental fortitude pushed to the breaking point.

Jennifer was muttering to herself, or maybe to me. "I do *not* want to hear about any haunted bullshit right now. Voices? In her head? In her head. No. No, no. I am not doing this."

I grabbed her arm. "Would you calm down? She literally just *disappeared*. Right in front of us! You saw it."

"I do not know what to do with this!" she hissed. "A dead person I can handle. No stuff or food or memories, that's a bit much but I can figure it out. *This* is supernatural. *I do not do supernatural.*"

I didn't reply. Didn't have the words.

Over her shoulder was the end point. The place I had wanted to reach. Where the side of the valley met the sky.

It was *close*. And for a moment, the insanity was forgotten. We could get a look beyond the valley. We could do what we came to do.

I beckoned to the others, and gently pulled at Tera's arm. A fierce look flashed in Jazz's eyes at the contact. But as he understood what I was doing, he relaxed. Just a little.

We formed a small, protective posse, winding our way up the bank. A hundred long steps later, we reached the peak of the pass, where the grasslands would start descending out to the world beyond. But with every footfall, the ground seemed to get a little harder to climb.

And then we reached the crest.

And my heart sank in confusion.

As far as the eye could see, a rolling expanse of wrinkled tundra awaited, vanishing into the distance. A wide, still river lazily carved through it, at least several miles away.

No roads. No towns. No civilization to be seen.

Jennifer to my left. Jazz to my right. Tera beside him, still twitchy from the adrenaline.

The four of us against a wilderness of nothing.

"We're going to die here," Jazz said.

I couldn't bring myself to agree. At least not out loud.

I sat, cross-legged, staring out at it. A plant prickled against my trousers.

*It can't* all *be like that*, I thought. *It just* can't.

The scope, the sheer emptiness, was unreal. "I've heard of places this remote," I said, "but I've never seen one before."

"How would you even know?" Jazz replied, perturbed.

Tera said nothing.

"We...we need to forage. Find food." I spoke slowly, thinking through the new reality. "We're alone."

"Yeah," Jennifer said, dejected, the wind out of her sails. "Come on. Let's get back."

"I'm getting out of here," Tera mumbled. "I don't like this."

Then I heard the whispers.

Nearly silent, clawing at the periphery of awareness, almost too soft to be heard. But they buzzed there, relentless.

"Hey, it's all right," Jazz was saying. "It's going to be fine. We'll go back, we'll take it easy. Okay?"

I looked down at the ground. And briefly set aside absolutely everything else as I noticed a fresh oddity just at the edge of my reach.

Wisps of a thin blue fog seemed to gather low to the ground, forming a solid line between us and the world beyond.

I squatted down, and reached towards it hesitantly. The closer my hand got, the more a humming started to form in the back of my teeth.

"What's he doing?" Tera asked.

"Don't, Noah." said Jennifer, noticing my interest. "Leave it. This is already way past the line."

I hesitated.

Tera was shaking her head. An insistent *no*.

Jazz just looked interested. Even downright curious. I upgraded him from *aloof* to *questionably sane*.

Leaving it alone would have been perfectly reasonable. And I *should* have done that. But something snapped as my thoughts raced from one impossibility to the next, and I quite suddenly couldn't stand to be dragged around by the world any longer.

I touched the fog, caressing its cold, damp strands.

The darkness was immediate.

And impossible to escape.

I flailed around in the black, desperate to find purchase

somewhere, anywhere. Whispers flooded by, ghostly, half-finished phrases swirling in all directions.

My hand brushed something familiar — gentle fingers, outstretched for mine — but then the fleeting contact was lost.

A gentle, two-toned tenor echoed softly behind my left ear, almost close enough to touch. But its words felt unreal, inside my head, one with my thoughts, even as it was speaking to me.

*You can't go there.*

Then, abruptly:

*Resetting to zero by zero.*

And with a tremendous shudder, my world turned sideways.

# FOUR

Darkness.

Twisting.

Falling.

*Resetting to zero by zero.*

Voices on all sides, calling out to me, their meanings impossible to discern.

Curving shapes indistinctly formed before me, quickly fizzling away into nothing.

A monumental pull backwards.

A gentle caress against my back, lumpy, but soft. A little crunchy.

*Crunchy?*

The thought whirled through me, dissonantly specific.

And suddenly, searing, overwhelming brightness.

Horrible, spindly textures caressed my face. I rolled over. Opened my eyes.

Lengthening grass strayed up to the clouds around me. I blinked, sitting up, making a few too many *uhm*-ing noises.

I was at the edge of a meadow, flora lazy waving in the wind, deceptively waiting, lulling me into a false sense of calm. *Nothing* about this was serene. This was a nightmare. Or a fever dream.

Jennifer coughed behind me, getting to her feet, facing off to the far horizon and sucking in air with a ragged desperation. My balance was off and the wobbliness overcame me as I reached her. The ground made for a sudden and unwelcome companion.

She sat back down, retching. "Why," she demanded, interrupted by a gasp to suck in more air, "the ever-loving shit did you do that?"

*Goes to show that I've got a friend.* "I had to."

There was no sign of Jazz or Tera.

Good? Bad? Didn't matter. Something was playing games, and it was clearly more than a parlor trick. We were up against something that couldn't even be fathomed.

My eyes settled on my trousers as I took stock. Covered in muck and debris. Feet were bare, cold, tingly. *Filthy.* Jennifer was no better. But at least we were together.

Finally, I finished my scan as a cold understanding settled in my gut. A hundred yards away, where the meadow narrowed, loomed a curving white block of concrete and glass.

"No. No way. No."

Jennifer didn't even look up as she hugged her knees. "What?"

I was at a loss for words.

In the blink of an eye, we had been transported, abruptly and impossibly, back to the very beginning.

* * *

It was a paralyzing sort of fear that carried us inside, seeking safety, or at least a retreat.

By mutual agreement we ended up in Jennifer's room. It was on the top floor, farthest from people and easy access. Not that it made a real difference, we knew, but the idea still appealed to a scared, primitive part of our minds.

Numerous more rooms were open as we walked the hotel's hallways. Nearly all of them had simply been left ajar and abandoned, which did not evoke a sense of calm. We spotted a few wanderers aimlessly trying to make some sense of their new world. We avoided them. Somehow, it felt like we'd learned *less* than nothing, except that the world outside was *not* what it appeared. Whatever kind of place this was, however barren and isolated and *haunted* it was, we had been sent back to the hotel. If we weren't safe *here*, then…

That line of thought had no ending that I could see.

The walk to her place was mercifully quick. And for a little while, it was easy to think of it as a refuge. Cold and alien, but a refuge. A cave. Shelter.

As we reached it, Jennifer held up her hands, still covered in drying vomit and bits of the forest floor. "Can you, uh…"

"Oh. Uh, right."

I grasped the handle and pushed, but I might as well have been trying to move a wall. "It's locked."

"No it isn't."

I looked at her. "Yes, it is."

"No, it *isn't.*"

"You try, then."

She reluctantly wriggled her hands, then sighed, grasped the handle and pushed.

The door swung open, gliding silently on its hinges.

I gave it a side-eyed glare as we entered.

Outside the window, the distant horizon still beckoned.

Jennifer watched me carefully for a lingering moment, then set her course for the refresher, and shut herself into it with barely a word. Muffled splashes from running water filled the air for a few long minutes. I thought it was a pretty decent way to process things.

My eyes drifted across the room. To the still-shut party door.

I tried to ignore it.

As the shower continued, lingering curiosity eventually got the better of me. I wandered over to Jennifer's dresser, and pulled the top drawer open an inch. It was lined with several pairs of socks, neatly arranged from one side to other.

I rolled it closed, disappointed with myself. Trust was one thing, but a sock drawer was personal. Intimate. Not a place for me. I decided that with her, that mattered.

The shower ticked off. I looked up.

She was watching me from the refresher, saying nothing.

I looked away. "Sorry." Then, "Feeling better?"

"Yes. A little."

She walked straight towards me, and at first I wasn't sure how to react. But then she made a brief, impatient noise, and I turned my back as she fished out a replacement outfit.

No reason, I thought wryly, to be anything less than a gentleman.

Amidst the soft sounds of rustling clothes, another memory percolated through my awareness, this time of a narrow tube cluttered with chairs and people. Windows lined the sides, showing bare rock as we skimmed past. A beautifully sweet, salty, savory smell lingered in the air. Thick, warming, and rich. As if by magic, I found the word, and put a name to it.

*Cinnamon.*

Someone had been talking on that train, maybe to me, maybe to someone else. I had been nervous, even anxious, but in a good way. I knew that the train would slow and I would get off of it, and there would be someone waiting for me. I knew that I wanted to avoid seeing them, if only to shed the tension. But it had to be done. Words had to be said.

The slice of time faded, the train receding into imaginary fog. Any fleeting warmth went with it.

Snug in fresh clothes, Jennifer sat on the edge of the bed. She had gone quiet, staring out the window. Her present line of thought was plainly written on her face.

"You know," I said, forcing a wistful tone, "I'm still not wearing any socks."

"What the *shit,* Noah."

I said nothing.

"Am I crazy? Are *we* crazy? Is there some kind of demon out there? Haunting the borders? Is this a goddamn demon hotel?"

I tried to smile. "Certainly lends the cult theory some credibility."

She looked at me. "What do you really make of this? Honestly?"

I thought about it, trying to circle around everything I'd seen in the last few hours. The amnesia, the prepared, yet vacant buildings. The outside world that seemed infinitely untouched. The impossible...disturbances.

I blew out a breath. My hands wanted to shake.

"I think where we came from is a much more interesting question. What were we doing before here?"

"What does anyone do? We were living. I can remember a nice place, a park, not too different to here. I don't know where it was." She frowned. "The park had a ceiling, though."

"I think I remember one of those. It had big lights. And I think there was a very fat man."

She genuinely smiled a little. "Sounds about right."

"But," I continued, "if we were just living, what makes us special? Why us? Why here? I think we got ourselves into something really serious. Something that we couldn't let ourselves remember."

"Something like what?"

"It must have been really big. Like we ended the world, and we're all that's left. Not so that we could have a new start, but so that we could die happily and in peace."

Jennifer cocked an eyebrow. "That's as dark as anything I've got. Like a bookend for the garden of Eden."

"A...what?"

"It's an old thing I learned about, growing up. Like a...testing ground for life, to keep it safe and easy once the on-switch was pushed."

"What happened to it?"

"Outside interference, if memory serves."

I shook my head, strolling over to the window, plopping into one of the chairs. "Maybe we're all dead, and this is some kind of afterlife. Just for us."

Jennifer said nothing.

My eyes returned to the horizon line. Somewhere, far away, a thin blue fog had us trapped.

*Resetting to zero by zero.*

Not a harsh threat, but a firm, if unintelligible statement. And an inexplicably technical one, at that. *It* had the power to move us multiple miles in mere moments. I wasn't quite ready to take on something that could define reality itself.

When I met Jennifer's quizzical eyes, it felt painfully dumb to pretend that the world had been behaving rationally up to this point.

"I don't think we did this to ourselves. This is all too...perfect.

Too controlled. Somebody out there is doing this *to* us."

"Why?"

"Maybe we deserved it somehow."

"*Deserved* it?"

I nodded, a little half heartedly. Her tone was more thoughtful than doubting. But it still felt uncomfortable. "Do you think they'll make it back here okay?"

"Jazz and Tera?"

"Yeah."

She pursed her lips. "I'm sure they're already halfway back. Tera's going to be shaken up. But they'll be fine."

Doubt colored my thoughts. "Maybe. We should go back for them."

"It wouldn't make a difference."

"What?"

She was silent for a long, long minute.

"I think," she said, "that this place isn't what it looks like. I think it has rules."

"What are you getting at?"

Jennifer met my eyes, then twisted, facing the party door we had both been studiously trying to ignore. "Rules. It has rules we have to learn. We just got teleported halfway across the valley in an instant, and that was crazy. We thought that woman in there was dead before. What if we were wrong?"

"Again, what?"

"Let me ask you something. Has anything about this place made any kind of normal sense?"

I shook my head easily. "No. Definitively not."

"How long have *you* been awake now?".

"A few hours. But—"

"What did we see outside?"

"I don't know!"

She was persistent. "Have you, *at any point*, felt hungry?"

"I—" I paused. "No!"

"*Why* is there a restaurant with no food in a place where you don't get hungry?" Her voice was moving into deranged territory. "*Think about it*. About Tera popping in and out like a ghost, and about that magic fog out there. All of it. You heard those whispers too, don't deny it. But none of it went right until one of us reached Tera. And we didn't get brought back here until— "

I saw where she was going. "Until I touched the thing."

She seemed to deflate.

"Yeah. Until that. I think touch matters here. In a special way. I think it…*grounds* you."

"This is pretty thin."

"You can't tell me that *something is not right here*. And after seeing what we've seen, I don't know if she," she jerked her thumb over her shoulder, "is actually dead. Or at least…not in the normal way."

"Yes, weird dead is much better than normal dead, I'm sure."

"I'm not screwing around, and you know it. When I first found her, I did a little dance, I tried calling out, I tried outright shouting. I even messed with the lights. But I didn't touch *her*."

"She wasn't *breathing*, Jen."

She walked over to the door, and shoved it open. "What if we weren't breathing either? Before we woke up?"

I swallowed, resolving to avoid the knot settling in my stomach, and got up to follow. She had a point. I didn't quite understand it, but it felt like she had a point.

The other room was exactly as we'd left it. Right down to the figure in the sheets. Despite the cool knot in my chest, I refused to look away. "So you think she will…*wake up*, if we…?"

"I hope so."

"I don't want to touch a dead body."

"Neither do I."

I closed my eyes. Counted to three, fighting with myself.

Every rational part of my mind rejected the concept completely. But there was a little voice, hiding out in the back of things, which held the opinion that the rational part of my brain really ought to have been miles away on a grassy hilltop.

I decided, grudgingly, that the little voice knew what it was talking about.

"Fine," I said. "Okay. *Okay.*"

I walked forward, one foot in front of the other, until I was just a few feet from the body. This close, I could make out individual wrinkles around her eyes.

I carefully knelt down and reached out, gingerly hovering inches away from the woman's skin. The surface looked pale and pasty.

Electricity seemed to tingle in my fingertips.

I brought down a finger, and gently tapped her through the blanket.

I exhaled, and the waiting adrenaline bled away.

She was warm. None of the cool stiffness that instinct told me to dread.

Jennifer slowly, carefully, came down beside me, pulling the blanket back a little.

I unfurled my fingers. Looked at Jennifer. Looked back at the woman. I rested my hand on her shoulder.

She inhaled as if her life depended on it, violently trembling, thrashing around. The sheet clung to her skin, clammy and taut, holding her in place, which only made it worse.

The woman looked at me. Looked at Jennifer. Looked back at me.

She screamed.

# FIVE

"Hey, hey! It's all right! You're okay. *You are okay!*"

Jennifer was trying to calm her down, holding the older woman's shoulder. It didn't work at first. She kept crying out, panicking, struggling against the younger woman's grip. But slowly —slowly!—gasps started interrupting the screams, becoming choked noises. Watching it was fiercely uncomfortable.

Crazy eyes became a little steadier. She was starting to see past the panic.

Jennifer, to her credit, kept talking the whole time. I kept my distance.

The woman never really *relaxed*, but the panicked nerves did subside. It was replaced by something more disturbing.

When her gaze finally focused enough to settle on us, there was something dark brewing behind her eyes. An anger, a *resentment*.

She locked eyes with Jennifer, brow furrowed above that glare. "I know you."

She angled back to me. "But who the hell are *you*?"

"I'm Jen," said Jennifer. "and that's Noah. We're trying to help you."

"You're in your room. Three thirty-one. You're safe." I said, doing my best to sound reassuring.

The woman squinted. "Why?"

I looked up at Jennifer. "You two are definitely related."

Jennifer grasped her hand, ignoring me. "You're safe," she said, gently. "Do you remember your name?"

The woman looked around again, taking in the view of the outdoors as she straightened, swelling up with new energy. The glare faded, replaced by a softer confusion. The transformation was disconcertingly quick. "Can you stop staring at me?"

Jennifer looked at me. "Out."

"What?"

"Wait in my room. I'll sort her out."

"Okay, okay!" I retreated.

The door slid closed, and some part of my brain simply didn't know how to process what I had just seen. It felt deeply unlikely that what had just happened, *had actually happened.* That woman had been as dead as a rock, I was sure of it. That demanded answers, and I had half a mind to storm right back in and ask for them. But I held back, understanding the abrupt exile.

We had seen this woman at her most vulnerable, before she'd had a chance to prepare for the world. It was a private time, one only rarely shared. And we had forced ourselves into it. We might have brought her to life but that still entitled her to privacy.

My unspoken questions became what I hoped was just another encouraging smile. Nobody was there to see it.

When the refresher door eventually clicked shut and the muffled sound of running water started, Jennifer joined me, closing the party door behind her. My curiosity was tingling. As were my ankles, where dried muck was still clinging on. I would have to take care of that.

She collapsed into the opposing chair, looking as if she'd just understood how tired she really was.

"Her name is Selena. I think she'll be all right. I pointed out the useful stuff."

"Even the socks?"

She found the energy to give me a look. "Yes. What do we *say* to her?"

"We try not to scare her."

"I don't think we can get away with hiding anything about this place. Or that we *should*."

"Me neither."

We stared at the walls for a long, long minute. It seemed to stretch out into forever.

Then a series of shouts, accompanied by excited footsteps pounding down the corridor.

A male voice, young. Unfamiliar, and muffled through the walls. The volume must have been impressive. "Food! There's food! And people! And everything! Wake up!"

I wanted to discount the very notion. It didn't make sense. We'd both seen the village. We *knew* what was down there.

Unless our hosts had finally arrived.

I made it to the door in three seconds and had it open on the fourth.

The source of the outlandish claims had already come and gone, his voice retreating around a distant corner of the hall.

The image of an aircraft descending, with uniforms bearing giant stacks of griddlecakes involuntarily sped through my mind. It was absurd. By any sane measure, I should have gotten up, chased down the runner, and demanded to know details. But I didn't. It could wait.

I turned around and closed the door.

Jennifer just watched me, chuckling half-heartedly. "Sounds like we just got a whole new set of things to figure out."

"Jazz and Tera are going to be *so* confused."

"Yep. We should head down. Can I have a cocktail? Do you think they'll be serving those?"

I surprised myself with a modest, even slightly demented grin. If it hadn't been obvious to me before, I knew right then that I had a friend.

It was several more minutes before our neighbor emerged, tentatively pushing the door aside. It was like meeting an entirely different person.

Gone was the bleariness, doubt, and suspicion. A mask had settled into place behind her eyes, carefully keeping her emotions and desires in check. An impressive transformation.

"What happened to *you?*" she asked, looking directly at me. Her voice had taken on a more clipped, melodious tenor. More assertive. More direct. I realized she was talking about my clothes. And my distinct lack of footwear.

"I went for a walk, intending to be very organized about it." I answered truthfully. "The forest had other plans. Feeling better?"

"Yes, quite a lot, thank you. It's Noah, yes?"

She smoothed out the wrinkles on her shirt. Her body language was calm. Quiet. Even tastefully so. But when she got going, there was not going to be any stopping her. I could see that. I *knew* it, just by looking at her.

"Yes," I said. "At least for now. Names are a little changeable around here."

"Mine is Selena."

"You can remember it?"

"Yes."

"What else can you remember?"

"Nothing I care to share."

Jennifer got up, interceding before I could press the point. "So, right." She gestured out at the wilderness. "Welcome to the valley."

"The valley?"

"The one and only," I chimed in.

"What would you like to do first?" Jennifer asked.

Selena actually thought about that one. "Well first, I think I'd like some breakfast. What's good around here?"

"There's a village down the hill. There's been some excitement, from the sound of it."

"A village?"

I pitched in. "There isn't much. It's like a resort. A very *quiet* resort."

She processed that. A look of distaste was subtle, but plainly shown. "Is there anywhere else?"

"Not that we can get to easily."

"Then it sounds nice."

We made an odd trio as we left the room behind. The hallways were, naturally, empty once more. It was threatening to become a pattern.

Whoever the mystery runner had been, they were long gone, back to what I daydreamed, impossibly, would be a smorgasbord of food, entertainment, and luxury.

Deeply unlikely.

If the village had simply flourished with the same instantaneous, reality-contorting magic that had moved us kilometers in an instant, then...

*Whatever is running this place, it actually wants to keep us here,* I thought.

Which meant our well-being was entirely out of our control.

And it would be entirely reasonable for me to enjoy things at a more leisurely pace. I felt no need, at all, to let my movements be dictated by some enigmatic puppeteer. And damn it, I was still dirty. And damp.

As we walked, nearing the landing, I made a decision.

"You two go ahead. I'm going to be a few minutes."

"You sure?" Jennifer asked.

"Yeah. I need some time for me. You'll be okay, right?"

"I'm sure we'll be fine," said Selena. Polite, perhaps quizzical.

Jennifer just nodded. She understood.

My door was a short walk from the stairs. I counted up the rooms as I walked. Two-oh-seven. Oh-eight. Two-twelve. Two-fourteen. And finally, my own.

Where its neighbors had been left open, it remained dutifully shut. Waiting for me.

I lingered over the handle. Its cool metal swivelled away with a gentle twist and barely a squeak.

The room was precisely how I had left it. Right down to the mussed sheets and halfway-drawn curtain. A check of the drawers found underwear, and indeed, several neatly lined-up pairs of socks.

I walked straight into the refresher, shedding the cultish garb as I went. This time, when I looked in the mirror, I was ready, and accepted the sight. It still wasn't me. But I could adopt it.

The shower was a warm, soothing spray, its twisting vapors escaping to mist up the room. The water was a tiny slice of heaven. But I didn't feel soothed. I felt defiant. Even *alive*, in the knowledge that as batshit as it was, there was *some* kind of plan for us.

Afterwards, I collapsed onto the mattress, relaxing in the little sanctuary someone had arranged for me. It was quiet. It was *mine*. My own.

Jazz and Tera would be reaching the village about now.

Reconnecting with Beans. Seeing *whatever* it was that had happened. Helping themselves to some coffee, if there was any fairness in this place.

I smiled wide at an empty ceiling, and it quickly devolved into a long, mirthless laugh. The kind of laugh that can't quite be stopped. I laughed at the absurdity, at the terror, the incomprehensible rules.

It must have sounded insane. It felt *great*.

* * *

A polite chiming echoed through the building. It seemed to be coming from everywhere.

I blinked. Bleary. Edges of broken thoughts ached behind my eyes.

Hard to tell how long I had been out. The sun was further along in the day.

The chiming was obnoxious. I assumed Jennifer was at the door again in some concerned reprise.

*Great.*

I opened the door.

No Jennifer.

The chiming continued, patient. Maybe somebody had found the hotel's back office and pushed an annoying button.

I closed the door. Plopped down in a chair. Focused on what I was pretty sure was an oak tree, just outside, maybe thirty feet away. Its leaves waved carelessly, harmlessly. One of them seemed particularly enigmatic, dappled in the warm afternoon light. I must have looked very thoughtful, staring at it.

I snorted at the idea.

"Can somebody stop that noise?" I called out. "It's beginning to grate."

Nobody answered, of course. In here, away from everyone, there was only loneliness for company. And that damned pinging. A hug would have been nice. Maybe a glass of something very strong.

Outside, the sun exploded into monumental, unearthly brilliance.

I stumbled to my feet, blinded, trying to shield my eyes with one hand as I used the other to fumble for the curtain.

For an instant, I was terrified, convinced that it was all cyclical, and the universe was ready to kick us back to the start. That Jennifer and the rest of them were finished, already gone. That I was all that was left, that the pings were a countdown to the *end*, and the valley all within it would be consumed in a wall of flame.

But the world *didn't* vanish in a hellish fire. The moment passed, and took any ridiculous explanations with it.

The burst of brightness faded, resolving into a more coherent form, projecting a ghostly image where the sun's rays intersected with the window.

I stared dumbly as an unfamiliar face materialized in the glass. A million unlikely possibilities came and went in a heartbeat.

The traced out visage gained weight and definition, hardening into a man's wrinkled smile. He looked away at something only he could see, then returned and at long last, spoke.

I understood, somehow, that it wasn't just for me. He was addressing *everyone*.

As words began to leave his mouth, fireworks detonated in the back of my mind, as if life itself was having a celebration, and memories were slotting into place, one after another. My mother, wispy hair over gentle, distracted eyes. A grand park. Sweeping vistas of infinite stars. A glowing, crackling globe that brought life to everything around it. Ice, dripping lazily from thin pipes to form pools of pure water. The scenes flashed past faster and faster, gone too quickly to grasp. Nausea wasted no time in chasing the shock.

The face in the glass was still speaking, and it had *plenty* to say. I struggled to process it, fighting to listen to the words.

"…so, hello. I am Captain Franklin DeSanto. On behalf of my team, I sincerely apologize for the circumstances in which you've awoken. You may be experiencing severe side effects, like memory loss, confusion, hallucination, or sickness, but I can assure you these afflictions *are* temporary, and you will feel perfectly normal within the next few hours. We are doing everything we can to make you comfortable."

He paused. I wondered, absently, if he was doing it for dramatic effect.

"If everything around you has felt like a dream, that's because it *is*. You are passengers on the inter-colonial transport *C.I.S. Apollo*, immersed within our CarverNet reality simulation. The world you can see and touch is one of many that we make, and we will do our best to make sure that from now on you experience all of them the *right* way during your trip with us.

"I know this is a lot, and to some of you it may sound strange. Believe me, *that is normal*. You were scheduled to finish your acclimation and awaken in this environment three sols from now, approximately one week into our four-month journey to Luna out of Ceres Station. Obviously, this has all happened too soon, before your bodies and minds have had time to adjust. In light of these circumstances…"

# MESSAGE LOG

Archive for Inbound 11
Sol 5, 09:44 Local Time


*Jennifer Motley is writing…*

*hey*

*No keyboard*

*What am I supposed to do?*

*What?*

*Oh gods*

*It's reading your mind.*

*It's reading my mind how is this happening?*

*How can it be reading my mind it's only a machine wait we're in a simulation which means it can feed a world to my brain why not pull thoughts too oh god it's sending this shit.*

*Just look away from the chat*

*I think you can turn this off. Under honesty settings.*

*What the freck is this.*

*Is your name really Aidan?*

*Apparently.*

*I liked Noah. It suited you.*

*Is your last name really Motley?*

*Probably. The computers might be lying.*

*Remind me to turn this setting off. This thing is bullshit.*

*I saw an ad for a game. A big tournament starting in a couple days. Sounded fun, want to do it together?*

*Uh.*

*Not a hard question…*

*Smiley face*

*Did you just try to think an emote at me?*

*Hello?*

*Just tell me about it.*

# SIX

"Riots broke out on Deimos Station this evening as sudden shortages in hydroponics production were blamed on austerity measures. The Martian government has urged calm and resilience but has refused to back down. In zeeball news, the Harrington Squires moved up to ninth place in the rim league, knocking long-time rivals Pock United out of the bracket. It's an exciting upset for the team.

"We'll have Entecka on the program later to celebrate the release of their third album. The band made headlines last week when they played at a political rally against—"

The newscaster drolly read out the rest of the headlines with a fixed smile. They washed over our ears like so much white noise. I kind of liked it. As soon as the zeeball headline had finished, Jazz had gone right back to ignoring it.

"We should do skydiving," he said.

"No."

"But we haven't done *any* of the extreme runs."

"That's because they all look terrifying," I replied, entirely reasonably.

"Terrifying? In what way?" He challenged. "Terrifying in that you're scared you'll be scared, or terrifying in that you're scared you might have *fun?*"

We were staring at a holographic menu, a span of hard light shimmering in air just inside our arms' reach. Pictures of broad deserts, spinning asteroids, alien jungles, and artic mountains were all accompanied by vague descriptions.

The mountains had Jazz's attention.

Smaller menus, dropping down from their respective pictures, listed a dozen different prescribed activities and experiences that could be found in each locale, from the suggested skydiving to a long walk on a sparkling orange beach or the rather exotic idea of hypersled racing.

Some sounded more appealing than others. An assortment had already proven to be interesting ways of passing the time. The beach stroll had been nice, but even I found it dull.

But Jazz was pointing at a decidedly *insane* prospect. And I had to admit there *was* a small, needed appeal to it.

I held my finger over the option for *The Crisper: Skydiving Challenge.*

It wasn't the prospect of losing a race, I told myself. I'd just learned that the term *adrenaline junkie* didn't quite apply to me.

*Do I want to do this?* I asked myself.

*No, I do not,* came the answer.

I tapped it anyway.

As my finger reacted with the line of text, our world fizzled into a spiralling cascade of starlight, twisting my stomach into knots. I could do this a hundred times and *still* not get used to it.

Reality faded into an even, searing white, and Jazz's voice echoed in my ears, dripping with unrestrained delight.

"Hah! This, my man, is going to be *fun.*"

            *  *  *

The world snapped into focus.

We were horizontal, suspended among endless fluffy clouds. An unlikely blanket of thin blue fabric kept us separated from the vast drop below. It did nothing for the rapidly-gathering frost on my face.

Our arms and legs were splayed outwards, tethered to loose webs of stretchy fabric. A word came to mind from some forgotten bit of trivia:

*Wingsuits.*

I experimented with tugging around my limbs. Where the fabric ended, chunky gloves and boots were a welcome shield against the open air.

But in an instant that comfort was hardly the most pressing concern. Suspended in midair between us, a line of glowing white text asked a terrifying question:

*Ready? Say yes or no.*

Sweat started gathering on my palms. To my right, Jazz was studiously trying to maintain a poker face, less certain about what was about to happen. I called over to him. My face was almost a smirk.

"Still want to do this?"

He flashed me back a crooked grin. His reply was almost shrill. It might have been tinged with insanity. "Of course!"

He stared at the words. "Yes!"

The words changed.

*Player Two, Ready.*

*"What?"* he shouted. "Why am I player *two?"*

I frowned, closing my eyes. My bluff had been called.

"Fine! Yes!"

The words were replaced by a generic smiling face, which in turned morphed into a countdown. Starting from five.

Four.

*Oh,* I thought.

Three.

I called over to my opponent. "I am not good with heights! Not good!"

Two.

"Try to have fun with it, bozo!" He shouted back. "I'll see you at —"

The countdown vanished.

The thin blue sheet was gone, replaced with a heart-stopping void. From the vast puffy shapes floating around us, it had been obvious that were were at high altitude. But now we were staring at an entire layer of cloud *below* us, too. And beyond, the unknowable vast face of a planet sucking us down to our doom.

*Oh god, no. No, no no.*

We dropped with all the grace of poorly-mortared bricks.

The sky tumbled past, swirling around and around in bitingly cold air. The fall became a slow-motion somersault, diving from one invisible current to the next. I was convinced I was about to be sick. For the *second* time that day.

Jazz managed to do something that stopped his tumble and was yanked backwards, opening up a substantial gap I careered down and away towards a grand sea of fluffy silver.

I plunged into the cloud bank far too fast, flinching at the barrage of icy crystals slashing against me. The wingsuit helped, but it was little comfort for my face.

I shut my eyes against the blinding cold, forcing myself to stop flailing and to *think, dammit.* To fight the swarming panic. To remember that it was just a simulation. That I wasn't plummeting to my imminent death from ten thousand feet wrapped up in a glorified sleeping bag.

*Focus,* I thought. *I know this.*

Through the onslaught, a familiar hum tingled at the edges of my fingertips. The same hum I'd felt in a hotel room days earlier. The same hum that precipitated everything magical in this world.

I smiled, understanding what I was feeling, even if I had no idea what I was actually *doing.*

I splayed out my palms, until each fingertip felt the tiny vibration, then pulled my arms down, towards the distant ground.

The suit tightened in response to the virtual controls. Coarse nylon gripped the air, pretending to claw back some altitude.

I punched through the base of the cloud, leaving the mist behind. And before me, opening out into vast horizons, lay a sweeping, soaring collection of jagged peaks, mighty stones reaching ever skyward.

It was almost breathtaking enough to make me forget what I was doing.

I pushed out again, this time keeping my arms more tightly bound, and keeping my palms flat, dancing with the invisible tingles. Momentum shifted, following my body language first one way, then the next, up and down, side to side, swivelling and swerving on every axis.

My cheeks stung. My stomach was flopping. My lungs burned.

I grinned past all of it. And started to *fly.*

For a long, glorious moment, the air itself seemed to be at my command, gently leaving me to serenely bob and weave through the sky. I was no acrobat, but the hint of control was downright intoxicating.

Far above, Jazz had been figuring things out for himself, and was starting to pick up speed. I made the mistake of waving up at him—possibly with a rude gesture—and immediately sent myself spinning away into a graceless tumble that nearly brought up my lunch.

It took several precious seconds to pull out of the drop and level out. Grimacing at the idiocy, I yanked myself around until I was more-or-less back on course. Jazz had used the interruption to great effect, and had radically closed the altitude gap.

Great blue flags marked the path as we careened into the ice-bound mountains. The velvety white snow was stippled with treetops poking out into the air. From a distance it looked almost comfortable.

"I think I like this!" I shouted.

"Only because you're winning!"

Something clicked as we rounded a bend in the slopes, and my eyes widened in alarm.

The end of the course was in sight, a clearing nestled in the heart of the mountain pass. Green flares, bright against bluish shadows, smoked up to beckon us down.

But it was too far.

Or to be more accurate, I was too low. I wasn't good at guessing where my glide would take me; there seemed to be some unfathomable calculus dictating how far someone could go at a given speed. But it was unavoidably clear that I'd taken too long to get to grips with my suit, and the implications of that were... *unfortunate*.

A strong gust of wind tore across my flight path, threatening to toss me further out of the race.

I tried hauling my arms around to take advantage of the wind, but all it seemed to accomplish was to speed me up, not take me higher.

In a matter of seconds the edge of the clearing had come much closer, maybe a couple hundred feet away. The treetops poked out of the snow, branches jaggedly threatening to snarl anything that came too close.

A rock formation overlooked the southern end of the pass. The wind currents were brushing thin, feathery clouds off the top, at a suspiciously useful angle. I would need to drop lower to use it but the extra momentum might just make up the difference.

Far above, Jazz was gently gliding onwards. He'd reach the end with barely any effort.

I muttered a gentle curse into the wind, and went for it. The wingsuit stiffened and bucked in a vain effort to grab every available smidgen of lift.

My glide path took me across the valley, dropping lower and lower. A gust of snow off a tall pine lashed upwards, catching at my legs and coating them in fine powder.

Thirty feet to the cliff's edge. What had been gentle gusts from afar had become a raging whirlwind up close, but there was no turning back. I flapped my arms, hoping against hope it would do *something.*

Twenty feet. I looked up. The smoking flares were enticingly bright. Circling above, Jazz was flapping around, actively *trying* to lose altitude.

Ten feet.

Five.

The gust over the rocks was tremendous, catching me like a glove across my whole underside and thrusting me forward and upwards. I curled forward, trying to ride it, following some instinct as I glided just a little bit further. And for a brief, fleeting moment, it seemed to work. The edge of the clearing was within reach. *Just a little further.*

But then I flopped out of the current, and what little momentum I had gained was gone.

Just before I smacked the treetop, it became obvious that I was never going to reach the flares. The impact against the pine shook loose a cascade of powdery snow. I was still travelling forward enough to flip head to toe as the branches lazily tugged me out of the sky.

Time slowed as I tumbled towards the ground. As the world spun past, I got a glimpse of that smug figure coasting overhead. Circling lower. Coming in to land.

I had just enough time to close my eyes before the snowdrift swallowed me whole.

* * *

"You should have seen it! Boof! Like exploding a pillow!"

Jazz mimed the treacherous end to my skydiving career with a little too much gusto.

We had retreated to the tavern, mugs of zesty ale in hand, huddled in what had become our booth. It was near the back, where we had a fine view of the establishment.

Crackling, shimmering lamplight danced between the tables, sending shadows to mingle amongst our feet. The others were sat across from us, watching Jaz's animated portrayals with rapt attention.

I leaned forward, glowering. "Yes, yes. I'll have you know that falling into a snowdrift from the top of a sixty foot tree is surprisingly comfortable."

Jazz beamed. "It was less *falling*, and more *flailing*."

I crossed my arms. "I don't think I'll be doing it again."

"Sure you will, wunderkind," said Tera. "And I want to watch it next time."

I shrugged. "Please. The only way I would let you see something that horrifying would be to have you endure it first."

Jennifer smiled, distracted. "So what you're saying is Tera should go do it, and then do it better."

I held up my hands. "Sure. You try falling several thousand feet in forty-five seconds through frozen misery. It's called *The Crisper* for a reason."

Jazz nodded. "He's not joking. I've never felt that cold in my life."

Tera had seen fit to turn herself into a walking anachronism. Her hair, messy as ever, bore hot streaks of reds, purples, and teals, while a brown corduroy jumpsuit was matched to a gleaming chrome blazer. Now, with a dangerous smirk, she leaned forward. "I see. Then I accept this challenge, and look forward to doing it *entirely* perfectly."

"Five coins say you plummet to a harrowing death," I said, raising an eyebrow.

She grinned. "Make it ten."

"Too rich for my blood. Try to remember it's fake."

"Your entire *life* is fake."

I sat back, defeated, and shook my head. "Forget the bet. I'm just going to watch."

The chunky old place was warm, full of heavy beams and cosy soft things; somebody's idea of a hardy refuge. A lute player lingered somewhere, off in a hidden corner, practicing their art. Up at the front, the bar had been filled to the brim with casks, while a gentleman in a woollen suit poured a range of beverages beneath a mounted sword. When we had ventured in fifteen minutes earlier, he had whipped up an enticing, spiced concoction that warmed the soul. Two tables over, a card game was reaching a fever pitch.

It was world away from the sterile, half-formed shell it had been just a few days ago.

In the time since DeSanto's announcement, I'd barely seen Jennifer outside of occasional late-night messages. She had become a veritable recluse; Selena, who had turned out to be her aunt, was a more common sight out and about. But I while I was curious, I had left it alone. We all had plenty of distractions to go around.

She leaned forward now, putting on an air of wisdom. "I do believe I am in need of a fresh beverage. Waiter!"

A mountain-sized woman in crusty leathers strode up to the table, a pitcher of something frothy in her hand. With barely a word, she poured it into Jennifer's tankard, slopping some of the drink over the side for effect. She gave the younger woman a brusque smile, and lingered expectantly. I ordered something that I couldn't pronounce correctly, a sin which was rewarded with a hard glare. Jazz mumbled something, received a glare of his own, and the hostess left us in peace.

"Mead?" he asked, glancing over his shoulder at the retreating waitress. "Really?"

Jennifer was unfazed. "Really. And this isn't just mead. *This* is the Golden Ichor Supreme."

I raised an eyebrow. "That's a pricy drink."

"And I am going to *enjoy* it."

Which was a fitting thing to say. The whole village, it seemed, was practically dedicated to the fine art of hedonism. Games, movies, adventures, food and drink, experiences of all kinds, all were available as ready-made indulgences. Many were available for free. Nearly all offered something more premium for those willing to part with their money.

The conversation wound onwards, shifting from topic to topic. Jennifer, I noted, never let it settle back towards any of us for too long, always prodding a line of questions about someone or someplace else. She never looked at me directly, which seemed a little odd in its own right, and I wondered if there was something being left unsaid. But between them, the twins supplied enough conversation for all of us, talking about some piece of manga they had mutually rediscovered.

As they rambled, the burly waitress returned with food. I inspected the thing on my plate cautiously as she set it down. It was a round hunk of bread, with the middle carved out and filled with a chunky red soup. It felt hot and smelled sour. It tasted *good*.

Jazz took a bite of his sandwich; something unidentifiable was squished between pieces of thick toast. He screwed up his face at the flavor, and promptly put it down again.

"So I hear there's a tournament."

"Yeah," I replied. "It's a big one. We," I tilted my head at Jennifer, "Are going to try to win it."

"You two? Fine. Then I get Tera."

Tera shrugged. "Fine. I'm in."

Jazz nodded approvingly. "Now. What *is* it?"

"Well, it's big. Sixty people get to try for a big prize, which means thirty teams of two. There's three challenges, each one is different. We don't know anything else. Only thing they've said for certain is that there's no safeguards and you only get one chance to make it. They also told us the prize."

Tera made a small square of light appear next to her, and started a search. "What was it called?"

"The…solstice tournament, I think."

She buried her face in the screen without another word.

Jazz was thoughtful. "So what's the prize?"

"We get a tour of the ship. The real one."

He shrugged. "I think I'd rather just win cash."

"Really?" I asked. "You don't want to see the real world?"

"This is enough, and I like money."

Tera was absently tapping out a weird rhythm with her feet. "Even if you had a big bag of it, you'd just spend it on a pleasure palace."

"Immediately. And a few fancy drinks."

Jennifer raised her glass in a silent toast. I slurped another spoonful of my soup, wondering absently if I really needed to eat it at all.

"So," I continued, "What we don't know is what the first challenge is going to be."

"Who else is signed up?"

"Don't know. Beans, probably."

Jennifer grimaced. "He's *definitely* going to be in it. I am so going to kick his ass at…*whatever* it is."

I looked over, eyebrows raised. It was the most substantial thing she'd said in days. "What's he done to deserve that?"

"He's just an asshole."

"Find out his real name yet?"

"No, *Noah*, I haven't."

Jazz looked thoughtful again. "I think I may have to take part, just to watch that."

"You know that if you play, you have to *play*, right, and not just goof around?" I said.

"Tera can keep me focused."

"Does Tera *actually* want in?" I asked.

Tera shrugged, and absently nodded. Didn't say anything. Still engrossed in whatever she had started reading.

"I hope it's a real challenge," I continued. "Everything here has been so…*friendly* since…" I trailed off, then found my words again. "Since we woke up."

The table was quiet for a moment.

Jazz nodded, slowly, with a growing smirk. "Something with some real stakes sounds good to me, and if it comes down to it, I wouldn't mind winning again. I could watch you," he brought his hand up, and spiralled it down to the tabletop, "plummet from treetops all day long but it'd be more satisfying if I had a hand in it."

"Oh, my," I said, finding a drawling, high-pitched voice somewhere in my throat. "Such fightin' words. Well don't you worry, I'll make sure your family gets to watch when you *lose*."

Jennifer suddenly looked fiercely irritable, and shoved her chair back, crossing the distance to the exit so quickly she was nearly fleeing the place.

I looked at Jazz. "What? Was that too far?"

"Only if you meant it."

Tera finally looked up. Pointed at both of us.

"You guys are dumb. Five coins says she drops you from her team in this tournament thing. Which I am going to win."

*  *  *

*This is how it was meant to be*, I thought appreciatively.

The village square was a hive of activity. Hundreds of people strolled in all directions, popping in and out of existence on their way to and from different destinations. The sun gleamed overhead, but I could still feel echoes of the snowy cold.

Holographic billboards materialised over buildings. Smaller stalls, manned by AI characters, dotted the periphery, selling trinkets, rugs, posters, and a hundred genres of music. By the gate, familiar newscasters read out the day's headlines. As I strolled across the middle of the square, a glowing hologram of a smiley face fizzled out, replaced by a figure in something approaching formal dress. A fleeting hint of admiration compelled me to pause and watch for a minute. This was the captain's daily address. Every day, DeSanto would give his own update on the journey and current events, throwing in jokes and offhanded commentary. It got a regular audience, mostly older passengers. Knowing somebody was looking out for us made it that much easier to indulge in the luxuries of the place.

The lone respite from the chaos was the library, which had retained its sense of impenetrable calm and a distinct lack of advertising. It was a slice of dull sensibility in the bustling, rampaging drama of our private theme park. The kids and elderly ignored it, leaving a stuffy collection of business enthusiasts and introverts to brave its quiet chairs and unearthly hush. The village was like that. The people knew what they liked. Some of them dressed up. Some of them didn't bother with clothes. Some didn't even look human.

On my way out of the market, I paused at a stall run by a short dark-skinned woman in an arrestingly vibrant dress. Like most artificial characters, she could hold a conversation, but her range of topics was limited. To set the expectation that we were talking to a machine, her skin glistened with a hexagonal pattern that glinted in sunlight. It was a pretty look, but unmistakably synthetic.

I paused to order a woollen blanket from her, and kept going. In just a few days I'd already exhausted most of her potential for small talk.

By the time I had reached the hotel and navigated its stairs and hallways, the blanket was waiting outside my door, knitted into a pleasant green-and-grey plaid. Being wrapped up in soft fuzziness was just the thing I needed.

Suspended in the air beside my bed was a holographic display, a two-dimensional pane of interactive light called the Index. It was a hub of sorts, an interface into the secret layers to this world. And a terrific way to spend money.

I'd found myself in command of a tidy account balance to furnish myself with goodies like my blanket, but the ease with which they appeared on a cart outside my door was downright seductive. The range of options on hand for creature comforts was…extravagant, and after a few mildly expensive experiments I'd decided to avoid the worst of it. While the *bedouin-tent-covered-in-rugs* look was tempting, something about a simple cosy blanket made life easier.

An assortment of news headlines from far off places floated at the edge of the display. At first I'd found them enthrallingly foreign; now I ignored them. I just didn't care that the price of refined pelarite was up eight percent on the previous year, or that fourteen people on Deimos had died from a sickness brought from Earth in contaminated food. But that was no reason to avoid catching up on the state of the universe.

Earth, as the story went, got small. It happened very slowly, and then alarmingly quickly. At the tail end of that transition, the solar system, once impossibly vast and inaccessible, was suddenly and irrevocably brought within our grasp. Forty years of relative peace followed as the energies that would once have fueled inward conflicts suddenly found a whole new frontier to develop. Free of an increasingly pressurized home world, and given the literal space to rule themselves, colonies sprang up anywhere that offered even an inkling of prosperity. It wasn't an easy growth spurt for humanity, and endless political bickering kept Earth from ever truly exercising authority over its children.

Mars established its own government a hundred sols after humans arrived on it. The colonists' home countries were less than thrilled, but in practical terms there wasn't much they could do about it. Declarations of independence didn't change that Earth had a humanitarian responsibility to its colonies, so for better or worse, supplies continued to flow. The pattern took hold, with each exploration ship planting a unique flag on whatever piece of rock it found.

Most of those expeditions brought miners, explorers, and researchers, all keen for their names to appear in history books. As discoveries were made, trade routes grew to give those fledgling outposts of humanity true legitimacy. But even the so-called company towns of Deimos, Ceres, and Titan were still hugely dependent on the raw resources, both human and otherwise, that poured into them from back home. Mostly biologicals and bits of technical infrastructure, but also the softer comforts like entertainment packages and textiles. And where the comforts went, people followed. Survival was a solved problem, but *thriving* was a luxury reserved for the few.

Keenly aware of the opportunities unfolding before them, entrepreneurs started operating long-haul passenger services between the nascent colonies. And like the wind-powered Atlantic crossings centuries earlier, they were long, arduous, and reliant on things going more or less perfectly.

A remarkably clever and *exceedingly* fortunate woman named Eileen Carver was one of the early industrialists to notice the coming gold rush, and established Carver Interplanetary Services. The company operated three vessels out of a port on Earth's lunar station, offering a relatively competitive option for those trying to escape to, or escape *from,* the handful of significant outposts within the asteroid belt. The Ceres line, a trek that took nearly four months each way, was served by the C.I.S. Apollo. It did a thriving business amongst those who weren't quite convinced that they had seen the best side of life.

Nearly two hundred passengers had embarked on the present voyage towards humanity's home. Those aboard who were particularly well-off got to make the trip in actual cabins, with extra privileges to indulge in. It didn't describe those extras in detail.

The rest, those that couldn't afford a ticket worth half of a year's savings, were relegated to what the highlights article called economy accommodation. But it didn't matter much. Everyone got wired into the the saving grace of the whole affair: the CarverNet Reality Suit. Fitted at boarding time, a passenger would be put under general anaesthesia, deposited in their berth, and once their body and mind acclimatized, be able to traverse a hundred different virtual worlds during the journey. The marketing material especially liked to hype up the benefits to mental health. I had to admit that to my mind, all of those destinations *were* infinitely more enticing than staring at cramped, bare metal for months on end.

CarverNet was one of a new breed of immersion systems. The suit was a conventional *all-over* haptics-and-mask combination, and played some extra tricks with the wearer's wetware stack, connecting to back-of-the-neck spinal implants normally used by deep-range natives for rather more practical applications. The simulation could do a good job of managing a human's nervous system in many respects, including intercepting muscle movement. In our minds, we might be running and jumping and swooping and dancing, but in reality we would be stock-still except for the barest hint of those motions. Compared to the toys I'd known growing up it might as well have been magic, or perhaps even an experience comparable to organised religion. As Jazz had neatly summarized to me one day, we lived in a self-contained world, with only hazy memories of former lives, and had to take it on faith that descriptions of a reality beyond our own were accurate. Whatever the framing, for me, it was a place to call home.

I snugged the blanket tighter. Smiled absently. Reality had tough competition. And that brought me back, for the fifth night in a row, to the Index's subtlest of party tricks: it could tell me who I was supposed to be.

A floating panel listed out a scarce set of my personal details, every one stark and cold. A picture of my face headed the details. It might have been generous to call my captured expression a smile. *Smirk* might have been more accurate.

But it *was* the same face that had looked out of the mirror at me countless times in the last week. More or less. The captured version of me had a few extra wrinkles, and  a small scar under the right eye. There was no trace of either difference in this world. I made myself look. Made myself try to grasp it. Try to own it.

The picture had been taken somewhere industrial, full of harsh lights and hard walls. By the third day of staring at the picture, I had remembered it alarmingly well. The place had subtly stunk of *karackao* smoke. The photographer had been a one-time family friend, and had enjoyed the delicate leaf's….*stimulating* effects a little too often. I had paid for the ID picture and left before he could suggest less savory uses for a camera.

Below the headshot, listed in cold light, were the basics that told the world what to call me, how long I'd been alive, and at least in a literal sense, where I was going. And a few other details. Mother, father, home address. The people to contact if something bad happened. A set of plain facts with thin shreds of emotion attached.

Which was why, for the fifth night in a row, I was staring at my own name with familiar disbelief.

My name.

Aidan Whittaker.

According to the biography, I was twenty-four standard years old. From Ceres Station, Sixth District, The Strand, Level Two, Flat Eleven. Memories of the address conjured up vague scenes of pristine powder-blue walls framing a grimy railing and a sweeping, closed-ceiling promenade. Some good times had been had there. And some bad ones. It had been a home. One that I wouldn't see again for a long time.

The amnesia had been fading, day by day. But in its place I was left holding the loose threads of a new life, responsible for somehow reconciling them with the foggy entirety of an old one.

It all felt thin, fake. Even vaguely depressing. A name tag left over from the previous day.

A chat message appeared in the air to my left. Jennifer apologizing for her behavior. Asking if I was okay. Asking if I was still game for tomorrow. The keyboard floated into view beside me, having proved to be my ideal form of communication. I started typing back. A line, then a paragraph. Two, even. A long reply that asked too much. I erased it the moment it was finished. Instead, I left it to one easy line:

*Wouldn't miss it.*

# SEVEN

"Well. *That* looks awful."

The rain pounded the stonework in waves. The old temple dazzled in the slippery gleam, impervious to the wind raging around it. Endless jungle, cloaked in teal and purple, ensnared its foundations. What little daylight there was came in steeply from the horizon, interrupted only by the harsh peaks of distant ziggurats.

Hard to tell whether the day was coming or going. I figured it was going. More dramatic that way.

From our perch, twice as high as the canopy and sheltered by an overhang, the view was pretty good.

Jennifer was crouched beside me, scanning the vista in thought. Her appearance had changed, newly gaunt cheekbones flanked by an undercut of shockingly white hair. She was outfitted in black, with a thin, long jacket flowing around her legs. An alias, rendered in crisp lettering, floated beside her whenever my gaze lingered too long: *Trace.*

She looked *badass.*

My own outfit was a tactical jumpsuit that seemed to be made of a dozen layers of mesh. Fur-like threads shimmered along the outer skin in fluid waves, making it hard to tell exactly where my limbs ended and the shadows beyond began. I'd changed my complexion, adding dark face paint, and left my alias completely blank. In a game that seemed tailored to encourage showiness, deliberate anonymity felt like the most intimidating option. In theory, at least.

The briefing, as the term suggested, was unnervingly brief. Somewhere, out in the wilderness, was a gate which needed to be opened. Details were scarce. But we did know that it had two prerequisites. First, a puzzle needed to be solved. Second, there needed to only be one-third of players left in this vast arena.

I didn't like that math.

And *then* there was the other thing we had been told:

Players could be injured in this game, and sensations would only be partially dulled. A scratch would still feel like a scratch. A thump would feel like a thump. Any injury that would be crippling or even fatal in normal life would cause instant elimination.

I'd played games like this one before, and it didn't take a genius to grasp the implication: in this round of the tournament, it was survival first, and a race second.

"We have to move," 'Trace' said.

I nodded, not taking my eyes off the landscape. "Hold on. I want to remember this."

"'Cause it's pretty?"

"No, because people are dumb."

"You, uh, want to explain your thinking?"

I waved out at it. "It's a game. If *you* were running it, and told people what to do but not where to go, you would make that part at least a little obvious."

She considered that, then a sly grin started to cross her face.

"Yeah, okay. I got it now. How far do you think those ruins are? Way out there?"

"Maybe…ten miles? More?"

"Do any of them look closer or farther?"

I peered out into the rain. Shivered. "Hard to tell. Why?"

"We spawned in *this* temple. If other people spawned in those ones, then we've got a big arena to work with, maybe ten miles across."

My turn to nod. I was starting to like this version of her. "This could go on for a while if we all have to walk that far to find each…oh. We don't. We just have to find the gate."

"That will be around half the distance."

"So we're all probably starting in a big circle—"

"A huge circle," she interjected.

"Yeah. But if you just put the gate in the middle of it, it'd be boring. So it won't be in the middle exactly, but it'll be close to there. Off to one side. Right about…see that thing?" I pointed as best I could to something in the correct spot that looked suspiciously building-like.

She squinted. "I can see something pointy and white. Big, but not as big as a temple."

"That'd be about right."

"It's just a guess, but if we can think to go there, so will everyone else."

As we spoke, little oblong shapes, suspended from parachutes, lazily descended from the sky, a celestial garnish across the vast plain.

I looked at Trace. Trace looked back at me. We stared stupidly as they drifted down into the trees, not having a clue what they represented. Then, abruptly, we got it simultaneously.

"Supplies!" We said.

Trace gave me a look.

I returned it with a grin.

Our clothes were soaked through in seconds as we made our way down to the jungle's edge. I tried to keep a map going in my head, but when we dropped below the tree line it was almost an exercise in futility.

An opening in the trees to our right offered entry into the wilderness. The wet moss squished underfoot as we launched into ferns and brambles. Small creatures scattered at our approach, invisible save for telltale rustling in the undergrowth. Droplets of water tickled at the back of my neck.

What had seemed like a flat plain from above quickly proved to be anything but. Sudden boulders, treacherous ravines, and imposing rock walls made moving in a straight line impossible.

We hacked and stomped our way through the mess, trying vainly to stay on some imagined course. I kept flashing back to our misguided rampage through the much-calmer forest on the first day. Compared to this, that had been downright serene.

A narrow clearing in the brush drew us close, and as we emerged from the brush, an upright barrel waited with a parachute draped around it. We drew close, and my heart sank. It was open. And empty. Someone had gotten here first. Whatever had been inside, we were now at a disadvantage.

We moved on, a little more cautiously.

Twice we crossed trampled paths, which inspired us to move more timidly. But we didn't see proof of other people until the afternoon had more definitively become a sunset. As the clouds steadily thinned, the rain ended and the air lost little humidity, but I still wished it would stop being quite so chilly. Birdsong filtered through the trees once or twice. I thought it sounded a little reluctant. Too late in the day for a big performance.

We reached a small clearing at the top of a rocky rise, where the crumbling remnants of a long-forgotten statue rose towards the treetops. It was a great stone foot, terminated at the ankle, atop a paved dais. Thick, luminescent ivy swarmed up it, a beautifully coarse weave that, to my eye, looked like it was climbable.

I looked at Trace. "Good vantage point."

"Yeah, but exposed."

"Worth it?"

She glanced around. "I'm lost regardless. If *you* know where we are, lead on."

I shrugged. "Nope."

"Then up we go."

"You've played a lot of games like this, haven't you?"

She grinned ferociously. "Religiously, for a couple of years. You? You're not exactly shaking with fear here either."

"I liked the solo adventures growing up. But never multiplayer, and *nothing* like this." I shrugged, testing one of the vines. "But there's been a lot of that lately."

The ivy made for an uncooperative climbing partner, but with persistence and swearing we scaled the giant foot. At the top, where the ankle had sheared off, we had a cross section of exposed stone at least ten feet across. It wasn't quite flat, but it *was* level with the jungle canopy. We just needed a little more height to get a view.

With some raised eyebrows, Trace planted a foot on my hand, and climbed onto my shoulders awkwardly, planting her legs on either side of my neck.

"You're warm," I said.

"And *you're* wet."

"And cold. Just mentioning it."

"I'm happy for you."

"Can you see anything?"

She took her time before answering. "I *think* I can see where that river should be."

"How far?"

"A mile maybe? Or less." She pointed in a direction off to the side. "That—"

A scream pierced the jungle, cutting her off. A male voice, old and throaty. Maybe a hundred feet away, or twice that distance. Couldn't tell. Didn't matter. We were standing on the most prominent landmark around.

*Shit.*

I dropped to my knees, rolling over as Trace clambered down. She went prone and I flattened onto my back, praying that the ruin's bulk would conceal us. There was no time to do anything else.

Unseen footsteps sauntered out of the undergrowth twenty feet below. One person? Two?

My chest tightened. They were moving with all the leisurely patience of a comfortable predator. My chest tightened as I tried to form a telepathic link with my ally.

*Have they seen us?*

The thought went unanswered.

The cold stone was little reassurance. Without a weapon, we would be easy prey.

A vine at the far edge shifted, repeatedly. I imagined a hulking bodybuilder tugging on it, testing to see if it could take his weight.

I met Trace's eyes, wide in the gathering gloom. She hadn't made a noise. She understood.

The vine strained, giving out little pulses of light that threatened to flare into a glorious blue as the intruder puffed and pulled, climbing up.

I started scuttling towards the opposite edge, hoping we could shimmy down before they reached the top.

Then a sharp *snap* cleared the air, the blue glow vanished, and a heavy *thump* reached our ears as they fell back to the ground.

"Shit!" a voice called out. I didn't recognize it.

"What happened?" responded another. Higher pitched. Different accent.

"My back hurts."

A snort. "What were you trying to climb it for?"

The first voice was rueful. "Get some altitude. Find some fresh meat."

"You're disgusting, Terry."

"You love it."

Terry and the mystery man went back and forth for another minute, but they didn't have any success climbing after us. The standoff, as one-sided as it was, had shifted from curiosity to a strangely lazy form of tension.

Then the vines moved again, straining once more. I tensed, concocting a wild plan to launch myself at whatever came up over the edge. I'd have to be fast and hit desperately hard. I might get the first one in a single impact, but not the second.

My fingers tightened in place, my legs steeling into position, ready to lunge. Trace was watching me, shaking her head firmly. The adrenaline gathered to a central point in my gut, curling around like a spring.

But no face came up over the edge.

Instead, the owner of the high pitched voice muttered some kind of curse, and dropped back to ground below. Their heavier companion guffawed, and moments later, defeated, they retreated away, footsteps fading into the trees.

They were leaving. In, I noted with an unbidden smirk, the wrong direction.

Trace exhaled, shuddering with a suppressed giggle. I wanted to join in, as the coiled tension in my stomach imploded, leaving me hot, sick, and drained.

*Freck.*

Relieved, we made hearty progress onwards, in the emphatically *opposite* direction from Terry and his sluggish ally. As we entered a swampy section, the low brush gave way to moss and spikey bushes. And something entirely different forced us to pause all over again.

Three figures were cowering against a big tree, their backs pressed to the bark. At first I didn't understand, but then, as the ground moved, their situation became clear with revolting clarity.

The creatures were low and long, scaly, two stumpy legs in front and one in the middle of the back, with two tails coming off symmetrically, sweeping the ground behind them as low growls emitted from toothy snouts up front. Six of them, two larger, four smaller, were arrayed on the trio, closing in.

We peered out from behind a pair of trees.

"Okay," Trace whispered. "Here's the plan. I'll climb up into those branches and try to distract the…things…while —"

I ignored her and stepped out, waving to try to get the trapped players' attention. It worked. A small man, head to toe in flannel pyjamas and welding a steel club, nodded at me. So far the creatures hadn't noticed. Good.

Trace started hoisting herself up the tree. Fine. She would do something useful.

I found a rock on the ground, picked it up, and aimed at one of the smaller things. I started to call them *dragons* in my head. Then I paused as I saw the pile of eggs just before my feet, and understood. This was their *nest*.

A low growl behind me turned pounding blood into ice. I

turned, slowly, as another adult dragon edged forward.

Thoughts, strategies, wild plans flushed through my mind. I could throw the rock at the flanker and attack it, but that could go badly, and I would be weaponless. *Or* I could keep the rock and lunge at it wildly. *Or* I could back away, slowly, and hope it didn't pursue. *Or* I could scoop up the eggs and throw them at it like a madman. It would get pissed off—what parent wouldn't?—but it would have a competing priority which might give me a chance to do something.

I picked up the eggs. The beast's growling grew in strength with each addition, but instead of hurling them, I just tried to give them to it. A peace offering. One step forward, then another. It was progress.

I froze as the little man against the tree shouted out. "Look! Look! All of you! He's got your eggs! Go get *him*! We're not scary!"

I pivoted on the spot, astonished at the betrayal. But the trio, suddenly free of their entrapment, were bolting. Six angry dragons were laser-focused on me and closing in.

Mania in my eyes, I threw the eggs at them. Nothing encourages poor decision-making like bad odds.

I spun as the dragon behind me charged, then *whuffed* as Trace dropped out of the tree overhead, straight onto its back. The beast was dazed, wheezing, but its compatriots had escalated from growls into full-throated *howls*, and *I* was the main source of their ire.

*Shit shit shit shit shit.*

We tore out of there, downhill as fast as we could, frantically crawling and sprinting. Those angry, sweeping tails swirled the brush, gaining ground. A woman howled out into the sky somewhere to our right. The sound collapsed into a dying gurgle as we ran.

We broke from the jungle on a stony bank. The river was thirty feet wide, but shallow enough for wading. And deep enough for drowning. I splashed in, Trace hard on my heels. Behind us, a dragon snout emerged into the fading daylight, but went no further. The water, it seemed, was as far as it would go.

"Assholes!" I grunted. "Just trying to help them!"

Trace whacked me on the shoulder. It seemed fair. I hadn't exactly taken the encounter slow and steadily.

I shook it off. We had to keep going. The water wasn't as frigidly cold as it looked. As we waded downriver, the pebbles underfoot remained steady and sure. In a few spots the current accelerated, clawing at us as it whirled past.

It ran in a lazy curve, arcing around a steep hill with sides so sheer that in places it was actually a cliff. Dangling bits of leafy mass caressed the open air. But my eyes sharpened as they tracked downstream, suddenly picking out something a bit different against the darkening sky. Just past where the cliff was tallest, speckled vines ran all the way to the top, where a few very rectangular blocks of stone poked out over the edge. Memory sharpened as I remembered the once-distant building we had spied from the temple. We *had* to be getting closer.

Wind gusted. I cast a gaze around us, eying the jungle. We were running out of time. "The vines. Look." I said.

Trace eyed it. "I see it. But those glow a *lot* when you're on them. It'd be a *here-I-am-come-get-me!* flare for the whole match."

"Let's risk it."

To her credit, she contemplated the climb, looking up…and up, to the point where she needed to step back a few paces. "Do…you remember what happened when that oaf was trying to get up to us? The glow was really dim when he moved up it. Maybe the more slowly you move, the less bright it gets."

"Then we do it slowly."

"We'll light up the whole planet if we don't."

"Okay."

She sighed, weary. "Should have let me tell you the plan back there."

Reaching the vine wall, I grasped the nearest one, tugging experimentally. It remained firmly in place. Perfect.

"Plans don't get along with me so well." I said, and started up.

We made the ascent as quickly as we could, searching for hand holds. It was a much longer climb than the last one. At first I was dazzled by the waves of blue light that pulsed up and down the wall as we climbed, but I resisted the urge to appreciate its beauty. After all, it *was* just a massive beacon broadcasting our progress.

We slowed, testing the vines, using nooks in the rock where we could, to make the pulses weaker or nonexistent.

About two thirds of the way up, where a dense thicket of leafy foliage sprouted out from the stone, we stopped cold. We clung to the cliff face, looking down and trying to stay very, *very* still.

Far below, a troupe, maybe seven players strong, was marauding down the river bed. Their chorus of voices echoed carelessly up to us.

*Same idea we had,* Trace mouthed at me. I nodded unhappily.

We pressed into the rocks, hoping that at this distance we would blend in. And that *they* wouldn't look up. Not that it would matter if we let go. Vertigo gnawed at my calm.

The gang's discussion turned rowdy, and a figure at the head of the group shouted something indistinct to make the others shut up.

I looked at Trace. We knew that voice.

*Tera,* I mouthed. She nodded.

I peered more closely. Jazz was absent, nowhere to be seen. Odd. It didn't sit right. Either he'd already been eliminated or he was hiding. If he was hiding, was it from *them?* As Tera seemed to be leading the gang, that by itself felt unlikely.

A scuffle broke out in the canopy below. The dragons had arrived in force. On cue, two of the gang suddenly shifted and started moving, hefting small, flappy contraptions before them.

Then stones started hurling into the trees, and my mood dropped even further.

*Slings.*

They had weapons. Tera was leading an armed gang. They were fending off the beasts but there was no telling how they would respond to us.

Jennifer motioned at me as if to say, *come on!*

I shook my head, conscious about drawing attention.

She started climbing again on her own, slowly, one *very* precise hand-hold at a time.

Freck.

I knew she was right. They could be friendly but if they weren't, we were exposed. Vulnerable. I twisted, spotted one handhold, then another, took a breath, and climbed.

Each step towards the top had to be precise, avoiding contact with the much easier vines at all cost. A single nudge would—

I lost my grip, slipping. I flailed, grabbing onto the nearest thing with all the precision I could muster. And a bright blue shockwave rippled straight down the rock face.

I looked down.

The gang looked up.

They started shouting. A few used their slings to send rocks up in the air, but they fell pitifully short. Others started climbing. So did we. *That's that, then.*

It seemed to take an agonising eternity to rise another twenty feet, putting the top within arm's reach. Jennifer called out at the top of her lungs, "Sure, come closer! We'll wait! You'll look really nice on your way back down!"

At that the chase began in earnest, but then abruptly terminated as Tera barked something to the others. They paused, and I watched intently as the gang disengaged from the vines and, staring up at us, continued downriver. I refocused on the climb, reached up—*up!*—and finally grasped the rough plateau of paving bricks, pulling myself up and over. Ten feet to the right, Jennifer did the same a moment later. As we lay there, arms and legs complaining mightily, I crawled back to the edge and peered over.

Seventy feet below, the bright blue flair of Tera's coat was steadily disappearing downstream.

I chuckled to myself. We were clear for a second time. For a little while.

Now to see what all the trouble had been about.

* * *

Overlooking the jungle plateau sat a stately building. Its walls looked solid, but covered in a material softer than rock and considerably more uniform. Curved tiles neatly cascaded across the top in a sea of faded red. A grand door in the middle of the wall lay implacably shut; open windows above hinted at a darkened upper level. At the apex of the roofline, two pieces of wood jutted skyward, crossed at odd angles.

Trace narrowed her eyes.

"It's a mission. Or a monastery."

"A what?"

"An old Earth building. A home for religious people."

"Oh," I replied sourly, thinking back to irritating sermons relentlessly blathered at travellers in rusty markets. "Sounds appealing."

"No, not like that," she said knowingly. "It's more about philosophy and sense of self than being a preachy prick."

As we approached, I had to admit it was impressive in its own way, as much for its one-time grandeur as for how intact it appeared.

We tried the door, but while it did give a little, something on the other side held it firmly against us.

Locked.

We paced up and down the facade for a while, stumped.

Then Trace got it.

Near the far-right corner, a gnarled tree-like plant reached toward the roofline. Not quite reaching it, but close enough for a jump. With a boost, Trace reached the branches, and I scrabbled up after her. We shimmied up the rough bark until we reached the wall, and discovered that where the leaves brushed the building, a slim window had been concealed. I felt a pleasant tingle of understanding: this was an intentional way inside.

The window conveyed us into a musty records room, with wooden tables and shelves piled high with document cartons. A desk sat in the middle of the room with a silver candlestick set on one end. I grasped it as Trace poked her head out the door; the candlestick lit in my hand, showing a skinny flame that danced on its wick relentlessly. Its light was pitiful, but appreciated nonetheless. And I was pretty sure the base would make a decent club in a pinch.

"Nice." Trace said.

Outside the records room was an open colonnade that ringed a courtyard. Stone benches in the middle angled towards a blank wall at the near end. At the far end sat a tall rock pillar that might have once supported a long-gone roof. Arbors lined the back wall. I dismissed them as little more than decoration.

"Well," I said. "This is definitely a place."

Trace nodded. "I'll check out the middle. You take the edges, see what else is here."

A quick study of the rest of the building revealed bathrooms with crumbling floors, a kitchen covered in vines, and a locked gate made of creaking timbers. A quartet of posts linked with frayed rope stood at attention before the gate. Their purpose eluded me.

I finished my loop, and found Trace in front of the stone pillar back in the courtyard. As I approached, she gestured at it.

"This is out of place. It's important."

"Okay. Why?"

She made some odd movements with her arms, trying to convey something that was going over my head. "Its scale is wrong. Every other pillar here is two and half meters tall and about a quarter of that across. This one is only two meters even, and it's skinnier."

"You can just tell that?"

"Spatial relations is my thing, okay?"

I crouched down. "I'll take your word for it. What are these rings, here?"

"Hm." She pursed her lips, evaluating.

The base of the pillar, where tall grass poked through the paving, was decorated with three extruded rings. Distinct symbols were painted onto the front of each: the top featured a bird, the middle a sun, and the bottom a fist.

"Okay," I said. "This *is* definitely out of place."

"See if there's anything else," Trace replied. "I'm gonna try some things."

Using the candlestick as a lamp, I scanned the pillar in the failing dusk, trying not to focus on how the flame made the arbor plants twist their scrawny tendrils towards us. Brushing lumpy growths off the hard stone eventually revealed further markings on the back of the pillar, near the top: three dots, connected by a line to form a chevron. And above them what I, perhaps generously, interpreted to be a closed eye.

Trace made some interested, thoughtful noises, but before I could ask for an explanation, we were interrupted.

"Excuse me, folks, but it looks suspiciously like you're doing something *useful*."

A hulking figure sauntered out of a doorway to our right. It was carrying a crossbow, and lumbering towards us a little too cockily. "So," the interloper continued, voice artificially throaty, "I think you're on to something, and I don't suppose you'd mind telling me just what it is?" He raised the crossbow, and aimed it squarely at my chest.

Trace was defiant, standing tall as a gust swept through the courtyard.

Something clicked. I *knew* that voice. Or rather, I knew the inflection behind it.

I shuffled around, hands held high. "Hang on. *Beans?* Is that you?"

The giant lowered the crossbow an inch, peering at us. "Who… oh. Freck. It's you two." He almost sounded dismissive. "Nevermind." The crossbow dropped further. "Don't you have anything to fight with?"

Trace turned around and went back to examining the pillar.

I shook my head. "Nothing like what you've got."

Beans shifted incredulously. "It's a bloodbath out there. I've had to take out five goons already, and all of them nearly got me first."

I cocked an eyebrow, and used my hands to outline his girth. "Maybe you should try losing some weight. People might find it easier to pass you by."

The giant grinned. "On the contrary. I don't mind *at all* if they notice me, long as they freeze in place for an extra special moment when they do."

Trace glanced over her shoulder. "Are you *sure* that you were the victim in those fights?"

Beans shrugged magnanimously, waving the crossbow in a careless loop. "I never started the fights, but I never let them *finish* starting them, you understand."

She gazed at him levelly. "Uh huh."

Beans gestured at the pillar. "What have you got?"

I shrugged. "Will you feel like using that on us if we tell you?"

He shrugged in turn. "I probably won't."

I turned to Trace. "If he found us, the others will too. We don't have time to dawdle."

She nodded, and exhaled. "Okay. So this thing is the key out of here. Ninety-nine percent sure."

She grasped the middle of the three rings, and to my surprise gently sent it spinning.

As it came to a rest, a quarter-turn around, the sky spun to match, putting an end to the dusk, sending us all the way through nighttime and straight into the following morning. Sunlight lept through the clouds at a nauseating pace, sweeping down over the roof to blind us.

Beans gawked at the sky, letting out a slow whistle. "That's some *voodoo*. If this isn't the place…"

"Uh huh," I muttered, thinking fast. "You and anyone else with eyes."

Trace coughed. "So the middle ring sets time of day. The top ring…something to do with birds."

She sent it spinning. At first, nothing happened. But then, as it settled, birds of a dozen species started warbling an unfamiliar tune.

"Well," Beans said. "That's nice."

Encouraged, I reached down and brought the ring a little further around. As it coasted to a stop, the birds shifted their cacophony, dropping a few pitches and picking up a jazzier melody.

"So we have control over time of day and birdsong. Great." Trace said.

I adjusted my reach down to the sun ring, and sent it spinning again. As it coasted to a stop, the morning light whisked upwards, over, and down again to disappear. The stars raced to glow brightly in its absence as a pair of waxing moons brightened the horizon. The birds went silent immediately.

Beans leaned on the nearest wall for support. "You're going to make me sick," he said.

"Join the club." Trace had her eyes shut, controlling her breathing.

"Let's recap," I said. "The top ring controls the birds. The middle ring controls the lighting."

Trace returned to her crouch. "And the bottom ring?"

"Dunno," I said. "Let's find out."

Trace wobbled it in place. Unlike the other two, it wouldn't spin all the way around. "Okay," she said. "It's got a limited range of movement. Which means the ends of that range have a purpose."

"Try putting it all the way to the right." Beans said.

She did so.

We looked around. Listened. Waited. Nothing happened.

I spun the sun ring, and predictably the night-time reversed to become a clear-skied mid-afternoon.

A distant commotion echoed off the monastery walls. Beans straightened. "Don't go anywhere without me," he said. "I'll check it out." He disappeared around the corner. Heading, I knew, for the wooden gate. I wondered if he'd smashed it on his way in.

I looked back to Trace. "Try putting the bottom ring all the way to the left."

She did.

*This* time, when I wobbled the middle ring, the stone refused to budge and left my hand with a nasty sting.

"Ah," said Trace.

"Right," I said, hissing. "Right. Lesson learned."

Another minute's experimentation confirmed it. When the bottom ring went all the way to the left, it locked the time of day. When all the way to the right, it locked the *birds* instead. In the middle, its starting position, both could be freely altered.

"I don't get it," Trace said. "Why birds? I get the time-of-day. That's a pretty universal idea. But *what* is with the birds?"

A chorus of shouts, definitely closer than before, reached our ears. They didn't sound angry or jubilant. They sounded confused and worried. Beans was probably causing havoc.

"Honestly", I murmured, "It's such a random detail. Birds are nothing. They're background."

Trace slowly tapped the ground in thought. "Birds are alive. The sun is a natural object. The only thing they have in common is that both aren't thought of as man-made."

I shook my head. "That's true, but what the hell does that have to do with anything?"

"I…don't know."

A resounding crash echoed from outside the monastery walls.

I snapped my fingers. "The sun isn't important. It's there, it's not there. It's literally blindingly obvious. The birds *aren't*, so they matter more. Look at this." I pulled her around to the back of the pillar, pointing out the markings. Three linked dots and a closed eye.

Trace studied it. "You're wrong and right. Birds don't matter at all. The *notes* matter. These dots are notes."

"Notes?"

"Music. Pitches. Low, high, low. It's a melody. Spin the upper ring."

I reached down and twirled it. In moments, melodic phrases came and went. This time, we actually tried to listen. High-high-low. Low-high. Low-low. Low-high-low. High-low-low.

"Go back! Back a bit!" Trace called. I grasped the wheel, reversing it. The songs reversed simultaneously. Low-low-high. Low-high-low.

*Low-High-Low.*

"Okay," I said. "That's about it. Now the closed eye—night time?"

Trace rotated the top disk about a quarter-turn clockwise. The sky followed it dutifully, leading us into nightfall.

The birdsong disappeared right along with it.

She rotated it back to its prior position, and the sun swooped back up from the horizon to linger above the clouds. And the melody resumed.

We looked at each other, realizing the solution simultaneously. I'd just clicked the bottom wheel all the way to the right when the monastery gates unequivocally smashed apart, and a raging chorus filtered around us.

"Oh, aim on my cock, why don't you?" Beans roared, charging around the corner, and past us towards the cover of a bench. We flattened our selves into the arbors along the back wall, hoping to avoid notice.

It didn't help.

Tera's gang appeared, one by one, around the edges of the courtyard. I counted four, maybe five of them. Beans had obviously given them a good fight. The crossbow knocked a fresh bolt. But he was breathing hard and their slings were still patiently twirling. I tightened my grip on the candlestick, for what little good it would do me.

Tension lingered for a long moment.

"Hi guys." Tera called out from behind a stack of rotting barrels. "This is fun."

"Where's Jazz?" I called out.

"He didn't like my friends. This is us winning, by the way."

"Winning, huh? Really?"

"Really!"

"You owe me five coins!" Trace shouted.

"I do? Is that Jen? Jen, honey, you all right over there?"

My partner didn't speak up. Instead, she just tapped me on the leg. She had a plan.

Unbidden, a stone flew from the shadows and cracked onto the wall a couple of feet from my head. A simple message. We weren't going to win a fight.

I nodded at nothing without looking down. I trusted her.

"You know," I called out again, "this is great, but I think we're gonna have to decline your hospitality."

On cue, Trace spun the sun ring, its sibling now locked into the melody, until it settled into deep night.

Tera snorted. "Decline our hos—"

A grand portal of silvery water erupted on the far wall of the courtyard, interrupting the moment. *The gate.*

It glowed from within, piercing the night.

Trace tapped me on the leg twice more, and spun the sun ring as hard as she could, sending searing sunlight flashing across the world at a dizzying pace. In the strobing, disorienting chaos, she bolted for the gate, and I was a heartbeat behind her, hurling the candlestick at Tera's position.

The gang unloaded at us, but their aim was lousy. Stones smacked off the ground and whirled lethally through the courtyard. One soared before me so closely I could hear it carve the air.

Beans fired a bolt directly into an assailant, and I glimpsed their body splintering into pencil-shaped shadows as it fizzled from existence. Then he was up and moving behind us. Tera was striding out from her vantage point, lining up her own strike. She didn't even care about cover. We all knew it was down to this moment.

Trace leapt through the gate, vanishing into its cloudy depths.

Beans, his giant feet making a terrible thump with each landing, kept sending me off balance. Sweat clouded my brow as I zig-zagged forward.

*I'm taking too long,* came the thought. *Go faster. Faster!*

I was two strides from safety when the brick struck me squarely in the shoulder blades. The last thing I saw was the gate's luscious flutters disintegrating into the shards of an inky void.

# MESSAGE LOG

Archive for Inbound 11
Sol 9, 18:08 Local Time


*Donald McCann is writing…*

*Sorry you're out, mate.*

*Saw them nail you.*

*If it's any consolation I took out the chick that got you.*

*Thanks?*

*That rock frecking hurt.*

*You're welcome.*

*That was Tera by the way*

cannot believe she got me

never going to let me live it down

Ah

well

I've always wanted to do a moroccan backstab

A what?

From Night Bus to Elysium. It's a classic.

Never seen it

Doesn't that have the guy from IO Five in it?

You are in need of education

I'll show it to you sometime. It's a must-watch

There's some backstabbing?

Yeah, it's all slick, like a heist, except being done on the people setting up a different heist.

But the important bit is that this guy gets great one-liners in this revenge sequence *you know what, just watch the movie.*

*Maybe don't watch it with Tera.*

# EIGHT

I found myself knocking on the door to room three-thirty-one. It was a very different purpose this time. This time, I'd been invited for dinner, as anachronistic as the idea was.

Nobody answered my knock, but when I tried the handle, the door allowed me to open it. I assumed I was welcome.

Not much had changed at first glance; the lights were softer, leaning towards a hazy purple, but the main attraction was what had been the window. It had ceased showing the local wilderness and instead displayed a vast map of the stars. On closer inspection a thin blue line swept across it, tracing out a journey from start to finish, with a bright dot roughly a fifth of the way across. I assumed it was supposed to represent our flight path.

"It's a little bit cozier like this, don't you think?"

I looked around for the source of the words, then suddenly understood, and glanced up. The ceiling was dramatically higher than it had been before, providing room for a mezzanine overlooking the bedroom. It had to have been an *expensive* expansion.

Selena was perched on the railing, watching me idly.

"It'd make me feel claustrophobic," I replied.

"It makes me feel exactly the opposite," she said. "I like to be reminded that we're not going to be here forever."

She disappeared back from the railing, and sensing a quiet invitation, I ventured cautiously up a spiral staircase tucked into a far corner.

I emerged through the upper floor into a remarkably incongruous space. A small kitchenette and antique round table occupied most of the level, with the far end given over to a comically oversized armchair currently monopolized by Jennifer, who in turn was tightly focused on something to do with her Index. As I settled into a seat of my own, she gave a distracted wave, slowly disentangling herself from a world only she could see.

"Hey," she said. She sounded exhausted.

"Hey," I replied.

Selena snorted from the counter as she fetched dishes from a cupboard. "So *casual*. You two had fun today!"

"I didn't even qualify for round two," I said.

"Yes, but you solved the puzzle," she replied. "And made this happen." She did something I couldn't see with her Index, and the map on the far wall disappeared, replaced by a leaderboard. Names, some familiar, some new, filled every one of the twenty slots. Twenty players ready to move into round two.

And at the very top, in gold lettering, a five-letter name: *Trace*.

"I wonder who that could possibly be," Selena said, smirking. "I watched the spectator feed the whole time. It caught up with you the minute you reached that last ruin." She beamed, and I felt my face flush, embarrassed.

Jennifer seemed to try to hide even deeper in...whatever it was she was doing.

Selena, undeterred, filled a trio of bowls with a bubbling orange stew and laid out some pulpy, syrupy fruits on the side, inviting us to the table.

As she set the down the feast, I suddenly understood the implication in her earlier comment: Selena wanted to be reminded about leaving the sim because she positively *relished* it. To her, a kitchen was still a kitchen, and hot food was a non-negotiable tradition. As with all good things, that included an obligatory dose of snobbery.

"Wine just doesn't taste right here," she was saying. "It's just *wrong*."

"Never had the real stuff." I said.

She shrugged. "It's hard to get a good one. And harder still to *make* it, especially with hydroponics water. Great for growing potatoes and soy and lettuce, but grapes just don't get along with it." She sighed. "You would think they would perfect it to a science, but somehow they *still* can't do it properly. It's all about unpredictable acidity over time…"

She carried on. I was having a hard time sharing in the outrage.

Across the small table Jennifer's eyes had, perhaps unwittingly, glazed over. After the earlier marathon I couldn't blame her. But as Selena continued monologuing the food worked its magic, clearing out the cobwebs. Each spoonful of the stew prompted a burst of flavour to dance across my mouth. Tangy, sweet, nothing if not comforting.

When the monologue reached a natural pause, I jumped in, hoping that I could slowly steer the topic into common territory.

"So how do you know so much about wine?"

Selena paused. "I was close with a sommelier once."

My eyebrows sharpened. "A sommelier? You found one on *Ceres?*"

"Mmhmm. "

Jennifer's eyes narrowed at that. "Hold on. Just *how* close?"

She chuckled. "Close enough for really good memories."

"And when was this?"

"Oh, maybe four years ago?"

"Four years…you mean *Zack*? You got *close* with *Zack Davies*?"

Selena beamed, judiciously saying nothing. Jennifer poked her.

"You're full of it." She turned to me for the first time since I'd arrived. "She's married."

The older woman shook a spoon mightily. "For fifteen years and proud of it! But Jacob had his indiscretions too." She leaned in every so slightly, voice becoming conspiratorial. "A few times we even *shared* them."

"You and Zack? Not possible."

"Believe it, dear."

Jennifer looked at me for support. I smiled politely and had no idea what to say.

Selena turned to me with an air of elegant serenity, charging merrily beyond the subject.

"So, Noah, what's one of *your* stories?"

I fumbled my words. "I, uh, feel like we're getting to know each other pretty quickly here."

Selena smiled graciously. Maybe a little impishly. "Oh please, we did that part already and it didn't hurt anyone. I'm genuinely curious. Where do you come from? What are you doing here?"

I put down my fork. Considered how much of that I wanted to tell.

"In a past life, in real life, I got a scholarship in the Homeward Journeys program. It's a lottery for bringing in people from the outer colonies to expose them to the old cultures on Earth. So when they said I was in with a spot at Union College London, I couldn't pass it up. The opportunity to see something that wasn't a bulkhead or a rock? To feel grass? Really *feel* it?And maybe get towards a decent job at the end of it? When I told my dad about it, he had this look that I didn't understand. I can remember that when we were walking to the docks, when I was going to leave, he took me aside, and gave me a hug. He told me that he wanted me to have a chance to see something green, something real, something wild. The kinds of things that he knew from his youth. The kinds of things that didn't grow in hydroponics racks."

I paused. "I can't remember anything after that. Not saying goodbye, or boarding the ship. It's just gone."

Jennifer reached out, and gave my arm a squeeze. A little gesture of reassurance. I offered her a small smile of thanks.

Selena was nodding understandingly. "You'll find your way back home, I'm sure."

"Maybe."

"You will. But, I do have a question. Putting aside the benefits of a real planet, there's the institute on Ceres. Jennifer goes there. Didn't it have something to offer you?"

A sliver of bitterness tinged my thoughts.

"Maybe it did. But I grew up in the sixth district. Everyone I knew worked in the docks and processing plants, and school was all about training you for those lives. I wanted out, sure. But maybe because of that life, or maybe for other reasons, the institute never had enough open spaces for me to get in."

The older woman chewed awkwardly, not quite knowing what to say to that. I let it go. No point dredging up old grudges. "Jen. You're a student?"

She nodded, mostly matter-of-fact. Maybe five percent smug. "Third year in multi-gravitational architecture. It's what I was doing when you came in. After graduation I'll be qualified to work on designing new colonies or transport ships."

My fork paused on the plate. "Congratulations," I said, entirely honestly. "How did you get into *that?*"

It was her turn to shrug. "I shadowed a few people in that line of work just before applying. Those experiences stuck. It was the first *real* thing I wanted to do."

Selena smiled. "Jacob fiddled with a few friendly strings for us years back which meant we got to know some interesting people. The rest was all on her."

Jennifer snorted. "Fiddled? Do you mean that literally?"

"Don't ask if you don't want to know, dear."

A disconcerted look crossed her face, but she turned to me. "Sorry that I've been hiding for the last few days. I've been trying to catch up on the program."

"They still have you studying? Even here?"

"There's a huge pile of reading material in my Index and my lecturers left open the option of doing a project on this trip. So, yeah. I'm trying to keep on top of it. It doesn't help that I can barely remember half of the last two years."

"But you *can* remember some of it, right?"

"Yeah. And I want the rest of it back. That's what I was doing when you walked in."

"I don't know how you've got the energy to get into that tonight."

She sighed. "I really don't."

I paused, unsure what to say to that. It was a topic out of my comfort zone.

"So, you grew up in the sixth district?" Selena prompted, deftly sliding into the chat.

I nodded. "It wasn't great. You two?"

Jennifer shrugged. "The second district, on level seven. Close to some okay food and nothing else. But," she mused, "I only started living there when I was sixteen, so *maybe* that's not fair."

"Sixteen? Where were you before?"

"Earth."

"You're a planet kid?"

"Both of us." She gestured at her aunt. "And that's just *fine*."

They shared a look, and for a long beat it seemed like a difficult topic. Eventually, Selena said, "It wasn't a good time back then. Before the move."

Despite the words, her tone was almost *happy*. Detecting an invitation to pursue the line of conversation, I nodded, putting on a curious face that I hoped wouldn't get me evicted from the table. "What happened?"

"Earth," Jennifer said again.

Selena's smile dipped somewhat, in the light of old memories. "She's talking about the part of her life spent there, not the planet."

"I figured that," I replied.

Jennifer shrugged. "Do you want to hear the story?"

I looked at her, then back to Selena, then back again. I wasn't getting any signals that it was awkward territory, so I nodded.

Selena *hmm*-ed and gathered her thoughts for a few moments before leaning back with a subtle smirk. "So, as you know, Jennifer is my niece. My brother, her father, was always a smart boy. Except with the girls he wanted. He was an *idiot* with the girls."

"How dare you!" Jennifer interjected in mock horror.

"I stand by it." The older woman said, momentarily straight-faced. She looked back to me. "Steven had a knack for falling in with women who shared a particular quality with our mother: they all inevitably became his own private antagonists. Things seemed different when he met Clara. Not better. But different..." She waved away some figment of memory. "They had Jen after a few years. And then Jen turned out to...not be what they wanted."

Jennifer snorted. "*That* was mutual. They were both assholes. Mom especially. Dad was better, but he chose *her* over *me* almost every time. I actually ran away from home one summer but it didn't last. I went back—I was fourteen—but they never forgave me for standing up for myself like that. So when Aunt Sel and Uncle Jacob announced they were moving to the colonies a couple years later, I packed a bag."

I arched an eyebrow. "Didn't your parents object?"

She shrugged. "They made noises. Mostly about how terrible a daughter I would be if I went through with it. But hey! They never actually tried to *stop* me, which said everything by itself."

"And you just *left*?"

Selena nodded agreeably, thinking back. "The paperwork wasn't easy, but let's not get bored with that. I became Jennifer's guardian. The colony cruisers were more traditional back then, and more expensive, and considerably more dull. But we could afford the extra ticket and the company apartment was big enough for a teenager to have her privacy."

"*Mostly* big enough," Jennifer corrected.

"Mostly," Selena agreed.

"But it was still better." Jennifer concluded.

I looked between them, a little confused. "If your time on Earth was so bad, why are you going back?"

"Because," Jen finally said, almost but not *quite* impatiently, "I have unfinished business."

They left it at that.

* * *

The movie theater was in lively swing when we showed up. A velvety rope guided us in beneath the beams of roving searchlights.

It was a grand affair, with sweeping, brassy gilding and neatly stitched lengths of voluptuous red fabrics. The center of the interior was a curving wall of double doors. Donald 'Beans' McCann was waiting for us, and ushered us in with mock-impatience.

As promised, he had lined up screen two for us with, in his words, the all-time classic *Night Bus to Elysium.*

It was fun. We cackled at the gimmicks, and gasped at the frantic chases. We oohed at the spectacular scenery. We sighed when the reclusive casino owner finally admitted his love for a woman he would never see again. We smirked at the charming rogue deftly side-stepping the detective's questions, and by the time the motley gang had reached their destination, we were left wondering just who the hero of the story really was.

In the gusting rain, surrounded by steaming vents on the roof of a city's library, the plot drew to its grand finale.

Over the detective's shuddering prone figure, a pair of survivors lingered.

"You'll never know if it was me, or if it was you, or if it was me pretending to be you," the rogue whispered to the love interest.

"That's fine," he said. "I just need you to know that you weren't supposed to get hurt." He drew a blade with one hand, grasping her collar and planting a kiss on her lips. "But in these times, who could say that you and I are so very different, in the end?"

A few dozen paces in front of them, the object of their shared attention stumbled forward into the warm, bright confines of a spacecraft, waiting to take him to safety and prosperity. It wasn't a ride for them. There might, eventually, be another like it. In the bittersweet glimmers of their eyes, the unlikely pair knew that they had ensured a good man had made it somewhere better.

But it had cost them.

The camera pulled back as the detective uttered parting words between hacking gasps. A fitting finale.

Selena nudged me with a smirk. I resolutely returned my gaze to the movie, dismayed at her lack of respect for the theater.

The love interest kicked the squirming wretch squarely in the abdomen, keeping him down a minute longer.

That minute might be all they had. Vigilante justice never lasted. Backup would be along soon, and the chase would begin.

The rogue looked up at the retreating transport, rain getting in her eyes. She spoke, confident, even cocky.

"You know, Alan, I see a glorious future before us."

"Just the two of us?"

"Just the two of us."

# NINE

At just before mid-morning, I transited away from Green Valley to Arkadia II, a world of lush, neon-hued plateaus split by deep canyons. It was a pleasure garden, filled with race courses, quiet strolls, shooter games, and certain sensory treats that the younger ones among us were barred from exploring. I'd been there once before, and had decided that its garish palette was going to be my home away from home.

I meandered to a railing overlooking a sheer drop, footsteps clapping against damp decking, and ordered up a swirling, foaming drink from mid-air. Despite the looming drop, I was safe. If anyone were to climb over the railing, much like the wispy fog in that lonely hilltop, they would be teleported back to the path.

Long, indulgent sips made for a cathartic moment as I took in the stars and planetary rings that lined the sky. Fake or not, it was a hell of a thing.

I brought up a tool that I'd been hesitant about using, and activated it.

At elbow height, a canvas fizzed into view, and a brush materialized in my right hand. With several swipes through menus, subtle controls appeared around the fingertips of my left. I meticulously twitched my grip, the motions shaping the head of the brush *just* so, and tinging it with the right dose of blue, then orange, then purples and greens.

And gingerly, I began to paint.

One stroke, then another, then a hint of another. A swish of darkened blue to show where a canyon wall was cast in shadow. A tinge of green for the phosphorescing growth. Dabs of purple for shade, swept deftly left and right to blend into the scene. Bright hazes of orange pulled across the sky to land atop the mesas.

I realized that I was missing a tone, added a medium grey to my repertoire, and used that to delicately etch edges of shapes into the scene, adding definition and depth where the land met the sky.

It was soothing, in its way, but perhaps a little easy to produce. The perfection of the color, and with practice, near-telepathic adjustments to the brush meant that the picture was what I desired, yet irritatingly incorrect in a way that was difficult to put a finger on.

As I contemplated the problem, my thoughts drifted to what was coming.

My loss in the first round of the tournament meant I wasn't eligible for the second. But Jennifer, as a proud member of the scoreboard, had earned a dubious bonus: she could invite someone to spectate on her efforts and provide whisper-in-the-ear advice. She of course offered it to Selena, who declined, citing an allergy to sharing her niece's point of view.

So, for the second round at least, it was to me, simply because everyone else she knew was a competitor. In the game, I would see what she saw, hear what she heard, and speak to her privately.

Kind of an intimate thing, in my mind.

As if bidden by the mere thought, Jennifer transited in behind me, *wooshing* in through a portal.

"Morning!" she called.

"Morning yourself," I called back.

"Game starts in a few minutes. Ready for…hey. That's really nice," she said, coming alongside and eyeing my attempted rendition of the vista.

"Thanks. It's wrong, though. I think I need to start again."

"I didn't know you could paint."

"I'm not sure this version of the craft *counts* as painting."

"I still like it. Ready for the thing?"

"Yeah. Probably. How does it work, again?"

"I send you an invite and you accept it. Here," she said, making my Index ping promptly. "Just like that."

I opened it, hesitant. "Just like that? You sure you want me in your shoes like this?"

She clapped me on the arm and squeezed lightly. "Yeah. You're good at this stuff, and I think you're better company than *you* think. Let's do it."

"Okay. If you're sure." I wriggled in place, shaking my shoulders loose. "Let's see what it's all about."

I accepted the invitation, ordered up a drink to appear in my companion's hand, and let the brush vanish as I finished my own in silence.

We retreated to a collection of loungers beside a lazy pool. Lights glowed up through the water, casting caustics against our skin. Far off on the horizon, the sun finished setting.

"Aidan?"

"Yeah?"

"Sorry about Aunt Sel, last night. She struggles with over-sharing."

"It's fine."

"Really?"

"Really."

"Good."

She relaxed. Then:

"Tell me about painting."

"Painting?"

"Yeah."

"I picked it up back home, a few years back. I like working in physical more than here, but here is…"

"What you've got?" she guessed.

"It's what I can see. What I want to see, I guess. It used to be starscapes. A few ships, you know, from the docks, on quiet shifts. Gave me a minute to just be calm. I tried people, once or twice. Haven't done those too well. The subject matter, the tools, it's not the same here."

"If you say so. But I still think that's a nice piece. I'm glad you've got a thing."

"A thing? I guess I do."

"Yeah. I'm a huge architecture dork. I like music. Sometimes I dance. Sometimes I hang out with other dorks."

I smiled. "I like baseball too."

"*Ooh.* I think I remember that! *Nobody* out here remembers the old sports."

"I've never played it, the spaces back home were never big enough, but my mom always loved it. She got so excited whenever it came up."

She mimed swinging a bat. "We could get the twins to try it. Maybe set up a game if we get enough people. I know Jazz would love it."

"And Tera would get super competitive."

"It's a little scary when she does that."

"Is." I paused, awkward, as a thought coalesced. "Your study field, it's...you know something you want to do with yourself. You've got that angle already."

She was silent for several long seconds. I worried I'd misjudged things. Jennifer looked up at the sky as she found her words.

"Noah, buddy, I'm on autopilot half the time. I'm going somewhere but every time I make plans something comes along and upsets them." She gestured at the world around us.

I nodded lazily and toasted the air. "Then here's to improvising."

She didn't reply to that, and we lapsed into another momentary quiet.

"I went a to baseball game once," she said suddenly. "A long time ago."

"Yeah?" I replied, interested. "What was it like?"

"I didn't see the appeal, honestly."

"Really?"

She shrugged. "It was a lot of big noise, bad food, and not a whole lot happening. But," she added, "the crowd had good energy. They were really invested. So I think I'd get why your mom was into it."

"She loved her home team. They—"

We were interrupted by a chime. The game was starting.

I looked at Jennifer. "Here we go."

She looked back, and nodded, opening her Index and transforming her outfit and cosmetics, donning her persona as Trace. A few beats later, she smirked, and then dissolved into a cloud of smoke.

I took a look at the rippling caustics in the pool, exhaled, and did my part.

With a flick of the wrist and a few judicious taps on floating controls, I established the spectator connection. The world faded away to a white wash in that familiar transition phase between imaginary realms.

"You know, I've never had anyone in my head before." Jennifer's voice was alarmingly immediate, as if she was beside me, or as if she *was* me...

*No, idiot,* I thought. *You're actually* her. *Not the other way around.*

I cleared my throat. "My first time, too."

A pause. Then another. And then—

The game snapped into being all around us. My arm—Trace's arm—involuntarily flung out as she—we—tumbled head over foot and crunched into a massive rock, before sliding off it. She scrabbled at the surface, tugging at it until her gloves found traction. And suddenly those few fingers were an anchor, and we weren't falling anymore.

Or, I abruptly realized as I looked up, we hadn't stopped at all.

Vast chunks of stone rotated above us, drifting past in sheer mockery of common sense. Not just a few; there were hundreds. And between them, not a night sky, but no sky at all.

"What, what the freck—"

Trace was hyperventilating.

"Calm down," I said, thinking back to a training day from another life. "Be calm. It's an asteroid field. You've got this. It's zero-gee. That means you have no up or down. Forward is wherever you want it to be. Backward is behind you."

Her manic breaths were punctuated by uncertain giggles. "You're in my frecking *head*."

"It's nice in here. Try to focus."

"I think I can hear you breathing. In my *soul*."

"Do you believe in that kind of thing?"

"Do I—shit, okay, okay. I'm focusing." She said. "How are you not freaking out right now?"

"I worked at the docks back on Ceres, remember? We went zero-gee a few times for cleanup runs. You'll get this."

Trace was nonplussed. "It's frecking weird."

"*You'll be fine.* Just breathe."

I put as much confidence into my voice as I could muster. Wasn't sure she was buying it. But that was okay.

I felt her arms relax a little bit, her shudders softening, posture shifting. She got our feet under us, planted on the asteroid in a skewed crouch.

"I feel like I'm holding onto the edge of a pool."

"Okay."

"Can you feel what I feel?"

"Yes."

"If I-" she held out a hand, "wiggle my fingers?"

"Feels very wiggly."

"Funky," she said, processing. "Can you see what I see?"

"Kind of. It's like I have my own head on your neck."

"How do you like it?"

I swallowed. "I'm a little queasy, to be honest. You?"

"Not great."

A long pause followed that. Her breathing, *our* breathing, got deeper and steadier.

Without warning, she launched us off and away, hurtling into the slow-motion maelstrom. But in seconds, we were clutching to a rock that had been flying at us moments earlier. And with a few beats' hesitation, she did it again, leaping out towards another destination.

"What are you *doing?*" I asked.

Her response was with a smile.

"I'm *swimming.*"

As we twisted and kicked off from spot after spot, contorting and gaining momentum in three very slippery dimensions, I realised that in Trace's limbs there was a smoothness, a confident economy of movement that felt alien, yet calming. As much as my brain was telling me that these were my arms, my legs, my torso, it was unavoidably obvious with each exertion that I was just a clumsy voyeur.

"Wow," I said.

It took several tries to handle *landing* on a target smoothly, but in the starlight, in those brief gaps between hunks of space debris, we *danced*.

It was beautiful.

Then a bright-purple exosuit flew past us and slammed into an outcropping at bone-crunching speed. But it didn't splinter into death shards; instead, a few beats later, it got up onto a crab walk, woozy, and stared at us before floating over.

"Hey dude," Jazz said, entirely too cheerfully. "How's it going?"

* * *

One asteroid in particular, much bulkier than the rest around it, was the place to be. What got our attention was a beam of green light lancing out of the black to pulverize a distant player.

As we watched from a distance, looking for a safe angle on the destination, I decided that it was hard to grasp how we'd possibly *missed* it.

A second interloper got zeroed by the defenses as they went in ahead of us. They had been gliding in to land on the rock's surface but fumbled it, bouncing off and squirming for purchase but finding none. Barely had they cleared the lip of an impact crater than a fresh bolt of bright, green light swept out from the stone, shattering them into glass.

"Ouch," Trace said grimly.

"That doesn't look fun." I added.

"Good grief," said Jazz. "This has *got* to be the place."

We kept close to the surface, giving the deadly crater a wide berth. Before long, we came to a deep fissure in the surface.

"Inside?" I asked Trace.

"Yeah. Inside?" She asked Jazz.

"One moment, consulting with management." He joked. "Yep. Down we go."

To my relief, Trace was getting better with the lack of gravity. She had initially struggled with the intricate contortions needed to safely hit one spinning space rock after another, but had learned quickly and this kind of movement was agreeably simpler. Even Jazz, whose gymnastic imagination left much to be desired, was coping reasonably well.

The interior of the asteroid was hard stone, oddly warm to the touch. As we descended through the tunnel, solar light disappeared, gently replaced by a purple haze, emanating from glowing tendrils snaking through the minerals.

"Is he in your head?" Jazz asked.

"Yeah," Trace replied.

Jazz nodded sagely. "Weird, huh?"

"You got that right," I muttered.

Trace just rolled her eyes.

Jazz nodded again with a lopsided grin. "Well, I've got Tera. She says hi."

"Lovely. Wish you were here, and all that."

Behind us, the green light flared again, signalling the end of another player's efforts.

Jazz's tone was conspiratorial. "Dude. This is just like *Okinawa*

*Retaken*. You've got to come in sideways and sneaky."

"What?"

"It's a thing I watched last night. A bunch of terrorists take over a big resort island and the police are forced to sneak in through this super-complex play structure on a beach, and it's a whole thing to get through the obstacle course without being noticed."

"I take it a lot of people fall into the water?" Trace replied.

Jazz shrugged. "There's a fight with katanas on an inflatable raft."

"Ah yes, a classic showdown." I muttered. "Your aunt will find it irresistible."

Trace snorted, and carried on moving us deeper into the mass.

In the heart of the great rock we found a substantial, spherical cave, dotted with circular openings that led into numerous tunnels. At its center, a grand machine, with an evil red crystal glowing at its core. A mesh sphere enclosed it, and its equator was neatly defined by a solid ring with six lumps equally spaced along its perimeter.

Trace whistled. "Cool," she said. The lack of a comment from Jazz was surprising, but when we glanced back, he was gone.

We saw the distant specks of other players, maybe a dozen, close in on the core from other entrances. Shrugging off our friend's vanishing act, Trace kicked us forward, letting momentum carry her through.

The silence remained unnervingly ever-present, right until we collided with the mesh, which sent the most unpleasant vibration imaginable thrumming through our exosuit. It felt like even Trace's *blood* was rattling.

She hastily pressed up and away, so that we were floating apart from the menace but in reach of its surface. Our boots connected with something hefty, and an arm grabbed desperately at our legs.

We looked down, and saw an anxious face that I didn't recognize. Trace waved, and let them keep holding on.

"That's neighborly," I said.

She didn't reply, breathing hard, counting those around us.

Ten players had made it to the core, meaning at least some of the rest had either been picked off on the way in, or were lost out in the maelstrom. "Player versus environment." Trace said, dismayed. "But more than before. We should have seen that coming."

I snorted. "At least this time we're all making an effort at cooperating. Giant green death rays really do bring people together."

She gestured at the core. "What do you make of this thing?"

"Probably important," I said. "Everybody seems to be coming down to it. Feels wrong though."

"Why?"

"Too *obvious*. The last round was a hidden puzzle and we got lucky to even find it. This is big and bright and full of evil light shows. Let's be careful."

The lumps on the mesh cage bristled with dials and handles up close. Before long, clusters of players had gathered around each one, trying to decipher the puzzle. It seemed obvious that doing *something* with the machine would open the gate.

"Look around at the cavern," I suggested. Trace did so, surprised, but thoughtful.

"What are you thinking?"

"What tends to happen to big machines like this? In fiction, I mean?"

She snorted. "They usually blow up. With a big shockwave."

I let my voice carry a drawl. "Right. Is there anywhere that looks like it would make for a nice big exit? A dramatic escape chute? Somewhere nice and tidy to wait for the special moment?"

"You want to cheese it?"

"You don't?"

"It just feels like *cheating*."

"*I* feel like cheating is the only way anyone wins this game."

After a few beats of silence, she pointed to a round pit, shadowed in the cavern wall far below. "That looks about right."

"Shall we?"

She sighed, and shook her head, but worked our position around while clinging to the rumbling core, until the opening in question appeared above and in front of us, rather than below.

And she kicked off again.

Halfway to the far wall, where the clamor of the core was distant and there was nothing to do but wait for impact, a chime started sounding in our ears. "What's that?" Trace asked the darkness.

"Wait a second," I said, seeing a notification in the middle of my vision. I declined it. "Tera was trying to call me."

"Probably trying to distract you. Focus."

"Yeah."

We watched as another couple of players found their way safely into the cavern, migrating towards the glowing core like so many moths. Nobody seemed to know what *do* once they got there, though, and I started to wonder if it was actually a misdirection. Giant, well-armed asteroid with a glowing core. Clearly a place meant to be challenged. Unless—

Another notification flared up, bringing more insistent chiming along with it.

"Again?" Jennifer asked.

"Fine, I'll see what she wants." I said breezily. "We got this. I'll come back on in a minute."

"Uh huh."

I disconnected without another word.

The transition out of Jennifer's awareness and back into my own avatar's woozy, gravity-resenting feet was jarring. As I haphazardly got used to my own height, never mind my own limbs, my Index dutifully brought up a ghost of Tera's avatar, silencing the chiming. There was none of the classic sauntering smirk. She looked *unhinged.*

"Jazz is gone. Just plain *gone.*"

"What are you talking about?"

"I mean he's *gone.* One moment we're in the asteroid belt with you guys, the next I black out, and then I'm back in my own bed."

I shook my head. "I'm sure he's just still in the game. Maybe you hit a bug. His avatar will zip right back here when he's done."

She was adamant. "No, it won't. Look." She opened her Index and spoke to the voice interface, sharing it into the call so I could follow along. "Kay Tee, Find Tera Cooke."

Her Index changed to render a three-dimensional perspective map of Green Valley from the air, before zooming in on the hotel and swapping its color surfaces for a wireframe view. On the second floor, about a quarter of a way around the building's semicircle, a bright yellow dot pulsed. Right where she was standing.

She looked at me, but spoke to Kay Tee again. "Find Selena LaVelle."

The dot on her Index shifted slightly, moving up a level.

"Find Aidan Whittaker."

The rendered scene changed completely, fuzzing out before re-assembling itself into my lonely slice of the Arkadia II resort. High atop the edge of a mesa, a yellow dot glowed.

"What are you getting at, Tera?"

She shook her head, undeterred, and gestured for me to wait.

"Find Jennifer Motley."

The rendered scene changed again, and the label "Solstice Environment" came up, before illustrating a wireframe map of the asteroid belt. As we watched, one of the exterior defences on the vast central rock sniped at an unprepared late-comer to the party, neatly scything them out of the competition with a brilliant green flare.

"Okay," I said. "So?"

Tera held up a finger. "Find Jazaban Cooke."

The Index didn't change at all. Moments later it flashed up a message: *Passenger not found.*

"I've tried calling him, messaging him, pinging his avatar on the Index. I don't know *where* the hell he is. But he's not here."

I revised my earlier estimate.

She didn't look unhinged. She looked *scared.*

"All right," I said, holding up my hands. "Let me tell Jen. We'll get some help and figure it out."

I closed the call, worried, and rejoined the spectator invite.

My inner ear did a somersault as the whole concept of proprioception reshaped itself in an instant. No longer being in control of my movements wasn't too hard to handle. But the fact that it wasn't *my* body, with my normal proportions, was just plain *weird.*

Deep inside the cavernous, villainous asteroid, Jennifer—Trace in this place—was fiddling around down on the glowing mesh core once more, working some controls in harmony with a few others.

"Hi," I said.

She jerked in surprise. "Hi *yourself.* What did she want?"

"She's scared."

"Of what? Losing again?"

I shook my head. "Jazz is gone."

"He got taken out?"

"No, I mean really gone. Kay Tee can't find him."

She paused. "Huh. That's probably just—"

The core beneath us bucked and pulsed, shattering the vibrating mesh screen. Around us players evacuated in all directions as a part of the disintegrating apparatus struck the crystal at the centre, sparking a roiling red explosive wave. Trace frantically kicked off, trying to get some distance.

Far above, several gates shimmered into life, precious exits waiting to catch the exodus and pull us to safety.

It was not to be.

A few heartbeats later, the explosion caught up and seared through our exosuit, and I felt our body rip into shards all over again.

* * *

This time, when I re-materialized, I was ready for it, bracing myself before my legs reasserted their normal existence. I called Tera back, but didn't get an answer.

*Probably having a breakdown,* I thought guiltily.

Beside me, Jennifer stretched, huffing in annoyance.

"Look," she said, breathing heavily. "I know what I said that one time, but *come on.* The timing sucked!"

"Uh huh," I said, distracted. I walked off to the lean against the precipice railing, and spoke flatly to the invisible voice that always seemed to be listening. "Kay Tee, find Tera Cooke."

A swirling smiley face shimmered into view, before morphing into a spinning progress wheel.

From behind, my companion called out. "Talk to me, Noah."

"Have a look," I replied, focused.

A moment later, the midair graphic resolved into an error, and that ghostly tenor, echoing just behind my left ear, read it into my mind.

*Passenger not found.*

Jennifer stepped up beside me then, more alert.

"Kay Tee, find Tera Cooke."

Another spin of the wheel.

*Passenger not found.*

"Kay Tee, find Selena LaVelle."

Another spin.

*Passenger not found.*

# DEEP-RANGE NEWSCAST

Helios Network News
Sol 11, 21:17 Local Time


"…according to a report released earlier this afternoon, three smugglers have been arrested at the Luna hub on charges of illegally importing stocks of refined pelarite. The rare belt mineral is a lucrative commodity for Earthbound traders but is tightly regulated, ever since the famous accident involving the U.N.S. *Kazansky* six years ago. Ted, what do you make of it?"

The other newscaster's smile flickered. "Dangerous stuff, Camilla. Happily border agents were able to secure the cargo without any loss of life. I can only imagine how terrible it could have been."

"Terrible is quite the word." Camilla turned back to the camera. "Next, in a breaking update from Ceres, Station Minister Gordon

Kell has announced that he will be stepping down at the end of the current solar week. I don't need to remind you viewers that Minister Kell has gained a reputation for cracking down on corruption in his career, even to the point of hamstringing his own legal trade. What could have caused this sudden reversal out of public life? More on this story as it develops."

# TEN

The calls to Selena rang, and rang, and went unanswered.

Jennifer lost some composure as possibilities sunk in. "It's probably fine. She's probably gone to stretch her legs. I'll go make sure she's all right."

She opened her Index and swiped along to the session controls, then waited impatiently.

"…and?" I asked.

"Nothing. Nobody's answering. Nobody is *available* either. They're all gone. And this damn thing won't let me open a portal."

It seemed like a foolish exercise, but I checked my own Index anyway. She was right. I tried to summon a transit portal back to Green Valley, but it never materialized. Instead a gentle *beep* sound was all that I got for the trouble. And though I scrolled through the Index's options three times over, there was no *exit* button anywhere. I felt like a fool for not noticing sooner. Life had been good enough that I had just forgotten to care.

No communications. No portals. No tracking. Cut off.

*Shit.*

Our little corner of Arkadia, with its loungers and delicate pool, suddenly seemed very remote indeed. My mouth went dry, contemplating having to face a return to the first day in this reality, when almost all the things that should have made it lively and rich and real simply hadn't existed yet. When it had held all the sanity of a feverish nightmare.

Jennifer's breathing steadily picked up, and up, and up. She retreated towards the railing, eyes widening as our prospects sank in. "I'm not going back. I am *not* going back to how it was."

I went to her. "No, we are not. I mean, yes, looks like that, a little bit, but we're still here. That's something. That's okay. You're okay."

"It's happening *again!*" she shouted.

"Might be. Might not. We don't know yet. You're okay."

"I am *frecking not* okay."

I put a hand on her arm. "Yes, you *are.*"

"Are you getting it, you clod? We're in a prison. We *voluntarily* put ourselves here. A prison. And it's making people disappear. *Again. We have* to get out of this fairytale tissue-paper bullshit."

"Do you want to stand there waving about it, or do you want to be interesting?"

She wasn't listening. I went back to my Index. "Kay Tee, I need to talk to the captain."

The assistant chirped happily out of thin air. "You can always contact him via the captain's comments feed. Would you like me to convey your feedback on how the voyage is progressing?"

I stared at the Index in front of me in disbelief. "Uh, *yes.*"

Kay Tee was as chipper as ever. "Please, start recording your message now."

A cartoonishly proportioned camera popped into existence at eye level. I leaned into it.

"Captain DeSanto, please get your people to help us in here!" I

growled at it. "This place is breaking. My name is Aidan Whittaker
—"

I abruptly paused, changing tactics.

"That's Jennifer Motley behind me. We don't know you, you don't know us, and I…really don't know what I'm doing. Ah, okay, keep it simple. The world, our world, is breaking. We can't call anyone, we can't travel between places, and the Index is losing people. I'm sure you guys have this figured out but we really could…use some reassurance."

I couldn't think of anything else to say, so I waved to close the message. The camera disappeared promptly.

Kay Tee happily spoke up. "Thank you. Your message has been sent to the captain. As it is currently the night shift on board, the captain is asleep, and will see your message when he comes on duty in approximately six hours."

"*What?*" Jennifer and I nearly shouted in unison.

I caught my breath. Time to try it again. "Kay Tee, I want to send a message."

"To whom, Aidan?" came the synthetic reply.

"Any member of the crew."

"I'm sorry Aidan, but Apollo crew member personal contacts are private."

"Make an exception!"

"I'm sorry, but I can't do that."

I made a silent promise to sustain my calm voice. "How much would it cost to deliver a message to Ceres?"

"Interplanetary direct link costs two thousand and three-hundred solar equivalent dollars per message. One moment. I can see that your budgetary spend for this voyage has a borrowing limit of nine-hundred solar equivalent dollars, to be settled by Carver Interplanetary upon your arrival in a new banking territory. Would you like to apply for an increase in your credit limit?"

I paused, apprehensive. That was a lot of money.

"I'll split it with you," Jennifer muttered.

I considered it. Looked out at the landscape. Decided that it wasn't worth being trapped here.

"*Yes.*" I said, enthusiasm gone out of my lungs.

"Wonderful!" Kay Tee replied. "I have submitted an application to raise your credit limit to three thousand SED. The current waiting time for application review is two sols."

Disbelief started to morph into impotent rage. This was *worse* than a joke.

Jennifer grunted and stormed away. "I need a drink. A real one."

It *was* a small blessing that we weren't *quite* as badly off as we had been at the beginning. I mentioned as much to Jennifer. She kept walking.

As we followed the paths along the cliff's edge, it wound us past a colossally-sized ball of gnarled branches, dotted with glowing green fruits. Beyond it, hidden from prying eyes, was precisely what the situation demanded. In a clearing lit by webs of dangling balls of light a round bar waited amidst a ring of tables. The bartender wasn't human. A three-legged creature, with a skinny abdomen and long neck, craned above us. As I looked, a name rendered beside it: *Heri.*

As we approached, Jennifer spoke up snappily. "Heri. Hi."

"What can I do for you, esteemed patrons?" Heri replied, gravely, polishing a glass. The aroma of sandalwood danced in the air as he moved.

"Your finest whiskey," I commanded. "and this lady wants *real* alcohol. In our veins. Can you do that? My treat."

"I'm sorry, but alcoholic infusion is only available to premium passengers with an emerald-tier support package."

"What *can* you give us?"

"The tasting experience of a richly complex burgundy. And some advice, perhaps."

The way the bartender said it made us pause, and I cocked an eyebrow as he leaned in. "Go on."

"Stay away from the patrons at table five," he whispered conspiratorially. "A riotous bunch, those ones."

I looked at table five, bemused. A couple of kids in dripping-wet diving gear sat happily as if they'd just climbed out of a processing tank.

"Noted," I said. Heri turned to my companion with a knowing smile. "And for you, madam?"

"Golden Ichor Supreme. Straight-away."

I handed over a coin as Jennifer dragged me to a table. The drinks appeared as we sat.

"Think we should tell those guys?" I muttered.

Jennifer shook her head sourly, fending off anxiety shivers. "Not yet. They're having fun."

As if on cue, they noticed us.

"Hey!" a younger diver from their group shouted. "Aren't you Trace?"

Jennifer looked at him, distracted from her mood. "What do you want?"

"I want to congratulate you, man! Your exit from the first round of the tournament was, like, *inspired.*"

The diver peered at me, before suddenly cackling. "Oh yeah! And *you're* the rube who got nailed two feet from the gate!"

Jennifer shook her head, stress lines creasing her expression. Sensing an opportunity to reset the moment for her, I made my best effort at sounding gregarious. "All the more shame about the second round! Who made it through?"

"Twerko, Avalon, Beans, Cordite Realmz, Bugbug, and DeGausse." One of the others recited excitedly. "We watched everyone else get pulverised."

"What a light show!" The first one added, loudly.

Heri coughed pointedly behind us, and the troublemaker got the hint, lowering his volume.

"But I hear the next one is a doozy. The briefing is old-world fightercraft in a gas giant's atmosphere. They'll be in gunships at knife-fighting range, and wandering too low will get you crushed like a bug in the gravity well. It's *heavy* stuff."

He seemed proud of his pun. Nobody really laughed, but I rewarded him with a small snort.

"Where'd you find that out?" I said.

"The library back in the valley, man. There's a spectator station and everything. The acoustics are awesome for it."

"Guys," Jennifer interrupted. "Thank you for the chat, but get lost. It's a bad time."

They watched, befuddled, as we moved away to find another table. I made an apologetic face, but they didn't follow.

"Okay," I said, patience wearing thin. "That was harsh. Don't be a freckhead."

She withdrew into herself, her presence seeming to shrink. "I know. I'm sorry."

I tried calling Tera again. There was no answer. Ringing Jazz had the same result. As did an attempt to call Don McCann. At least *he* would have some right to be in better spirits.

"I'm sure Selena is fine," I said, trying to encourage her to perk up.

Jennifer said nothing.

I sighed. Looked at the bar. It wasn't right, just sitting here, but sitting here was all we could do.

Or was it? We had done this before. The results had been questionable, but it wasn't new territory.

"We'll find a way out of this," I muttered, watching Heri clean another glass. "We'll poke at the edges of this place until we find something. It's what we do."

Jennifer stopped, slumping down against a fibrous tree, deflated. She had a warble in her voice, no longer angry, but now verging on repressed hysteria. "No, we won't. We won't do a thing."

I sat beside her gingerly. "Hey, hey. We'll do it."

"We didn't even do anything last time! We walked for ages, reached the edge of the map, shit ourselves, got flung back to the start, and then *they* fixed everything for us."

"That's true," I admitted. "But the point is we *tried* something. Even if we didn't need to keep going, we still tried."

"You're a peach. But let's be real. We could just wait it out."

"*You* could. But what if it's something really bad? What if they can't fix it? We can't trust that *they*, out there, will make life perfect again."

Jennifer glared at the bar. "*Perfect?* This hasn't been perfect in the slightest."

"You know what I mean. Look, you're gonna get out of here, and study gravitational architecture, and graduate, and design ships. You're gonna do it. But that *won't* happen if you don't make your own way right now. You don't have to fix it, but you do have to *get up*."

She looked at me firmly, intently. Mutinously.

Then she got to her feet. "So, what. What can we do? Order drinks? Paint all day? We might as well catch a movie and wait it out."

"No."

"No?"

"No," I repeated, pulling her along until we reached the silver cylinder that marked a transit station. As we got there, its display flashed into existence. I pulled up the available leisure activities, swiped to *The Crisper*.

Jennifer started. "Wait, wait, wait, what—"

I pushed the button.

But where we should have been warped to the clouds far above a frozen mountain range, instead we remained firmly grounded on the jungle mesa, surrounded by orange and cyan plants and a bartender with a stiff disposition.

"Hmmm." I said enigmatically. "Come on."

"Where are—"

"We're stuck *here*." I interrupted. "As in, right *here*. Arkadia. In *this* version of *this* world. This is reality for us right now. We can't go to a different plane, we can't go to a different dimension, we can't call out. If you're so content with that, then sit around and mope. But I'm *not*. I need to fix this. Be interesting and *help* me."

Silence reigned for a few beats.

"I like this version of you." She said suddenly.

I smiled grimly.

"Good. Then get ready. We're going to find some comfortable chairs, get another drink, and find out what we don't know that we don't know, and break things even more if it gets us out of here. We're going to do research, and *mess with some shit*."

"I take it back."

A manic smile twitched my lips. "It's too late for that! If we really go looking through our Indexes, they've got to have more resources, in-depth documentation, anything, on how this place works."

"Makes sense to me," she replied slowly, keeping more alongside as we moved now. "Love it or hate it, there's something to this place. A *design*. I've never met a designer who didn't love blabbering about their own work."

"Yes, the calling card of the intelligent snob. It should be easy for you to relate."

She gave me the *dirtiest* of looks. Worth it.

It took a considerable amount of careful questioning, and presenting myself as a hobbyist interested in working for the company, but eventually Kay Tee put the so-called documentation on CarverNet in front of me.

While I tried to get my head around the immediate problems, Jennifer dove into the backgrounds of the crew and the Apollo itself. What I had to admit to myself, going from one documentation piece to the next, was that my understanding of the CarverNet simulation was deeply incomplete. Or, really, totally wrong.

Heri polished another glass as we sat at the farthest table possible from the divers. Some creature made a *hoo*-ing noise in the distance.

"Hey."

I looked up at Jennifer. "Yeah?"

"Remember how in the game, in the first round, we kind of read the world? Saw paths and hints in it?"

"Sure."

"This is just another game."

"Kind of." I sat back and thought about it. "It's not very game-like, but in principle it's exactly the same medium."

"What I mean is that we have to get out of it. We can't use a menu, and we can't reach the power button."

I understood. "So we need to make it break. Make it crash."

"Exactly. So how does it *work?*"

I consulted my light reading material, shook my head,

bewildered. "I'll get back to you."

"Mmhmm."

We were at it for a while, until the words on the Index started to blur together. For good measure we tried calling Tera again, with no answer. Jazz remained uncontactable. Selena remained absent. It was hard to deny the gnawing sense of frustrating futility.

When my eyes glazed over I stood up, walked a circuit of the bar, tried to ground myself. Decided to try to calm my nerves with an artistic break. Heri made for a fascinating subject, and there was a part of me attracted by the way his legs gracefully twisted and turned. Tripedal locomotion was pleasingly *foreign* to watch.

Out came the canvas and floating brush. A few lines, an easy profile. A dash of color. A swirl of something entirely *wrong*.

I cleared the canvas in frustration. Focused, played with different pigment combinations, looking for the right palette to capture what I was seeing. Cleared it again.

After another aborted try I gave up in exasperation. Painting was supposed to be calming, soothing, meditative. This was none of that. All I could think about was technical jargon, an impending sense of doom, and metaphors about reality itself.

Jennifer looked at me kindly as the tools vanished back into thin air.

I shuffled back to the table. Gave myself a shake. Time to stop playing.

*Sigh.*

* * *

"So what I've been getting is that we're in a world of two... *dimensions*. It didn't *actually* use that word, but it was the closest thing I could...I'm just using that word."

Jennifer nodded patiently.

"The first dimension is a central, shared world, full of places and objects which can be interacted with by anyone. When I," I grasped my now-drained cup, "move this across the table, the cup isn't part of me."

"Why would it be?"

"Sure, but let me finish."

"Sorry."

"This cup isn't part of me. As I move it, and let go of it, its position is changing for you, and Heri, and everyone else here. Even the diver dudes over there. It's part of the world, and is a sort of absolute, passive fact. I can move, you can move, but the cup will stay where we put it."

"This is sounding a lot like the metaphysics module from my first year classes."

I shrugged. "The second, um, dimension, is more, ah, *personal.* It's unique to me and my brain and my suit, and unique to you and your brain and your suit, and so on for Selena and Tera and anyone else. Even my neighbor—remember Abigail? That dimension is what the Carver people call the *perspective*, and in it, for me, I'm the center of the universe. When my brain says to walk forward, I perceive my legs moving, but the world is actually scrolling past me while I stay still. And when I grab this cup," I waved it again, "it becomes attached to me. Not part of me, but *attached.* When I move it, the world scrolls by the cup as I move it, so that I can take a drink from it and it doesn't look stupid."

"Neat," she said.

"Probably. I'm struggling to totally understand what it *means.*"

She pondered it. "It *sounds* like a system which is totally full of exploitable gimmicks."

"Think on it. What did you find?"

"Absolutely *nothing* of use about the Apollo other than what we already know. The captain's name is Franklin DeSanto, the ship's been in service for most of a decade…that's it. I can't even find out if we're both physically in the same *part* of the ship."

Heri approached from the bar, moving in a way that combined his prim attitude with the swagger of totally owning his place. His legs made a *shlepping* sound as they worked. "And how are you two doing?"

"Badly," Jennifer said.

"I'm sorry to hear that."

"Thanks, Heri."

"I overheard some of your chat. It seemed *very* interesting. I thought you two would be in need of some extra fortitude." He produced three glasses, which filled with an amber liquid on the spot. "Jumpy Juice. Our house brand, I'm afraid, but still a fine beverage for humans."

I accepted the drink, and moments later, felt a surge of alertness in my veins. "Thanks," I said, nodding to Jennifer. "It's got a caffeine infusion tied to it. Take a drink, get a hit in your fluids."

"Nice," she said, a little less moodily.

"Heri," I said, intrigued. "What do you know about CarverNet?"

He blinked at me. "It's quite a nice place to be, isn't it?"

"Do you know of any way out of it?"

"I'm sure you can leave any time you like. But I'm always here for you."

"But what if we *can't* leave? You know, by ourselves? Could anyone get us out?"

"Afraid that I don't know about that topic. But why don't you tell me about what's bothering you?" The alien gestured to Jennifer's sulking silence.

I sighed, giving up. "Fine. Do you ever get lonely?"

"Sometimes. It's a terrible feeling. My hatchmates used to leave me to fend for myself. They'd all go off to dance with their *zyrs* or work for the mother or play with each other, and me, I'd get left behind almost every time. I could have resented them for it, and I usually did, but sometimes it wasn't that bad."

"I know what that's like," I said. "Sometimes you want to be with everyone else, and sometimes you just want to be on your own. We loners have to stick together. Far apart."

"A resounding summation." Heri blinked, and saluted with his glass before taking a long sip.

"That's not a bad piece of backstory." I replied, saluting in return, remembering that I was complimenting a machine.

"Yes, well." The bartender bowed. "We all weave our sorrows into compelling tales. And you, my lady? What's yours?"

"My father is dying." Jennifer said, abruptly.

"What?" I said.

"He's dying. Errol's Lymphoma. Got a few months at most. It's why I'm here."

"I'm so sorry."

"My condolences. That's a terrible thing." Heri said.

"Yeah." Her voice warbled. "Yeah. We're going to see him. See him off. Not, like, murder him, but be there for his end, you know?"

I put a hand on hers, and squeezed. "Do you need a hug?"

She shook her head. "No, no, no. I'm fine. He was a prick. But he's still important. That's all."

"Do you need to talk about it?" Heri asked, gently.

"I, uh, yeah, sure. Therapy from a computer. Right now. Sure."

Heri froze in place for a fraction of a second, then resumed movement as if nothing had happened. "Mister Whittaker, do you know of this disease?"

"No," I replied. "It's a new one to me."

Jennifer's voice was dulled, withdrawn. "It mainly affects zero-gee workers who don't handle radiation protection wisely. I don't know how he got it."

Heri nodded sagely. "It's a very rare concern, as I have been told."

"Yes. You only have to already have a single undetected tumor, and then the next time you get a flush of VacStrat, bad cells get washed around your system. Then, next time you go for a space walk, if any part of your suit is below spec, and you get exposed to direct gamma radiation from something like a bad thruster failure, well, you've had it. Your body just goes nuts on itself. You can treat it, you can fight it, you can suppress it, but the bad guy is already in your bed and getting him out is impossible. You basically need a bunch of your insides swapped out all at once, and the cloning process to grow the new parts takes time. Too much for most people."

I was silent for a long minute, visualizing it. Heri, to his credit, said nothing.

"I-" I started.

"I just don't know what the hell he was doing that he could have gotten it. He *hated* zero-gee."

"Um." I finished. "Um."

Heri bowed. "Hopefully you'll be able to find out when you see him next."

"Heri," I said, running a little thin on patience, "Can you give us a minute alone?"

"Of course." The alien rose, bowed again, and retreated to tend to the bar.

Jennifer was shaking her head. "It doesn't matter. I'm not even sure I want to be there."

"Is Selena making you go?"

"No, I wanted to make the trip. I'm just not sure I want to go there *for him*."

"Oh."

"Look, let's talk about something else, okay?"

I nodded. "Heri's conversation skills are pretty good, aren't they?"

She swallowed over a lump in her throat. "Yeah. Very good. I forgot what I was talking to for a few seconds."

"Hey—"

"No, enough. No more on that right now." She got up, and started pacing. "Let's go back to what you were talking about before. About how when you pick up a cup, it's part of you?"

I drained my cup of its last dregs, then handed it to her. "That's right."

"Okay." She inspected it, frowning. "Now it's attached to me."

"Yep."

"What happens when we're both holding it?"

"Don't know."

I wrapped my hand around hers so that we were both grasping the little piece of ceramic. "I guess it's attached to both of us."

"Yeah. So what happens when I move it—"

She pushed her arm, moving the cup, and my hand moved right along with it.

*"Ah."* I said. "Do we become attached to each other?"

"Maybe. I need to think about how that might or might not help."

"How in the stars *could* it help?"

Jennifer reached over, and tried to push my hand directly. It didn't budge. She nodded thoughtfully.

"Okay. Everything that's designed into a system like this one is intentional. It's what the architect thought everybody would want to do. But that means there are going to be edge cases, where people can do things that *weren't* intended, places where all the rules don't quite line up, and those spots are where things get weird."

"You're saying that moving me *through a cup* is one of these edge cases?"

"I think so. Get up."

"Why?"

She leveled a look at me.

I stood up.

Jennifer walked back to Heri's bar, and returned with a mug, placing it on the ground between us. "Let's do something nobody would ever do. Try to pick it up with your toes."

I obliged, removing my shoes and trying a couple of different methods before wrapping my big toe and its nearest neighbor around the handle.

She squatted and tried to pick up the mug. It raised up, bringing my foot with it, and bending my knee as my leg rose. I nearly toppled over and she grinned, returning it down.

"Okay," she said. "Now try to *stand* on it."

"Um." I said. "Why?"

"Just, come on."

"Fine."

Against my better judgement, I swirled and levered my other foot atop the mug, so that I was perched rather improbably on a tiny, wobbly piece of drinkware.

Remarkably, it didn't break.

Jennifer picked it up, and took me right along with it as if I weighed nothing, and waved me around like stick.

"What the hell?" I shouted. Heri looked up, aloof. The divers stared at us from their far table.

"*Wow*," Jennifer grinned.

As she swung me around and around in figures of eight, I wanted to vomit. I seemed to be magnetically glued to her arms. When she left me still for a moment, at a near ninety-degree angle away from what should have been *up*, I released my grip on the mug. Suddenly free of the broken physics, I fell to the floor, crunching my face into the hard planks. It was a mercy that only a whisper of the impact came through as pain.

"Dude," said one of the divers, approaching. "Is that your secret? Are you, like, a superhero?"

Jennifer shook her head and waved him off, before pulling me away hurriedly and leaving him behind in confusion. We retreated down the paths until we had a little more privacy to experiment. As we reached a railing, Jennifer shared her theory.

"I've never seen a piece of work where somebody didn't take a shortcut somewhere. Remember what I said ages ago, that touch matters? Gravity here pays attention to what you're touching, or if you're on a planet and not touching anything, it just defaults to *down*. But that means that if you're *only* attached to a cup, your gravity re-orients to be relative to the cup, making you movable by whatever the *cup* gets attached to, like me. And the cup has no concept of conveying *mass* from one attached object to another. To me you only weigh as much as the cup."

"Makes sense? I think?" I muttered.

She shrugged with the trace of a smirk. "Third-year in multi-gravitational architecture."

"Right."

"I'm just saying. Intelligent snob, and all that."

"Let me try with you."

"Okay."

She removed her shoes and perched on the mug, balancing awkwardly. I reached down, grabbed the vessel, and swept it off the ground easily, lifting my friend high into the air.

"Waahahaho, wow, okay, *careful!*" she called out.

I spotted my goal and marched towards a railing. Jennifer's eyes widened as we got close. "Wait, what are you—"

I grinned. "Want to find out what happens when someone goes outside the borders?"

I waved the cup out into the empty air, where a sheer drop into the canyon waited.

"Noah, okay, this isn't funny."

"Totally right," I replied, "it's *revenge.*"

On cue, she wobbled, and fell off.

"Oh, shit." I mumbled, watching.

She plummeted down for several heart-stopping seconds, and then vanished as she hit the rock face, abruptly *snapping* into existence behind me and swinging for my shoulder.

"Jackass!" she shouted as the hit connected, and I jumped in surprise.

"What can I say," I shrugged. "Now we know something new."

"Yeah, that you can't be trusted."

"Well, yes," I admitted.

"Wanker."

"Fronk."

"Jerk!"

"Poser!"

"Gumball!"

I chuckled.

She looked murderous, but then broke down, and joined in.

For a second, we forgot why we there, doing what we were

doing.

Heri found us, and handed us each a glass with something blue in it.

As the laughter subsided, we had a moment where the earlier tension had been shredded. I looked at her. Actually *looked*. I saw another glimpse of her real fear. It wasn't of heights.

I took a sip, and raised an eyebrow in thanks. There was a distinctive cooling tang at back of my mouth. Felt a telltale looseness in the back of my mind. Real alcohol.

"Some liquid courage for the lovely couple." Heri said, and winked, retreating without another word.

I examined the drink, letting its rush tickle my thoughts.

"This is nice," I said.

"Yeah," Jennifer agreed.

"You have that premium package, don't you." It wasn't a question.

"Yeah." Jennifer said again.

"I thought you didn't want a drink."

"I changed my mind."

"Nice. Did you tell Heri that we were a couple?"

"Nope."

We each took a long, appreciative swig.

"I have to fix this place. I have to." I said. "I don't know how it's broken, but I need it. I really need it, Jen."

She tilted her head, savoring a fresh mouthful. "Why?"

"It's the best I've ever had it." Another swig. "They *can't* take this away from me."

She saluted with her drink, but shook her head. "The real world can get better than this."

"Not the one I've known."

"Then, here's to living in your head as often as possible." She toasted the sky, and set about draining her glass.

I consulted the horizon through my drink. Dwelling on how the light bent through the one side, then back through the other, rippling along into a doubly-refracted mirror of itself, warm hues bluntly submerged into a cooler interpretation. Filtered. Processed. Changed.

Layered.

I sat bolt upright, finishing my drink.

"Keep your glass," I said. "I know how we're getting out of here. We need to continuously layer physics in a way that lets us both be in control simultaneously."

Jennifer peered at me cautiously. "I'm starting to think giving you alcohol was a mistake."

"The cup trick."

"What about it?"

"We need to both be the holder and the held. We need to make a paradox."

"Uh huh. And *how* do you propose we do that?"

"Well," I said. "How good are you at holding yourself upside down?"

It took a while to work it out. We sourced some robustly-sized tankards from Heri, which had actual handles—critical for making the exploit workable with our pitifully small human extremities. One of us would find their perch, gripping the handle with their toes, and clasping the other vessel at face level. The other would try their best at a hand stand—no easy feat!—and waddle over to insert themselves into place. It took a *lot* of tries. I fell over nearly every time. But just when the intoxication was wearing off, we succeeded. The moment the loop first closed properly, with Jennifer's toes grazing my hands, and her fingers brushing against my now-aching bare feet, we *knew*. Gravity re-defined itself instantly.

"Whoa", she said, startled.

"Whoa is right," I replied.

We were a closed loop. From my perspective, she was being pulled up, while from hers, the same was true of me. We tried moving, and with some experimentation found that if I tried to bend to the left, and she tried to bend to the left, we would start rotating in place, counter clockwise, totally oblivious to whatever pretence of gravity ruled the rest of the place. It was rather like the zero-gee work I had done in a former life, or more immediately like the asteroid field challenge we had been exploring a mere hour earlier. Jennifer grokked the comparison quickly, her limbs working to reprise what she had described as *swimming* from that same challenge. The harder we leaned in response to each other, the more we picked up speed, until we were moving dizzyingly fast. Jennifer eventually threw out a hand to steady us, but the moment she touched the boardwalk, the regular rules re-asserted themselves, and we were hurled into the planking with heavy *thuds*.

"Well," I said, when we had gotten back up and started the trick again, "We're not dead, but we are breaking every single law of physics. So that *is* new."

Jennifer snorted. "Let's do it a little differently this time. Let's try to…get out into the scenery."

"Out *there*? Over the canyon?"

"Yes."

"What if we fall?"

"Yes, *Aidan,* what if we fall?"

"I'm sorry." The apology was trite, but accepted.

"Don't worry about it. There's nothing for us to touch out there but ourselves."

The idea filled me with unbidden concern. In true zero-gee, the idea of being without a stabilising handhold implied inevitable death in an uncontrollable drift away from the nearest source of light, heat, and air.

*But this is all a game,* I reminded myself. *It's all a giant game.*

The idea wasn't reassuring. We did it anyway.

Apprehension gnawed as we floated out over the open air. What a sight we must have been, a pair of wormy shapes flexing around each other with no regard for reality. Dangling upside down from nothing but our own audacity, it dawned on me that we were doing something a little bit beautiful, if utterly demented. The boardwalks and bushes and loungers fell away below, leaving us far, far above the floor of a luminescent canyon. If we rotated the color palette a bit, I mused, it wouldn't look that different to the first location from the solstice tournament.

I was so caught up in lazily watching the world spin by, and Jennifer so distracted by maintaining momentum, that we almost didn't realize that we were about to drift into a rock face.

We wriggled to avoid it.

We failed.

I scrunched my eyes up, everything in my brain telling me that it was going to *hurt* with the momentum we had gathered.

The impact never came. But when I opened my eyes, what I saw wasn't much better. I was outside of the world, upside down, somehow just *within* the rock face but able to see out through it. Jennifer was on the other side of that paper-thin mirage, clutching an outcropping with one hand and a cup, half embedded in stone, with the other.

She had anchored us there, straddling the border between the intact world and beyond, having broken the hack completely.

"Hey," I said.

"Aidan?" she called, wide-eyed. "You still out here?"

"Yes," I said. "I'm in the cliff."

"What—" Her eyes widened. "*What?* Oh, hell."

"Yeah." I said. "You wouldn't *believe* what I'm seeing back here."

I forced myself to turn away from her, and glared out at the abyss.

Outside the lines, beyond the borders, the world was *broken.*

Colors swirled and phased, smeared around in swirling, hypnotic repetition, pulled from the edges of the surface into the void as concepts like shadowing and perspective and *not being able to see through rock* ceased to apply.

"Um." I said, swallowing. "Jen?"

"Yeah?"

"If you let go, you'll probably be okay. It'll just snap you back."

"What about you?"

"I have no idea, gotta be honest."

"Let me try to pull you back through. I've just got to—"

"Wait, I—"

Her grip on the tankard under her feet, between my clutched hands, slipped. And with it, our little excursion was torn asunder. We came free from each other's grasp. But she didn't teleport to safety. And neither did I.

Free of anything to provide momentum, I simply drifted.

"Jennifer!" I shouted. But she didn't respond.

"Jen?" I called again.

She couldn't hear me.

I had broken the rules. I was outside her world.

She looked scared.

The deeper beneath the surface I moved, the more previously-defined shapes succumbed to the overwhelming cascade of infinite and depthless light. This was a perspective no brain was ever meant to see or interpret. The longer I took it in, the choppier it became, reality itself developing a stutter every time I looked around.

The stutter became a halting jerkiness.

The jerkiness, too, degraded, until the world in my eyes barely kept up at all.

And then, finally, it couldn't cope. And the entirety of my vision, of Jennifer perched far above in a rock face, completely and finally smeared into a wash of ugly, stretched darkness.

A *click* registered in the back of my mind.

My arms had weight. My legs followed. I was upside down, I knew this. Then right and left, up and down, all twisted, and as the sensation of polymers on skin rushed into awareness. An adrenaline-spiked heartbeat took an eternity to complete. I vomited, sending sick smearing across my face as I fought to get control of stiffened, forgotten muscles.

It had worked.

I was out.

# ELEVEN

I bolted upright into a pitch-black space, skin clammy. I swung around, *thumping* a suddenly-painful hand into a *very* hard wall.

*"Ow!"* I shouted out.

I suddenly understood why I couldn't see, and felt around by my head, finding a metal block covering my face. I could feel breath escaping from small, precisely-machined holes in the front. Other than that, it was smooth.

The trace of vomit stung. A gentle spray touched my lips as the expelled mess was pulled away, destined for some recycling system.

Revulsion gathered as I pictured myself cocooned, mummified in this machine.

There had to be a release latch. It wouldn't be long before it reset and sucked me back inside.

Moving my hands further down, I felt where the helmet met the rest of the suit, joining at a collar piece on my neck. I put all my focus into my fingertips, searching for—

The tiny *click* was felt, more than heard, as a small lever relaxed. The helmet slackened, peeling away from my face. I eased it off, over the top, gingerly removing the contraption. Cool air rushed into the gaps where skin had been swaddled in silicone.

A soft light overhead glowed into life, austere in its effect but suitable enough. I was in a tiny room, cramped. Most of it was taken up by a convoluted-looking chair, which had been cradling me moments before. Opposite the chair, spanning nearly the total width of the space, was an unmarked door. The walls were dark grey metal, panelling running on all sides. A shallow shelf beside me was bare. Below it sat a cubby, where snug webbing kept a large, hard-wearing bag tucked out of the way. I reached for it, and jerked back, a tether binding my arm to the wall.

I let out a word that was not kind.

*What the hell kind of rig is this?*

I felt back behind my neck, to where the suit's spinal link would have lived, relieved that it had separated from the contact pads in my skin. There was no immediate danger of being pulled back into that damaged dreamland.

I got to work on the rest of the haptic suit, peeling its tight layers off; they came away with a sickening *squench*. I had nothing on underneath, shuddering as new sensations tingled from skin that hadn't been unprotected for at least a week. The little cabin assaulted my mind, textures, sounds, and smells intruding with unreal clarity.

The tether remained attached to a cuff on my left arm, even without the suit to contain me, and on closer inspection I found that it had been delicately inserted into my skin. I was no expert, and couldn't make it out, but it didn't hurt when I moved around. A handful of flexible tubes, some clear, some opaque, connected to it. I decided to leave the cuff in place, but unplugged the tubes one-by-one, finishing with the tether. Blood didn't start spilling out, so I figured I was okay.

*Now,* I thought, naked and cold and stuck in a closet, *where the hell am I?*

Once freed from its cubby, the bag unfurled into something that looked vaguely familiar. I dug into it, extracting a few token items, including a printed, framed picture that I recognized as my family. They were discarded to the floor. In the bottom of the satchel waited a thin, tightly folded change of clothes over a pair of worn boots. The ensemble offered little comfort against the cool air, but was better than nothing.

Deciding that the tiny room had exhausted its secrets, I tried the door. It slid open as I bolted free of the imprisoning equipment.

A duo of overhead panels warmed to life in the stillness. The air smelled metallic. A familiar hum of air scrubbers gently underscored a deeper vibration that sent occasional creaks through the alloy plating. My room, really my *container*, was attached to the side of a hallway, was roughly eight feet wide and nearly four times as long, with nearly a dozen doors matching my own lining it from end to end. A few skinny tables and chairs had been bolted down in the middle of the space at a halfhearted effort at sociability, but all evidence indicated that it was a wasted effort. At one end a hatch promised to be an exit with bright lettering; at the other, a pair of partially-walled-off stalls had been fitted. I explored at that end first, dismissing the unfamiliar and unresponsive bank of controls.

"Hello?" I called out, my voice disconcertingly deep and resonant. "Anybody?"

No-one answered.

My movements were sluggish, matched with an inner ear that was deeply confused about which way was up.

*Okay,* I thought woozily, *You're out. You're clear.*

*You're free.*

*Get moving.*

I had to find the crew. I had to find Jennifer, and get her out too. *In that order,* I told myself firmly.

The first obstacle was the exit, itself a large door with a shiny wheel in place of a handle. A sign beside it gave me a clue as to my home zone—*Block 12, Group B*—then repeated itself in two other languages I didn't recognize. Below the sign was a red alarm button. Pushing it did nothing. As if there was no expectation that anyone would be in a position to use it.

I tried my hand at the wheel, spinning it with limbs that felt oversized. I didn't recall being especially tall, and in CarverNet, I had certainly looked *up* at people more than once. Nonetheless it was hard to get a good sense of scale. It was hard to just get a good sense of *up*.

The door's seal broke as the wheel reached the end of its turn, prompting unseen bolts to retract with a soft *thunk*. Beyond was a small antechamber. Opposite my entrance was another just like it, with the label *Zone C* emblazoned overhead in crisp red letters.

Halfway between sat a floor-to-ceiling ladder and broad hatches at both ends. A strip of yellow paint, complete with the word *caution* in curving letters, encircled the upper one. A strip of green paint encircled its lower counterpart. On the wall, facing the ladder, waited a third door, left blank, with no obvious markings. A small glowing touchscreen beside it patiently waited for someone to input a code.

I attempted to decipher the interface's few icons, but it refused to reveal any secrets or allow me to progress any further. After a few failed attempts, an error message flashed up: *Transit code required. Please make sure you are entering the correct code for this artery. That means you, LAWRENCE!*

I gave up with it.

Beyond the Zone C door was a hallway identical to my own. The pods were all locked; I tried all of them, up one side and down the other.

Returning to the antechamber, I pondered the meaning of the different paint colors. Red was evidently just for signage. Green was impossible to tell, but usually meant environmental things. Yellow by contrast hinted at something utilitarian, or dangerous, or mechanical.

Meaning, crew-only.

For a moment my resolve flickered, but there wasn't really an option *except* to venture onward. I had already gone too far outside the lines. At this point, even if things were perfectly fixed, I would need to get help to get back inside the sim.

I tested the ladder, and finding it secure, climbed. The hatch above had a weird mechanism, its handle twisting and sliding across grooves in the face of the round plate. Momentarily stumped, I retreated, got an eyeful of the whole assembly, and understood that it was an *are-you-sure* sort of lock. Not a true obstacle, but one that needed care and attention.

I climbed the ladder once more, grasped the handle, and slid it all the way across the hatch face before giving it a ninety-degree twist. The lock released with a *thunk*, and the steel plate slid aside, the air beyond cold and still. Above was a long, skinny shaft lazily lit by a quartet of glowing stripes down its length.

This was not high-end decision-making, and deep down I knew it.

I steadied my grip, and put hand over fist again and again, putting as much surety into my movements as I could muster. Once I'd gotten started, it got easier.

And even easier, with some progress.

By the time I was halfway up the tube, I was virtually *flying* along from rung to rung, and got it at last. I wasn't climbing *up*. I was climbing *inward*. Block twelve had to be on a rotational arm, which made sense for passengers wanting gravity. And *that* meant that I was going towards the spinal core of the ship.

A long-forgotten admonishment brushed through the back of my mind:

*You are being aggressively stupid, Aidan.*

"Oh screw *off*, Gregor." I muttered, surprised at myself.

A vision of Gregor Chumak, one-time best friend and next-door neighbor from years gone by, flashed before my mind's eye. He and his overwrought moustache had always had fine advice for me. Advice that was routinely ignored. I missed him. In all probability I would never see his face or hear his annoyingly deadpan tone again. As I reached the ladder's top, now actually floating, I dug up more old memories from Ceres, this time focusing on days spent doing honest work at the dockyard.

It wasn't unusual for ships to house a transit corridor within their rotational core. It wasn't always done, but it made sense. A rapid mover could launch from one weighted area, zoom *up* into the gravity-less core, skim along, and then *descend* into place at its destination.

Unfortunately, I wasn't *in* a mover pod. There was no telling *what* lay ahead. And I had no map to guide me.

It was almost, but not quite, pitch black in the open core. I floated out into it, letting my eyes adjust. A ripple of warmer air passed by, but for several beats I might as well have been floating in an inky nothing. Then, out of the sides of my vision, I started to make out the shape of the walls, the grids of guide rails, the ductwork and intricate clusters of cables. Far away, down the shaft, I spotted a red glimmer, and started climbing towards it. The weightlessness wasn't unfamiliar, just unsettling in the near-perfect gloom. In point of fact, it made the travelling notably *easier* than it might otherwise have been. A guide rail made a good aid for steady propulsion, though it also brought a lethally intense awareness that a mover going past might terminate my misguided expedition rather efficiently.

*Just keep going, Noah,* I told myself. *Just keep moving.*

Twice I thudded into support beams blindly. I kept going. I had to find someone.

The red light grew closer, bringing a trickle of hope as I reached it sooner than anticipated. The darkness had played games with any comprehension of distance.

The light belonged to a dormant mover idling on the rails. At a guess, it was a cube. Keenly aware that at any moment it could be called away by a well-meaning interloper, I blindly searched along its exterior, one side after another, finally identifying an escape hatch after a few slow minutes. I kept expecting it to launch off in a new direction, crushing me into a bulkhead.

*Take it slow, stay calm, it's the night shift, nobody is going for a ride.*

The hatch gave way as I fumbled with the mechanism, and the mover's well-lit interior waited happily below. Maneuvering inside, I was gratified to find that the control screen was unconcerned with access codes or identification or anyone named Lawrence, and with a few taps and a bit of guesswork sent it gliding along at a merry pace. The speed increased steadily, darkened silhouettes flashing by outside the open hatch, and I watched anxiously as the machine shifted course, shimmying sideways, rotating at a disorienting pace, and then sliding downward into a confined chute. I got the distinctly unpleasant sensation of being gradually glued to the floor.

Finally, the door opened, sliding into the wall, and I was greeted by something *entirely* different.

Strings of lights haphazardly spun across the corridor, woven over and under numerous wiring ducts, and cast their homey glow onto rows of synthetic plants tucked in pots along the sides. A bold mural of swirling flowers and stars had been painted across the wall opposite, its creator evidently having some unique artistic tendencies. The air was warmer, thicker, and more humid here. Something strong and sour floated in the air, maddeningly tantalizing.

Slowly, with effort, one foot went forward, then the other. I found myself once again using the friendly, unbothered walls for support.

Gravity in this zone was stronger than I was used to, and I stumbled along, each step causing my blood to pump harder than it ever had.

*Maybe this was a bad idea.*

I kept going, pushing through it even as lightheaded nausea loomed. The source of the aroma was key. Hot food meant someone was awake.

On the left, at the end of the hall, the web of twinkling lights gave way to a much brighter, much whiter, round room with a table in the middle. Cabinets lined the wall. Merrily humming away in front of a counter with a steaming pouch of something orange, a tall, fair-haired woman in a ruffled green jumpsuit turned around, absentmindedly venturing to her seat.

She had just moved to sit down when she glanced up and froze, spotting me leaning in the doorway.

"Oh, *shit.* Are you okay? How did you get here?"

My breathing was weak. "I got out. The Carver sim. It's broken. We were all trapped in there, but I got out. Are you on the crew?"

She abandoned the snack.

"Yes. Madison O'Connell, engineer on this ship. Who are you?"

"Aidan Whittaker. I was in, uh, block twelve."

She hauled me across to the table using muscles that were far more at ease with things than mine were. I was grateful for the chair's support, slumping into it. She thumbed a button on a device strapped to her belt, and Kay Tee's tenor rang out on unseen speakers.

*"Emergency crew meeting needed in the galley."*

Madison leaned in intently. Her voice was soft, understanding.

"All right, Aidan. We'll sort you out. We'll take care of this. Tell me *everything*."

* * *

I fidgeted on the cold plastic of the chair, recounting the last hour of my life to Madison's searching gaze.

When I had finished, she slowly nodded. "Okay," she said quietly. "We'll fix it. I'm glad you're here and alive. What you did to *get* here was stupid. Going into the shafts unannounced is a great way to end up dead. *Actual* dead."

"I worked the docks on Ceres," I said, a little defensively. "I've done stuff like that before."

"Then it's an outright *miracle* you survived this long." Her look softened. "I'm sorry. You've been through something very, very far outside most people's lives, and it's good that you're here. We'll get it fixed, okay?"

I nodded.

The door swished open, and a newcomer stepped in, all angular jawbones and wrinkled forehead. He looked alarmed, tired, and annoyed. I recognized him from his daily presentations in the Green Valley marketplace.

"Morning, Frank." Madison waved him over. "We've got a passenger out of the 'net. This is Aidan. Says he forced his way out of the suit, looking for help."

I nodded, raising a hand to shake his in what I thought would be a welcome gesture. "Captain DeSanto—"

"Call me Frank," he said, waving it off briskly, fetching something from a yellow box on the wall. He rounded the table and pressed an injector gun to my skin.

"Hey, hang on, what—" I interjected.

He depressed it, and a sense of cooling refreshment fizzled through my arm. He pulled back. "This is a vibrastim. It'll wake you the freck up. I'm appalled that you've had to come this far and we'll make it right. I'm sure Maddie has been interrogating you already?" He glanced at her, and she nodded. His gazed refocused on me. "Are you all right?"

I flexed my arm, perturbed. "I've been better."

"My people will look after you. If you have the energy, what's the short version of all this?"

"I really don't know where to start," I said.

"Just the gist of it," he replied, "We'll go over what you've already covered amongst ourselves."

I breathed slowly, feeling a little more strength in my core. I *could* tell the story again. A shorter version.

"The CarverNet stuff, it was just…breaking. We couldn't transit between places. The Indexes couldn't find people at all. Nobody can call each other. At least one of my friends outright *vanished* out of it completely. Kay Tee was useless at being any help." It was a rush of statements, coming out faster and faster.

"Okay, okay." He said, hands held up. "Where was your pod?"

"Um." I thought back. "Twelve. Block twelve."

DeSanto turned. "Madison, check it out. Wake Ricky and

Milo."

She nodded, rising, and leaving briskly. "Wheel four. If something fell over we *should* have gotten an alert, but we'll have to see what's what."

DeSanto returned his attention to me. "Aidan, I want to reassure you that we'll get this sorted out. Never mind the hour, thank you for bringing this forward. Ah! Lawrence! Good. This fellow is one of our passengers. Check him over and find him a place to put his feet up, if you pretty please."

As Madison set a brisk pace out of there, a surly, bulky man in pyjamas meandered in, unimpressed.

"I see," Lawrence said, yawning. "And he's not one of the golden ones, either."

He huffed, but pulled me to my feet, supporting my weight with a gentle touch. "Come on, up you get."

I glanced back at DeSanto as we lumbered across to the far passageway. "I have a friend who helped me get out. I need to tell her what's happening."

DeSanto frowned after us. "What's her name?"

"Jennifer Motley. I don't know where her berth is."

"We'll look for her after we've solved this problem."

As we rounded out of sight, and reached a door marked *Medical,* Lawrence grunted. "Right. I overheard some of that. Your name is Aidan? Time to have a seat."

Within was an examination chair and a small working office. He perched on the desk as I reclined in place as instructed.

"Yes."

Lawrence puffed out some breaths between pursed lips, taking in the state of my still-attached cuff from the haptic suit. "The others are a little slow on the uptake, but I know perfectly well you had to have experienced some pretty messed up shit to get dropped out of the sim. And the gravity difference won't be helping."

"Yeah." My mouth was dry. "That's a way of putting it. Do you have any water?"

He fished a pouch out of the desk drawer, and handed it over. The drink within was *real*, more real than anything I'd had in a lifetime. It satiated a need I didn't even know I'd had.

"This tastes amazing."

He shrugged, but said nothing.

I drained the pouch and handed it back. It was the first real thing I'd had in days. "Thank you. Who are you?"

He grunted. "Lawrence Kaplan. I'm the ship-board doctor."

"Aidan Whittaker," I replied, becoming more cogent as the stim shot did its work in earnest. "Frecked-off passenger. That's how I'm feeling."

Lawrence chuckled at that, perhaps a little mirthlessly. "Don't worry. Maddie is good at her job. Whatever went wrong enough to get you here, she'll find it and solve it."

"That's reassuring."

"It should be. She's the second best at her job."

"Who's the first?"

"The engineer," he rapped on his makeshift seat, "who built this desk. Who, incidentally, was her predecessor. Maddie knows her trade, but Raj was a true artisan."

"I feel great."

"Frank gave you a stim, right?"

"Frank?"

"The captain."

"Yeah."

"That'll be why. You'll crash soon."

He pulled a gadget from the drawer and pressed it to my wrist. "Your pulse is high-but-steady, blood oxygen looks a little low, but that's normal for someone as sedentary as yourself."

The remark stung a little. Mostly because there was truth in it.

"Can I just sit here for a minute?" I asked.

"Of course. Should come naturally. Take off your shirt?"

"Um. Why?"

"I need to see your cannulation cuff clearly."

"Oh."

I did as he asked, watching as he inspected the connectors. "The desk doesn't look that spectacular to me."

"Ah," he said, tone getting intense, feeling carefully around the cuff.

"What?"

"You're an idiot."

"*What?*"

"You pretty much tore this out of the wall." It wasn't a question. He looked up at me with raised eyebrows. "You're lucky that the suit wasn't running the pumps when you did it. Could have been really messy. You might have lost blood."

"Great," I said, picturing it.

"I don't like idiot patients," he continued, "Chances are that those tubes you yanked out are spewing nutri-juice all over your pod right now. We'll have to clean that up. Might be me. Might be Ricardo."

"Ricardo?"

"Ricky. Our sparkling fresh tech apprentice," he clarified.

"Right," I said, none the wiser. "I'll promise not to do it again."

The doctor grunted.

I looked around at the bulkheads, eying the wall of certificates and photographs. "How big *is* the crew?"

Lawrence shrugged. "There's six of us. Don't let the titles fool you, we all play double duty at times."

I stared. "Six crew, including the captain, for a ship carrying *two hundred* people?"

He gave me a sad shake of the head. "Look, Mister Whittaker, I recognize the optics of it. But those two hundred passengers are in a self-contained world. From the moment we leave to the moment we arrive, we might as well just be hauling freight."

*Freight?*

"I don't think I like that very much."

"Apologies. I tend to be blunt; it is a defining quality. We're in a spinning cigar, flying through the big empty for months at a time. The captain, the pilot, the medic, the engineer, the tech, and the hydroponics whiz-kid. Unless you're having a health problem, we leave you alone. The only time this place *isn't* quiet is when somebody's having a domestic spat or we're in dock."

I paused at that, considering the point. "If it's that quiet, why don't you use the sim with us? The CarverNet suit?"

"Sometimes we do. Anonymously. Your vitals are excited and your heart is going to have some trouble in this gravity without help. You can have another stim when you need one. Take it slow on solid foods or you'll be a double idiot."

"Okay…"

He stood, satisfied, and pulled me to my feet. "I expect the others will get the simulation fixed, Frank will do an announcement, so nobody else does something like this. When it's all sorted out, we'll get you back inside, safe and sound. Tomorrow, maybe, if it's a big job. I'll put you in an empty crew bunk for now."

"I don't want to just sit around!"

Lawrence paused, gave what I'm sure *he* thought was a reassuring smile. "Look, it's just going to be a tech fault, and the techs can fix it. In the meantime, put your feet up and take it easy."

I nodded grudgingly, and we departed the small office, heading down a corridor and down a flight of stairs into the outer deck, leaving behind the smells of Madison's abandoned snack. He delivered me to a cabin just a little way down the corridor. A loudly painted sign on the door called out its former owner.

*RAJ, THE ONE AND ONLY!*

It was sparse inside, most traces of its former occupant packed up with their departure. As I evaluated it Lawrence fished a blanket out of the footlocker and showed me how to turn on the entertainment screen. "I'm going to check in with the captain. Stay here, look after yourself, and Elsie or myself will be down in a few minutes to get you settled in for the night. Try to relax, yeah? Help yourself to a vid or two."

"Hold on, I—"

"Don't worry, you'll be fine."

He flashed me a thin smile and vanished out the door before I could get another word out.

Quite suddenly I was alone again, with no idea what to do with myself.

*Some welcome. Handed around and deposited like an unwanted bag.*

Irked, I approached the console. Jennifer had to be dying to know what was going on, and the interface might make it possible to tell her. I got to work.

The room's last occupant had been playing a recording of a rock storm tapping against a window, and quite by accident I resumed it, the noise echoing from the hidden audio panels. Frustrated, I looked around, trying to get ahold of myself. Tried a breathing exercise that Tera had shown me. In, and out. In, and out.

In, and out.
Calm.
*Relax.*

# TWELVE

I was not calm. I poked around in the cabin, exploring its nooks, its crannies, getting to know it. Behind the mattress was a small, overlooked figurine of a lanky four-legged animal that I didn't recognise. A refresher, small but private, was tucked behind the back wall, accessible by a skinny door.

The infotainment screen bore a superficial similarity to the CarverNet Index, but it worked very differently. I managed to find a messaging service that mentioned CarverNet as a feature, and wrote a quick note to Jennifer, then tried to send it. The panel promptly came back with a discouraging note:

*IDENTITY PROTECTION DATABASE ERROR: UNABLE TO DELIVER TO RECIPIENT. YOUR MESSAGE HAS BEEN MOVED TO THE STANDBY QUEUE AND WILL BE DELIVERED WHEN ACCESS TO THIS USER IS NEXT AVAILABLE.*

I uttered a soft curse and stepped back, hoping she was coping. Ideally Heri would be talking her ear off.

Still jumpy from the stim, I abandoned the cabin and ventured out into the hall, debating how far I could reasonably wander before somebody would appear to usher me into another box.

The corridor's curve was less pronounced than the deck above, meaning that I was further out from the ship's core, and from what I could see it seemed to go in a straight circle all the way around. A painting hung carefully, if wonkily, on the opposite wall. It was of a blue-striped bird, perched on an unfamiliar kind of tree over a gentle meadow. Somebody evidently had a taste for art.

Footsteps clattered down the stairs. One of the crew ducked down into view, another woman, younger and warm-skinned, waving as she approached.

"Hi there. Lawrence ditched you, right?"

"Uh." I said, trying not to make a bad impression. "He did."

She stuck a hand out. "Elsie Green. Pilot. Frank just told me about, well, you."

I took it. "Aidan."

"Keeping your spirits up, yeah?"

"I got the impression I should be pretty hammered into the deck right now, but I feel okay."

"Whaddaabout up there?" She pointed at my head, speeding past the words. "Do you need anything? We can warm something up if you're hungry? You do, er, eat, right?"

The thought of a hot cup of something warm, sweet, and bitter sent a tingle through my taste buds. "As far as I know. I think I can wait on that, though."

"Dandy. Just ask, okay?"

"I appreciate it. I'm, uh, feeling a little uncomfortable."

"Was it Lawrence? If so, don't worry about it. He has trouble making people like him. He cares about how we work, but not about how we *work*, if you follow."

"I...do?"

She beamed. "Good start. You can say if you're not feeling right about something, yeah? No sense being anything but honest when you're aboard this beauty."

*This...beauty?*

A remarkably coherent thought formed as I remembered what her job was.

*Elsie, pilot.*

"Right. Um. Can I ask you about the ship? If it's all right?"

Elsie considered that, then tilted her head in a curious nod. "Don't see why not. Whatcha want to ask about?"

"My friend and I were really interested in your ship, but my Index was all full of marketing fluff. I guess they don't want us freight-class people thinking to much about anything other than CarverNet. So, ehm, how does the Apollo work?"

"Big topic. Don't think I can go into heavy details, but sure. Come over here. Look at this." She beckoned me into a closet and went to a panel on the back wall. She unlatched it smoothly, setting it down with unlikely strength. Behind, thick cushions framed a big window made of thick poziglas. "This is a really good spot to come to sometimes." Elsie said. "I keep it to remember where we really are."

I leaned on the edge of the bulkhead, gazing out. Beyond, maybe a meter or two from my face, raw vacuum beckoned. Far away—though scale was impossible to grok—a densely-packed quartet of wheels spun past. Chunky, boxy sections were grafted onto the thick stems that linked each wheel's perimeter to the core. They all rotated at similar, but not quite identical speeds, so from our perspective, they irregularly crept past our viewpoint with no regard for sensibility. Beyond and below, an enveloping field of stars glittered in the dark.

"That's quite something," I said, quietly reverent.

"Yeah," Elsie whispered. Then she brightened. "Those four wheels are modular gravity spaces. The first two you can see are all cargo. Hard goods, mostly. Alloys, personal tech products, mining equipment, spare smelter parts, that kind of stuff. Wheels three and four are for passengers. We rotate them in the opposite direction for inertial symmetry, and at slightly different speeds to suit different gravity needs." She paused, sizing me up. "You're a colony kid born and bred, so you would have been on wheel four, which is rotated at eighty-two percent of Earth standard. A little heavier than station standard, but familiar for your muscles. Over the journey we speed it up little by little, so your heart gets ready for pushing blood around when you're planetside."

"Neat," I said. "I hadn't read about that trick anywhere before."

"We mainly advertise it as a perk for the higher-end tickets, but everybody gets the benefit."

"Sneaky," I mused. "Those are the engines behind wheel four?"

"Yeah! We've got the main engines and fuel back there, plus some of the power banks, and if you look closely on the spine," she pointed proudly, "those are our docking thrusters. The big guys get us moving really fast—cruising speed is about forty thousand kilometers an hour—and halfway to arrival, we do a flip using those little ones and the big guys burn hard all over again to brake."

"That's really cool," I said, entirely honest. "A friend of mine would love to know about all of this. You two could probably talk for hours."

Elsie chuckled proudly. "Maybe we will, once shit is fixed. I don't know the first thing about how the sim works, but the techs know Apollo inside and out. Me, I just fly her."

I gestured at the cushions, then considered the lights, plants, graffiti, and other efforts. "I get it. It's a home. And those paintings make it better. The one with the roses was nice."

"Oh, thank you! I do one every run. There's one of a squirrel up on level one that's my favorite so far."

"A what?"

"Squirrel."

"What's that?"

"Huh." She paused. "Colony kid. Right. A squirrel is a little animal that's native to a few continents on Earth. Mostly ignored by the locals but I like them."

"I'll look for one when we get there."

"You won't have trouble, I'm sure they'll take a liking to you. Anyway, with the artwork, I used to keep going by it and finessing the little details all the time, you know?"

"I do, yeah. Getting it right is addicting."

"Dandy." She smiled, putting the hatch firmly back in place. "There's more to it, of course. Come on, let me show you." She guided me back to the galley, and sat me down at the central table, bringing holographic projectors to life overhead. A cupboard hung open behind her, with something in green foil glinting. A bag of snacks lay abandoned on the table, its label crinkled but legible:

*CYBERFISH! HOT, COLD, SOUR AND SWEET - THE SNACKING SENSATION FOR YOUR CIRCUITS!*

Elsie rescued a handful and started munching. Offered me one. I ate it. Went back for another.

The projectors warmed up and a lively animation of the Apollo fizzed into view.

"Pretty," I said.

"We're in the crew module here," Elsie pointed, "forward of the hold wheels. We're spinning like they are, but where the others are kinda made of skimpy chunks on the mounting pylons, we're a solid block from the core all the way out to the lowest deck. Up towards the core, you've got a lot of storage and support systems, and here on the third deck, which is this one, you've got a lot of functional spaces like the galley, the bridge, the spa—"

"The spa?"

"No," she chuckled. "I was just seeing if you were listening."

"That's disappointing."

"Yeah," She continued, "you're tellin' me. But we have a hydroponics garden and a storage room that Frank set up with lot of pretty lights and a decent-spec display and sound system. We use that on the weekly movie nights."

"Ever watch *Night Bus to Elysium?*"

"A run or two ago. It was okay." She pointed to the screen. "You go out another level, and you're into crew quarters, and then you're swimming in endless hardvac after that."

I considered that, mapping what I'd seen onto the rendering before us. "You must get sick of this place after a while."

Elsie shrugged with a *some-of-this-some-of-that* gesture. "Apollo grows on you."

I changed the subject, happy that she was indulging in my curiosity. I pointed at a long spire out in front of the ship on the diagram. "What's this bit? I haven't see that design before."

"It's new," she said proudly. "Corporate had it installed last time we were at Luna. It's a point-deflection slingdome."

"A *what?*"

"*I know.* Maddie can talk your ear off about it. Basically you've got that long spire, right, which goes way out, packed full of sensors. Once we're away from a dock, it unfurls this really big, thin umbrella in front of the ship. By itself, the umbrella just shoves tiny pieces of spacejunk out of the way as we fly past. But for more substantial stuff, we have this reservoir of ferrofluid that gets accelerated out really fast along the outer surface of the umbrella like a shovel. It gets timed to grab debris and just—" She mimed the motion with an exaggerated swirl. "—sling it away from us. Then the ferrofluid gets sucked back into the spire for the next hit."

"Cool," I said, thinking it sounded insane. Conventional wisdom said that a shipbuilder covered the front of a ship in slabs of ablative plating and just expected that the vessel would bash its way through any junk it encountered near a port. But I had replaced a *lot* of those smashed and scorched plates in the last few years. This system, if it worked...

The pilot seemed to read my mind, and stepped away from the projection to find more snacks. "It's worked a charm so far. On this run, anyway."

"Elsie," I said, looking away from the schematic. "Lawrence talked about us, the passengers, like we're cargo. Even with as small a crew as you are, it kinda seems like you..."

"Have nothing to do?" She grinned. "Not true! We earn our keep by keeping an eye on things."

"She means," Lawrence's chimed in dryly from the doorway, "That we're lowly stewards."

"And just where have you been, doctor grumps?"

"Sorting out Mister Whittaker's pod. He left a mess behind. Are the others back yet?"

"No. I've been talking *Aidan* through how a lot of the ship is laid out."

"I worked on a refit for a heavy miner a year ago," I explained hesitantly. "I was interested in how a passenger ship like this one worked."

"Ah," Lawrence nodded, thoughtfully, and a little wryly. "A

passenger ship without any of the usual passenger facilities, you mean."

"Yeah."

"Decent enough topic. The answer is, it goes perfectly until someone makes a mistake, and then, well, we're here to sort it out. A human crew to take care of human error, if you like. Ah, finally, somebody *practical* is here."

Clomping boots announced the presence of newcomers to the deck long before we saw them. Madison poked her head in, followed by a skinny man I didn't recognize.

He waved and spoke with a lyrical accent that I pinned as Ceresian instantly. "Aidan, yeah?"

I raised a hand in a confused greeting. "Yeah."

"Ricardo," he said, striding across with an exertion to shake my hand. "It's a pleasure. I understand we have you to thank for raising the flag tonight."

Behind him Madison crossed straight to the counter, briskly assembling a drink for herself. She combined a scoop of powder with steaming water and stirred her cup with fierce intent. We watched in expectant silence as she finished the ritual and took a long, slow, appreciative sip. When it was done, she looked up, surprised at the watchful gazes, then quickly nodded at her companion. "Ricky, this is Aidan Whittaker. Aidan, Ricky Fields."

"We, er, just met." I said, a bit lamely.

"Is that stim doing the trick?" She asked.

"So far."

Madison turned to the others. "Right. Where's Frank?"

Elsie shrugged, shaking her head. "Not sure. I think he's writing up some paperwork."

No sooner had she finished speaking than the man himself strolled into the meeting. "Milo was looking for you, Lawrence," he said. "Another migrane."

"*Another?*" The medic muttered. "That kid's gonna need the real stash of goodies at this rate. Permission?"

"Approved, just get him on his feet. I'll sort the forms." DeSanto replied.

I started to feel overwhelmed. Too many new faces, too quickly.

Madison cleared her throat. "We've got a handle on it, Frank."

"Okay," he said, expression brightening. "Do tell."

She frowned over another sip, summing it up in her own mind before manipulating the idling hologram to illustrate her report. I got the impression that she liked putting on a show.

"From what it *looks* like, a micrometeorite punched through the edge of wheel four's base ring, went in through the cabling ducts, and buried itself in load balancer three." She illustrated the path across the spinning wheel. "The trajectory meant that it avoided big-pressure areas, and when it got into the ducts we care about, the polyflex housing on the data lines swelled and plugged most of the gaps that the little bastard left on its way in, so it was such a slow leak that we never got a decomp alert. Probably still wouldn't for another couple of hours. It's real one-in-a-million shit." She didn't look entirely convinced as she said it.

DeSanto frowned, but didn't say anything.

Against my better judgement, curiosity got the better of me, and I spoke in the lull. "I'm not supposed to know any of this, I know, but, er, load balancer? What does that have to do with what I saw in CarverNet?"

Ricky cleared his throat. "The sim is run by banks of server nodes in each cluster, which provide the processing for each environment you occupy in the sim world, and they get fed by all the little processing boxes in the passenger berths. In the middle you have the load balancer node, which acts as a hub, making sure that not too many passengers are managed in the same server node at once, transferring sessions between nodes—"

"Moving you from one world to the next," Madison interjected helpfully.

"—and syncing passenger data between each server so that everybody can find everyone else in there." Ricky finished, getting the hint and softening his technical explanation for my ears.

"And, you, what, found a rock in the middle of the box?" Elsie replied, doubtfully.

Madison held up a small white pebble, dulled on most sides, shiny in a band around the middle. "Exactly. Little shit was face-first into it and tore half the fiber links on its way in, both in and outside of the tech room. We're gonna have to do some surgery to close it up properly before we can take out the dead cabling and get replacement parts in place."

"How long?" DeSanto asked, frowning.

She shrugged. "Couple hours. Less, if I have extra help."

Madison looked at the doctor, who shook his head. "Not me. I've just done my bit for the moment."

The silence was awkward. I coughed, and spoke up. "I could do it."

She looked directly at me. "Kid. Aidan, sorry. You said you worked the Ceres docks. Can you handle zero-gee and hold a wrench in a vac suit?"

DeSanto held out a hand in a firm *stop* gesture. "Maddie, he's a *passenger*. He's not trained or certified and he didn't buy a ticket to help with repairs on the damn ship."

I cleared my throat, unsure exactly why I was so earnest. "I'm happy to do it."

DeSanto looked at me. "There is no pressure to contribute to this."

I nodded. "It's fine. I'm already drawing outside the lines here, and the sooner the sim is back and working, the happier I'll be. And technically I didn't even pay for most of my ticket."

Elsie chimed in. "He seems like a decent enough fella, Captain."

The captain sighed, gave his pilot a look, and made a *go on* gesture at the engineer.

As I wondered what it was I had just volunteered for, Madison eyed me with an approving look. "That's the spirit. Come on, we'll get you suited up. Familiar territory. Then we'll have it all right as rain."

# THIRTEEN

Ricky clapped me on the shoulder as the mover shot us upwards towards the core. The vac suit chafed, its layered fabrics and seals an irritating restriction. The hood was loose down my back, faceplate gently bouncing against my spine with every movement.

As the gravity thinned, we got out, stepping into a hallway lined with cages upon cages of appliances, cabling, tools, and piles of snacks.

The tech shuffled forward, calling out, "Crestville nodes should be in locker eight, I think. Upper shelves."

"Very good." Madison replied. "Get a few thirty-meter fiber rolls and a sealer kit. Twenty-mil spools should do it. Try lockers nineteen and, uh, way at the back of twenty-three, I think."

We split out, and I accompanied Ricky to locker nineteen. He opened the big cage and meandered inside, picking out a few of the more middle-weight bobbins from a shelf before handing them to me to carry.

*Yes, indeed*, I thought. *I'm a professional at wrench-holding.*

He retrieved the sealer kit from the other locker, and I appreciated that he had the harder job. It was a hefty-looking toolbox and he seemed to struggle with it, but refused help.

We regrouped a few minutes later, Madison lugging a small cart with an empty bucket, tool pack, and technical-looking box with a darkened readout on its front. I assumed it was the replacement bit of kit they had described. The load balancer.

The mover returned to us a moment later, with Lawrence at the controls. We piled in with the newly gathered goodies, and he punched in coordinates for the wheel four tech ring, adding a passcode. I tried to make it unobtrusive, but followed his hand as his fingers tapped in *8801*.

*Good to know.*

Gravity faded out beneath us as we entered the ship's core and re-oriented, then asserted a shade of itself under our feet as the mover shunted down the same lengthy tunnel I had been crawling by hand not too long before. The hatch was tightly closed now, though, giving no indication of the darkness screaming past.

It was probably best not to dwell, I decided, on the image of being hit by it.

I tried to find another topic in my thoughts, but the silence in the cab was just as disconcerting. Ricky seemed primed to talk about something, but kept refraining, held back by some unseen tension. Instead, he guided me through sealing up my vac suit and turning on the air pouch on my waist.

Claustrophobia loomed. The poziglas face shield would fog with a heavy breath, obscuring the others. A speaker in the hood offered a link to the outside world. It was tinny and weak but I was glad of it all the same. *It's not,* I noted with a mix of calm and  discomfort, *that much different than the sim suit.*

The mover slowed. We had arrived.

The tech ring was cramped to begin with, and three people in bulky suits did nothing to help with that. Racks of compute tech ran the walls, and I had an uncanny realization: this was the true heart of the world that I had been so deeply enthralled by. One could look at a given node and think, *Green Valley, Genesis, Arkadia, Dharma.*

Ricky noted my interest and filled in a few gaps. Each gravity wheel had blocks attached to it. The six passenger blocks were limited to wheels three and four. I had been in block twelve on wheel four, and blocks eleven and ten had been my immediate neighbors. Each block had two levels, one for habitation, and one for infrastructure: air, water, heat, septic, networking, and power. All of the above were connected into the Apollo's main utility grid, but some things, like water and heat, were mostly handled locally within the block for modularity. *Networking,* though, was central to the wheel, and fed down to the tech ring that wrapped around the base of it. In the tech ring for wheel four, the servers I was looking at joined together passengers from blocks ten, eleven, and twelve into a single shared world. Blocks seven, eight, and nine, over on wheel three, existed in a separate virtual silo, merrily enjoying their days in blissful isolation.

Madison pulled forward the damaged node, a metal cube that had a dozen trunks of cabling lying on the floor around it. The last trunk, still attached, she uncoupled dispassionately. It had a much messier removal, spindly threads of transparent fiber all wildly disorganized, the victim of a bad and sudden haircut. I followed it with my eyes to where it disappeared into a panel in the back wall. The panel itself was warped, a telltale hint at the damage within.

When the balancer node was free, Madison spun it around and unlatched its outer housing, then gingerly lifted the casing off to demonstrate the issue.

"Freck," Lawrence muttered. He was right.

The logic boards within were torn to pieces. The remains of a large chip sat glinting in the light, half-pulverized into sharp splinters.

"Wow," I said. "That's just *gone*."

"Poof," Madison agreed. "Totally smashed. I've seen junk punctures before but this was insanely unlucky."

"Does seem a little unlikely to have happened by chance," Lawrence muttered.

Madison gave him a look. "Weirder shit has happened."

"Not to us," he replied darkly.

I cleared my throat. "What do we have to do?"

Ricky looked up, banging his head into a shelf. "Ow! Fr—"

His transmission cut out. A moment later he was broadcasting again, his tone rueful. "You and me, we'll be in the wall replacing damaged fiber links. If we're lucky, it'll just be the trunking lines within this module and we won't be re-stringing half the wheel."

"Okay." I said, feeling a little out of my depth. "How do we get back there?"

As Madison set about unpacking her replacement hardware, Ricky led us to a skinny airlock buried behind a stack of flimsy boxes. An ominous frowny face had been painted across the outer door. He ignored it, instead turning to a side hatch not unlike the one Elsie had shown me before. But where her hatch concealed a cosy window seat, this one opened to reveal a space between the bulkheads, full of straps, bolts, and many, *many*, cables. It was cramped, dim, and eerily quiet. I could hear my own breathing in my ears a little too loudly.

We found the problem easily enough. A mass of shattered glass fiber on the floor, a torn rubberized housing. The tiny space rock had pierced the wiring on a curve, and we could easily trace it to the entry wound in the outer hull: a small, lopsided hole that had taken a lot of air with it.

"What a mess," Ricky muttered. "Come on. Let's get on with it."

"Your accent," I asked quietly. "You're Ceresian?"

"You got it," he said, then looked at me. "District three. You?"

"Sixth," I said.

"Rough," he replied. "Good for you man, getting out of there."

"Yeah." I said, interested. "What'd you do? To get a job out here?"

"I made tech apprentice level four. This is my first full run on a long-haul liner." He sounded undeniably proud.

"Very nice," I said. "You must have been excited to get it."

I could feel the shrug through his voice. "It was a step up. The alternative was another quarter on an ice hauler. And I liked Frank more than the other guy. Hey, careful in here, don't rip your suit. Lawrence will bitch at us both if you suffocate."

I took the hint and focused. It needed several minutes of careful tedium through clumsy gloves, but we tackled the job in a steady cadence. The patching gun *hissed* as it built a new, bubbly seal around and across the wound in the ship's side. When it was fully covered, Ricky flicked some kind of switch, and the gun's extrusions changed from white to silvery, and instead of foaming, remained flat and glinting as he drew them across the seal like metal tape.

"I haven't seen that trick before," I said.

Ricky was steady in his movements as he answered. "Always something to learn, *bratan*. It's a metallic polymer tape. You bind the goop in place, give it an extra layer of airtight coverage if we do it like *this*," he stepped back, "and abracadabra!"

"Nice," I said.

We got to the *real* problem next. I would extract an old, torn cable from the mess, and Ricky would run a new length in its place in between cleaning up bits of debris. The crew on the other side would grab and pull each thread until it was snug. Repeat a few dozen times. It was slow work, and I was deeply conscious about the lack of air mere millimeters from my face, but there was something pleasing about seeing the job go from chaos into repaired, constructed order, knowing that I was healing a world as we fed the foamy conduits through mounting clips and gaskets to meet the banks of real hardware. When we were confident that it was settled and we hadn't missed anything, Ricky handed me the patching gun and stepped back as I applied some extra sealant around the gasket. It had remained in good shape through the impact, but the extra patching couldn't hurt. When I was done, he inspected, and nodded.

"Calling the princess of the Apollo!" Ricky sung over the comm, "We are done. Start pressurizing, pretty please?"

From her distant, unseen seat, Elsie offered back a snort and made some noises in the affirmative. Ricky clapped me on the shoulder, then collected his box of scraps as we trudged back to the others.

When the airlock's inner door had sealed behind us, I was relieved. Lawrence had gone, and Madison was down to her jumpsuit, socketing the last cables into place on the replacement device. As she powered it on, she nodded to herself, and pulled out a small pad to bring up its interface and get it talking to the stacks of equipment.

"Good work," she said, distracted. "Take a minute if you like. I have to take this thing through setup and discovery." She paused, tapping away. "Aaaand, *there*. Might take a few minutes for it to sync with everything." She looked squarely at me. "Thanks for the help, Aidan."

"Indeed," Ricky smiled. "Saved us a fair bit of time on this fix.

You're a decent hand at this."

"Don't think I really did much, but happy to do it," I said. "The trip is going to be a lot nicer with this stuff working."

Madison nodded. "Lawrence went up to your pod to get it sorted out for you to go back inside. He just pinged me, you're all set. Elsie's coming by to grab you while we clean up here. You can go back in if you're ready."

I nodded, agreeable. "I like the sound of that. It's been, well," I paused, changing course with my words. "Good luck."

"Thanks. Ah," Madison smiled at her pad. "There we go. It's all set. Signals are syncing, there's traffic. The sim should be back to normal."

"Good," I said fervently.

"You like it that much, huh?" She asked, eyebrow quirked.

"I do," I said. "I know it's a fantasy, but it's fun. I can *live* there, you know?"

She gave me a thoughtful look and a tilt of the head, but said nothing.

The mover arrived at the hatch speedily, with Elsie waiting inside to chauffeur me up and away to paradise. I left the vacuum suit in a neatly folded lump on the floor and entered, relieved.

"Don't take this the wrong way, *bratan*," Ricky said, "But I hope we don't have to see you again."

The doors closed, whisking us away.

I idly watched Elsie's hands move across the display, entering destinations and quick passcodes, feeling a mix of sadness and eagerness. Comforts and luxuries, escapes and delights, all the *fun*, was waiting.

We didn't have much to say. I was tired now that the stim was wearing off. I was ready to relax, and unwind, and not care about wrenches and bobbins and sealant guns or server nodes.

The mover swished to a stop, and the doors opened onto the octagonal antechamber. It was brighter now, welcoming and warmed up for human use.

To our left:

*ZONE 12 C*

And to our right:

*ZONE 12 B*

The console's familiar warning to Lawrence glowed idly. Zone B remained quiet, clean, and still. My pod door sat patiently ajar. The suit was folded and set before the chair, blocky helmet beside it, tidily inviting me to closet myself away. My minds' eye saw beyond the hardware, to a hundred worlds of opportunity and discovery and indulgence.

*It's okay,* I thought to myself. *The little field trip is done. We've got everything up and running, and the sim is working. Drinks under Arkadian sunsets. Long walks on the crystal beaches. Painting. Movies. Games. Beans' stupid references. Bliss for three wonderful months.*

But staring at that little bleak closet, with a cradle ready to absorb my body, *fun* was not the pre-eminent idea in my thoughts.

"Are you all right?" Elsie asked kindly. "I know it's not the most inviting thing ever."

"It's fine," I said slowly. "When I'm in there, I won't know any different."

*Who am I trying to convince here?*

"I'll help you get plugged in. It'll feel pretty weird, but you'll get comfortable pretty quickly. You'll have a hard time doing all of it yourself."

"Will I need to go under like last time?"

She gave me a lopsided grin. "Probably not, but we'll see what your vitals say. Besides, I've seen your movements, you're not exactly the image of grace, mister. Your brain still thinks you've got sim limbs."

"Gee. What a compliment."

"Mmhmm. Do you need some privacy to get the suit on?"

"Yeah." I paused. Contemplated the outfit's purpose. "Not entirely sure why though."

She shrugged. "If it helps you be you, you can have it."

"Thanks."

She patted the door and turned to go, giving me the space.

I paused as I held up the suit, feeling its neoprene layer and soft mesh of haptic vibes. I glanced back at her retreating form. "That thing over there, is that a shower?"

"Yeah."

"Would it be all right if I used it? It'd be really nice to feel fresh before going in."

She nodded understandingly. "All good. Let me go open the water lines. We usually keep the 'freshers off during flight. The cradles do that stuff for you anyway. Saves power, less maintenance, less bitching." She tossed me a spare fob. "You'll need this to use it once I've got them running. The light will come on when it's ready. I'll wait outside."

She retreated to the antechamber and disappeared down the ladder and through the green ring, leaving me alone in the cold and quiet hall. The line of identikit berths sat, waiting, a cold, sterile counterpoint for that plush hotel in a distant valley.

It was quiet. Still. Calm. I smiled, inhaling the scent of antiseptic, faint traces of body odor. A subtle zing of ozone. Hardly the stuff of dreams, yet nuanced and lively all the same.

The shower's light glowed, beckoning. I felt, more than heard, the subtle rush of water through tubes in the bulkheads. I went to step inside, but paused, lingering. A little voice had emerged in the back of my thoughts. It had an idea. I didn't quite like it, but felt irresistibly drawn to exploit it.

*What are you doing?* I thought at myself.

*Just having a look,* I thought back.

Instead of undressing, I turned, giving in to the compulsion, and tried the key fob on the nearest pod.

It opened with a soft *click*, its overhead light glowing into life from the darkness within, and I saw before me a sight which was equal parts uncomfortable and addictively empowering.

Reclining lazily, wrapped up from head to toe in their black and silver suit, a pudgy figure lay softly, breathing evenly. They were open to me, immersed, entirely unaware.

*Exactly like I will be.*

I stood there, a transfixed voyeur, aware that I *should* have closed it up and walked away, but instead I lingered, supported by that soft cushion of anonymity. I wasn't sure what I was feeling, but I didn't like it. Nonetheless, I felt a compulsion to *know*. To have that inkling of invasive sight, seeing them at their most vulnerable.

The small status screen twinkled by the door, the figure's name softly glowing in the corner: *Jose Peto.* A shrug seemed fitting for this inattentive audience. I really *didn't* know them.

The moment of power was a little thrill. I quietly tried a few other pods, drawn in by the morbid sight of people in different states of exertion. They were all limp, their limbs abandoned by their minds, yet their breathing was a giveaway as to their state of exertion. Some were heavy, some were slow, one was staggered. The concept of CarverNet as a paradise, once a magical delight, slowly morphed into an unsettling inversion.

A couple more pods. More anonymous, passive people packaged in dark boxes. *Simra Muir, Emmanuel Arroyo.*

I froze when I opened the third door. *Tera Cooke.* I shut it immediately, without a second thought. Some boundaries had to be left uncrossed.

I ventured down towards the exit, looking for my chaperone. As I reached the hatchway I hesitated, turning back, and gave in to one more temptation.

The last pod on that side, closest to the exit, was for *Jazaban Cooke.* Guilt attacked my thoughts as I went to close it, but something stopped me. Something in the back of my mind, some instinctual construct, felt *sick,* and it took my conscious mind a few beats to understand:

The figure in *this* chair wasn't breathing. Wasn't moving at *all.* Cold, still, part of the furniture.

A piece of cargo.

I flashed back to finding Selena's prone form waiting to be pumped full of stimulants, but *this* was no sim. This was no fantasy. This was no game.

This was a body. I couldn't *see* him, inside that suit, but everything in my brain told me what he was.

*A body.*

Emotions flattened. Time slowed.

*Do I touch him? Do I check to make sure?*

The answers came to my thoughts smoothly, unbidden. *No. I know for sure what this is. And I know I'm out of my depth for handling it.*

"Elsie!" I called, hoarse.

She rounded the corner at a brisk clip. "Wha—" she broke off, registering. "What the hell do you think you're doing?"

I wasn't listening. This was *real.*

"I think he's dead."

"Get out of there. It's not your pod, it's not your space. What are you *doing* violating them like that? And—" She halted mid-rant. "*What?*"

"I think Jazz is *dead.*"

Elsie glared at me, which rocked me more than it should have. But she pushed past into the pod, focusing on its occupant and checking his vitals. After a minute she backed away, slowly. Gingerly.

"Oh *shit*," she breathed. "Oh, *shit.* Freck, *shit in a handbag.*"

"I was talking to him just *two hours ago.*"

"We'll deal with it. *You* should get back in the sim. This for the crew to deal with."

"No, absolutely not. No way am I gonna do that now. I was talking to him *two hours ago.*"

She held out a hand, stern. "Fine. But give me the fob. Now."

I handed it back gingerly. She took it, and went briskly to the wall panel. "Frank," she said, speaking into it, "Get Lawrence and get down here. We have a dead passenger and Mister Whittaker will be staying awake with us for a while longer." She released her finger from the panel, terminating the conversation. "For whatever *that's* going to do for us."

She steered us away from Jazz's pod until it was out of sight. "We'll sort things out. But this was wrong. Poking at people's spaces. I didn't think you were the kind of person who would do that."

"I was just fascinated by it," I said, plaintively, searching for an explanation that wouldn't make it worse. "The sight of it. I spent a lot of time with those people, all while they were looking like *that*, absorbed into the ship. I just couldn't look away."

She relented a little. "I think, maybe, I understand, but from now you've spent your credit with me." She shook her head. "Freck. To think I gave you a passkey."

"I'm really sorry."

A rumble grew near the transit doors, signalling the imminent arrival of the others.

Elsie took a deep breath, and looked at me, hard.

"Tough shit."

# FOURTEEN

We regrouped in the galley.

"This is for the log. On behalf of Carver Interplanetary Services, I have confirmed that passenger Jazaban Cooke, berthed in cabin twelve-bee-seven, is deceased in transit." Frank said, heavily. "Thank you, both, for finding him. Does he have any kin aboard?"

"His sister," I said. "Tera Cooke." Madison nodded at that, checking her pad.

DeSanto sighed. "Lawrence and I will pull her out and convey the news. We'll host a farewell service in a couple hours."

He looked directly at me. "Holding a small service for the death of a passenger in deep flight is obligatory, but you don't have to attend it."

"I knew him," I said, feeling sick. "I'll be there."

"If you feel that's best. I'm sure Miss Cooke will appreciate it."

He looked at his crew, his face a definition of stoicism. "This is the first recorded passenger death aboard the Apollo in her seven years of flight. We will ensure it is the last."

* * *

I retreated to my borrowed cabin. Or at least, I *meant* to. I found myself staring through the open door into the little space, replaying what I'd seen in my mind's eye, over and over. Taking in the little closet with the reclining suit sitting there, dreadful and still. Like *meat*. Or a *doll*.

I couldn't get over it. It just *could not* be real. Jazz had been alive and snarky and having a good time that morning. I'd been zooming around a damned asteroid field with him!

I felt the sting for Tera, who any moment would be finding out for herself. We weren't *great* friends, but we *had* circled up together.

The bunk before me just looked cramped and forbidding. Too much like the little sim cradles. It was as if a fog had settled in my thoughts, and all I could process was whatever appeared in front of me.

I abandoned the cabin.

The infinitely looping corridor was full of fake plants, little sculptures, and pinprick lights dotted along the walls and ceiling, a sky full of tiny stars just within reach. It had *Elsie* written all over it. The simple warmth cemented an idea that had been growing: the crew had to have been living here, together, for *years*. They had to be like a family. It gave Lawrence's wistful tones about their departed crewmate a more real flavor. Something homey. Something personal, beyond the veneer of workplace friends.

The thoughts helped a little. The sickening, gnawing, churning pit in my stomach relaxed bit by bit.

I passed a room marked *Hydroponics Alpha*, and although the door was locked, a broad window beside it offered a glance at rack upon rack of leafy greens immersed in nutrient mixes. A large chart was attached flat to the far wall, illustrating different tests evaluating…what, exactly?

I pressed my face to the window, squinting.

It was illustrating a mix of edible enjoyment as compared to atmospheric conversion rate. For various strains of the karackao plant, going by the taped-up graphics.

I snorted in disbelief, and put a few dots together. Lawrence had mentioned a hydroponics whizz-kid, and there was a name I hadn't met yet. Whoever this Milo was, he had been putting a lot of time into finding the most practical way to grow his own highs.

Across from the lab was a door with a little plaque beside it:

*Elsie's place. Beware, ye nosy fiends!*

I shook my head and carried on, pondering things. I passed a few more closed cabin doors, each unmarked, wondering just what it was that I was really doing. I had the odd feeling of being a voyeur in someone else's home, yet I was here as a customer, or perhaps a client. Yet I wasn't *their* client. To them, I had been cargo, as Lawrence had put it. Now I was their *guest*, as much as anything else.

In their home.

In their lives.

I mentally toyed with the image of me wearing the dress uniform of a ship's captain, stewarding my crew through the deep reaches of space, the proud, public face of my family to governments, traders, and adventurers of the frontier. Someone with credit. Someone with a *reputation*.

It was a compelling vision.

It faded with the realization that this had to be *weird* for my hosts. They had been minding their own business, tucked into their little world for weeks at a time, and now I was suddenly in their midst without warning.

*That*, I thought wryly, *could apply in both directions.*

Warbling, scratchy strains of some somber musical piece escaped from an open doorway. I approached quietly, not wanting to disturb, hoping to take in the sonorous melody on my own.

As I got closer, muted voices filtered out under the music. Curiosity piqued, I strained to listen, and carefully made out the words. I wished I hadn't.

"Are you *sure*?" Madison's voice said. A tinnier version of what I recognized as Lawrence's clipped drawl replied.

"I don't know *what* killed him, Maddie."

"It could have been a heart attack."

"There's no signs of anything amiss in his body chemistry except some raised, leftover adrenaline, which can be explained by the activity he was doing in his last hours."

I swallowed, mouth dry, listening.

"What about a seizure? Aneurysm?"

"No sign of it. It's like he just switched off. Heart stopped beating one moment and never restarted."

"Why didn't it raise an alarm? We should be hearing klaxons the second anyone starts flatlining."

"I just *don't know*."

Neither one spoke for a solid minute. I was turning to leave when Madison spoke again, very quietly.

"The CarverNet suit moderates bodily functions."

"Maddie…" Lawrence replied, trying to be comforting, while, I imagined, standing beside a corpse.

"We need to raise it with the suit engineers," she said, painfully slowly.

"Maddie, the suit *doesn't* interfere with nerve signals directed at cardiovascular or respiratory systems. It's explicitly designed to isolate them. The sims literally can't touch those signals. You know it, I know it."

"I know, I know…" she sighed. "But what if? What if, even if it was never intentional, what if the suit killed him? One moment he would be there, enjoying himself, and the next his heart would just stop getting told to beat and his lungs would stop getting told to breathe. He'd have just *stopped*. Dammit, I'm gonna be sick."

"The only way that could have happened is if someone did it on purpose." Lawrence's voice was flat.

Nothing was said for a long moment after that. After several beats, I decided I was better off *not* waiting around to hear it.

I retraced my steps back to Raj's cabin, processing. This was totally different territory. Lawrence was suggesting *murder*. Who would zero a guy on a ship out in the middle of nowhere? And why? It seemed preposterous, but then, that was the point.

*But what did Jazz ever do?*

A little emotion started to take root, one that I hadn't truly experienced lately.

Fear.

I needed a real friend. I needed Jennifer. And, if things were genuinely *dangerous*, then she was safer out *here* than in *there*.

Staying put would accomplish nothing.

I made good progress around the deck, avoiding the stairs up to the next level, just seeing what I could see.

Taped up on a wall was an oversized print, featuring two figures in relaxed chairs, looking out onto what I knew to be an ocean. I'd seen them a thousand times in sims. But somehow, here, that printed picture was magnificently more enticing. It had been *shared*. It was of somewhere *real*. And it stung, because I couldn't truly relate to it. I wanted to, I desperately *wanted* to.

I added it to my personal list of things to do when I eventually arrived on Earth. Number one: try real bread. Number two: stand in an ocean.

*If* I survived to get to Earth.

*If.*

"Hey mook," a voice called behind me. I turned. Ricky was waving from the cupboard nook.

I sharpened, realizing that I had to present a more stable version of myself.

"Hey," I said.

"You all right?"

"Yeah," I replied. "I'm, ah—" I couldn't find the words.

"It's all right. I've been there."

"Have you?"

He leaned against the wall. "Yeah. Not too long ago. Friend of mine. I'd rather not talk about that if it's the same to you."

"Yeah, okay. Sorry. Um."

He smiled weakly. "Don't worry about a thing, *bratan*."

"Yeah." I took in his posture, shifting topics. "How is it that you're not struggling with this gravity like I am?"

"Muscle and bone mods." He flexed an arm. "My stem cells do funny things now, but instead of killing me with cancer, I can just walk around planetside without collapsing."

"That's an *expensive* therapy."

"I saved up. Listen, I'm going to do a thing in a little bit, do you want in? It involves liquid courage."

I shrugged. "Maybe. I had a question for you, actually."

"Ask away, my dear compatriot."

"I can't remember going into CarverNet. If you were going to put someone into the sim, or take them out of it, how does that… work?"

"Why are you asking about *that*?" he said. There was a tone to his question, somewhere between suspicion and uncertainty, I thought.

Maybe just nervous.

"When we first woke up in the sim, it was missing stuff, and we couldn't remember ourselves, everybody had amnesia, and it was all really frecking weird. I was wondering why, and what you guys *do* to us. To passengers, I mean."

"Ah," he nodded, thinking. "That's fair."

He cleared his throat. "When we bring you on board, there's the getting suited up and there's the cannulation, which is Lawrence's piece but we all help, and that takes a while, but then it's set and forget for us. When you're all prepped and sat down in your pod chairs, it...well, the concern is mainly psychological, you understand." He paused, a little uncomfortable. "This is a skinny-crew ship. Passengers are in the sim for a *long* time and we need them to want to spend most of the trip in there."

In the distance, from the direction of Madison's cabin, footsteps clanged as someone climbed the stairs.

"I get that," I said, trying to make Ricky feel comfortable. "I really don't mind having a look behind the curtain. I really think the sim is a great experience, and I'm just curious about how it works."

He looked relieved. I wondered whether it was a touchy subject, but kept silent as he carried on.

"Okay, but you didn't hear this from me. When people go into the suits fully conscious they get itches, they get irritable, they get claustrophobic because they have context of the outside, right? They *know* they're in the suit. Deep down, they know it. And it gets extra hard for them because the suit does this thing with your spine implants where it kind of *borrows* control over your body. Makes you feel like you're moving without *actually* moving. That sends people into panic attacks if they're not ready. Sometimes even traumatic memory repression. That's a shitty thing for paying customers. So we do this slow therapy while you're unconscious, like a warmup, where your brain gets used to being in the suit, and," he gestured at me, "you guys back in ten and twelve missed some of that when you woke up early. But, uh, yeah, when everyone comes on board, once you're in there and conked out, we just switch the sim on or off for you. When we get to Luna we'll do it in reverse, you'll go to sleep in the sim and wake up in the real world just as we're getting docked." He shrugged, then gave me a weak grin. "Questions? Comments? We value your feedback."

I shook my head. "I'll write a strongly-worded letter when it's all done, but right now I'm just taking it as it goes."

"Very good, my man. Very good." He rifled around on a shelf, extracting something. "Listen, *bratan,* I'm going to go up to the galley and pour myself a glass of *this.* Want to accompany me on such a fine endeavor?" He showed me the bottle, with its logo peeking out. My eyes widened.

*Sapphire Class Nihonshu*

And below the title:

*Excellence of our stars*

"That's quite the drink," I said. "Thanks. I'll save my glass for after the service."

"Suit yourself," he said. "I'm not a fan of funerals."

I frowned. "I thought it was just a memorial. A few words in a chapel, that kind of thing."

Ricky shook his head. "I just re-read the policy. We're too far from port, and the company won't let us hold human remains in storage for three months. It's going to be a burial in hard vacuum. And I, for one, don't have much stomach for it. A simple toast in the galley for me and anyone who comes, thank you very much."

"Enjoy," I said, a stone sinking in my chest.

"I will." He replied, and walked off, bottle in hand. I shook my head, watching him go.

I retraced my steps towards Madison's place. When I arrived it was vacant, with the door ajar. Taking a deep breath, and knowing that this was going to earn me some severe dislike, I ventured inside.

Displays lined the left wall. They were locked, waiting on a passcode. On a hunch, I entered *8801*.

I had to pause in disbelief for a moment when it worked.

I scanned through the screens, one after another, looking for passenger lists. One was waiting, already scrolled to block twelve with a highlight on Jazz's name. I quickly used it to search for Jennifer's berth, and the system returned her record nearly instantly:

*Block Ten, Zone A, Berth Four*

She was showing as steadily immersed with normal vitals. I memorized the location, repeating it to myself a few times, then sent the search results back to Jazz's listing. I glanced around the little workshop, uncertain what I was looking for. It had some character: no plants, but a stack of actual, physical books; an archaic record player set aside on a cabinet; a few stuffed toys perched along the top of the bench. Homey. Soothing, even.

Then I spotted the row of key fobs hooked onto the wall by the door. They were identical to the one Elsie had lent me.

Perfect.

I snagged a fob and ducked out, mercifully unobserved, and keenly aware that I was burning *everyone's* trust at this rate.

Guilt pursued me, but so did satisfaction. I told myself I would make it up to them if I could.

I found a different set of stairs up to the third deck which deposited me near the mover, bypassing the galley. Nobody crossed my path, though voices echoed as I reached the big mural and parade of potted plants. I reached the mover door, and pressed the *call* button, waiting for one to arrive and praying that there wouldn't be anyone in it. I didn't want to have to invent an explanation.

Glasses *clinked*, foil crinkled. Booze and snacks. Dainty little indulgences that might have been alluring but now couldn't be further from importance.

Finally, the mover arrived, and the door slid open. It was mercifully empty as I slipped inside. Voices abruptly grew louder, and I pressed myself against the mover's wall, trying to be out of sight and avoiding drawing attention. Madison and another figure, who I assumed to be the mysterious Milo, crossed by the mural without so much as looking over at me.

When they had gone, I exhaled, and punched in the trusty code. The mover's display unlocked, and I selected my destination:

*ZONE 10 A*

It took an age, and I prayed that nobody would intercept the mover with a pickup call of their own. But it zoomed along happily and arrived without incident.

The door opened into inky, repressive darkness, but after a few unsettling seconds the lights noticed my presence and came to life. Ricky's words danced across my thoughts, and the prospect of a sudden memorial service felt *wrong*. As if somebody was working too hard to move past Jazz's death. A moment of doubt flickered across my mind, but it was dismissed just as quickly. Distrust and anxiety overruled any fledging congeniality I felt towards the crew.

I found my target easily. Extra-easily, as it happened, because in this area, instead of pods, the hall was lined with actual *cabins*. One, just down and to the left, had the name *LaVelle* on dimmed signage beside the door. I recognized Selena's surname, and paused, abruptly thoughtful. If I walked into their space and invaded them like the pods back in block twelve, it would mean crossing a very personal line.

But Jennifer had to know. And dammit, she would have invited me in.

Their cabin was nice. Off-white hard bulkheads, with crash webbing holding baggage firmly in place. A poziglas mirror, large enough to be useful and small enough to be ignorable. A spare guest chair, bolted to the floor. Two occupied suits, breathing steadily, reclining on ergonomic cradles. A generic impressionistic painting firmly secured against one wall. Acoustics felt uncomfortably dampened; even the thrum of the air processors was muffled, and my own breathing sounded thin to my ears.

It wasn't *quite* a picture of comfort and decadence, as I might have guessed from the spaciousness. Ricky's commentary about the psychology of the environment came back to me, and I realized, taking in the modest, spartan room, it was a different kind of luxury:

Privacy.

The kind of precious perk that they might only enjoy in the hour before they arrived. It must have cost a fortune. Not that it was being respected at the moment.

I studied the two figures before me. They were obviously

Jennifer and Selena. There was no doubt about *that*. But which was which? The virtual recreations I had known were of similar height, similar build.

Then I spotted the control panel, and went to it.

As I crossed the room, for the first time since waking up I saw my *real* reflection in the mirror, and paused.

Pasty skin, just like in CarverNet. Absent the aspiring reddish waves that I sported in the sim, my real hair was shaved down to stubble. My jawline was exactly as it *should* have been, but I had softer, rounder cheeks, and older eyes.

I did a little jig, just to be sure that it was real. Waved at myself. Pulled a goofy face. Satisfied, I leaned away from the shiny surface and nodded. "Good to see you, Noah."

The nod faltered.

*That* was an odd feeling: defaulting to an arbitrary invention rather than my own name. But it felt nice. It felt like a good version of myself. A little smile reflected in the mirror, somewhere between reconciliation and acknowledgement.

*Maybe it's not* that *odd, in the scheme of things.*

Disappointingly, the control panel's display was locked. The code from the mover did nothing, and a few different attempts at passwords accomplished just as little. I even tried an alphanumeric conversion of the name *Apollo*, which should have equated to one-one-six-one-two-one-five-one-five-one-two, but that did nothing. I tried it a few more times, just in case I'd entered too many or not enough ones.

I gave up with the control panel, and studied the chairs, hesitant, thinking about what Ricky had told me.

*Once you're in there and conked out, we just switch the sim on or off for you.*

I thought about my own exit. There, I had needed to get control over my own limbs to tear the suit off. Here, no such requirement existed, because I was *already* on the outside for *her*.

I realized, as a I stood between the two cradled figures, that one was breathing more intently than the other. Knowing Selena's perennially cool nature, I decided that it was as good a tell as any.

Leaning over the figure I presumed to be Jennifer, I reached out to the collar on the suit's neck.

*Could it be that easy? A little clasp, just like my own suit?*

I went for it, feeling around, and settled gratifyingly on the shallow locking clasp that secured the helmet into place, and flicked it open.

"What the *freck!*"

The voice was muffled by the hood, but recognizable nonetheless.

I carefully pulled the blocky headpiece up and away, discarding it to one side, and eyed a familiar visage blinking up at me, trying to focus.

Her hair was cropped very short, but otherwise there was no mistaking that face.

Jennifer swallowed. "You. Um. I'm gonna be sick." She sharpened. *"Aidan?"*

"Yeah."

She squinted in the mottled light. "Prove it."

I paused, caught off guard. "Uh. You told me about your dad."

She paused, then nodded. "Took you long enough. Why—can't —I—move?"

She shook her head in frustration. "I'm waving my arms. Are they moving? At all? Freck *me*, this is weird."

I fiddled with her neckpiece's latch, wiggling it until it *clicked* and came away, mechanically disengaging the suit from her skin. Instantly, her left arm flew up and *thwacked* my side, sending me stumbling backwards to jostle Selena's quiet figure.

"Shit! Sorry!" Jennifer called, taking control of her other limbs more gingerly.

I rubbed my side. It was mainly my pride that was wounded. "Are you okay?"

She nodded, testing that she could stand. "Frecking disorienting having the world pulled off your face!"

"I know."

Jennifer wobbled over, helping me up. "I guess you'd know about that by now."

"Kind of. What we did on Arkadia worked, obviously. What's the state of things in there?"

"The sim came back online a while ago, it's all back to normal. Except we still can't find Jazz, but I guess they're still working on some things. Tell me already, what's been going on out here?"

"*About* that, yeah." I said, flashing back, feeling ill. "I don't know how to...he's dead, Jen. And I think either the suit killed him, or someone killed him *with* his suit. *And* I think they sabotaged the ship to do it."

Jennifer stared at me.

I shook my head pre-emptively before she could speak. "It's not a joke. I found him. His *body*. He died while he was jacked into the sim. *While we were playing the game with him.* The medic on board is suspicious. He thinks it was deliberate."

She didn't say anything. Just looked at me, looked at the door, looked at her cradle, looked at Selena's calm, steadily sleeping form for a long time.

"It's all shit, isn't it," she whispered. "Please tell me, be as honest as you can: is the guy we, you and me, mutually know and hang out with, *dead*? Really, genuinely dead?"

"Yes," I said. "The captain, DeSanto, is waking up Tera right now and filling her in."

"Gods," Jennifer said, still quiet.

"Come on," I said. "Let's get back to the crew zone. I didn't tell anyone I was going to wake you up, but it was the right thing to do. They'll understand."

"Noah," She spoke slowly and deliberately. "Will Sel be safe if I leave her here?"

I nodded. "I think so. As safe as anywhere else."

"Okay," my friend said. "Good. Then, ah, find my clothes while I get this shitting thing off, will you?"

# FIFTEEN

We retreated to Raj's cabin, avoiding any awkward encounters with the crew along the way. I put something lighthearted on the infotainment screen to lighten the mood while catching Jennifer up on who was who and what had happened, but despite my best efforts at staying focused, physical distractions abounded. Despite the horrible circumstances, this was our first time actually being in the same physical space, and for me, the first time on this ship where I'd truly been alone with somebody trusted. Even the simple smell of her body odor, unremarkable in any other moment, gave her a real *presence* that just didn't exist in the simulation. It spurred a warm, intoxicating sense of affection.

For her part, Jennifer had been smiling a little more easily than she ever had in the sim. Human contact, as innocent or complex as it could be, had a healing effect on the soul. There was a fleeting moment of easy, genuine goodness between us as she took a seat on the bunk.

"Frank DeSanto is master of the show. This is his boat," I said, forcing myself to stay focused by pacing rapidly up and down the small room. "Elsie's the navigator slash pilot. Madison is…I don't know what she does, exactly, but it's something technical, and she seems to know about everything, even though she's still in her first year here. Lawrence is the resident medic, Ricky's apprenticing and Milo does something with hydroponics. I think. I don't really know him yet."

Jennifer tilted her head. "You've only been out here for a couple hours. Did they just give you a tour?"

I shrugged. "Kind of. I helped fix the sim. They're a family and some of them struggle with oversharing."

"I guess on this kind of ship social skills *could* get a little bit deficient."

"You said it. That's the crew."

"Then, er, who is Raj? We seem to be in his space." Jennifer asked, musing on the topic.

"Somebody who moved on to other adventures, from what I gather," I replied. "They miss him."

"And how about you?"

"What about me?"

"Are you okay?"

I paused to give that one a moment.

"No."

"That's a first."

I smiled weakly. "Yeah." The smile faded, and I used the infotainment console to find something calming. The guide, a primitive version of Kay Tee, suggested a musical performance that I had never heard of. It began playing.

The words came together as I sat on the bunk.

"He was *our age*. It feels like we're still kids, Jen."

"I know."

"I need a friend."

She clapped a hand on my shoulder. "Let's fix this shit."

Her hand felt good. We said nothing to each other for a long, long moment.

I knocked on the bunk frame. "You ever think about living like this?"

"You're fancying becoming a strapping ship captain, aren't you."

"With a girl in every port. It has to have crossed your mind too."

"Maybe."

The door slid open without warning, and Madison looked in, aborting her planned message the instant she laid eyes on Jennifer.

"Oh." She said, without missing a beat. "You must be Miss Motley. Aidan mentioned you. He *didn't* mention that you were awake too. "

"I wasn't," Jennifer said, simply.

After an extended pause to consider that, Madison turned to me. "*Ah.*"

I cleared my throat, and handed over the borrowed fob. "Here, you'll want this back. I took it from your work room."

She took it. "Thank you. Ask permission next time."

"Can I borrow it?"

"No."

"I overheard you talking to Lawrence earlier."

"Oh?" Madison replied, her tone icy. I decided to risk it.

"I agree with him. That it all looks really suspicious."

"Do you?"

"I do, and you should, if you don't. What does it for me, is a few things." I ticked off my fingers as I went through it.

"One, you didn't get an alarm. You said it yourself, you *expected* to see one. Two, the timing with the frecked hardware in the tech room was just too close for comfort, but, third, I don't think that could have caused the issue directly, otherwise a lot more of us would be zeroed right now."

"So far, so reasonable," Madison said, calmly.

"And fourth," I continued, "It doesn't *look* like an attack. It *looks* like it was meant to go unnoticed for as long as possible, while a big and loud and dramatic distraction meant everybody would be looking somewhere else. By the time you were in port, unloading everyone, and found him, it'd have been so long that you'd have chalked it up to a freak byproduct of the meteorite strike, or a heart attack, or any one of a dozen unprovable things. But instead, his sister noticed *immediately*, and raised the alarm, or at least *tried* to raise it."

"Hold on," Jennifer said. "I'm still getting my head around all of this, but even if you're right, and it's a bad event with bad intent, well, I'm still catching up, but that sounds like a complex strategy. How would someone *know* to zero somebody at just the right moment?"

"They couldn't, if it was a coincidence," I said, grimly. "And that's what makes it all stink even more. It's too damned unlikely, all of it."

Madison looked thoughtful, but burdened. She shook her head. "I hear what you say. I get it. It looks and sounds really unlikely, and it probably is, and it's downright conspicuous that this much has gone wrong on this run. But there's only nine of us awake on this ship, and three of that number only started participating *after* the incident. You're suggesting that someone in our crew deliberately murdered a passenger."

*Yes,* I thought, anxiety starting to be traded for irritability. *That is exactly what I am suggesting.*

Jennifer's expression was slowly slipping from thoughtful to standoffish.

I kept my face a mask. "Is it a crazy thing to say?"

"There is another possibility," Madison replied, thinking. "We could have a stowaway. If someone *really* wanted to, they could smuggle themselves in a long-store container. We've got a hundred or so of the things strapped down in wheels one and two." She slowly nodded to herself. "I'll need to check the cargo blocks. Make sure that it is or isn't a real possibility."

"So you're taking this seriously?" I asked.

"I hope it's not true. But you *are* right about at least one thing: the meteorite strike was an extremely unlikely coincidence. We're moving really damned fast right now, to the point where the slingdome would easily scoop away a bit of debris like that pebble. It would have had to come in at a very steep angle at *just* the right instant to hit us at all, never mind actually hit something that sensitive. But it's not impossible."

"Lawrence sounded pretty skeptical of it all on the comm." I offered.

"He's skeptical of *everything.*"

"In some ways," Jennifer ventured, "the idea of a killer on board is more comforting than the alternative."

"The alternative?" I asked, incredulous.

"Yeah. That the suit, that CarverNet killed him by *accident.*"

"I have been thinking along those lines too." Madison admitted, "But I can't figure out how that could possibly work. The sim, the equipment, it's all designed to support basic bodily needs and unconscious functions, not *influence* them."

"Don't know about that," Jennifer said. "I have felt a need for some unconscious functions during some pretty intense, uh, moments in there."

That got an unwilling smirk. "We'll take that as a compliment." Then the older woman sighed. "But I hate the idea that one of us would be sadistic enough to do this. It's just horrifying."

Jennifer leaned in. "I'm sorry. I know, Aidan's told me this already, but this is coming too fast. Is this real? Is he really dead?"

The older woman nodded sadly. "Yes."

"Gods."

"Has anyone looked into *why* somebody might want to do that to Jazz?" I asked.

"I had given it some thought," Madison said. "But we didn't know him. The only one who might know isn't ready to be asked that."

"Tera." Jennifer said, quietly. "This must be a nightmare for her. How is she?"

Madison sighed. "Miss Cooke is awake and has been informed of her brother's passing. She is not in a great place."

"I can imagine. Where is she?"

"The captain's quarters. He's taking her through what has to happen. It's a delicate conversation so please don't interrupt it. Speaking of which, I'm due at the farewell service in twenty minutes. It's at the midships airlock. You don't have to come."

I grimaced, anxiety pulsing in my gut. "Ricky said it would be an actual burial in space."

"It is. Has to be. We don't have the facilities to hold on to… him…for three months."

"It's too fast." I objected. "Like you're trying to get rid of him. Get rid of a problem."

Madison paused, stiffening for a fraction of a second. "It's the captain's decision. But it is a respectful process. I've been to one of these before." She looked uncomfortable, then quickly added, "Not on the Apollo, of course."

I looked at Jennifer, something unspoken passing between us. "Are you coming?"

Jennifer looked back at me levelly. "I'd stay here, if it's all the same."

"That's probably for the best anyway," Madison said. "You're fresh to all this. The others don't know you're up here, and that may be a useful thing for us."

"Us?" I interjected, jumping on the change.

The engineer held up a hand defensively. "Look, Mister Whittaker, Aidan, you're upsetting the natural order of things on this ship. I have to admit, though, that however unlikeable your ideas about murder are, something *is* happening, and as I can only draw a meaningful line to my own people, I would like to keep you safe. Simultaneously I don't hold any expectation that either of you want to go back into the sim before we have an explanation."

Jennifer hunched her shoulders forward. "You got that right. This doesn't feel real yet, but you're making me believe it."

"Mmhmm." Madison's tone softened. "Let's take it one step at a time. We've got a ritual to observe. Do this part right."

* * *

The midships airlock was a zero gravity block situated on the Apollo's spine between wheels two and three. Anxiety sat hard in my stomach, an aching ball of tension, and of anxiety.

And revulsion.

*Everything* about this was happening impossibly quickly.

When we arrived, a small group was waiting, floating in front of the inner door: Frank, Lawrence, and a third who I didn't recognize at first, until I did. She looked *different* to her CarverNet avatar. Gone was the shock of playful hair, reduced to a plain blonde. Her facial shape, with tighter cheeks and higher, narrower eyes, bore traces of outer-belt ethnic complexity that had been absent from her avatar as well. But it *was* Tera, without question.

Between the lot of them, at waist height, was a solid white body bag.

*This is real.*

Bile rose in my throat.

I nearly turned around, unable to deal with it. All that stopped me was the look in Tera's eyes as she recognised me. The gaunt stare, laced with shock and anger, pleading for someone or something familiar. I clambered along handholds to close the distance and gave her an embrace, trying to channel whatever comfort I could. As I enclosed her very solid frame, for one brief moment the anxiety and revulsion didn't matter. Couldn't matter. The person touching me was a good person. In the span of an hour, she had been forced to go from enjoying a lazy trip with her brother to saying goodbye to him permanently. And now, at this sudden juncture, she was so very alone.

As we hung like that in a clumsily anchored hug, I couldn't take my eyes off the body bag. Its bulk casually, listlessly *waited.*

"Shall we begin?" Lawrence asked. His soft tone hit my ears with a resounding heaviness.

At the words, we separated, and I gave Tera what I hoped was a reassuring nod and a squeeze on the shoulder as the various attendees settled into polite positions. Madison, I noted, found a spot that kept her at the furthest distance. I got the impression she was here, more than anything, simply out of a sense of duty. Everyone waited, respectful, until Tera finally, horribly, nodded to the captain.

The white bag loomed with evil patience. I wished it would move, twitch, or betray any kind of life at all.

*Freck,* I thought. *This really is happening.*

DeSanto gave it a gentle push, and it floated away into the airlock, which in turn closed itself dutifully. The outer door opened, but instead of the bag simply floating out whole, it lingered there, implacable, until after a long, long pause, a quiet thrum began, and it started visibly vibrating.

The captain spoke into the echoing silence, reverently reciting a solemn verse.

"There is a ship on our seas, sailing in the dark. Our kin is aboard, a bearer of our spirit. We call on the moons and the stars, the gods of our time, to mind him in their patient light. Should we join him tomorrow, we ask the same; for now we remain, charged to hold the memory of his name."

He looked expectantly at Tera, who was plainly, silently, letting tears shine on her face. When she shook her head, he bowed his own. "We *remember* Jazaban Cooke, whose soul, voyage, and story we honor as we commit his remains to the empty places. The stars create us, and the stars accept us." He straightened, and his last words were much softer. "*Facilis itineri.*"

Through the inner door's window, the vibration strengthened to a peak, then ceased. We watched, each with their own thoughts, as the bag smoothly disintegrated into a cloud of shining white powder.

At Lawrence's instruction, the airlock's ventilation released a short fluff of air, which smoothly carried the cloud onwards and out from the hull into the inky void. In long, gentle moments, the specks lazily dispersed in the night, an ephemeral offering to distant twinkling deities.

It could have been beautiful, if it hadn't been a friend.

I felt twisted, in denial, and angry, but most of all, simply numb. It was unreal that I would never see, hear, or play with him again. I intellectually knew that it had to be *a fraction* of whatever Tera was experiencing, but in that moment it was hard to be empathetic.

DeSanto pressed the controls to re-seal the airlock. "I have now spoken those words three times in my life," he said heavily. "I dearly hope not to do that again. My condolences, Miss Cooke."

Tera just floated there, staring out into the black, distracted and subdued. Withdrawn, even.

"If you need to talk," I said, "I'm here."

"I know."

And that was all she said. We lingered in place, watching the flecks of white dust vanish from sight, until Madison steered us away, escorting us back to what I was starting to think of as *home base*. She deposited us in the crew module, and departed to search the cargo blocks as she had promised.

We walked through the galley, intending to reach the cabin I'd been stashed in before, but stopped cold as we caught sight of Jennifer standing before the hologram of the Apollo, still lazily floating above the table.

Tera recognized her after a heartbeat, and the two exchanged an awkward, quiet hug.

"I'm so sorry," Jennifer said after a long moment, holding her close. "He was an amazing guy. We're here, okay?"

The other woman said nothing. Just looked between us, and stared at something only she could see.

We remained like that, in the quiet, for a very long time.

# DEEP-RANGE NEWSCAST

Helios Network News
Sol 12, 04:14 Local Time

"Hi Camilla, I'm live here at Luna's Cameron Station where demonstrations against the utility union have turned violent. It's the sixth day of the strike and water rationing has pushed some of the populace right to the edge. A man who I believe worked in a water processing plant was beaten by the mob here in the zocalo. A gruesome scene to be sure, and one the locals are none-too-happy about."

The feed switched back to the anchor desk, where the host's smile was thin and unwavering. "Do you think there's any merit to the riots?"

"I think holding water hostage is a dangerous ploy. The utility unions here hold a staggering degree of power to bargain with the administration, but depriving the entire station of supplies of something so basic treads into dark territory. We'll be here on-site to monitor the negotiations when they happen."

The newscaster's expression faltered. "They haven't begun negotiations yet?"

"No. As far as I can tell they've made demands, but aren't meeting with the station administration."

"Truly concerning!" Camilla said. "You would think that with such a strong position they would press their case. Perhaps something more underhanded is at play?" She returned her attention to the camera. "We'll pick up more on this story as it develops, folks. To all you watching on Luna and around the system, stay strong, and stay safe."

# SIXTEEN

In its fuzzy, holographic indifference, the Apollo's schematic floated over the galley table, spinning onwards.

"How did the service actually go?" Jennifer asked, nervous.

Tera leaned against the bank of food cubicles. "They turned him into dust."

I coughed. "It happened far too fast. I didn't even know for sure it was *him*."

"I'm sorry I wasn't there. It was just…" Jennifer trailed off.

"Yeah, well, far as I'm concerned you've had enough of that kind of thing in your mind already."

A single tear left Tera's right eye. But she rebuffed an attempt at further consolation.

We didn't say anything for a long, long moment, watching the hologram's lines get traced out over and over again.

"She's a really ugly ship," Jennifer commented, eyeing the hologram in an anxious effort to change the subject. "That dome thing up front looks neat though."

"She's a *real* ship," I answered. "Not some diagram. And these people call her a home."

"I'm just saying that I could have made her prettier." She shut her eyes. "I need to tell Aunt Sel about all of…this."

I sighed. "It won't let you send messages back into the sim. I've tried."

Both women grimaced, but had nothing else to say.

I was contemplating raiding the cupboards when DeSanto walked in. He waved a gesture to us to continue whatever we had been doing, and quietly closed the door behind him. We looked at him silently, and he looked at us, any surprise at Jennifer's presence hidden behind a stoic mask. He turned to a small screen embedded in the wall and tapped a few controls. Soft music began to play. Something soothing.

He crossed to the counter and produced three bags of rations. Handed one to each of us. A host's apologetic courtesy to his guests.

Within each was a soft, baked pouch with a flavorful filling. Savory and sweet. The first *actual*, substantial food any of us had eaten in weeks. Jennifer made inhumanly short work of her portion.

The quiet sound of chewing permeated our little group for a stretch.

Finally, DeSanto cleared his throat. "I thought you all deserved —"

Tera cut him off. "I want to know what killed my brother. Was it an accident? Was it a glitch?"

He took a moment to collect himself, then nodded. "That's a reasonable thing to ask. I don't have an answer for you right now."

"Are you hiding the answer because you don't think I'll like it?"

"*No.*" His reply was quiet, emphatic, and calm. "But I can tell you that he didn't suffer. He enjoyed his time aboard."

"He was having fun, Tera." Jennifer interjected softly. "He *was* having a good time."

The younger woman's shoulder's vibrated with contained rage. "How could you know? How could you possibly know?"

The captain's voice was gentle. "I know that he was spending time with the people who knew the *real* him. They might not have known *him* like you did, but they knew who he wanted to be. I know that because all three of you are here."

"What does that mean?"

DeSanto gave her a soft smile. "I don't take part in the sim anymore, but I do know what it does. I know the gift that it gives you."

"*Gift?*"

"Mister DeSanto—" Jennifer tried to cut in.

"*Captain* DeSanto." He responded firmly. But then he relented. "I've been master of this ship for six of her seven years. But it's Frank, please. Death is a hard topic and you all deserve to be treated better than this. And yes, I meant *gift*. If you'll forgive the detour, I'll explain."

The others said nothing. I nodded warily.

Frank took it as approval and offered a kind look to Tera. "There's a proposition by a first-generation Martian, Aaron Andersen, who passed away some twenty-four years ago." He shook his head. "That was a long time, now."

Jennifer made a *go on* gesture. He nodded, and spoke reverently.

"Andersen's idea was this. You have a man in a room. He has a box. He opens it. In the lid there's a mirror. There's something inside this box. It's a rock, a hunk of stone, jagged and rough, ugly to the eye. But when the man looks at it in the mirror, the rock is smooth, round, and sparkles in the light. Now, depending on the man, he might dismiss the box, or he might covet it, or he might see a vision to be chased. Andersen called it the mirror of the eidolon.

"I think on this a lot. What I've found, as the years have gone on, is that Andersen's mirror describes the difference between *presentation* and *belief.* That is what we apply with CarverNet. An alternative place where what you believe about yourself can be what you present about yourself. A narcissism that lays bare who you are. It's a tremendous therapy, because we couldn't ask for a better way to hold a mirror up to someone and show them their psyche. Of course, my employer's idea was to extend that into *retail* therapy, which is a terribly effective business model."

Tera spoke very softly. "Get to the point."

He nodded apologetically. "The CarverNet sim is a hedonistic dreamland full of delights. It is a taste of paradise. All of you," he pointed at my chest, and looked proudly between the lot of us, "have lived in it, and two of you *left* it willingly. I'm certain Jazaban had people who cared about him because you're here, talking to me. And that matters."

We were all silent for a long minute.

"I don't think I feel very comforted," Tera said at last. "But thank you all the same."

Jennifer spoke up. "If you don't mind me asking, what's your story?"

"Twenty-eight years working for Carver," Frank replied. "I've been running the Ceres route almost since it opened, and was executive officer of the *Copernicus* before being given *Apollo.*"

I ingested that and updated my assessment of him. He was a lifer. This was his *career*, not simply a job or a trade.

"I guess the crew are like your family?" Jennifer mused.

He smiled sadly. "Yes, though not entirely by choice. You make do with the people that travel in the same skies and thank the stars when they're a decent sort. I take it that your Aunt is well?"

"That's right," she answered, guarded. "She's particularly enjoying the food-and-drink parts of that mirror of yours."

"Good, well, hold onto her if you like her. That is an extra-special privilege."

"I think I understand," she said.

"You don't." Tera mumbled flatly, staring into her minds' eye.

"Maybe she does." Frank nodded plainly. "I definitely looked for people to surround myself with when I was younger. It's worth it when you can have it. And please," he spoke more quietly now, "Tera, my sincerest condolences and apologies for your brother. That should never have happened on my ship, and I won't allow anything like it to happen again."

"It was a nice poem you read before," she muttered. "I heard it read out when my neighbor died, years ago."

"The wayfarer's prayer." He replied. "I'm fond of it. Oh, that sounds rather dark, doesn't it? Well, I think it's a good prayer, for what it is. It's an old one. Predates you."

We looked up as Madison barreled in, stopping only to make use of the drinks machine. "Hey, Frank."

"Madison."

"Are our lovely guests treating you well?"

"They are. I think we're all due for a bit of therapy by now, but this is as close as we might get."

"Oh. You told them about the mirror of idols theory. Right."

Frank sighed, long and low. "It came up."

"Of course it did." she said, leaning against the wall. "I've been looking around for signs of a stowaway."

"Why?" He asked, puzzled.

"I had a chat with Mister Whittaker here. The likelihood that the earlier damage to ring four was coincidental is somewhere adjacent to zero."

He looked at her for a long moment. "Right."

"What are you saying?" Tera asked.

"Nothing for certain." Madison assured her. "Not yet."

The captain was thoughtful. "What did you find?"

"I've been up through the cargo blocks. There's no signs of a stowaway. But I *did* find something odd in block two. There was an extra container back there. One not registered on the manifest." She held out her hand and opened her fist, revealing a small woven parcel. Within was a lump of shiny blue stone.

My eyes widened.

Madison nodded. "This is refined, crystalline pelarite. Not a rare sight on this ship but we tend to have records on it."

Jennifer looked confused. "It's a mineral. Why is that important?"

"This stuff is used in the manufacture of pseudo-ceramics. It makes it possible to produce modern supercapacitors. Anything that's self-contained and needs to charge, discharge, and moderate a lot of energy at short notice. Ships, stations, you name it. Apollo couldn't fly without this stuff being available in the assembly line."

Jennifer nodded. "Okay. You're speaking my language now."

"You're not speaking mine," I said, stepping over to peer at the crystals more closely. "Like she said, what's so important?"

The engineer coughed, shifting uncomfortably. "There's another use for this. Milo, er, enlightened me to it. Make it into a powder, dust it into your nutrient mix, and you can get a coffee plant to hybridize with cannibis and downright thrive. Your people, out in the belt, call it *karackao*."

It clicked. "Oh."

"What?" Jennifer asked, clearly not following. Tera shook her head.

Frank chuckled quietly. "Karackao leaf gives you an intense

caffeine hit combined with a lazy high. It makes the world calm down in a get-your-heart-moving kind of way. Stoned and energetic, if you can imagine."

"It gets you horny, Jen." Tera said.

"Oh."

"Right," Madison said. "And imports of this rock are regulated to hell and back in Earth territories. There's a lot of money behind this stuff."

"Why regulate it?"

Frank cleared his throat. "Because in the fine powdered form you need for…that…pelarite is explosively combustible. I allow Milo his experiments but even we have rules about that."

The engineer put away the pebble. "This stuff is serious money, and there's damn near three hundred kilos of it. I'd take a bet that it's undeclared. Somebody is smuggling it."

"Milo uses it? Could it be his stash?" I asked.

Frank shook his head. "No. He's honest with us about the extracurriculars he brings aboard."

"I used to hear about this stuff getting snuck out," I pondered. "There's a few gangs back home that get named a lot. La Fraternité, the Ostapenkos, the Seomuns, the Afterburners…what?" I looked around at the faces evaluating me. "I read the news, okay?"

Madison's tone was cold. "I won't have their dirty business on my ship."

Frank contemplated that for a few beats and stood, an odd look in his eye. Without a word he strode out of the galley with unmistakable *purpose*, leaving the four of us behind.

"That was dramatic," I observed.

"Is that stuff *really* an aphrodisiac?" Jennifer asked.

"A damned powerful one," Tera said, smiling slightly, lost in some memory. A roomful of raised eyebrows greeted the statement.

The smile faded.

"Okay," Madison said, a little awkwardly. "I'm going to start questioning the crew. If any of you have something to come out with, speak." She paused. Nobody volunteered anything.

"Fine." She pushed up and stormed towards the door leading to the medical office. Managed to get one footstep beyond it.

An alarm, searingly loud, blared suddenly as the bulkheads around us shuddered. My gut recoiled at the implication. *Not another frecking problem!*

Kay Tee's familiar tenor provided a terse description over the intercom.

*"Transverse impact alert. Pressure loss detected, central engine compartment, deck two. Evacuate to safe areas immediately. Pressure seals will engage in three seconds."*

Madison was planted in place, attention refocused in an instant, fob brought to her lips. "Elsie, talk to me."

The pilot's voice came through a tiny speaker. "We've been hit again. I'm seeing red all over the engines and we're leaking heavy propellant into vacuum."

"Kill power to the whole module. I don't want a single spark back there."

"What can I do?" I asked. "I can help."

She just shook her head firmly, with her hand up as if to keep us quiet. The move broadcasted *not now, I need to think.*

Frank's voice proceeded his arrival by milliseconds as he burst back in, eyes sharp. "Details. Now!"

"Another impact, engine block." The engineer called back. "Elsie says it's the fuel tanks."

"Get everyone *but* Elsie. Doesn't matter what they're doing. Personal time is over. No exceptions. Let's go."

Madison glanced at the three of us. "You three, stay here, stay safe. Keep calm, feed yourselves. We'll check in."

As we processed the instruction, she pulled the fob from her pocket and tossed it to me. "Here. Keep this on you."

They disappeared out of sight with admirable speed as the klaxon continued to blare.

Just like that, the three of us were alone again.

Tera watched them go, practicing her brave face. "Right. Right, right, right."

The klaxon stopped, its message having been heeded.

I paced back and forth, from the drinks machine to the little beanbag seat and back, thinking. Emotions, thoughts, plans, all swirled around my head in bits and pieces.

Tera spoke into the void. "Do you two think there was something behind Captain Philosophy's little lecture?"

Jennifer looked at her, surprised. "Maybe. I put on my sexy coat and call myself Trace and I feel powerful. I feel like all the things that I wish I could forget about don't matter."

I muttered my own contribution. "All I could think about while he was talking was that you two cared about Jazz and each other, and all I wanted to do was fix the damned mirror."

Jennifer was kinder than I deserved. "It's philosophy, Noah. Makes your head spin even on normal days."

"Yeah, well. Maybe Trace is who you really are. Maybe Jennifer should forget about the things that she doesn't want."

Tera gazed away into some middle distance. "I wish, I really wish I could flip a switch to do that."

"Maybe for a while," Jennifer muttered. "Not forever."

"I know what he looked like when he was dead," the younger woman replied. "I knew him from a little kid, and I'm never going to not know that."

I gave her a kind look. "He did nothing to deserve it. His story was good. And you're still here. You're a good person. Don't be something else."

"Something else?"

"Something that would make him sad."

She looked so very tired. "You didn't know him."

Jennifer's voice was gentle. "We knew the version of him that he wanted us to see. And I liked that guy I saw. That matters."

"You...might be right."

"The people around us are who we've got. That's us, here. The three of us."

I reached over, patting Jennifer's shoulder. "Aye. We'll make it work."

Tera leaned on a chair, but didn't quite get into physical contact range. Still, the engagement was good. It meant she wasn't going to do something rash, all alone.

It meant she wasn't like me.

I pointed at the floating hologram. "At risk of changing the subject, the three of us, we've got a long way to go. We're moving really damned fast right now. There's that big new shield at the front meant especially to prevent hits like the one everybody just ran off to see."

"And?" Tera said, eyeing it.

"That second hit just now wasn't an accident. No way. Not this soon."

"Maybe it just *was*. It's space. Things go wrong out here."

Jennifer shook her head. "It happens, but this might be the unluckiest ship I've ever heard of."

A sudden wave of inspiration flashed into my mind, and I pushed away from the table, veering towards the door, determined to take advantage of the impulse.

"Hey." Jennifer said. "Are you going somewhere?"

"I need to see something."

"What?" Tera said.

"The glitch that broke the sim before was caused by a really special bit of space junk hammering CarverNet hardware into little pieces. I'm going to look around it again."

"Alone?"

"I can't risk either of you to check this out."

Tera stepped forward. "You're being dumb. Say you find something sketchy. Then what?"

"I show it to the crew."

"The crew. You find something *sketchy* and show it to the only people who could have made it happen."

I switched to Jennifer for support, but she just nodded. "She's right. You shouldn't go poking around like this."

Frustration boiled. "I can't wait. It all feels wrong. All of it."

"I agree. But why do this without real professionals watching out for you?"

"I'm going to do this," I said, stubbornly. "I'll try not to die."

"You've lost it, mate."

"I don't think I have. Somebody on this ship is dirty, we see evidence, and now there's suddenly a major emergency to focus on? No way. This feels deliberate. I don't know *how*, but something else is at play and we might be able to see for ourselves. Get a step ahead in this game."

"Jazz is *dead* and you're calling this a *game?*" Tera asked, incredulous.

"Yes. I'm sorry. Can't do it any other way," I said. "I'm going to go see what there is to see, while the killer is occupied. Jen, you coming?"

"*Killer?*" Tera eyed me, something starting to seethe in her eyes.

"Yes, Tera. *Killer. Get with it.*" I was disappointed with myself for the rebuke, but it spilled out under its own momentum as I rounded on her. "It can't have been an accident. Accidents like Jazz just don't happen. And now? With what we just saw? It's not a bad hand of cards. It's not a cruel accident. Jazz was *murdered* and the sooner you grasp that the better."

She shrunk back like a wounded animal. "How can you say that to me?"

"I'm sorry. I know it just happened. But it's never too soon to start looking around. Get suspicious. Don't let these people pretend that they're all-knowing and all-good."

She nodded, slowly, head tilting at me.

"What if it's *you?*"

"What?"

"What if you killed him? I never actually *saw* you while we were all supposed to be in that game. Gods, your pod was right across from ours!"

Jennifer laid a hand on her arm. "He was in my ear the whole time."

But the younger woman wasn't listening. "No! What if he did it? He got close to us! Got to *know* us! And magically, when we've got a problem, he can just pop out of the net when none of the rest of us can? And you went to his *funeral?*"

Jennifer shook her head, coming between us. She glared at me. "Just—go. Don't let it get interesting. We'll head up front and find the pilot. Somebody has to be looking out for you."

"Piece of shit!" Tera yelled.

I tried to ignore her. "Fine. Elsie's nice so be nice. But be a pain in the ass if I don't come back, okay?"

I walked out without a look back.

# SEVENTEEN

I retraced the steps we had taken before, punching in the code: *8801*. It was proving to be a useful code.

A sour feeling clenched my stomach. *Who the hell does she think I am?*

The mover deposited me in the wheel four tech ring. I stood there, alone, surrounded by merrily blinking lights. Immersed in the hard truth of a lovely fiction.

Inspecting the server racks came naturally. Dust and finger marks were everywhere, a testament to the flurry of activity it had witnessed. The new load balancer, held in a big blue cube, purred away merrily. Somewhere in there a hundred people were having a dandy time. All the cables were neatly tucked away inside the walls and conduits.

An odd pair of forgotten pliers had fallen behind a stack of cable spools. I picked it up, inspected it, set it aside. What the hell *was* it that had driven me back here, running off again on a misguided excursion?

Nothing was immediately obvious. I thought back to the earlier repair effort, being inside the walls, stringing up cable after cable.

The equipment was tightly packed, nestled neatly into their spaces so no cords would ever need to clutter the walkable area. It was hard to fathom any kind of space junk puncturing the room and *not* hitting something important.

I eyed the tight, upwards curve of the tech ring. Walked its entire length until, several seconds later, I was right back where I'd started.

Hmm.

As the stacks beeped and whirred, a heat exchanger in the wall behind me hummed to life. There was nothing remarkable about it; a room full of active machinery needed to stay cool somehow. The heat from the room would be slowly absorbed by a coolant gel and circulated into fins along the external hull, radiating away into the night.

The more I ignored it, the more it niggled. I started paying attention, examining its mesh front.

The heat exchanger was built into the *wall*. Not the floor, which would have made more sense. More surface area, more likely to be unobstructed by superstructure. But building it into the floor would mean interrupting the already-cramped walking space for the precious squishy people inside.

The *walls* in a tight ring like this one faced fore and aft. Fore to the other swirling rings, crew ring, and slingdome. Aft to the engines and the big empty. The engines that had us moving extremely fast. The engines currently swarming with people.

Things clicked, and I looked askance at the new load balancer. At the patched hole in the bulkhead behind it. Imagined the *second* patched hole behind it. In the *wall*.

The hole that shouldn't rightfully exist.

I took the mover back to the midships airlock. Searched the lockers, found a vac suit and a few extra air bladders. Considered using the big exit, but decided there was a smarter idea. Elsie wouldn't approve of what I was about to do. That bothered me.

Returning to the tech ring, I snugged into the suit. Donned the headgear and sealed it tight. Linked up the bladders into the oxygen line for good measure. Looked at the load balancer. Imagined its many lazy worlds. Questioned my sanity again.

*Arkadia would be a perfect escape from all this.*

A hard ball of ice settled in my gut.

*This is not escapable.*

I found the little airlock, and worked its controls, stymied by its requirement of a passcode. The borrowed digits *8801* were, for the first time, of no help.

I removed the helmet, leaned in close to the control display, considering the crew and their various levels of attentiveness. Decided that most of them didn't care enough about security to mind the little details. Shifting to squint at the display from an extreme angle, I crouched and bobbed until its button shapes were fully covered by glare from the overhead light. And there, at that angle, years of oil from repeated touches revealed the digits. I donned the helmet again and started trying combinations.

*7215…No luck.*

*2157…Not that either.*

*2751…Nothing.*

*2571…*

The panel unlocked.

After a moment of stupefied paralysis I hooked my suit to the tether cable, took a deep breath, and cycled the airlock. Vents in the antechamber began sucking the air into storage tanks.

My fob buzzed as a tiny speaker crackled to life. Lawrence was speaking from some distant corridor.

"What do you see in there, Maddie?"

"The ignition shell for engine three looks like it's had it. There's no way we're going to use this thing again without a real rebuild."

"Can you do it?" Frank was asking.

"No. Not safely. Best I can do is kill its fuel feed, stop it from lighting again. No telling *what* the hell else got messed up out here too. Gonna be a while, guys."

*Better to stay silent for now,* I thought.

When the door opened, I was, for the first time in a long time, face to face with barren emptiness. No cushions, no decimeter-thick poziglas, no strings of lights. It gaped, engulfed, and waited.

*Freck.*

The tech ring was wrapped around the base of the great spinning wheel. Its gravity was somewhat weaker than it would have been further out. The angle the meteorite had come in at meant going outside and climbing sideways along the ring wall until I reached the wound. The problem was, naturally, that I was on a spinning ring, with centrifugal force pressing me against the floor. This was playing a dangerous game with inertia; if I wasn't careful, the forces pushing me to the floor at the moment would send me cascading out into the void. The tether would save me, but it would be a mess I did *not* want to contemplate.

But I had to know. I had to be sure. Because although the math and perspectives of overlapping hulls and relative momentum made my head hurt, I was *damned* sure that the angle of the first hit was an impossible feat.

I gingerly leaned out of the hatchway, scanning the gloomy hull. Light from the sun reflected at an oblique angle, but this far out it was hardly a searingly bright presence.

Hefty bolts secured the outer hull into place, and they made for a pretty decent set of handholds. I slowly edged out with a death grip, straddling one bolt to the next, working my way around the side of the circle.

*Whatcha doing, buddy?* Came the unbidden thought.

I giggled a little. I'd worked in zero gee before, but this wasn't that. There was a *chasm*, a true bottomless pit below me as far as my mammalian brain was concerned. And I was clinging to a sheer cliff face with only a smattering of flat stumps to keep me anchored.

So far, it all looked normal. There was nothing suspicious about any of it.

As I continued around the ring, I looked up, craning my neck to peer around the ship's core. It loomed above, parts of it freely spinning from my perspective, while my wheel merrily stayed still. Six spokes ran out to the outer edge of the wheel; as I climbed around a huge pipe, I paused to take it in.

The pipe, or rather, the *artery*, was several meters in diameter, and ran straight out to one of the passenger blocks. I realized that it had to contain the transit shaft, plus a service tunnel, power, and other utilities. The block that it served was a tall, hulking chunk of plating clamped implacably against the wheel's outer cage.

"Paging Doctor Kaplan," Madison said over the fob's speaker, her voice echoing up to my ears.

"What did you find?" Lawrence's voice.

"Our little friend frecked more than the ignition shell. There's a few droplets of blue goop floating around in here. Could be oxygel. I can't see the source."

The fob was silent for a long moment.

Then Frank spoke again. "Could it have been leftover from Ceres?"

"Possible. Their dock techs aren't the best or brightest I've ever met."

That stung a little, but I silently agreed.

She continued. "…but if it isn't, best friend number two hit one of the tanks, we're gonna be in trouble."

I forced myself to stop visualizing all the different ways that meant the ship could explode, and *focus*. One ludicrously dangerous thing at a time, dammit.

The climb continued, until I reached the spot where I was sure the entry wound had to have been. I stared, inspecting the various lumps and pieces of plating, searching for it.

Nothing looked like a punched hole.

I started feeling around, and suddenly switched my attention to a different kind of thought process when a bulky surface extrusion lazily *flapped*, riveted metal wrinkling away at my touch.

*Now* that, I thought, *is suspicious.*

Beneath the dull shroud, a small, spider-like device was clamped into place. By a single…*leg*? I wrenched it free surprisingly easily, and spotted the telltale puncture hole underneath, now full of sealant.

For a fleeting second, vindication filled my bones.

The moment I'd processed what I was looking at, a small thruster on the machine's underside burst into life, propelling it away from the hull, taking me with it. I flipped and flailed, torn free of the handholds, and in the moment of sheer panic let the contraption fly loose as my hands scrambled for the tether.

The side of the ship drifted out of reach.

*Freck, oh freck, oh freck.*

Blood surged, pounding my ears as the void pulled me loose, breath coming hot and fast. Worse than the instinctive terror at spinning free of the ship was the sheer silence beyond the flimsy vacsuit. I was alone, and I was going to die.

Then the thin cable snagged at the end of its run, yanking me back in place, stopping my flight away from everything that could keep me alive.

It took a very long minute to stop hyperventilating.

When I did, and found the concentration to start climbing, hand over hand, along the tether back towards the hull, self-destructive frustration boiled.

Whatever that *thing* had been, it was clearly there in secret and it was just as clearly some kind of weapon, meant to disappear into the void once used. Untraceable, unpredictable, unprovable.

And I had just helped it vanish. Like some kind of idiot savant.

I stopped beating myself up as I realized that not *everything* was gone. The shroud that had covered the machine was still attached to the hull, caught on a *real* piece of superstructure.

I clawed up and over to it, gingerly retrieving the thing. This had been a weapon *planted* to cause a specific kind of damage. It was *meant* to blow up the sim. On command, at just the right moment, so that someone could lazily tie Jazaban's death to a more severe accident. And while they did their work, the suit would have kept him quiet, isolated, and helpless through every last heartbeat. The cowardice of it was infuriating.

"Wrap it up, Milo." Frank was saying through the fob. "Engine two looks safe, Madison. Wherever your blue goop came from, it's not here either. Would someone please go check on our guests up front?"

Elsie chimed in, more clearly than I had expected. "They're with me, Frank. Take your time back there."

I took that as my cue to finish up, and retraced my path back to the airlock. It was slow going with only one hand available, and I was a little more carefree than I should have been, but I had a purpose. I had *proof.*

That was a complicated question, I realized, because surely more than one such device had been strapped to the hull and used already. And if one was *here*, one was on the engines, then for all anyone knew the ship was infested. Reveal that knowledge to the wrong person and it was as good as zeroing myself then and there.

Handhold by handhold, I ticked names off my list.

I had to trust *someone* on the crew. Elsie was a genuine soul, near as I could tell. Madison I couldn't quite draw a line on, but she was nothing if not resourceful and up front about things. Then again, she was also a skilled engineer with a deep knowledge of the ship's workings and activities. If anyone would know how to invent a precision strike tool, it would be her.

Milo I didn't know. It could have been him, it could not have. I would need to introduce myself.

Which left the captain, who conveniently vanished moments before another calamity struck. Moments *after* being confronted with evidence of contraband.

The captain who had known his ship considerably longer than his engineer.

*That* line of thought left me puzzled as I reached the airlock. DeSanto—Frank—certainly would have had the know-how to install something like this, but he genuinely didn't seem like the kind of person to *attack* his own pride and joy. Unless it served his...what? His code? He certainly seemed like the type to follow a code.

It could have been Lawrence. Big, surly Lawrence. Who had expediently removed the victim after death.

As the doors sealed and air valves slowly cycled, repressurizing, I glanced up to the ceiling, and felt like a moron. A small, glassy dome looked back down at me, the telltale view of a camera.

*Freck.*

The inner door opened, and Elsie stood there, glaring at me.

"Aidan," Elsie said, "You're a damn fool."

"I can explain!" I said, waving up a hand to ward her off. "I was thinking about what you told me about the Apollo, about how her bow thing works. The shield. And then I was thinking about how everything was laid out, and I had a hunch."

I waved the piece of fabric at her, its printed illusion dull and unimpressive under the lights. "This was covering a thing, a gun, strapped to the outside of the hull. It was concealed so that you'd never notice it casually."

Elsie rocked back in disbelief. "A printed cloth? You went on a spacewalk and you're justifying it with a piece of *cloth?*"

"Uh," I paused. "No. Look, this thing, this *gun,* was perched *directly* over the penetration spot. The one that we came back here and fixed before. I think it caused it."

"A gun? A gun, strapped to the outside of my ship in the middle of deep vacuum. First you violate people's privacy and now you're coming up with lunacy like this. What the hell is wrong with you?"

"That's, uh, a different topic. I'm *not* making this up. This tarp is all that's left."

To her credit, she didn't *immediately* close the airlock on me. She closed her eyes, trying to be patient. "Let me see."

I handed it over. "Look at it. Tell me you aren't suspicious that this exists."

"Okay," she muttered, studying it. "Weird print. I'll give you that. So where's the gizmo itself?"

"Flying away out there." I replied lamely. "It tried to take me with it."

The pilot looked at me if as if her world had gone crazy. "Weapons. You're saying somebody strapped weapons to the outside of our ship, facing inwards, and *hid* them."

"Yes."

"Maddie's the only one qualified to go looking for them."

"Then she might have put them there. A perfect position to prey on people out here."

Elsie's hand reached up, slapped me, and *pointed*. "You're out of line. Maddie wouldn't have done anything like that. She just wouldn't. We'll wait for her to get back and then see what she thinks."

I nodded reluctantly. "Okay, then. Fine. If you're absolutely certain."

"I am. Let's go."

The mover took us back to the crew module dutifully, As I shimmied out of the vac suit, Elsie simmered, bundling it under her arm. I kept quiet.

We arrived at the deck three aft corridor. Galley to the left, stairs down to the fourth deck on the right. Elsie turned, and glared at me, jabbing me in the shoulder. "Wait *right* here. I'm going to put this suit away behind a *locked* door and I'm not showing you which one. You had better be here when I come back."

She went down the stairs.

Only a little repentant, I lingered for a minute. Then, as I heard trusted voices from the other direction, moved towards them. *I had seen it.* I had seen proof that Jazz hadn't simply been ended by an accident, or a glitch. He had been murdered during a carefully timed and planned diversion. Whatever else was at play, Tera deserved to know what I knew. Elsie's wrath could wait a little longer.

The lines of friendly plants and paintings guided me in towards the galley, where Tera and Jennifer went back and forth, voices indistinct. Anxiety rose with each step. I didn't *want* to have this conversation, but I absolutely *owed* it to her. Some things were just important.

A shadow moved at the corner of my vision, and I paused mid-stride to glance around.

Something hard *thwacked* me across the shoulders and I fell to the floor, stunned. I tried to get up, struggling, but was firmly pushed down, flat to the ground, the assailant's weight pinning my torso with such strength that even *breathing* was painful. The shout died in my throat as something metallic clicked against the back of my neck, and the sight of the galley's doorway washed into a blurry mess.

As the pressure on my back released, hopeful safety drifted farther and farther away.

I was being dragged coarsely, roughly, with little regard for my face as it scraped against the deck.

Nobody came to stop it.

I tried, one more time to shout, to call out, to summon help. Or even to roll over and see the attacker. But the drowsiness came flooding in. I fought it with every ounce of willpower.

There had never been a real chance against the chemical intruder pumping through my veins.

Thoughts fogged as my feet scraped over the mover's threshold.

My world dissolved.

I prayed that Jennifer would be all right.

# EIGHTEEN

Hard. Metal. Warm.

I came to, scrunched in a curled-up shape in pitch blackness, flat on the floor, a massive headache throbbing. I pushed upright, looking around, and banged my head on something hard, but yielding. I squashed bubbling panic, wishing that I had something on me more robust than a fob.

*The fob.*

I patted my pockets and came away disappointed. The little gadget was gone, and with it, an easy way to call for help.

I felt around, finding a tube encapsulating me. I pressed up against it with growing force, and when the seal gave way, shoved *hard.* It rolled off to one side, and a rush of cooler air met my face.

A lone cold light overhead glowed to life at the movement.

Whatever the *thing* was that I'd been hidden in, they had stuffed me in a damn closet. A hint of indignity swirled alongside the anger. They had meant to hide me, and silence me, and get me out of the way.

*They.*

Elsie had known what I'd found, and where, and had been right behind me before I'd gotten hit. But if she really had bashed me on the head and injected me with something, then I was a terrible judge of character.

There was no way I was going to stay put. The closet, unfortunately, was locked. I paused, old knowledge coming to the fore.

I knew locks. Archaic mechanical tumblers, biometrics, passcode pads, near-field hashkeys, even simple magnetic trap-latches. I'd met most of them at one time or another. But those had been on Ceres, where things like apartments and shopfronts were so commodified that if somebody or something was locked away during an emergency, it didn't matter to the station as a whole. People valued their privacy and protection more than their safety. Not so on a freighter like *Apollo*. Which meant that the lock here would be little more than a simple courtesy mechanism with a pass code or fob to release it.

I started feeling around, then pulling away the surface of the bulkhead behind where the bolt ought to have been. I could recount more than a few well-paid thrills facing down far more complicated obstacles than *this*.

The polymer lining beside the door gave way, coming free of its housing. As promised, the guts of the lock were laid bare in the wall cavity. I got to work on them.

My thoughts flashed back to the airlock camera. Somebody had gotten spooked. That much was clear. The thought brought a grim curve to my lips.

*Good.*

But whether I would be able to *do* anything about it was entirely dependent, I realized, on how long I'd been out. If it had only been a few hours, there was a chance that getting out would nudge the killer further off balance. But a whole day or two was a lot of time to frame *me* for everything. Tera herself had counted me as a suspect. That hurt, but even I could recognize the potential in that version of events.

The lock's electrical circuit finally collapsed, and I was free.

Outside, the hall was gloomy and deserted. A deep rumbling vibrated through the soles of my feet.

"Hello?" I called out. "Any of you pricks out here?"

There was no answer. A pipe spewed steam from a broken joint.

Arrows on the wall promised an exit to my right. I obeyed, hopeful that I'd be able to find something. I did.

Clutches of wiring hung loosely, dust layering their tops. A lone yellow light spun lazily on the ceiling. At the end of the corridor was a wall full of diagrams and blinking dots. The signage was different, more technical, the surfaces harder, and interior bulkheads outright missing or abnormally full of gaps. Valves and gauges dotted the tubes. A place for working, not for living. I did the math and decided I had to be near the engines. The back of the ship, where people didn't go regularly. The part of the ship which had just been damaged. The part of the ship which reportedly had highly explosive oxygel floating around.

*Not good.*

"Anybody back here?" I shouted.

The engines thrummed in reply. The bulkheads had nothing to say.

Pipes and heavy ductwork criss-crossed the passages, the apparent byproduct of years of low-budget fixes and half-baked retrofits. I jammed my foot on a box of spare screws, sending a shock radiating up my leg and eliciting a curse.

"It's a miracle any of this *works*," I muttered, ducking under a pipe before climbing *over* a clutch of cables strung across at knee height. A left turn, a right turn, a long saunter. When I'd climbed over the same duct three times, I realized that I was going in a loop, and started to explore the side nooks. One contained a box full of dusty noodles. Another was a small refresher, quietly and carefully preserved amidst the outer chaos.

I found the transit station squirreled away into a corner behind a corner within a nook beside a vast blue tank full of valves. Getting to it bore disturbing similarities to a universal pest; I was like a flea, scampering around the inner workings of monstrous machines of thrust.

Plans today did *not* include flea impersonation.

The mover descended into position, swishing open to spill a reassuring glow into the hostile clutter. Inside, I directed it back to the crew module's middle deck, and watched with relief as the door closed on the dark, cramped maze. The feeling of travelling back out of the ship's nether regions came with a feeling of relief...and of dread.

"Okay," I said, trying to pump up my spirits. "Hotels, diners, valleys, closets. I am *not* going to be buried away in some forgotten nook and ignored. Let's go. I haven't hit anybody in a long time, but I'm going to make an exception. Come on!"

The mover twisted as it arrived into the crew area, and slung itself downwards as rotational gravity re-asserted itself. "Okay," I said again. "Here we go. Here we go! Time to—"

The door slid to the side, revealing a pitch black chasm.

My enthusiasm for a confrontation died in my throat.

This wasn't right. This didn't make sense.

There was no party to interrupt, no casual scene to storm into.

"Hello" I called. "It's Aidan! Anyone out here? Jennifer?"

I paused, too long, for a reply. None came.

"What the hell is going on on this ship?"

The demand sounded cheap in my own ears.

The corridor held its secrets. Gathering my courage, I stepped out into the forbidding dark. One step. Two steps. Three.

On the fourth, emergency floods snapped on at the hall corners, bathing the corridor in an eerie pale green that left murky shadows crawling in the corners.

My breathing picked up as unsettled anxiety began to supplant everything else.

I gingerly took a left turn and side-stepped down the hall, finding my way to the galley. The heart of the crew's home.

It was deserted. More than that, it was packed up tight. No cupboards had been left ajar, all the little supply cabinets had been locked. Even the cushions were tidy.

*That's wrong,* I thought. *Something is very wrong.*

I went to the hologram controls on the central table, and tried to bring up the display. The controls came to life at my command but instead of the usual spinning illustration of the ship, the projectors just spat out a text message:

*Mister Whittaker,*
*We've left her safe and intact*
*Stay out of trouble and keep her that way*

Bits of floating dust glimmered in it, fuzzily drifting through.

I stared at the message, befuddled, trying to understand. A fog in my thoughts was making it hard to *think.*

A clanking sound echoed from a distant passage. I spun to face the door that led past the medical office and down to the fourth deck. Blackened gloom lay beyond it. I picked up a metal mug from the counter, an artifact of Madison's caffeine habit, and whacked it against the wall, creating an ominous clang of my own.

Whatever was down there, it stopped making noise. It could

wait.

The galley's three exits ringed its perimeter, making a hub for anyone coming or going. One to the mover, one to the medical office, and one towards the front of the ship. It was a good place to set up. I needed the lights on.

Having been through the first two exits often enough, I left through the third.

The front of deck three was one straight hallway, wrapping all the way around. A hydroponics bay, the captain's cabin, others that I couldn't make out. A chunky, circular door with a pill-shaped window at head level dominated the corridor. Deciding it had to be the bridge access, I leaned in against its smooth, metallic bulk and *shoved.*

It lazily opened, rolling to the side within the wall. Alarms rang in the back of my head.

*The bridge is unlocked. This has gone from unsettling to just plain wrong.*

Lights brightened a little with each footfall further inside. A stale *tang* drifted to my nose.

"Frank?" I called.

No reply.

As my eyes adjusted, and the overheads glowed, the bridge was gently revealed.

Four stations. Three split along the sides, one forward and in the middle. Heavy grating underfoot, with hundreds of cables running underneath. Cool blue accents. A wide window at the front gave my first unrestricted view of the nose spire, lancing out into the black far overhead. The sun, a distant, glimmering ball of white gold, gleamed in at an angle.

I sat at the forward station, creaking its stiff padding. Staring out at that inky, everlasting emptiness, a shiver ran across my skin, and a shudder followed. Even by the standards I had endured this was too damned weird.

A smile crept across my face despite myself. I was on the edge of a plan. It began and ended with the phrase, *I've had enough of this gods-damned ship.*

I made myself focus on the spread of controls before me. It would be best to not break things.

I'd never flown a ship. Never been in front of controls like these. But certain things tended to be *known* through sheer cultural osmosis, and even I could tell that the levers on the right side of the panel meant these were flight controls. That meant…

*The conn,* I thought. *This is called the conn.*

This was Elsie's station.

Elsie, being the pilot, would need to have an overview of everything at all times. This station would be a good tool.

*Just don't break anything.*

I tapped at a few buttons, and a transparent sheet lit up in front of me with a swirl of color, resolving into coherent text and shapes. Deciphering the interface, I found a messages queue, but it was empty.

Disappointing.

Searching further bore some fruit, and with some trial and error a status view replaced the empty inbox, scanning the ship's condition. My gut tightened as the results were rendered in cold light.

Power draw was minimal across the ship. Engineering was spiking erratically, but not triggering any warnings. The gravity systems, too, were managing normally. Life support, again, normal. But as I watched, there were no spikes, no twitches, and no indication of liveliness.

*Where the hell* is *everyone?*

I tabbed over to a different view, one that overlaid power draws across a map of the ship, and frowned.

The crew module was dark, with barely any draw at all outside of the bridge deck. The main core was a steady amber, likely evidence of the big rotational motors doing their work.

The second cargo wheel was more intriguing; block four was a bright green blaze on a sea of dim ochre outlines. I made a mental note to explore it.

A quick, but mildly accidental flourish of the controls brought up a quick actions menu, and from there it was straightforward to accomplish my original task. The pale, sickly greens vanished, replaced by friendlier, more normal lighting within a handful of heartbeats.

I sighed with relief. It was the little victories that counted.

Now I needed to know what was going on.

With some experience using the interface under my belt, it was easier to explore the different functions. The power readouts were replaced by a journey progress view identical to the one projected onto Selena's window, with a flight path charted across a twinkling backdrop.

Then I realized what the display was actually showing me, and froze.

*Impossible.*

I refreshed the display, hoping it was some kind of mistake.

*Two and a half months.*

*I've been blacked out for nearly eighty sols.*

*How the hell am I still alive?*

The indicator said that arrival at Luna was only twenty-eight sols away, far less than the hundred-plus I'd thought we'd had before us. It seemed impossible. The excursion in hard vacuum felt like it had only been minutes earlier. What had *happened?* What had I *missed?*

How long had this chair been empty?

The questions mounted too fast to count them.

Where was Jennifer? Or Tera? Plugged back into the sim world, believing me long since zeroed?

If I went through the crew cabins, one by one, what would I find? Corpses? Or worse, empty dioramas left over by a killer that had roamed the ship, one at a time, disposing of each inquisitive soul as they started putting pieces together?

A vision flared, of one little farewell ceremony after another, each member of the crew turned to dust until only the captain himself remained, a broken recluse living alone with hundreds of silent, unaware and unprotected passengers available for his whims.

The prospect was beyond grim.

I shook my head, and stood, refusing to entertain it, retracing my steps to the door. I leaned on it, a tingling growing in my hands, and felt lightheaded, even nauseous. Something, deep in my gut, felt *wrong,*

I found a broadcast panel. Thumbed it on. Spoke aloud, hearing my voice echo back from the corridor.

"This is Aidan on the bridge, calling literally goddamn anyone."

I wished for a change. Hoped the gods would pay attention. But this time, for better or worse, I was expecting it when nothing but silence came back.

*Think, dammit. Two and a half months, gone.*

Jennifer was the priority. I had to find out what had happened to her. I went to leave, reaching out to pull the door closed from its slot in the bulkheads, wondering what the hell to do. In eleven weeks, anything could have happened. For all I knew, I was the last survivor aboard a ghost ship. There wasn't even a *hint* of what to do with myself.

*I could go back inside.*

It was unbidden, but tempting, in a way. The ship was safe. It was secure. The best way to not break anything was to go right back into CarverNet.

In a little box. In a pod. Strapped into a suit that presented its occupant for a lazy, effortless murder.

It would be giving up.

It would mean walking away from whatever had happened here, with no guarantee of coming back out.

*At least it would be fun.*

Then, as my head gradually cleared, and my breathing slowed back to a normal place, I felt it.

At first I put it down to the threat of a panic attack. Enough of those had come and gone for their symptoms to become familiar.

But something niggled.

I looked down at my hand, then up at the door, and withdrew my fingers, then grasped it again. A preposterous thought slowly coalesced.

A tiny tingle was dancing on my skin.

It could have been a mislaid electrical ground. It *could* have been an injury.

Both were wrong.

I *knew*, without any proof at all.

*I'm in a sim.*

It was the same tingle that *CarverNet* gave when a participant's hands were ready to use an imaginary control. The same tingle I'd experienced countless times in as many places, from a tankard of mead to flexing a wingsuit. It was so ingrained, so familiar, that it hadn't even felt *weird*.

I slowly, dementedly, started chuckling.

This *was* a sim. But not CarverNet. Not as I knew it.

This was some kind of training tool. A private version of the Apollo, faithfully, perhaps artistically laid out, for crew members to play out scenarios.

It was a *game*.

I left the bridge, walking more assuredly.

In proper context, the empty halls put a whole different framing on what I was seeing. Nobody was answering because there was *nobody else here*.

And the more I looked, the more I realized that it was a more generic version of the ship. As I rounded the passage, the telltale spray painting on what had been Raj's cabin was nowhere to be seen. Gone too were the dainty lights and paintings that Elsie had added.

It was a version of the ship that had never been occupied by those people.

Immediate priority was to get out.

But I had two problems. First, the only world-breaking exploit which I knew about couldn't work with just one person. And the second, which I confirmed after several seconds of experimentation, was that I had no equivalent of the CarverNet Index. No interface to tell the machine to release me. At first that seemed unfair, but then I realized that it actually made a depressing amount of sense. There was, I admitted, a tiny chance that I was deluding myself.

The message in the galley, at least, made more sense now. It wasn't a helpful, snarky note. It was a warning.

*Stay out of trouble and keep her that way.*

The possibilities were all ugly.

The whole crew had seen Tera by now. Madison and Frank had both seen Jennifer and had clocked that she meant something to me. Elsie wouldn't have been far behind on that uptake either.

I dismissed that last idea. She wasn't that kind of person.

What in the stars had Jazz *done* to earn being murdered in total isolation?

There were no answers. None would be forthcoming here.

Block four was considerably bigger on the inside than the passenger blocks. Two levels tall, floor to ceiling cargo containers nestled and bracketed into a vast steel superstructure. Some were red, others green, most white.

The lights were up full, which made for a happy change. Soft music echoed from somewhere around the curve.

*Lots of good stuff in these*, I thought, *forgotten and locked away for months on end. Like me, if I don't break out.*

"Hello?" I called, climbing up the big metal frames to see around the bulky blocks. My voice started going deranged. "Anyone waiting up here? Any plots? Quests? Menial shit to put me through?"

At first, there was nothing.

Then came a snarl. And *something* clanked out, nails tapping *hard* against an unseen floor.

*What.*

I backed away, slowly, returning to the mover. The controls to bring it to life couldn't unlock fast enough. I was only two taps in when an idle snuffle came from behind, and my arm involuntarily seized up.

I turned, slowly, gingerly, eyeing a four-legged creature slowly stalking forward, pointy jaws bared, fierce teeth beneath a long snout and thick, matted fur from eyes to tail.

It was hideously alien.

The slow snuffle became a *snarl.*

"Hey hey, hey! Easy!" I said, blood pumping, holding out a hand to try to calm it. I'd met a *dog* once before, but nothing like *this.*

The beast sauntered, tilting its head as if evaluating me. I flicked my eyes to the control panel, and that was enough for the creature to decide that I was prey. It leapt forward, jaws opening wide. Teeth sunk into my hand, and two fingers disappeared behind them, torn free into its gullet.

I cried out, flailing, trying to hit it in the head. When a weak blow connected, its jaws opened a fraction, and I yanked my bleeding, torn limb free, scrambling backwards into the mover. The beast started forward again, savoring its time, *knowing* I was weak.

I stumbled back, slapping the control panel. The mover door slid shut to the sound of satisfied crunching.

I held up my mutilated hand, the stinging static of blood stumps etching itself across my psyche.

*I've had enough. I've had* beyond *enough.*

The wound stung with an *agonizing* edge. The bite was deep, with bone and muscle torn raggedly and deep gouges raking everything that had survived.

Breathing. Fast, hard. Too much. Too heavy.

*Please, please don't be real.*

Through clenched teeth, I used my good hand to tell the machine to abandon the creature and take me back to safe territory.

This was bad. This was *mean.*

If my belief in a sim world was wrong, the next part was *really* going to suck.

As the door slid open onto the crew deck, I made my way to the medical office, sucking in air as the wound raged. Inside I thrashed around, hoping there would be a tool, or a stim, or something handy which Lawrence might have used. Although there was an examination table, and cupboards, and what looked like an injector in a red container with a big white cross on it, the instructions were gibberish.

The wounded arm refused to stop throbbing long enough for me to think clearly.

*Just make the pain stop.*

I glared at the instructions through the stings, threw caution aside, and pressed the tool to my arm. With a squeeze and a hiss, screaming nerves quieted, cooling goodness flooding through my body.

Blinking away the adrenaline haze, I inspected my hand as well as I could, knuckle bones glistening under putrid shreds of skin. It felt real. It *looked* real.

Around bends and passageways came the unlikely sound of the mover door swishing open.

With it, the lights dimmed again, reverting to that grim pale green.

"What the hell *is* this?" I giggled, delirium edging out the fear.

A quiet, cold, growl was all that came back.

*No.*

Nevermind the improbability of it. Disregard the sheer absurdity of what I was pretty sure was a *wolf.*

It was here. And its claws were tapping out a methodical beat.

The raw panic soared through my mind. I retreated as fast as I could manage. From here, the only way to go was down. The medical office was stashed towards the aft end of the third deck, and just behind it stairs left down to the fourth, which only had the one central corridor. My progress was an ugly recreation of my arrival in the crew module days before. Across from where those aft stairs met the lower deck, another set led back upwards, towards the front of the ship. I eyed it, adrenaline surging, and made a split-second decision. Bolting right, I ran for the workshop two doors down.

Crashing echoed from above as the wolf found the galley. I kept going, scrabbling along, suddenly seeing the trail of bloody droplets in my wake.

Tools were available, laid out on the bench with precision. I grabbed a pressure wrench and reversed course.

As I returned to the four-way junction a harsh *clank* rang out behind me. Then it rang out again, and again. Mechanically approaching.

I spun, brandishing the wrench with my good hand. "Come on! Try me!"

Thirty feet away, the pale lights ended in a wall of inky dark. At first, only the metallic glimmers of flooring and doors glinted in the dark.

Two of those glimmers blinked.

*Freck this.*

I bolted for the stairway leading to the front of the ship. I burst out into the forward corridor, picking a direction and running.

*There.* The bridge door in its stupid round glory was there, half-open and waiting. I kept going, a plan for sanctuary forming—

And stumbled to a stop.

Beyond the bridge, the wolf waited, center of the passage, watching me with that evil tilt of the head.

I made a decision. Bolted for the opening.

The wolf reacted, charging me. It moved a *lot* faster than I thought possible.

I scrambled, moving my legs as quickly as I could, holding the wrench aloft. My eyes seized on the promise of safety. Time slowed as senses heightened. I *heard* it bearing down on me, sniffing, snarling growls of anticipation rumbling out of its gullet.

It was close.

Closer.

*Close enough.*

Jowls pulled back as it sought another bite.

And I was through the door.

It was overwhelmingly fast. But I didn't have to move, I just had to *pull.*

I could feel its breath as the heavy blast door *clonked* into place.

A split second later a heavy *thud* rang through.

I locked it.

Made *extra*-sure it was locked.

I slumped against it, eying the bridge, having absolutely no idea what to do. The beast, hurt though it was, let out a heavy howl that resonated through the plating, and something started *thumping* against the door. Gentler at first, then more firmly, more intently.

Crushing. *Bashing.*

Ideas of a sim were forgotten.

Plans for survival didn't matter.

Broken illusions and death were the only things out here, and there was no escaping it.

This was beyond sanity. And I was *done.* I didn't know how to fight that thing. It was capable of *ending* me and it *would not stop.*

*Thump.*

The thought flashed through my mind, cold and pure.

*What if it* can *end me?*

I got up, sucking in air, looking out at the window before me, at the conn, at the distant sun. I waved one half-destroyed hand at it, and would have flipped it off if I'd still had the finger. An insane tingle stabbed across my thoughts. I burst into uncertain chuckles.

Another *thump.*

A little thing, so far, so very far away, its brilliant gleam dulled by distance and space dust and the poziglas. A shudder ran down my spine.

This wasn't a game. This was how they got rid of me.

A grate at the front of bridge, behind the conn, twitched, metal scraping as it moved. And then the sniffing. The wet, intent sniffing, that snarled as it found my scent.

It was inside.

My legs turned, my arms reached for the door, and fled.

Or at least, I tried to. The big bridge door was locked.

A claw scraped as the end approached.

The big latch gave way, but my one good hand had the force of weak jelly, and the door barely budged.

Another *snarl*. Louder. Closer.

The gap wasn't big enough.

Hot, wet breath on my calves.

And finally, without any reservation or defense, there was *liberation*.

I gave in, collapsing in deranged giggles as unreality faded to a crushing, sucking black.

# NINETEEN

The mask was pulled from my head without grace. A woman's voice echoed from somewhere. Intent. Anxious. "Freck, freck, oh freck."

A rush of cold stinging air. Nerves pricked up as the skin-tight silicone loosened away and limbs regained both mass and control.

I blinked, bleary, still clammy as the adrenaline faded. "Jen?"

"She's safe," Madison said, her words clearer now. "I've got her with the others. Are you okay?"

I was lost for words. There were so many.

None of them fit together.

"No…" was all I could get out.

I tried to stand up, ripping away from the tethers. I was ready for the flimsy limbs and fuzzy sensations, but the shift wasn't any easier on my eyes. "That was a gods-damned nightmare."

Madison helped steady me. "You're out, now. You're out. You're all right."

I flexed my arm. "There was this *thing,* a wolf, I think, and it could use the movers and it was hunting me, and everyone had disappeared…I knew it was a sim, I *knew* it, but it got to me." I trailed off as her eyes moved quickly at my words, her head nodding slowly, worried. She pulled me over to a small console beside the cradle that had supported my trapped body.

"Look at this. You were in a real shitshow. You've got *all* the complications switched on. Alone in the dark, random start, hibernation start, canine cargo, delayed fireball countdown, and… *oh*." Disgust dripped from her words. "Look at this. Aggressor intelligence, injury persistence, tactility scaling, it's all been maxed. Who did this? Did you *see* who did this?"

I blinked, shook my head, felt discordant shame turn to anger as I scanned the readout.

"This thing frecked with my head."

Madison started to shake her head but stopped partway through. "Your friends are safe. I promise. But you're kind of right. It's a psych tool. It's meant to test everyone's mettle and suitability for long, lonely flights where things can go wrong, help you develop coping strategies. Look," she pulled up logs from past runs, each tailored to a crew member. Certain scenarios were brought in and left out, different modifiers were higher than others. I got control of my breathing long enough to focus on Lawrence's last session, dated half a year earlier, featuring the same challenges I'd faced. His wolf had boasted only modest intelligence.

I looked at her, then back at the screen. Wanted to curl up in a corner and hide. "I don't know what I'm doing here. I genuinely don't."

"Well, you weren't *supposed* to be *here*."

"Yeah." I swallowed. The words started coming out in a rush. "I'm supposed to be a happy kid having a fresh start, not dealing with shit like this. I'm supposed to be able to do this *right*, be…" I lashed out, punching the cradle. "A friend of mine is *dead* and this *thing* is here, punishing me for trying to do anything about it. I'm just, I don't know why I'm here and I think it's time for me to go. I can do that. I can get out of this and I want to do that right now."

Madison watched me ramble, pursing her lips, and slowly shook her head.

"What?" I asked.

"This is disappointing."

It was my turn to be silent.

She put hands on my shoulders, steadying me. "Whatever life you're trying to escape to, it's not coming back. Your buddy is a cloud of ice crystals about a hundred thousand kilometers away. *He's* not coming back. Somebody put you in that machine and they meant to leave you there. It was *lucky* that I heard you. You have to be your genuine self, right here and right now. Nothing else matters. Do you get it?"

I blinked past a bleary, wet haze in my eyes. A lump was in my throat. "I don't want to do that. I don't want to be who I was."

She pulled me forward, touching her forehead to mine. It was a weird, but also weirdly affectionate gesture. "Aidan," she said with deliberate calm, "tough shit."

It was a long moment of incredulity, peppered with defiance and laced with an icy calm.

I wanted to shout at her. I wanted to argue, I wanted to bargain for a way out of what was coming.

*Enough,* said a little voice in the back of the tempest. *Enough.*

I pulled back, blinking away the haze. "I am starting to get angry."

"That's better."

"How long have I been here?"

"The sim was running for two hours."

"*Hours?*"

"Of the regular Earth kind, yes." Something indecipherable

crossed her face. "At first, we didn't come looking. Elsie brought me a tarp, told me what you'd found while extra-vehicular. I would tell you that was spectacularly stupid, but I doubt you'd listen." She leveled unimpressed eyes at me, but a small hint of a grin quirked at her lips.

"And the tarp?" I asked.

"Nothing like it should be on my ship. But I remember plenty like them from the port on Ceres. There are not a lot of conclusions to draw from that, but it means that somebody was in a rush. They were improvising when they covered up…well, a gimbaled railgun, is my guess." She held up the shiny ball bearing, recovered from the destroyed load balancer hours before. "It's the right kind of ammunition, it's sneaky, and there could be dozens of them on the hull. So I took the tarp to Frank. He's the captain, and the captain gets to decide how to handle a problem with his crew. Then *you're* nowhere to be found, Elsie throws a fit, and we're out searching for you."

I grimaced. Flashed back to the device that had rocketed away into the dark. The memory was fuzzy and had only lasted a moment, but I was gratified that her hypothetical was so close to mine. The prospect of a hundred such spider guns being lined up, ready to fire on command and end any one of us, grated. It wasn't the lethal threat of the thing, I realized. It was the *cowardliness* of it. The uncaring, unconcerned, unpreventable *intent*.

*We're waiting to be slaughtered.*

*So why haven't they been used?*

Then something clicked. Another spider gun *had* been used, on the engines, just before I had decided to go exploring. Just *after* contraband pelarite had been found.

"So," I said, working through it a little further. "These railguns. They can clearly kill something. Why stop at putting me in a sim?

If we could all be killed, why not do it?"

The answer crystallized even as I said it. *Because you weren't marked to die. You just got in the way.*

Madison nodded. "Some kind of code of honor bullshit, I'm sure."

I coughed, and massaged my virtually-eaten fingers fervently. "We have to stop this."

Her expression darkened. "I have a monster in my home and the list of candidates is not very long. Let's get back to the others."

My shoulders shrugged off the weariness and anxiety as best they could. A phantom ache pulsed through my hand.

"Where are we?"

"Deck two. Behind central storage."

"Right."

I scanned around for my clothes, but gave up. They might as well have been thrown out an airlock. The sim suit would do.

*Fine.*

The door beckoned. We left the training room behind and immediately came face-to-face with rows of metal cages, filled to the brim with spare parts. I knew this place. We had visited it long before, when I had blithely volunteered to hold a wrench or two. The transit alcove awaited on the far side. We walked briskly.

"You were all down, investigating the engines before." I said. "How did it look?"

"Bad."

Once in the mover I punched in the unlock code with a manic fervor. My rescuer raised an eyebrow, but remained quiet. Sensing that time for telling me to mind my own business was thoroughly gone, I worked the controls to bring us down to the habitation decks.

My fingers froze millimeters from the last button as Madison's fob crackled to life. The audio was tinny, distant, as if being recorded from across a room, but the words could just be made out.

A firm, gravelly tone came through. "You son of a bitch. The hell are you thinking? The hell are you *doing?*"

The response was an unfamiliar, singsong-y lilt. "What I *need* to be doing, Captain."

"Don't give me any of that shit. This is *my* ship, and I won't have you threaten *my* people like this."

The second voice turned dark. "Do *not* forget your arrangements, Franklin."

"Okay, so explain it to me: what in the whole goddamned solar system makes you think you have the right to tell me what to do?"

*Milo?* I mouthed. Madison said nothing, her face a mask. The singsong tone returned.

"The family has taken quite a risk investing in your services. Our product pays quite handsomely, and in addition to your share we are *entitled* to your generosity and accommodation."

"My *generosity? Freck* the Seomuns and freck your product. You were supposed to be an idle *drifter*. Pick up, live with you for a trip, drop off, never see again. Nobody said anything about any of *this.*"

"My remit expanded just before we left the station. His presence aboard was not anticipated."

I looked up at Madison, whispered, "Who are they talking about?"

She looked back angrily, shaking her head.

The distant argument continued as the captain barked back his reply. "I don't give a shit. This stops, all of it, right now."

"Put your other guests back to bed, Franklin, and nothing further will *need* to happen. It will be smooth. We'll have an understanding."

There was the sound of a door closing, and footsteps. Then the speaker stopped transmitting.

"I don't get it," I said after a long moment of mutual silence. "Why would they broadcast that?"

She breathed back, "That was Frank. *Frank* was broadcasting that."

"But why? You heard it. He's part of this."

Something tightened in her eyes. "He didn't know if he'd be able to tell me in person." She reached past me and pushed the onscreen button. "We need to go close this down *now*."

"Madison," I asked slowly, and with a non-too-convincing calm, "Would Frank know where *my* people are?"

"He does. Which is why we need to *stop all of this, now*."

"We need to get everyone safe *first*."

"Safe from *what?*" She leveled an incredulous glare at me. "We've covered this. Nowhere on the ship is safe right now. If you want to keep your friends *safe*, we need get to the man telling the *captain* what to do."

I shook my head. "Where are my people?"

"Raj's old cabin."

"Fine. Then when this door opens, you go for Frank, I'll go for them."

"If you've got to do it that way, then do that," she said, a fire growing in her words.

"I have to," I said. "They come first."

As the mover slowed to a stop, a pleasant little chime sounded, and the door slid to the side, opening onto a murderous shout echoing in from around the bend.

"—of a bitch! *You?*"

There was a dull thudding sound and a gasping moan.

We reached the galley door and pressed ourselves to the sides of the corridor, peering inside without interrupting. Frank was clutching his gut, leaning against the table. Lawrence was towering over him. Elsie was behind him, against the wall of food lockers. The entrance opposite ours contained a figure I guessed to be Milo, and with some twisted sense of relief, Jennifer and Tera as well, lingering out of the light. I made eye contact with them, making a gesture to get to us but quietly. Tera tilted her head at me ambivalently. Jennifer ignored the whole exchange.

"Did you kill that kid?" Lawrence roared, stealing attention back to himself. "Own up to what you did!"

"Now, now, doctor," A smooth lilt, now clearly Ceresian in origin, spoke from an unseen corner. "I'm worried you will have the wrong impression of the good captain. Let's get out in front of this: He's guilty of plenty, but he's not a *killer*. A distinction *I* can't rightly claim."

Lawrence slowly turned, incredulous, advancing on the smaller man. His fists loomed, each with the bulk of a ham. Ricky stepped into view, smirking, a bundle of energy, shifting and bouncing on his heels. His voice was loose, unrestrained, sing-song. "Come on, big guy. Don't tell me you don't like it."

The doctor swung a heavy arm, but hit only air as Ricky lithely twisted to the side, creating a void. Another punch was thrown. Another miss.

Lawrence lunged forward, blind rage clouding his focus, but barreled into the counter as his target swirled, planting himself beside the big man's bulk. As the doctor stumbled, something flashed in Ricky's hand.

Madison shouted out, "Lawrence, move!"

But the doctor was more startled by the warning than able to heed it. Ricky pirouetted, jabbing a loose fist into the big man's lower back, before plunging an injector in after it, and deftly pulled away before spinning back around to resoundingly kick the collapsing doctor into the wall face-first.

Lawrence impacted with a crunch, unconscious before he hit the floor.

A lot of things happened all at once.

Frank straightened, wheezing, and charged at Ricky, but the Ceresian was faster. A smirk and a straight punch to the left temple sent the captain tumbling, sputtering. Madison barreled into the galley, a fire raging in her eyes.

I hung back, out of sight. This was going badly. Across the way, Jennifer did the same. I approved.

A heartbeat later Tera was striding forward into view with a piece of pipe clutched in her hand. From her spot at the table Elsie ran to Frank's dazed side.

And then the tableau froze in place as Ricky held up another device. Unfamiliar, but freakishly simple to comprehend. A small grip with a trigger and a tiny display on top. It looked like a strange little weapon, but the longer I looked at it, the more I understood. This was his weapon. This was the tool for calling on instant, invisible death.

The smirk was infuriating. He knew that he owned the room.

"Now, now," he deadpanned. "Let's not get all hasty. Nobody here has been given a sanction and I have no desire to end *any* of you, yet I *will kill every soul in this room* if you don't all just settle down."

"You killed Corben!" Tera shouted, the words strangled, finally having had enough.

*Corben?*

Ricky was pleased. "Yes, that's *exactly* right! He was soothingly quiet when he went. I wouldn't try it!" he intoned, voice taking on a deadly calm. "I have two railguns facing this room and I can target them on command. You'll have a slug through your chest in milliseconds. Not long after that, you'll be breathing vacuum. Am I clear?"

Tera hurled her pipe at him. To her credit, it was well-aimed, and though he swiveled his torso to avoid it, the impact still struck the hand clutching the trigger. It sent him off balance, but he was quick. With several rapid steps backwards, he yanked Elsie up with fierce strength. She grabbed the nearest thing, a multi-pack of cyberfish, and smacked him with it, but the attack didn't even register as he pulled her into a one-armed choking hold.

The room slowed again.

"Ricardo," Madison said very slowly and carefully. "Don't do this. You've already done enough. It's just us here. Nobody outside this room knows who you are. What are you going to do? Barricade yourself in a closet for three months?"

"Freck that," Tera snarled. "I'm going to *end* you."

The retreating figure had reached the far exit. "That *is* a good point, Maddie. But the question is are *you* all going to listen to reason? I'm inclined to think otherwise."

From his prone position on the floor, Frank kicked out a leg. It connected with Ricky's shin, but didn't knock him over.

The assassin shook his head. "Please don't. I rather liked you, Franklin." His face contorted then, tinged with dismay. But it was gone just as fast, replaced by a mighty smirk, and with a last step he yanked his captive backwards out of the galley. Turning back at us, keeping her struggling form sedately wrapped in his left arm, he held his right aloft.

The trigger gleamed.

*He wouldn't,* I thought, staring fiercely at it. I locked eyes with Jennifer, and frantically making a get-out-of-here gesture.

*He won't. He can't.*

Ricky stared at Madison, and Madison stared at him, something unspoken passing between them. And he squeezed the trigger.

For a long fraction of a second, nothing happened.

Then it did.

A tiny hole burst through the floor, punching through into the ceiling and beyond. Air sucked through it with fierce momentum.

Nearly instantly, a vacuum alarm sounded, emergency lights started flashing, and a familiar two-tone voice enunciated a terrible message.

*"Transverse impact alert. Pressure loss detected, decks two, three, and four. Central storage, galley, and living corridor are affected. Evacuate to safe areas immediately. Pressure seals will engage in three seconds."*

Ricky was gone. And Elsie with him.

"Get out! Out! Now!" Madison shouted frantically. I leapt forward, gusted by the swirling, escaping atmosphere, crossing the distance to the table and throwing an arm around Frank. As we struggled towards the exit, I saw Tera go for Lawrence, while Madison grabbed a chair and shoved it into one of the doorways. The other two hatches slid shut, one after another, but the last one, our own entry point, clanged against the chair. Wind rushed from the outer hallway as Frank scrambled feebly through the gap.

Another *slam* echoed from beyond as I helped Tera drag Lawrence's bulk out to safety, and the wind slowed. My arms strained at the heft, acutely conscious that the easing tempest was just a pleasant sign of impending suffocation.

And then Madison was *there* again. With the extra hands we had the doctor moving across the threshold, and then finally beyond it. Tera was last out, and pulled the chair free. It clattered to the deck as the hatch sealed.

The exodus of air ceased.

For a long, long minute, we sat there, collapsed against the bulkheads, gasping in the thin oxygen. I fought to keep calm. To know what I was doing. To do what had to be done next. I went to the doctor.

"He's breathing." I reported between overwrought breaths.

"He's out cold." Madison said. "I don't know what the hell was in that syringe. I need to get him to the med room."

"If it's the same," I wheezed, "that I was stuck with, he'll be awake in an hour."

"Let's hope it's only that long." She looked around at the three of us. "This is insanely bad."

Frank cleared his throat. "You're more right than you know."

We all looked at him.

He locked eyes with his engineer. "He'll take the bridge, and then start coercing us into submission. One by one, until we're no longer a threat. It's their way." He grunted, rubbing his throat where it was starting to bruise. "The little prick is enhanced. Should have guessed."

"*Who's* way?" Madison asked.

"The Seomun family. He's one of theirs. They twisted my arm into letting him on board for the duration."

"What does he have on you? We heard your broadcast."

He shook his head. "He thinks he owns me. The engine hit was the same thing. I tried to control him, and he thinks he can punish me."

"Because you're a smuggler." Madison's tone was frigid as she put the pieces together.

He pointed at her. "I will make no apologies for that."

The look between them could have shattered ice.

"Not today," Madison finally said. "Fine. But you *will* explain yourself to me, to the rest of us, and to these two when this is all over."

The captain coughed weakly. "We'll get there when we get there. Ricky's already got the bridge by now. We need to move, get somewhere else, before he starts holding us at gunpoint."

"We *need* to get to Jennifer." I said.

"Plus one from me," Tera muttered. "Jen's a thinker, not a fighter. Ricky could tear her in half."

"She's with Milo, she'll be safe," Frank said. "And Ricky won't care about her."

"*We* care about her," I said flatly.

"I'm going to kill him," Tera muttered.

Madison growled out her words. "That's fine in my book. But we have to *get* to him first. *And* overpower him."

"Are you hiding an exosuit or web stunner somewhere?" I asked pointedly.

"No. But we have to do it, and we have to get out of *here* first."

Frank grunted in agreement and stood up, limping to the emergency bulkhead sealing the other end of our little piece of hallway. He popped open a little panel in the floor, digging around for a manual release. A few moments later, he appeared to find it, and slowly heaved, lifting the heavy plate up until it allowed half a meter of clearance. Tera wasted no time crawling through. We lugged Lawrence's limp form under the creaking, straining metal, until it was just Frank left.

From the other side, Madison and I took over the lifting duties. When the hefty load was in our hands, Frank released it, and slowly shimmied under feet-first.

The bulkhead was heavy. *Very heavy.*

The captain's torso was coming into view.

A tiny voice in my mind wondered what his life's path had cost him to get him here. He had tried to look out for his people. I decided that earned a little more patience to hear him out.

Then his head cleared the gap, and we let the big door *clunk* back into place.

The new surroundings were an improvement. Potted plants and strung-up lights framed a mural, and opposite it, the mover patiently waited. Around the corner lay stairs down to the lowest level, and we tried to go that way, but were immediately blocked by more spinning lights and a newly-formed wall slammed tightly across the lowest step.

We were trapped.

"Well, shit." Tera said.

"That hit must have turned part of the hallway into hard vac. Deadly if anyone was in there." Madison said grimly.

"What now?" I asked.

"Service tunnels?" Frank asked.

"Service tunnels." Madison agreed.

"What tunnels?" Tera asked.

"The transit shafts are pressurized." The engineer explained. "Aidan crawled through one to get to us before. We're on deck three. The shaft over there doesn't go down to deck four. Underneath the mover capsule there's a big hatch that opens into the tween-deck crawl space. It's all about utilities, power, water, data, pneumatics. It's a crawl but we could get where we need to go."

Tera sat on the steps beside Lawrence's unconscious form, examining him. "Go do whatever. I'll wait with the big guy. He tried. He actually tried. Didn't hesitate for even a second."

Madison led Frank and I back up the stairs to the transit access. With a tap on its panel its door slid to the side, the lights brimming with a friendly glow.

The machine's lights and control panel abruptly died.

"Excuse me, folks!"

The smooth lilt came over a hidden intercom.

"I'm afraid this is my command now, and while under my authority no crew member will be authorised to use the transit system. But it's hardly a permanent rule, my friends!" Ricky mused. "I rather feel like you all have a choice to make. Submit, acknowledge my, eh heh, *diplomatic* immunity, and remain pacifistic for the remainder of this trip, or I can force you, with my own hands, into a sim chamber where you can wait out your life in isolation at my mercy."

The transmission ended, but then quickly added an afterthought:

"Or I can just kill you."

I locked eyes with Madison.

She was *furious*.

"Come on." Her voice was taut. "There's another way in." She led us away from the pod and knelt down, counting floor panels in the dim scene. "If he doesn't want to let us have *our* ship, then we'll take it apart."

On the third panel in from the edge, the engineer pulled out a small tool from her belt and started wedging it into the edges, prying the piece of flooring loose. Frank tilted his head as we watched.

"Maddie," he said, "We'll still need a ship to live in afterwards."

"You gave up your rights to it, Frank. I'm doing this."

She finished her efforts and the panel came away, clattering as it was discarded.

In the void it left behind, broad enough for a small person to fit through, a dense nest of wires and soft tubing waited.

Madison screwed up her arm into a fist, and started punching the cords away, knocking them loose from mountings and cable ties. One swing after another, until she finally gave up, straightened, and *hopped*, bringing her feet down and tearing through into a more sizeable void beyond.

A line of emergency guide lights died with the impact. It was disconcerting to wonder what else had just been terminated.

The engineer's head poked back up through the gap then, mussed and covered in oily grime. With a click of her tool, a tiny little light blazed out into the corridor, first onto Frank's resigned face and then onto me.

"Lawrence isn't going to fit through that." I said, eyeing the hole.

"Fit through *what*?" Tera called up from the steps.

"Madison's taking apart the ship."

"Oh, good."

"It's tight in here," the engineer said, slithering down into the hole. "But we can get through the walls. I just need to…" She felt around. "Yes, okay. Storage four-two should be through these. Give me a couple minutes."

Frank leaned back on the wall, out of the way, and sighed, looking at me.

"I'm sorry, kid. This is a whole lot more than you should ever have had to see."

"I'm still here." I replied coldly. "You'll forgive me if I don't tick the *satisfied* box on the departure form."

"You know, Mister Whittaker, I rather think I'll understand."

The sounds of a raging mechanic echoed out of the hole.

I retreated down the stairs to Tera's crouched form. "How is he?"

"He's pale, but breathing okay. He's gonna be angry when he wakes up."

"Okay! Madison called, as a *thunk* vibrated up my leg. "I'm through. First panel down, three more to go."

I looked back at the doctor, then at his ersatz carer.

"And how are *you* doing?"

"I'm angry."

"That's understandable. And?"

"And *what?*"

I searched her eyes, shaking my head. "You slipped up. I noticed, even if they didn't."

"What are you talking about?"

"Who the hell *are* you? Why did you call your brother Corben?"

She looked at me, pain written in her eyes, and took a deep breath.

"It should be obvious. That was his name."

# TWENTY

The emergency lights glared fiercely.

The words came slowly, haltingly, and very quietly.

"My husband's name is, was, Corben Torvalds. Mine is Rachel."

Some piece of unseen tension gave out, and she collapsed against the bulkhead. The rage had gone out of her with the admission. Frank watched from his perch.

I softened. "Your *husband.*"

"Yes."

"Why hide it?"

"You might have trouble with this, but we're living a lie to be able to *live.*"

"Please, explain."

Tera—*no, Rachel*—closed her eyes. "Corben went to SolPol a month ago, turned in all of his friends. Including a trio of mid-level Seomun regulars."

"Oh." I said. "*Oh.*"

"Absolute bastards." She said, bitterly. "Absorb the bad kids and twist the good ones until everybody feeds into them. We didn't live in the nicest parts of the station but we were doing okay for ourselves. Their people made passes at me now and then, but they didn't bother us for real. But Corben, well, you know him. He wanders into the wrong bar and sits at the wrong table and by the time it closes he's best buddies with everybody there. It looked like nothing, but we all knew who they were. Everyone did."

"Those kinds of people are hard to miss." I agreed.

"It was pancakes and jazzy juice all day long with them. He's practically in love. One of them even comes around for dinner a couple times. It's okay, you know? We think we're going to have a protected life, be left alone. Then he sees them throw our neighbors out of their apartment because the big guy wanted it for his side girl. Not even for himself, just his freck toy! It was *wrong*. We were going to be quiet and leave it alone. We had a good thing and there was no reason to ruin it. The same thing could happen to us if we spoke up."

"Corben didn't see it the same way." I said softly.

She nodded sadly. "He had to do something about it. Next thing I know there's a death mark on his head and we're being quarantined by SolPol, given new identities, and being shipped planetside." She looked up the stairs to where the captain was watching us, silently. "I just can't believe they followed us *here*. We were supposed to be *safe*."

The hallway was quiet after that, save for the sounds of muffled destruction.

Frank nodded solemnly in the lull. "I am so, *so* sorry for what happened to you."

"Go freck yourself." She replied coldly. "Maybe you're not the reason they *found* us, but you sure as shit let them get close enough. Freck! We were going to be *SAFE!*" she roared the last word, somewhere between anguish and fury.

My throat went dry as it clicked. Even in private, in CarverNet, where it was the two of them and the two of us and nothing but lazy comforts for our souls, the fiction had been studiously maintained. Even at his *funeral,* of all horrible things, she hadn't revealed the lie. She had kept it quiet. Kept it secret. Kept it private. Suspicious of everyone, all the time because that kept *them* alive.

And it hadn't mattered.

"Ricky killed him." I was as matter of fact as I could be. "Focus on *that.*"

"I am."

"Can you be *you* right now?"

She glared at me. "As opposed to…?"

"As opposed to the moaning girl I met in the woods a week ago."

"I'm going to rip his throat out."

"He looked *really* strong, Ter—, er, Rachel. And he doesn't even need to *see* us to kill us. This isn't like the tournament. This is real."

She nodded. "I know. I don't know how, but if I can't do it, someone else is going to do it for me. To be determined."

I sighed, and looked at Frank, then back to her.

"I really hope Jen managed to get somewhere safe."

Rachel looked down at Lawrence's softly breathing form. "Me too."

A voice crackled from Madison's fob then, in its resting place beside her pit. The tone was mildly sassy and oozed swagger.

*"Hi,* Ricardo? Buddy? Whatcha doing?"

*Jennifer.*

We stared at the little device. I went to reach for it, but Rachel grabbed my arm and shook her head. I understood. We needed to be silent. We needed to move without arousing interest, or detection, or attention.

"Who is this?" Ricky's lilt answered, full of curiosity.

"You can call me Trace," Jennifer said. "I'm the voice of your conscience. Just checking in."

"That's funny. I like you."

"I'm a bundle of jokes all day long. You want to tell me what's going on?"

"Well," the assassin replied dryly, "I'm currently holding your pilot hostage and deciding how best to live comfortably for the next several weeks."

"Sounds like you've got a puzzle."

"I suppose I do!"

"Just a thought, take it or leave it, but you might find it easier to manage that second thing if you weren't doing the first thing."

A smirk in the reply. "The mighty trouble with that, *Trace*, is I don't think most of the people on this boat like me too much. It's understandable."

The fob went dead.

*What in the stars is she playing at?*

Madison's head popped back up, out of the hole she had carved, hair frizzing with static electricity. "It's tight," she said, wearily, "but we can get through."

"We need to get to the bridge." Frank was quiet, but unwavering.

She shook her head. "We will, but one thing at a time." She pointed at him. "*You* stay here with those two." She pointed at Rachel. "Don't do anything stupid that could kill *us*, please. Follow us when the big guy wakes up. Aidan, you've been useful in tight spaces before. Coming?" She ducked back down and disappeared.

"Yes ma'am," Frank muttered, shimmying over to mind the doctor's unconscious bulk.

I looked at Rachel, clapped her on the shoulder, and scrambled up, then down into the abyss.

It was an exercise in contortions, shimmying through dusty lattices of rubber vines into a coffin-sized gap. Something in the back of my mind felt *icky* just contemplating it.

Then my eyes adjusted, and I made out the hand beckoning me forward.

I waved at it, then slowly stood up, until my nose was just clearing the opened floor. "Hey," I whispered. "Pay attention to what you hear."

Without waiting for a reply, I scooped up the fob and vanished into the guts of the ship.

The ambient smell of stale tech assaulted my nostrils. Musty. Sour. A little burnt. Negotiating the crawlspace on my back was tricky, but before long the dim glow from the newly-created exit came into view, and I slid out of the wall, feet-first, covered in dust and grease.

It was a storeroom. Deathly quiet.

Madison put a hand on my shoulder in the dark, causing me to jump. "Hey!"

"Okay, okay." she grimaced. "Sorry, just wanted to find you."

"You did."

"Are you with me? Up there in your head?"

I nodded. "Yes."

"Good. I'm struggling to figure out how we survive this."

"Obviously a hard question."

"Ricky is strong, smart, and a good fighter. And he has weapons on the hull. If we do anything to draw his attention, he can find us. Your take?"

"Dunno," I said, "but we need to get everyone together and out of sight before taking him on. If we leave anyone exposed and compliant he won't see it as submitting, whatever he says. He'll see it as…*convenient.*"

"Are you sure about that?"

"Yes."

Madison started moving away. "Step one is sealing the hole he just put in my ship. The entry wound on this deck is the only one that matters, so we fix that and then it's just a manual job to open all the slammers between us and him." She flicked on her little pen light, angling it away to the far wall, searching. "The vac suit you stole is on my workbench, and there should be a spare patch kit there too. Don't be nervous. Should be closest if we go….*that* way. There should be a little hatch around *here*…somewhere. All the rooms on this deck should have emergency exits between them in case of something like a fire. It's in the specs, at least. Help me look?"

"Right."

We searched around in the gloom until I found a light switch and got the overheads on. After that, we spotted the telltale recess after about ten seconds. It was concealed behind a large set of shelves, kept from easy discovery by a crate of rations marked with a garish logo.

*Kronk Beans! Very Kaffeinated!*

With the stimulating snacks hauled out of the way, Madison handed me the light and dusted off a small groove, then with a grunt found the catch and flipped the handle up and out. A small hydraulic *hiss* accompanied the motion. We clambered through on hands and knees, and once through I found myself looking at one of the crew quarters.

It was *filled* with sports paraphernalia. Half a dozen sports teams from a dozen cities. The more I took it in, the more the sight redefined itself, not so much evidence of *fandom* as a collector's stash. Souvenirs of places long-since visited.

"Lawrence." Madison said, noticing my stare. "You can practically smell the sweat."

"Everybody's got a thing."

"Come on. Elsie's place should be through the next one."

"Wait. I'm roasting alive in this suit. Where are his clothes?"

"Is this really the moment?"

"I don't care. All I need is something different."

The dresser drawers were tucked away. Any discomfort felt at going through someone's belongings paled beside what would happen if we slipped up. I looked at Madison, and she shrugged, busying herself with moving the desk out of the way.

I stripped out of the sim gear, relishing the dry air, and threw on the stolen clothes.

Nothing fit. The shirt was so baggy on my frame that it restricted my movement even more than the suit designed for that explicit purpose, and the lower half of everything was just too *big* to stay up.

"Um."

"What?"

"These don't fit."

"Go without. I don't care. We've got shit to do."

*Freck.*

I put the suit back on. Revulsion simmered as the haptic mesh re-asserted its grip, waiting for an opportunity to trap me again.

I shook myself. As the woman said, there was shit to do.

The next hatch was found tucked behind a poster of an odd figure. It was wearing a ribbed, grid-like helmet and holding aloft a long stick, bent at one end.

"What's this one?"

"No clue. Not my thing."

"Right."

I was pulling the poster to one side, trying to remove it without destroying it too much, when the little fob crackled to life once more.

"Hi again," Jennifer said, channeling her Trace persona, "I've been thinking. What does holding Miss Greene hostage do for you?"

Ricky's tone was dry. "Do you have something to share on the topic?"

'Trace' chuckled easily. "You're going to need her alive and cooperative to put this ship into dock. You're no pilot. You don't even know the first thing about procedures and codes. But you can't keep her tied up for three months. She and everyone else will need to be entertained, and fed, all of that."

The assassin's tone darkened. "*Any* of you can be ended with the flick of a switch, and some of you will be. As for my lady Elsie, with enough time and focus, she won't need to be herself."

"You're frecking pathetic!" The shout was tinny and distant, but the pilot's voice was unmistakable in the transmission's background.

"One moment," Ricky spoke flatly. A short, sharp sound clapped through the fob. "Mmhmm," he said. "That's better."

"I've heard she's quite the sprightly soul." Trace commented grimly. "I don't think she'll be so cooperative."

"She doesn't need to be *zesty*, merely skilled. You haven't—" Ricky's voice swerved away from us, and we listened raptly as he rounded on the pilot once more.

"Elsie, darling, behave. I love your spirit, you'll be great fun, but this is setting a poor example. *Listen.* I have talents and tricks, and I don't want to hurt you, but I *will* break you. I know you. I know that pyschosexual domination will work wonders between you and me."

There was the sound of something being dragged. "I can kill every one of them out there. I can kill your *family*, and when at the end of it, by the time we arrive, your body will be my plaything and your psyche will be my *property*. You will perform."

Revulsion swirled, but I held my tongue. It'd wouldn't help to lash out.

"Gods," Madison whispered. "Is he serious? If he *touches* her…"

I forced myself to say nothing.

"You have to be joking," Jennifer's voice responded at last.

"Oh! My, what an oversight, broadcasting that. Hum, no, that was entirely real, and from the look of it, I'm afraid I'm going to prove that to her in a moment." Ricky suddenly brightened. "But this isn't a challenging topic! My curiosity is piqued. Who *is* this mysterious Trace? I don't know your voice, so a passenger, surely. But…" He trailed off for a moment. "Your name *is* familiar. I'm sure it will come to me."

Access to the next room was blocked by a hulking obstacle. With a mighty string we shoved it clear, and the hulking obstacle receded. Twisting and contorting myself around the skinny gap, I hauled myself up and through, dodging the bunk frame that had so fervently resisted our entry.

Even if I hadn't already been told, this was unmistakably Elsie's signature. No doubt about it. Lighting nets were strung across the ceiling behind a mottled blue canopy, sheer and soft to the touch. The effect reminded me quite strongly of CarverNet's *Arkadia* environment. Elsie, it seemed, was a fan of the look too. It might have made for a cosy nest in different circumstances.

A muffled broadcast of wet, snarling, chuckling sounds echoed from the fob, and noises of grunted pain, from a higher-pitched voice, seeped through the muddy mix. Hard to tell *what* was happening, but none of the possibilities were good.

I helped Madison through the gap, and together we hauled the bunk out of the way more completely.

Elsie, sensibly, had not seen fit to cover up the other hatch, and Madison turned to me as she got into position.

"Wait here," she said through clenched teeth, working the latch. "My bench is behind that wall. When I'm through and got the gear, I'll let you know."

I obeyed, staring at a parade of sketched artwork and desk filled half-dismantled toys, trying to take it in, but all I could see was the vision of Elsie being degraded, violated, tormented, until the oppression became intermingled with reprieves, and kindnesses, and reassurances, until she was equal parts terrified of and desperate for the smallest act of approval.

Even when Ricky left, she would live with that forever.

A cold anger started to burn. The image, the progression was unthinkable, yet I could think it. I could *see* it. There was something *menacing* in my mind which could conceive of such things in detail and find a pleasing rhythm in such total domination of another person.

But the difference, I told myself, between my mind and the assassin's, was that *I* would reject that inner monster. He had no place in me. Not as a focus, nor as a tool.

I told myself that little lie again, and again, until finally, I decided that the monster *was* useful after all. And that it was time to feed it.

I shivered in the haptic suit. It erased any defense. Made me vulnerable. Raw.

There was a wild, primitive strength in that. The engineer's words echoed. *You have to be your genuine self, right here and right now. Nothing else matters. Do you get it?*

I picked up the fob. Fingered the button.

Spoke very slowly, and very, very icily.

"You don't want to go down this path, *bratan.*"

A few beats of pure silence went by.

"Aidan? Is that you?" Ricky's voice was pleasant, cheerly surprised. "You're up and out, brother! Well done. How was the sim?"

"I grew up in the docks." I growled. "I grew up around ships, in the zocalo, in the little world owned by the Families. Just like you. Just like Corben. I know what makes you tick inside. I know what *they* make you. I tasted that life too, and I hurt people. But I walked away. That's something your breed of scum has a hard time fathoming." I took a breath, and thumbed the button again. "Enough of *you,* enough of the *dregs* of Ceres playing at owning our lives."

The fob was, amazingly, silent.

A corner of my thoughts wondered what Jennifer made of that.

Madison poked her head back around and I let my thumb off the broadcast button.

"Keep going," she said. "I've got the stuff, I'm gonna seal this. When I open the hatch into the corridor he's gonna see a little alarm flash up there. Keep him off balance, thinking about *you.*"

I nodded as she disappeared, replacing the panel behind her.

Seconds later, the muffled thump of a door sliding open quietly announced that the engineer was getting to work.

The fob in my hand finally crackled to life again. "*Bratan.* I much prefer talking to you. That's a fantastic set of words. If only you were enough of a man to give them weight. But we both know I hold the cards, the deck, the game, and the whole match in my pocket, and you, nothing. Hiding in a closet, desperately hoping to make something of yourself. I could tear your head from you with a flick of a—".

I cut him off. "You *listen* to me, *Ricardo.* Elsie is off limits. If you *touch* that pilot, I will let Rachel put you out of the airlock and she'll do it so that you hit space in tiny little pieces, just like Corben. Remember him? If you *violate* that pilot, I will let Lawrence make sure you're awake for most of it. And if you disregard *me*, I will personally use a plasma torch to remove your crystallized parts one at a time while you watch. We *do not hurt the good ones*, understand?"

After a long pause, the reply came, sounding taken aback.

"You're not my better, Whittaker." A pause, then a curt addition: "But I like you."

The fob lapsed into silence as I glared at an illustration of a flower.

Hot rage settled, heartbeat by heartbeat, into cold resolve. My life had been carved in two parts by Ricky's manipulations. I had tried to forge a new start from it, a new *person*, who had never lived with twenty-plus years of life in a remote cesspit full of mercenarily-minded grifters and wealthy lunatics dripping with sociopathy. A person who had never been one of them.

*I am an artist, dammit. I am an honest person. I will do it right.*

I exhaled slowly, steadily. As much as I wanted it to be true, it simply couldn't be. Time to be truthful with myself.

*I am an artist. I am an honest person. I will do what is needed.*

One more time.

*I am an artist. To an honest person, my name is Noah. I will do what is needed.*

The final version coalesced, stark in the face of what lay ahead.

*I am not Noah.*

*I am not an honest person.*

*I will do it right.*

The door creaked open abruptly, but instead of air being sucked out, Madison's fingers lunged through ahead of her face in a grim replica of a scene that seemed to have happened quite a long time ago.

"This deck is safe," she said. "Good work."

"You did the hard part."

She looked at me askance. "No, I think you did."

It wasn't worth arguing. Time for the next step: get everyone and get out of sight.

We made short work of the pressure doors, which Madison called 'slammers', opening section after section of the corridor as we made our way around the deck's infinite ring. Beyond the storeroom, scalding steam sprayed out of the ceiling where the galley shot had hit a line. We gingerly gave it a wide berth.

We finally reached the bulkhead blocking off the stairs up to the galley. Madison worked her magic with a grunt, and the big metal plate slid into the ceiling.

A very groggy Lawrence blinked out at us from where he was splayed across the steps. Moments later Rachel scrambled down behind him. Frank followed, but clapped a hand to my shoulder to lean in close. His breath was hot.

"I was listening. Whatever way this plays out, that woman gets the final say."

I nodded, and he pulled back, moving to confer with his engineer.

Ricky's voice came through the intercom, bright and clear.

"Oh! What's this? No, I told you before. I was very clear: if you try anything, I will end you."

We froze, looking at each other.

There was no time.

"Move, move!" Madison whispered, ushering us away. I helped Lawrence forward as he started to get some presence in his muscles. He kept fading in and out of consciousness every other step, but started mumbling the names of equipment and drugs. The emergency lights pulsed on, then off, and on again, in a slowly breathing darkness that made the distance vanish as much as it terrified those within it.

"For all who are listening and may care," Ricky's enigmatic voice continued from one unseen speaker after the next. "Someone aboard my ship has queued up a long-range broadcast. One Jennifer Motley. Would that be you, my lady Trace?"

Blood ran cold.

As we passed the spray-painted tagline across the door to Raj's long-vacated cabin, a smirk entered the assassin's voice once again. "*Unfortunately*, I'm afraid that goes against my no-tolerance policy."

A tiny, evil rumble zipped through the floor plating.

As I shared a look with Madison, Kay Tee's duo-tone tenor smoothly doled out an update. "*Transverse impact alert. High-gain transceiver is reporting an error. Medium-range LIDAR array is reporting an error. Immediate maintenance attention is recommended.*"

"Mother frecker," Madison growled.

*He's insane*, I thought.

Ricky's voice returned to the intercom. "There we go. No more need for *that*. Let's look you up, now, Miss Motley. Who—Oh! Habitat cameras! Marvelous. Elsie, darling, you should have told me about these sooner. Let's have a look and see where everyone has gone."

Our group reached the opposing pair of pressure seals. I thought back to the sim, trying to remember the layout, and nodded. We had a choice to make. Behind both doors were stairs up to deck three. The route to the left would take us forward, towards the bow and the bridge. Going right would take us to the medical office and who knew what else.

"I spy someone poking in the doctor's cupboards!" Came the assassin's voice again. He almost sounded bored. "A new face. You *must* be Jennifer. Do you have any advice for me? That won't encourage me to dispose of your irritating commentary?"

Frank and Madison didn't hesitate. They went to the left.

I met Rachel's eyes, and left her holding Lawrence upright as I went right.

I mimicked the steps Madison had demonstrated. Find the pneumatics panel…*there*. Claw around the edges, open it with brute force. Pull the levers to release the door.

There was no time. The barrier slid away, and I charged up the stairs as fast as my feet could carry me. The sinking realisation came by the third step: Elsie's stim was fading. Muscles that had been boosted for hours were starting to come back to reality.

*Go. Harder.*

"Oh! This is *different*. More like it!" Ricky said over the intercom, new enthusiasm dripping from the syllables. "Milo! My guy. What an enterprising idea." His voice shifted, taking on a conspiratorial edge. "Milo, it appears, is building a tidy little explosive! Excellently inventive. I treasure that kind of *bombastic* thinking. He deserves some credit."

The sound of one person clapping echoed throughout the halls.

*Milo. Jennifer was with Milo.*

I ran up the stairs, scanning wildly for the medical office.

"Now, now, Milo, darling," Ricky continued. "I'm going to need you to put that canister down. Just set it on the side. *Do it.* I will not ask again."

The door was there, *right there*, where Lawrence had deposited my groggy form several hours earlier.

I reached it first, pounding on it.

"Okay. Make your peace." Ricky said sadly. "I didn't want this."

The office door opened. Jennifer's ashen face stared into mine. She squeezed her eyes closed.

A tiny, terrible vibration rumbled through the deck.

Pressure doors didn't close on us, and no air rushed from our lungs.

Her eyes opened.

Kay Tee spoke flatly into the void.

*"Longitudinal impact alert. Pressure loss detected, deck three. Hydroponics beta, crew utility, and prayer room are affected. Evacuate to safe areas immediately. Pressure seals will engage in three seconds."*

"We're still alive?" I asked dumbly.

Jennifer was numb. "Looks like it." She shook herself. "What the *hell* is happening?"

"We're going to die or wish we had."

She grimaced. "What can I do?"

"Help me find a, dammit, a subdermal injector and, freck, tetraketamine. I think it was tetraketamine."

We poured through the lockers, first finding the injector. The drug was harder to find, but we eventually got hold of it and several other small vials, and took the whole clutch with us.

As we fled the medical space, I spotted the tiny camera up in the corner. If Ricky was watching, he was being uncharacteristically quiet about it. If he wasn't watching…

The mental image of him alone and distracted with Elsie churned my stomach.

Jennifer eyed the injector clutched in my fist. "Are you going to use that on him?"

"Yes."

She hesitated for the briefest fraction of a moment. "Good."

In a recreation of my path through the torture sim, we took the deck four stairs, pausing just out of sight of that deck's cameras. The surviving crew were perched on the matching steps up to the front of the ship.

*Good. Out of sight and closer to the bridge.*

The emergency floods blinked on and off, hiding us from each other in a slow strobe.

"Hold there!" Madison whispered, projecting it beyond full volume. "He can see the corridors. *Only* the corridors."

"Can he *hear* us?" I whispered back.

"Not unless you're going to hold another radio show!"

"Jen!" Rachel called. "Are you okay?"

"I'm fine!" the other woman answered.

"I thought you were going to die!"

Jennifer was matter of fact. "So did I."

"My name is Rachel!"

"What?"

"We'll cover that *later*," I interjected. "Short version is Ricky was sent by a crime family to kill Jazz, actually called Corben, for betraying them. Corben was her husband, not her brother."

Jennifer processed this, eyes moving frantically. "Okay. Fine. Explains things, I think. Feels a little gross. Where were *you* all this time?"

"He drugged me, got me in a private sim, got me out of the way."

"Oh." She nodded. "Makes sense. It's a good move. Okay." She closed her eyes, and took a few deep breaths. "Lay out the game."

I nodded. "He's a killer from a crime family. He has the bridge. In the sim, I explored it, used some of the stuff in there, so I know what he's got to hand. He can see a map of power draw anywhere on the ship. Any system, down to the room. He has guns strapped to the exterior that can aim themselves in almost any direction and fire remotely. He's killed two of us and hurt two more. He's a good fighter and probably has enhancements. And now he has cameras too, at least in some places. We can't fight him up close and if we go to gear up, he'll kill us at range. We're all just…inconvenient for him. This is a game to him. The only person he needs, he's already got. We can't let him remain."

She took it all in, and closed her eyes, thinking. Focusing. Then she opened them. "Let's move. In the dark, right?"

We counted the beat of the blinking hazard lights. Three beats on, three beats off. Three beats on again, three beats off.

The darkened hallway was roughly four meters wide. An extravagance for its crew.

I nodded, and we lined up.

*Three beats on.*

*Three beats off.*

*Three beats on…*

The light blinked off, and we bolted across the gap, stumbling through the black until we collided with the others on their steps, clambering up and away as the illumination came back.

"Ough!" Madison objected.

"Where's the doctor?" I asked, realising that Lawrence's bulk wasn't among us.

"We put him in Milo's bunk." The words were bitter. Angry.

I withdrew as much as the crowded stairs would allow, understanding. "…Right."

Jennifer had pretty much landed on the captain, but he didn't object, just graciously helped her up.

She dusted herself off. "I've worked through it, and I have a plan," she announced, standing tall in the amber flares.

Frank's eyes were hard. "I'm listening."

She told us, explaining each step, and the critical piece, in detail. And as she went through each aspect I remembered her education. Her *actual* area of expertise, out there in normal life.

"We need a distraction to keep him from thinking too much," Madison said thoughtfully, when Jennifer had finished.

I stood. "He's going to be watching *me.*"

"How?"

Jennifer patted my foot, but said nothing.

*This is it,* I thought.

I took a deep breath. This had to work. Or it would be the last thing I ever did.

At least my last act would be true to myself.

Holding the fob to my face, I pressed the button.

"*Bratan.*"

"Aidan! How can I help you?"

The reply was immediate, but broadcast over the intercom. This time, it was for the whole ship to hear.

I strode out into the corridor amongst the crew cabins. Assertive. Calm. Collected. Walking the length of it a ways, then spotting a tiny camera tucked into the ceiling, waving, and going back the way I'd come.

I clicked the button. "I wanted to have a look at your handiwork."

"Really? That's kind. You were threatening to turn my parts into frozen dust just a few minutes ago."

"The threat stands."

"It was a shame what I did to Milo. You didn't know Milo, did you?"

I sighed into the microphone. "I did not."

"He was very giving. He was good in bed."

I reached the stairs where Madison, Frank, Lawrence, and Rachel were crouched out of sight, and climbed past their bewildered looks. It came easily, sauntering by as if they meant nothing.

"Are you in the habit of executing all of your lovers?"

The playful lilt returned. "*Lovers?* Oh, no, we frecked a few times. Everybody here has at some point." His voice took on a mocking impression of Frank's enigmatic cadence. "That's just life, out here in the empty places, frecking each other until you can freck each other *over*. It's a load of shit. "

I emerged onto deck three in the forward ring corridor. It was dark, the lights forgotten, except for a glowing red stripe down the middle of the floor, bisecting the loop and brimming with angry, passionate glows.

The lone exception was the bridge, its cheery light spilling from the slit in that big round door.

I deliberately ignored it, forging a relentless path along the fore side of that little red line.

*Don't give in. Don't slip.*

Ricky needed to know that he wasn't the center of my attention. That I walked freely in his world. That he was beneath me.

Partway around the deck's upward curve, hydroponics beta came into view. I strode up to it, peered through the big plate window.

Equipment and plants plastered every surface. Halfway up the outer wall, plants, vegetables really, had torn free and squished against a large steel planter, pinned against a single point.

Sticking out from behind them was a pair of legs. A glistening chunk had been carved from the right thigh. The more I looked, the more I started to recognize glimpses of a human torso beneath the wreckage. It had become a mashed and broken plug, a little too late to keep the room's air from emptying into hard vacuum.

Disgust tickled my throat. And behind it, a calm admiration.

I pressed the fob button again. "Do you think Milo suffocated first, or died from the shock?"

"He died knowing that he brought it on himself. All that matters."

"I think he died knowing that you were going to freck him again."

That got an unwilling chuckle. I continued, staring at the body, eying the window's reflections. My allies were moving freely.

I moistened my lips, bringing the fob close until it could detect a gentle whisper. "I didn't know Milo. He wasn't a friend. But I know Elsie. I know Madison. I know Frank, and I know Jennifer. I even know Lawrence, and plenty of others that I met in an imaginary world. A fabulous world. I rather liked it. You broke it. You broke *me.*"

I started walking back towards the bridge door with deadly calm.

"I owe you some thanks."

"And why?" Ricky asked, idly amused.

"First, a basic physics truth." I cleared my throat. "It is generally impossible to reliably be certain of both the position and velocity of a given object. This has, er, many points of comparison. But here's an easy one: who I am, and who I *will be*, are mutually exclusive. I know that. Because I want to be a good person. I want to have a family. I want to explore, I want to discover things."

I parked myself in front of the bridge door, now staring at the window as Ricky stepped up to it on the other side.

We locked eyes.

"Is Elsie there?" I asked through the little fob.

He held up his own, gesturing curtly. "Yes."

"She's a good one, isn't she? She doesn't know how to fight back."

He nodded, head tilted. "If you don't mind, I have to get back to helping her understand that."

"Good." I stepped back and moved on. "You should know this first. I'm a mean, selfish bastard, deep down, and always have been. I didn't want to be. And I know where you come from. You're just like me. You want to be a name. You want *recognition.* You want the person in front of you begging for your kindness before you shove them down to service you."

Ricky sneered at me through his words. "Do you have a point?"

"Simple," I said, rounding the corner back into the stairwell, and letting my voice drift away into a whisper as I disappeared from his view. I surveyed the now-empty corner, nodding. The crew were gone, disappeared into a brand new hole where several steps had been dismantled.

I spoke very, very precisely to Ricky. "I want you to beg for *my* kindness."

I released the transmit button. My left hand trembled despite efforts to steady it. Whether it was happening from rage, or from anxiety, was impossible to tell.

Silence reigned as I followed the crew into the guts of the ship. As I wormed my way through the displaced metal and into a service tunnel, I grasped Jennifer's waiting hand. I brought up the fob one more time, and whispered again, intently.

"I'm going to *hurt* you, Ricardo."

The intra-deck space was cold. Hard on the knees and stomach and other unprotected places. We shimmied along head to toe for several meters, until at a junction Lawrence and Franklin veered right, while Madison, Jennifer and I crawled left.

The intercom, muffled and echoing through these recesses,

boomed with frustration. "Where the hell are you?"

Jennifer whispered to the engineer. "How much further? What do you need?"

Madison glanced around, thinking. "We're practically underneath him now. Another few meters and we'll be there."

The three of us crawled the lingering distance speedily, until the engineer stopped, and started feeling around the plating above her, nodding.

"TALK, dammit!" Ricky shouted out, his pacing feet tracing impatient paths above us.

Madison bit her tongue, but looked back at us. She patted the end of the tunnel beyond her.

"We're up against the inner hull here. So count back…one, two, three, five, *ah*. All these cables coming out there, over my legs, that's the underside of the conning station."

"That's our way in," I nodded. "There's a hidden entrance into the bridge here."

"How big is it?" Jennifer asked.

I thought back to the torturous training simulation. It was almost ironic. Ricky had given me the perfect tool. "Big enough."

Madison fished a small device out of a pocket and connected it to a dangling cable.

Ricky came on again, audible through the plating now. He was rattled.

"You don't frighten me, Whittaker. You can't take me. You talk an interesting game, but we both know you couldn't make good on the best of days. I'm going to have a little demonstration of exactly how useless you are."

Madison held out her hand and whispered at me. "I can get what I need right here. Aidan, once I take this plate off, he'll be able to hear us. No talking, you have to be *quiet*. Try not to freck up."

I nodded, and gave her the fob. She switched it off.

The pair of them pressed to the side as I squeezed past, crawling clumsily to the head of the line. Madison wriggled until her shoulder was between my legs, adjusted herself to avoid crushing anything useful, then went back to work.

The muffled rant above restarted. It had evolved into raw *frustration*.

"You all don't seem to *get* it!" Ricky snarled. "There is no fight here. I control your lives. Even this one, right here, that our very vocal guest cares so much about. We'll get started with demonstrating what that means now."

There was the sound of scuffling through the plating inches from our faces. "Come here, girl. Don't fight it. Don't fight *me*. This will be good for you. You'll enjoy it. Why don't we indulge ourselves? Right here, for everyone to listen. We can do this in your very own bunk…*next* time. Hey! I said *don't fight me*. Remember, Elsie, I *own you*. Give me your name. *Say that I own your name!*"

There was a loud *thud* as a body landed on the floor, shaking dust loose into our faces. Then boot steps, and *another* thud.

Jennifer spoke quietly into her fob, putting on her best *Trace* persona.

"Ricardo. Is any of this *really* called for? Does any of this *really*…?"

She stopped talking. Didn't seem to know how to finish.

Madison finished her work, and put a finger to her lips. We pushed, slowly, prying the floor free. Beyond, the glare from the bridge overheads was blinding. I was coming up right behind the sheet metal on the back of the station, shielded from the rest of the room by its bulk.

Elsie cried out, pained, as another *thud* sounded.

I wriggled up, slowly, as smoothly as I could possibly manage, flashing back to the motions Jennifer had demonstrated during my time in her head.

I stared at the engineer, stuffed into the crawlspace, busy with her small screen, refusing to be distracted.

*Good.*

Elsie moaned.

Madison finally looked at me. I met her gaze. She nodded, once, and tapped one more button.

On cue, the lights cut to minimum brightness, and Kay Tee's doubled tenor pleasantly chimed.

*"Dark cycle started. Have a good night."*

Soft opera began to play across the intercom, a lullaby-like tune with tinging bells.

"Ah, finally. Somebody makes another move!" The assassin rose, looking around. I peered out around the edge of the console by a mere inch, and got sight of Elsie, who was flattened prone on the floor. I held a finger to my lips as bruised eyes widened. Lumpy blue and black marked her face. She had not cooperated. It was costing her.

That cold, calm fury boiled.

Ricky strode around the room, oblivious. "Don't you all get it? Why? Why not come out, submit, and enjoy a quiet ride onwards? Throwing punches? Building bombs? Trying to psych me out? This isn't even your ship! You own nothing! You're all hotel keepers, on shitty salaries, hauling frecking bodies for months at a time. Why not admit that? Why not go off, leave here, and start *living your damned lives?*"

"Because," a deeper, harsher, angrier voice cut in from the other side of the bridge, where the captain's cabin awaited. "This *is* our life. Get the hell *out* of my bridge."

Frank charged, swinging a swirling, pointy lump on the end of a lengthy bit of cable.

It impacted Ricky's shoulder with a heavy *thump* and he stumbled back into a workstation, his head colliding with the heavy frame. For a moment he looked genuinely surprised.

Another swirl of the makeshift flail, and another *thump,* this time deep into soft gut tissue as the captain advanced, cornering the invader. *Another* hit cracked against bone, this time taken on the smaller man's off arm. It would have been enough to send any normal human screaming to the infirmary.

The fourth swing never landed. Ricardo's arm shot up, intercepting the hit and seizing the weapon. He stood, shaking off the hits, and lashed out, striking Frank in the throat before grabbing him by it, and lifting him off the deck.

"Franklin. I admire this. I want you to know that." As he started to squeeze, horribly slowly, Frank wriggled, flailing, to no avail. He might as well have been fighting a machine. I nudged Madison with my foot.

*Now,* I thought. *Now!*

The bridge door rolled open, and Ricky stopped murdering his one-time captain long enough to turn and look.

But, predictably, nobody was there.

*Now for the party trick.*

It was imperceptible at first. Then, slowly, with the subtle sense of being pulled towards the wall beside me, gravity faded out of existence, and we all started to drift off the floor. Zero gee.

*No up, no down. Backward is behind me. Forward is in front of me.*

*Momentum is all that counts.*

*I'm going to do it right.*

Nothing to be said. Everything to be done.

Using the top of the conn, I swirled up and over, twisting around, borrowing a motion that Jennifer had taught me so many hours before, and kicked off in a tight somersault. Felt the impact as my feet, with all of *me* behind them, compacted Ricky's stomach. He swung, but hit nothing, unable to find any leverage as we bounced apart. He glided backwards, flailing for purchase, but found none as the bridge doorway came and went.

And then Rachel was suddenly *there,* swinging into place behind him. As they collided, he tried to twist, to bring murderous hands to her head, but she was ready, and her arm snaked around his neck.

A flash of metal in her hand.

Ricky stopped his struggling. He met my eyes.

I would have liked to think they were full of admiration, or some cocksure understanding of honor amongst kin.

But he just bore the glare of disbelief.

I just watched him mercilessly as the artificial gravity started to re-assert itself, rotational engines getting back to work far above.

Nobody took their eyes off the bastard until, slowly, steadily, and quietly, he slumped to the floor.

It was over.

# TWENTY-ONE

I found spare clothes in the captain's cabin. They fit poorly, but they did stay put when worn.

When I returned, the bridge was quiet. Very quiet.

Frank sat on the floor against a wall.

Elsie paced, fuming, but not finding any words.

Rachel and Jennifer were talking quietly, stood over Ricky's placid form, shallow breathing his only sign of life.

I leaned over the conn, staring out the forward window at the long, blinking spire pointing out into a field of stars. It was possible that the pose was meant to be enigmatic. For the most part, it was only to control my breathing.

*In, two three…*

*Out, two three…*

Madison found the environmental controls and restored ordinary lighting and temperature across the crew module. It was a relief.

The engineer sighed, and walked over to her captain. Squatted down with a sigh.

"Okay, Frank. Time to explain."

He nodded slowly. Sadly.

"The money," he croaked. "Two more runs and I'll be able to retire. Actually *retire*, Maddie. I could look up Jeanine. I could meet my daughter. I could live planetside."

"I believed in you," she said quietly. "You were supposed to be *better* than the rest. A man who did things right."

"I was," he said. "But I have limits. They told me they needed to get someone to Luna this trip. And the day we pulled into port, Ricky came *recommended*. I never thought…" Frank gestured around us. He didn't need to finish the sentence. "But the responsibility is mine."

Elsie spoke for the first time in several minutes. "Is anyone *else* here on the take? Anyone?"

Frank shook his head. "No. I would make a point to not formally notice."

I muttered Ricky's mocking line. "Frecking each other until you can freck each other over."

"It isn't like that," Frank was trying to sound righteous, but the effect was undone somewhat. "My crew, taken care of. When I move on, Maddie would be a shoe-in to run this place. She still is. We look out for each other, Mister Whittaker."

I held up my hands. "You're right. It's not my place."

Out in the hall, Ricardo's unconscious form was right where it had been left, but his watchers were gone. It didn't matter.

"Aidan did good with us today, Frank." Madison was quiet, calm, but firm. "You saw it. You heard it."

"Hmm."

He was thoughtful, but neutral.

That felt fair.

In the lull, Elsie stopped pacing and came up beside me, close and quiet.

"Thank you." Her words were barely a whisper. "I don't know if you knew, but you had him rattled. He…meant…what he said about doing things to me."

"He was drawing me out. Bluffing."

"No." The reply was barely a whisper. "Just after you talked to him the first time, it set him off. He actually *did* the start of…to me. He…" she trailed off, halting, quiet. "He forced me to… *taste*…he would have kept…" She screwed up her face, killing the words, until she had control. "You understand. I know you *understand*."

I looked at her. Then at the skinny figure lying helpless and alone thirty feet away. "I'll remember that."

"Good." She brushed away the strands of hair dangling before her eyes. "Get off my station. I have work to do."

I voided my post, letting her settle into place at the conn, working the controls like she'd invented them.

Diagrams and updates flew past, status charts being generated and stuck into place across the big display.

I watched, silently, as she methodically sorted through one task after another, building a mask over her emotions. A coping mechanism.

A full, unperturbed minute passed.

Finally, she stopped.

"Okay," she called out, louder, calmer, firmer. "Time to hear exactly how frecked we are."

The captain accepted Madison's outstretched arm, rising to his feet. They both approached, gathering around.

The women joined us from their conversation out in the corridor, with a very groggy Lawrence in tow. He nodded to each of us in turn.

"It looks like you all managed to get my tetraketamine in our friendly neighborhood asshole," he remarked, gesturing at the limp form behind him. "How much did you use?"

Rachel handed him the empty injector. He peered at its setting. "Seven milligrams."

"Is that a lot?"

"It's a lot more than I'd give you."

"Is that a bad thing?"

He shrugged. The woozy look hadn't gone from his eyes, but there was an attentive sharpness behind them. Elsie waved off his approach, and he dutifully gave her space as he shifted his attention to Frank.

The pilot cleared her throat. "Okay. Here's the summary. Ricky's little treats have put a lot of holes in my baby. Half of hydroponics is hard vacuum. Water lines across deck three got hit. The system sealed off those pipes when it saw the pressure loss so we still have some water going around up here, but we lost a lot of good liquid to the great outdoors. Deck four is hanging onto its atmosphere by a skinny patch, and it looks like that's leaking too, slowly, so we'll need to do that better. The cargo and passenger blocks look fairly untouched, thankfully, so we're lucky there. Nobody back there should be any the wiser. But we have a very big problem with *power*. One of our capacitor banks up front got hit at some point, and electrical breakers to the ones in the engine block are still closed. Between them, we're only able to handle about half of our grid capacity. We're on the edge of a brownout."

"Anything *else*?" Madison asked, through gritted teeth.

"Yes. The main engine diagnostics came back. You were back there before, you saw some of the damage. From what the system can tell, we're bleeding helium *and* oxygel from the main tanks into god knows where, and the cameras are showing what *looks* like damage to the ignition shells on engines two and three."

Frank stared at her between raspy coughs. "Describe the outcome for me, please. Be blunt."

The pilot nodded reluctantly. "We have about three months left of inbound flight eleven. In about four weeks, the flight plan would tell us to flip the ship, periodically lighting all four main engines for deceleration and correction, bringing ourselves to match velocity and trajectory with Luna over the following several weeks. The problem is that I don't think we have those engines available to use. Not safely, anyhow. If it was just damage to the pipework, that would be one thing, but there's *fuel* floating around loose back there. Besides the possibility of rapid disassembly if the wrong stuff mixes together near a power source, we are *leaking propellant*. We could reconnect the power and light the other two engines, but even if we didn't blow up we might not have enough fuel *left*."

"Okay." He said, heavily. "Please find us an alternative plan."

"I'm working on it."

"Good. Lawrence, help me get Milo out of—"

"You're gonna do *nothing*, Frank." Lawrence was firm. "The bruising on your neck is bad, there's a welt on your head the size of my hand, and I haven't even gotten a look at your abdomen yet but if it's not black and blue I'll eat one of those awful fish packs." He softened infinitesimally. "Milo isn't going anywhere. We'll go get him after I get *you* on my table. Elsie, you should come by too, when you're ready."

The doctor hauled the captain up, and one step at a time, they departed, giving the rest of us curt nods on the way out.

"Gods," I said. "Yeah. I can help do whatever you need. I can get Milo. Just point me to a vac suit."

Madison shook her head. "No, that one is on us. We'll handle all of it. You've been through more than enough. All three of you have."

"I genuinely want—"

"I *know.*" Her words were kind. She put a hand on my shoulder. "You've proven yourself in my mind, at least, but you *aren't* a member of this crew. Milo was one of ours. We'll handle it. And then we'll figure out how to deal with the rest of it." She looked at Rachel and gestured to the unconscious assassin contemptuously. "I'm going to let *you* decide what to do with him."

Jennifer took my hand. Spoke softly. "Come on."

The three of us left the crewmates alone on the bridge. As we stood over Ricky's softly breathing shape, Tera—*no, Rachel*—shook her head. "I don't know. I want to frecking *space* him, but I don't know. I don't actually want to kill *any* one."

Jennifer wrapped an arm around her. "We could lock him up for a while. Make him face SolPol's people when we get to the other end."

"*If* we get there," I muttered grimly. "Thanks to him, that might not happen."

"So what do we *do* with him?" Rachel asked, face a shifting mask of emotions.

"Help me get him up." I said. "We'll put him in one of the sim suits for now. The training room. One deck up. That'll keep him in one place while we decide."

It was surprisingly difficult for even the three of us to carry the limp body out of the hall, through the galley, and into the mover. Being able to prop him up against its wall was a small blessing.

When the mover opened onto the broad, open storage racks, I did a small double take. The space had been neatly carved into a small fraction of its former self by more of the big protective bulkheads. But before they had closed, the rushing of escaping air had wreaked havoc. Cables, filters, bits of pipe, pieces of computing hardware, tanks of ferrofluid, even what looked like a crate of spare water pumps were scattered across the floor. It made for a challenging obstacle course. Jennifer went out in front, clearing rubble as we dragged our cargo.

In the sim room, I lumped him on the floor, then found a pressed and dusty clone of the now-familiar CarverNet suit. With a grimace, we stripped him, and pulled, tugged, snugged his bulk into the skintight mesh. Finally, when it looked like it was on correctly, we heaved him up onto the same cradle that had been holding *me* not too long before. We left off the headpiece.

I pulled the different cords in, linking them up. The cuff on the suit's arm accepted the connection happily, and Rachel found a button for power as Jennifer snapped the collar tight. I watched idly as she stopped to connect a few other things on the cradle that I didn't recognize.

*Cozy.* In a matter of speaking.

The small status display lit up, and with a few taps I had the suit in *standby* mode.

*Right Leg: Connected*

*Left Leg: Connected*

*Right Arm: Connected*

*Left Arm: Connected*

*Torso: Connected*

*Head: Disconnected*

*Nerve Traces: Connected*

*Core Bodily Functions: Stable*

*Nutrient Flow: Stable*

*Waste absorption: Connected*

*Motion Suppression: Active*

*Simulation State: Awaiting Scenario*

"Okay," Rachel said. "He's not going anywhere."

"Let's get some air," Jennifer suggested.

I cast a lingering look over his slack face, and nodded. "Let's go."

* * *

Raj's cabin made for a claustrophobic refuge. A movie played on the infotainment screen, something Jennifer had picked out. *Hunt for the Winter Lion.* Near as I could tell it involved four fiercely competitive brothers searching for an old man they had met in a long-forgotten tavern.

Nobody was paying attention.

"This happened so fast." Rachel muttered, perched on the end of the bunk. Her legs were tucked up against her.

"It did," Jennifer agreed. She was leaning by the door.

"This was the longest day of my life." I said. I was on my back on the floor.

Rachel sighed. "I'm glad he can't hurt us anymore."

"For now, yes." Jennifer nodded. "But we can't leave him like that. It's the same problem *he* had with us. Sooner or later we'll need to…do something."

"Just breathe for a minute," I pleaded. There was no greater sensation in my bones than simply being *tired*. Every one of us was breathing just a little heavily. Out of our element. Practicing for where we all wanted to be.

The movie hit a dramatic bit overlooking a steep, terraced hillside. A figure in dark robes with a long sword in one hand approached the heroes.

Jennifer reached down, extending a hand. "The bed looks more comfortable than that."

I took it. She was right.

"I have a question for you, Noah. Okay?" She put a hand on my shoulder. "All that stuff you said, taunting him. Was any of that real?"

I was quiet for a long moment. The fatigue was catching up.

"Yes."

"Are you that kind of person?"

"No."

"Explain that to me."

It was a long minute before I answered. Hard to find the words.

I opened my mouth. Closed it. Tried again. "I have not necessarily always been a good person."

"Go on."

"I…know the part of life that made Ricky work. I know that same part of life is what Jazz, or Corben, ran away from, and it got him killed. It's like there's a little monster, tucked away inside you. It wants out. It wants to tear things apart. It doesn't want to be told *no*. Ricky's people feed that monster, dangling carrots in front of it. But people like you, like Jazz, like your Aunt Sel, or like Elsie, you don't hear it. Or if you do, you're really good at ignoring it."

"And you?" Rachel asked.

"I fed it a little bit today. I don't want to do that again."

"But you could."

"I don't want to." I gave them both a bittersweet smile. "I rather liked being Noah. For a while. A different me who could live like the shitty things didn't matter."

Rachel watched silently. Thinking.

Jennifer gave me what I'm sure she thought was a reassuring squeeze.

"The man I know is sweet, stoic, relentlessly warm to be around. I'd rather like to spend more time with him."

Rachel spoke, clearly, precise. "All those things. Is that *you?*"

I shook my head. "I don't think it matters. But I could be that for you." I nodded at her, and glanced at Jennifer. "And for you."

"Why? Because we're 'good ones', as you put it?"

"Something like that."

"I guess we'll manage." Jennifer said.

"If we live through it." Rachel added. "I don't know how to do any of this without Cor. He…we could die out here, if they don't find something." She hugged her knees. Alone. "I wasn't ready for any of this."

She scootched in for some kind of distant group hug.

I exhaled. "How could you be?"

"I don't know if I'm ready to *live* alone like this."

"We're not ready to die out here," Jennifer rubbed her elbows. "It's not time yet."

"What if it is?" the younger woman asked, not bitter, but with more than a trace of caustic solemnity. "Three months of this and then…what?"

"Then we get to know if we're going to be okay."

Jennifer launched up, anxiety simmering, and stared at the

movie without really seeing it.

"Are you thinking about your father?" I asked delicately.

"It's hard not to. Gods, *you* just lost your husband and *you* had to come out of a torture sim to out-talk a lunatic. You both could be red paste right now. And Jazz, Corben, I don't even know where to begin. And all I can think about is whether or not I'll get to see my dad before he dies."

Rachel squeezed the other woman's arm. "Jen, it's okay. It's an okay thing to worry about."

"I know. But it isn't."

"If you don't get to see him, will you be okay?" I asked.

She looked on the verge of tears. But they never came.

"I suppose I will. I'll have to be. And so will you, Tera."

Neither of us corrected her.

Rachel just rocked back and forth.

The movie played on. A little while later, it got to a really good bit.

* * *

Madison came by, telling us that they were hosting a ceremony for Milo. Jennifer attended. I declined. One of those farewells was more than enough for me.

I kept Rachel company for a while, but she wanted time to herself.

Exiled from the cabin, I walked, relishing the simple activity as if it was the most refreshing thing in life. Past deck four's now-significantly-more-robust patching job. Around the haphazard gaps left torn in the stairs and walls. Through the galley, where packets of snacks were strewn far and wide. Past the repaired chaos of deck three's hydroponics farm. A formerly-locked door had been left ajar. I poked my head inside, peering through dark blue drapes to find crushed petals of a yellow flower left forgotten on the floor.

I kept going.

The captain's cabin was open, and I poked my nose inside. Frank was reclining on a small built-in loveseat, bandages wrapped thickly around his neck and torso.

"Mister Whittaker. Come in."

I did so, finding a seat opposite.

"How are you?" he asked.

"I've had better days."

He sighed. "So have I."

"You look alive."

"I almost wasn't. Lawrence even found it in himself to be sympathetic."

"Wow."

"It's why I hired him." He coughed. "I'm supposed to be saying those terrible words over Milo's body right now. Madison will be doing it for me."

"The woman is in charge."

"The engineers always are."

His words drifted away. There was little else, it seemed, for him to say on the topic.

I made a face at the wall. "I wanted to *be* you, just yesterday." I wasn't sure why I said it. It just came out.

"Why?"

"You had the respect of your people. A command. A captain, out here in the dark."

"Then I apologise for setting such a lousy example."

"You were right, you know. Your theory."

Frank crooked an eyebrow. "Oh?"

I nodded. "The person you are, when there's nothing to hold

you back, that's *real*. Real as anything. It's therapeutic. Giving that gift to people, well, maybe there's something to that."

Franklin sighed. "Don't live my life, Aidan. For all his bullshit, Ricky wasn't wrong. The cost to hiding from reality is enormous. The time we spend out here will never be gotten back. My little girl grew up while I wasn't looking."

"I understand."

"No, you don't."

"I don't?"

"You can't. You might have lived quite a life but you haven't lived this one. Take my word for it."

"Don't you think it's worth trying out, at least?"

"I think I'm a tired, beaten-up relic with too many regrets." He waved me to the door. "Maybe it is. For you."

# TWENTY-TWO

Elsie rounded us up, one at a time, returning everyone to the bridge. When all the survivors were present, she parked herself on her station's chair. Madison took the seat nearest the pilot.

"Okay," she said heavily. "We have another plan. It's a bad plan. But it might save us."

"Do tell," Lawrence said.

The engineer gave him a look, but spoke so everyone could hear. "All we have left is about a dozen ion thrusters for maneuvering and, reliably, about thirty-eight percent of our electrical storage capacity. We're currently moving at about forty-five thousand kilometers an hour, and the thrusters, all combined, are an order of magnitude less powerful than the main engines, which we have determined are unsafe to use." She gestured to Elsie, who took over the explanation.

The pilot nodded. She looked ill. "If we stick to the original schedule, then we would be due for a long brake fairly soon. Doing that with thrusters won't work like you'd expect because we'll be going too fast, we'll overshoot and cross Earth's orbit before it and its moon are in the right place to meet us. We need to burn the thrusters steadily for an extra fifty sols longer than the normal deceleration plan. That, for anyone counting, means that to meet our original plan, we would have had to have started burning the sol before, er, yesterday. However, if we start in the next few hours, and actually take the deceleration a little more *gently* than we need to, we can still adjust our flight path to intercept Luna about two Earth weeks later than planned."

The room was very quiet. A little ray of hope.

Maybe. More for some than for others.

I looked at Jennifer. She looked troubled, but stayed silent.

Elsie took the lull as a cue to continue. "This plan should work. We don't have a high-gain array to use anymore, but the low-gain will still work for basic messages. We'll be able to broadcast out to tell Luna about our arrival window change. We should only get there a little late, and hopefully without moving so fast that we're smashing the station into rubble." She shrugged, and there was a chorus of grim nods in response.

Madison took over. "It gets worse, if you can believe it. The bow LIDAR array is in a bunch of little pieces, so our fancy new slingdome won't work as well as it should either, meaning that the front of the crew module is going to get hit with a lot of space junk over the next few months. We can't guarantee that it will be safe up here." She shook her head at the increasingly tormented looks facing her. "That's less important than the power problem. Given the damage to the grid, and the overall power draw we've got, and the lack of extra super-capacitors and generation cells from the engine unit, we're only *just* running an energy surplus as it is. We could stay at cruising speed, carrying on as we are now, until long after we run out of every other resource. But over the kind of sustained thruster burns Elsie's going to do, we're going to be in the red very quickly, and by five weeks from now we'll be grazing the bottom of the barrel. By the end of week six, we'll be depleted. We can't replenish our power stores faster than we'll drain them.

"The idea is this: If we slow the habitation ring rotation to around sixty percent of normal to reduce motor upkeep, that will help. If we kill some of the fancier features on the bow spire and let the forward hull take the hits, that helps a lot too. But then comes the funky part: We have to retreat to the passenger blocks and close the environmental circuits in most of this module. No lights, almost no heating, no hydroponics, no plumbing, maybe *one* air reprocessor up here just in case. We don't even spend energy on scheduling a counterspin, we just turn off the motor and let friction slowly kill the module's gravity. We set the course, trust the computer to get us there, and wait it out in the sim."

She stopped there to let us digest it.

The idea of hiding in CarverNet while our fates rested on everything going *perfectly*, with no room for escape, ate at my composure. On a deep, unwavering level, it scared me.

"Can't we get there sooner?" Jennifer asked.

Elsie nodded, but held up a hand. "We can, but we can't. It's about redundancy. We're talking about burning for *over a hundred sols*. If we plan to use all of the thrusters all that way, then the moment we start decelerating we're committed, because we can't..." She shook her head. "If one fails, the calculation changes. If something falls over and fires too early or not at all, the calculation changes. If we don't have a backup we can't recover from that. I'm sorry. We can't do it with that risk."

Frank spoke kindly. "We all want to get there as fast as we can."

"All in favor?" Madison asked, grim.

Elsie raised her hand.

The others, one by one, followed. As did I.

Eyes laid on Jennifer, who turned to look at me. I looked back, understanding. Either she risked missing her father completely, or she *would* miss him completely. She knew it. She had no choice. She had to be okay with it.

In the end, ever so slowly, she put her hand up.

The plan was agreed.

"Freck." Madison muttered contemplatively.

* * *

I took Rachel aside as the others came to terms with the plan. We rode up the mover together, to deck two, and negotiated the scattered piles of debris until we found our way to the door. She went in first, and waited in the corner. I went in second.

Ricky chuckled at us. "*Finally.* I was starting to get *bored.*"

His arms were docile, rendered helpless, muscles isolated from his nervous system by the machine. I pulled his display close.

I gave him a pleasant smile as I started filling in scenario settings. "*Bratan.* You should know something."

*Environment: The Crisper, Hiking Simulation*

Ricky spat. "Is it that you're too much of a coward to try me in a fight?"

*Injury Persistence: Maximum*

"It's that we won't put you out the airlock."

*Tactility scaling: Maximum*

He sneered. "You don't have the stomach for it, do you?"

*Carnivorous Cargo: Enabled*

I put a hand on his arm. His face flinched at the contact.

*Alone in the Dark: Enabled*

"No, they don't." I said.

*Adversary Intelligence: Maximum*

The smirk disappeared as he squinted at me, considering, A shadow of something crossed his face. Might have been acceptance. The bluster slipped from his tone. "They aren't killers."

*Respawn on Death: Enabled*

I agreed. "They are not."

*Respawn Iteration Count: Infinite*

He said nothing. I looked at him, up and down. Finished my work.

"Ricardo, you and me, we understand one another. There are rules for us. Rules we obey. The only one that really matters is the only one you forgot. We don't hurt the good ones."

I picked up the blocky helmet. As I lined it up with his head, I leaned down, close enough that my breath tickled his lips. "I told you that I would hurt you."

As the helmet descended into place and clicked shut, entombing his senses in its grasp, I treasured that last glimpse of his eyes. They had finally, gratifyingly, borne one simple expression: *Fear.*

Rachel walked closer, inspecting my work. She nodded.

I pressed the *Begin Scenario* button.

We turned off the lights as we walked out.

# TWENTY-THREE

Closing down everything in the crew module, turning off the lights, and the air, and the heat, was like a gut punch for Elsie. But she did it with an enviably resolute steadiness. Frank, for his part, had accepted the plan with the stoicism befitting a ship's captain.

As we waited for the mover to zip down the length of the ship, I looked at Jennifer and squeezed her hand. "Are you okay?"

"Yeah." She said, pretending to be cool and collected. "I will be. You?"

Her eye was twitching. She was definitely nervous.

I put on a brave face. "Same. I hope."

"Obviously. We'll be fine. We'll make it."

"Knowing what we know, I don't know if I'll ever be comfortable in there."

She gave a weak smile. "Drinks on Arkadia? Racing through the oceans on Titan? We'll keep it interesting."

"You make a good point."

We arrived at block twelve. Rachel, Lawrence, and I stepped out. Behind us, Madison and Frank lingered with Jennifer. She would be escorted to block ten, in a different part of the ring, before the crew united in block seven. I gave a little wave as the door closed. As it zipped away, a pang of sadness filtered through crowded thoughts.

And then it was just three of us.

*This will be fine.*

"Come, honored guests." The doctor drawled, tired. "In you go."

No pomp, nor circumstance. Just the resignation of someone who had a duty to perform.

Muffled sounds of an older man cackling away welcomed us into Zone B's hall of sim capsules.

Rachel stopped.

I looked over, uncertain. "Ready for this? We'll make it work."

She shook her head. "He won't be in there."

"We will be, okay?"

She started at the wall of closed doors. "I keep having this little hope that what was in that bag was wrong, that it wasn't him, that it was some horrible mistake. That he'll be inside when we go back in. But it's just a fake prayer, isn't it?"

Lawrence shook his head. "I'm sorry."

"Was he in one of these?"

"Yes."

Rachel took a low, slow, shaky breath. "Show me."

"Of course."

The big man quietly stepped over to the first pod on the left. Used his fob on it, pulled it open. The little overhead glowed to life.

The words still shone on the little display:

*Jazaban Cooke*

The cradle behind them hung empty, waiting. A small rucksack was tucked into the cubby below. Rachel stepped into the little space, looking, feeling. Touching.

She pulled the bag free. Kept it close.

"How do I change his name on here?"

Lawrence showed her.

She did the work. Stepped back.

The correct name was now displayed in its place, a patient little memorial.

*Corben Torvalds*

It wouldn't last forever. Nobody else would get to see it. Those details didn't matter.

She backed out of the pod. Screwed up her courage. Her expression was closed. Armor had been replaced.

Lawrence closed the pod. Our own were waiting.

I asked if I could have a shower quickly. He indulged my request, but they didn't leave me any privacy. I didn't care.

The easier gravity was a delight for tired limbs, and meant that the forced spray of water was always accompanied by a strong current of warm air. The shaved stubble on my scalp bristled as the wash reached it. All that had happened, and I still couldn't remember losing my hair. Probably never would. There were likely lots of little holes like that. Pieces of myself that would have to be repaired with something new.

A few minutes later, the water turned off, and I was just left with the warm wind wicking the last droplets away.

I stayed in it as long as I thought I could get away with, dreading the end of the moment. I wished for some other plan. For *any* other option.

But this was happening. No use fighting it. No use fighting space, or the laws of physics or the only plan that *might* keep us alive.

*I have to let go.*

Claustrophobia nibbled at my calm. I didn't want to surrender myself. It felt like…*dying,* almost, in the vain, almost spiritual hope that while our souls experienced delights, our bodies would wait, patient.

*Alone.*

Surrendering or not, we would have to trust that Elsie had gotten it right. That eventually, one day, we would come back out of that world.

It did not come naturally.

My pod was, of course, exactly as it had been. My suit waited, neatly folded. Stepping into it, I wriggled around until it was tucked against all the right places, cupping certain spots *just* the right way. A lump formed in my throat with each *click* as I nestled back into the cradle.

Rachel watched silently from the corridor, her own pod open and waiting. Lawrence approached without preamble, his bulk making the tight space feel even tighter. As he checked and re-attached the support feeds to my cannulation cuff, I snugged the gravity webbing back into place.

"Ready?" he asked.

"No." I said. "But I'll see you on the other side."

"Fingers crossed. We'll do our best."

"It's been a pleasure, Lawrence."

"No it hasn't, Mister Whittaker. But I appreciate the thought."

I put on a brave face as my limbs lost their weight.

The suit's neural fabric synced with my spinal implants. Anxiety tortured my thoughts, but there was calm behind it. Acceptance.

Faith.

I relaxed, surrendering to the mask as he snugged it into place, reality dropping away into empty darkness.

I was afraid.

It was time to go.

That simple greeting, inevitable as the stars, waited for me.

*Welcome to CarverNet*

# FOUR MONTHS LATER

Elim Rasmussen sipped his tea. Delicate porcelain clinked as the cup reached its saucer.

It was a ritual. Essential to keep oneself centered. That was turning out to be important today.

He stood in his office, still relishing the title that he had earned just two months prior. *Dockmaster.* It was a good title on most days.

Today, maybe not.

Far below the vast poziglas window, his eyes rested on a sight that had brought him all different kinds of stress, meetings, and anxious inquiries. It was nearing its moment of truth.

The battered, broken hulk lazily drifted in, guided by little sentry drones that clamped to the hull and propelled it into position. Elim took another sip, calming his nerves. First this one had gone missing, then it had arrived two weeks *late*. It was totally unresponsive to pings, and when it had reached the station perimeter it *ought* to have at least shown signs of life. It had been his new hire, of all people, who noticed that the freighter was broadcasting a loop on the *low-gain* bands.

He monitored the feeds from the drones as the vast ship finally aligned with the station, slowly, *slowly* easing into umbilical range. As long as nothing exploded, scraped, or otherwise caused havoc, well, it was better to be recovering a ghost ship than no ship at all.

The telescoping scaffold extended, visible at this distance with enough squinting. It crossed the gulf between station and vessel. The metal rods latched into place on the newcomer's hull, and the umbilical unfurled, tugged down the length of the connection until it met hard metal.

The dockmaster held his breath as his systems spoke to those on the ship, negotiating approval to unite their atmospheres.

It was taking too long. Something felt wrong.

*Come on, come on, don't be a dead one.*

He exhaled in relief as the routines completed their handshake, and status updates fed through to his displays, mirrored from his staff's terminals two levels below.

*Seal established successfully.*

*Pressurizing…*

*Umbilical pressurized.*

*Opening airlocks…*

*Airlocks open.*

*The Apollo welcomes you to board. Captain Franklin G. DeSanto is commanding.*

The dockmaster picked up his fob.

"Somebody go find Miss Carver. My office. We've got her missing freighter."

Then another message, longer, less formal, and written very personally to him from a passenger aboard that ship, appeared on the display. As he scanned it, taking in a story that had implications he did *not* want to investigate too deeply, his brow furrowed.

The teacup returned to its saucer.

He picked up a handset. Something wired. Something secure.

"SolPol office. Yes, I'll wait. Greaves. Hi, it's me. Wake your people up and get them to dock eight. Right the hell now."

* * *

I brought the injector down slowly, carefully, learning a foreign form of a familiar medium. The thin, needle-like head inserted a droplet of paint into the fluffy canvas, where it was absorbed by the waiting fibers. Blue meshed with neighboring black and white, just down from where a clutch of green cells had just been deposited.

I shifted the color wheel on the injector again, pulling in a dash of yellow to get the pigment just right. Laid out several more little deposits of color to fill in a tiny gap. Finishing touches.

It was a strange way to paint. More akin to tattooing than brushwork, but still, there was an easy delight behind it. Much easier than the physical therapy, which in turn had only been half as hard as the remote classes.

I lowered the injector. Surveyed the little canvas, pleased. It would do. I let the ink dry, carefully wrapped it in a papery sheath, then slid it away into my bag.

I looked out the window at my muse. Out there, in the dark, a vast bluish-green marble hung, unendingly tantalizing.

Today was the day. In a couple hours a shuttle would take the last of us planetside.

An old to-do list echoed in my thoughts, bringing a sense of euphoric anticipation that twitched my lips.

Number one: try real bread. Number two: stand in a real ocean.

I couldn't wait.

Messages waited in my inbox. One from Jennifer, of course. I read it, felt sad as I progressed through its contents, and finished it with a bittersweet note. Today had been a particularly important day for her too. But not too long before we'd see each other again.

On to the next. My father, sending his daily update from back home. Not much new had happened, other than that his work friends had gotten a little excited watching a zeeball match and spent the night with the constabulary.

On to the next. Eileen Carver, again. She had visited all of us in person. Somewhere between truly conciliatory and proactively, maybe cynically congenial.

I read her message, eyebrows raised. Typed up a brief reply.

*Miss Carver,*

*Thank you for the offer. Captain O'Connell's recommendation of course conjures a sense of appreciation, but I must decline the opportunity. If a life out in the stars crosses my career again, I will keep both of your names in mind.*

*All the best to you,*

*Aidan Whittaker*

I read it twice.

Pressed send.

Looked around the guest room. Picked up my bag.

Onwards.

I turned off the lights as I walked out.

# ABOUT THE AUTHOR

J. J. French is an author and composer. When not pursuing creative endeavors or indulging in computer games, he can frequently be found on a sofa somewhere, enjoying cups of tea and the occasional peanut-butter-and-jelly sandwich. He lives in England with his family.

# COPYRIGHT

This is a work of fiction. Names, characters, organizations, places, events, and incidents are either products of the author's imagination or are used fictitiously. Any resemblance to actual persons, living or dead, or actual events is purely coincidental.

under which it was purchased or as strictly permitted by applicable copyright law. Any unauthorized use or distribution of this text may be a direct infringement of the author's rights.

Thank you for reading! The process of taking this story from concept to this sizable concoction of words frequently seemed impossible, and the resulting novel's existence is no less than surreal. We're getting to the genuine end of the book now; it's kind of amazing that you're reading this. Nobody reads the dry stuff at the back of a book.

Anyway, a few acknowledgements to wrap things up:

To Lucy: Thanks for being such a relentless critic.

To Kevin, Alex, and Leah: Thanks for the endless chatter about movies and TV shows all these years. I hold you responsible for a *great many things*.

To my family: Thanks for the encouragement and support over the years. Means a lot.

To you, reader: I hope you enjoyed your time with Noah, Jennifer, and all the rest. You're probably hungry, so go get something to eat. I recommend a packet of cyberfish.